THE CRITICS RAVE ABOUT STOBIE PIEL!

BLUE-EYED BANDIT

"Kudos to Ms. Piel for providing a love story with humor, passion and some whimsy. It's an all-around great read."

—*Romantic Times*

FREE FALLING

"Ms. Piel has written an innovative story, blending history and romance into a sweet tale of renewed love."

—*Romantic Times*

THE WHITE SUN

"The consistently entertaining voice of Stobie Piel takes us on another roller–coaster ride of excitement through the stars."

—*Romantic Times*

THE MIDNIGHT MOON

"This distant time and place Stobie Piel depicts will capture your imagination-and the romance and triumph of its characters will touch your heart."

—Susan Wiggs, bestselling author of *The Lightkeeper*

"Ms. Piel keeps us on the knife-edge of curiosity as she tantalizes us with her imaginative plot."

—*Romantic Times*

SWEET DANGER

"It may be dangerous, but I cannot imagine anything so compelling as when love claims you completely." Rafael paused. Suddenly, it was important that Evelyn consider him handsome. He removed his spectacles and set them aside. "Can you?"

She looked up at him, her eyes wide. Her voice came as a whisper. "No."

Somehow, suddenly they were closer to each other than he remembered. Her face seemed bare inches from his. He wanted to protect her, to earn her friendship and respect, to prove to her that no matter what he had done in the guise of the Renegade, the quiet, restrained schoolmaster reflected his true self. Instead of speaking, he reached to touch her soft hair, untangling it from its loose binding. It fell in long waves around her face and down her back as she stared up at him, shocked and enchanted.

His fingers grazed her cheek—the softest skin he had ever touched—and he bent closer to brush his mouth over hers.

Other *Love Spell* books by Stobie Piel:

BLUE-EYED BANDIT
FREE FALLING
THE WHITE SUN
THE MIDNIGHT MOON
MOLLY IN THE MIDDLE
THE DAWN STAR

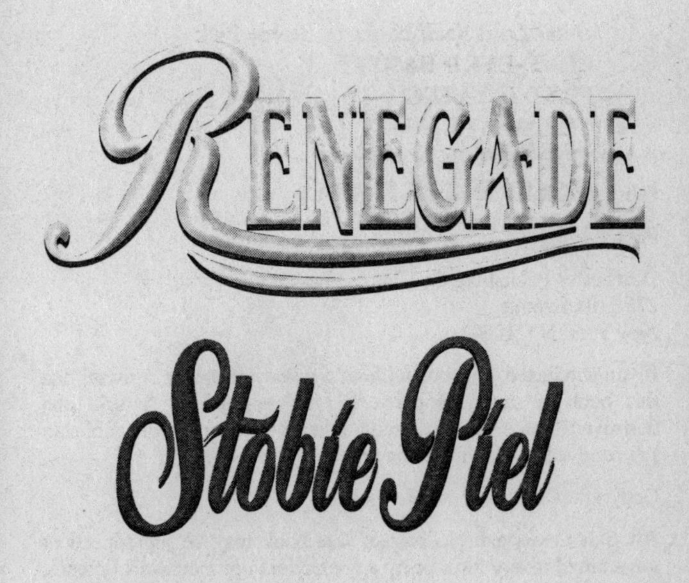

LEISURE BOOKS

NEW YORK CITY

At the heart of every story I've ever written is the belief that for every soul, there is one perfect love, a soul mate. This book is dedicated to mine, wherever you are.

A LEISURE BOOK®

February 2001

Published by

Dorchester Publishing Co., Inc.
276 Fifth Avenue
New York, NY 10001

ISBN 0-8439-4828-0

The name "Leisure Books" and the stylized "L" with design are trademarks of Dorchester Publishing Co., Inc.

Printed in the United States of America.

Visit us on the web at www.dorchesterpub.com.

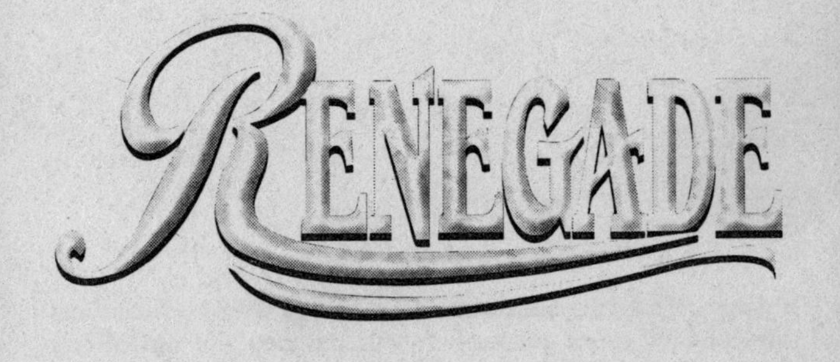
RENEGADE

"It's something that's in the air. The sky is different, the stars are different, the wind is different."
—Georgia O'Keefe

Chapter One

New Mexico Territory
1880

The Atchison, Topeka, and Santa Fe Railroad was barely a month in operation, and already it was late arriving. Rafael de Aguirre checked his pocket watch, then seated himself on an adobe bench to wait. Captain Westley Reid was meeting with the governor of New Mexico and had enlisted Rafael to greet his wife when her train arrived.

Rafael heard the first sounds of the train's arrival before anyone else. Being nearsighted had few advantages; acute hearing was one. The train pulled slowly into the station, but Rafael remained seated. The first class passengers would be last to leave; they generally lingered aboard, waiting for porters to gather their belongings and assemble trunks in the station.

Rafael stretched his legs out, crossed at the ankles. His long black hair fell over his shoulders, reminding him he'd forgotten to tie it back. But if Westley Reid's elegant bride intended to make her home in New Mexico, she might as well get used to Indian hair.

The coach passengers began unloading, tumbling from the train as if it had been a prison from which they had suddenly been released. They looked uniformly tired, cramped, and uncomfortable. Some carried carpetbags, but most had no belongings at all. Rafael saw Mexicans, Indians who had come south from Colorado to work on the new rail, and a few Chinese. Santa Fe was growing by leaps and bounds, taking on a new flavor from its Spanish-Indian beginnings. Maybe the mix was for the best, but already the class separation seemed more distinct.

He glanced toward the first class car. Only porters and servants had emerged, busy with the lavish bags owned by the wealthiest passengers. To his surprise, a young Mexican family emerged. They bore no bags, and their clothing appeared unkempt. The woman held a newborn baby wrapped in a lace-trimmed bunting. Only the blanket around the child seemed fitting for the lavish accommodations from which they'd just come.

Rafael watched as the family walked to the area where the coach passengers gathered. They seemed to be searching for someone. A young woman stepped down from the train and waved at them, smiling. Rafael caught his breath and stared.

Beyond anything, beyond anyone he'd ever seen, this young woman enchanted him. He adjusted his spectacles to be sure he saw her clearly. Her dark hair was tied in a loose knot behind her head, but long, waving tendrils had escaped and fell in disarray around her beautiful face. She wore a cream-colored gown that was bunched and wrinkled from the long hours she must have spent in the cramped coach seats, but somehow she looked fresh and happy. The woman beamed when the mother revealed the newborn, then hugged the two as if close kin. She gave the father a small bag and bent down to speak to the older children. They spoke to her hurriedly, and she responded in halting Spanish.

Rafael found himself walking toward her before he realized he'd left his seat. He stopped and stood staring, his heart pounding. This was something he'd never felt before. It had been long since a woman had caught his eye, and *never* had one affected him this way. Whatever had brought this enchanting girl to Santa Fe he would soon learn, but some inner voice assured him that her true purpose would be found at his side. He waited, spellbound, as the family she conversed with departed. The woman stooped and lifted a small bag, then hoisted it to her shoulder. No one joined her from inside the car; no one greeted her at the station.

But someone would, now. . . .

He stopped before her, and she looked up at him. For an instant—the most perfect moment he had ever known—he saw the same look of wonder and recognition in her eyes. He felt as if an invisible cord bound them together, a cord that had always been there between them, and now in this sweet moment, they together had found the person at the other end.

He smiled and held out his hand. "Allow me, dear lady."

She seemed surprised, but she handed him her bag. Rafael took it and slung it over his shoulder. She appeared bewildered, but more than that . . . enchanted. Her gaze shifted subtly to his mouth, then back to his eyes, and he found himself moving closer. He took her narrow, gloved hand in his and drew it near his chest. She didn't back away, and her breath came in tiny, swift gasps. For a moment, they stared at each other as if no one else in the world existed.

Her brow furrowed as if she fought to regain composure and found the task near to impossible. "I don't know you." It was a sweet voice, gentle, and his heart warmed at its sound.

He drew her hand to his lips and kissed the back of her gloved fingers softly. "You will."

A strange madness had overcome him. He could see nothing but this woman, barely remembered why he was at the station at all. Impatient to be rid of the task, he recalled that he had promised to retrieve Westley's bride and deposit her at her husband's home. Then he would take this beautiful, ethereal woman back to the pueblo where he lived and learn everything about her.

"I have a duty." He didn't want to waste time

on Westley's task, on anything but this woman before him, but he had to. "I must find my friend's wife and deliver her to her husband. Then you and I . . ."

She was trembling. Rafael snapped back to his senses and laughed. This seemed so powerful, so *different*. He touched his mouth, feeling shy yet eager. "Forgive me." Excitement rose inside him. "I am not generally so . . . unrestrained, I promise you. But perhaps I should introduce myself. I am the Tewa pueblo's schoolmaster, Rafael de Aguirre." He took her hands in his, standing so close to her that he could perceive her swift pulse, her warmth. Her fingers tightened around his. "I don't know your name."

She opened her mouth to speak, but no words came. Her surprise endeared her to him still more. She wasn't used to such a bold greeting and probably had no idea how to react. Yet he sensed without question that she shared his attraction. He had no idea what had come over him. Perhaps his Argentinean father had passed his latent romanticism down to his son—Allejandro de Aguirre had fallen in love with the daughter of the Tesuque pueblo's chief and finally absconded with her against the tribe's wishes. Allejandro had moved his family into a tiny, abandoned pueblo between Tesuque and Santa Fe, and named it Tewa. Soon after, he'd invited both Mexican and disaffected Zuni to join him, fulfilling a lifelong dream of bringing together people in a cooperative society based on respect and the wisdom of his wife's people.

While Allejandro had died before fully reestablishing the small pueblo, Rafael had followed his example and established a school for Tewa's children. His success was so great that Zuni from both the Tesuque and Pojoaque pueblos had begun sending their children to him.

His father's dream had seemed near fruition until, thanks to some kind of eastern political maneuvering, Westley Reid's father had been given the pueblo as a "gift" after the Mexican-American war. It was to decide the fate of this "gift" that Westley had been sent west and was today in consultation with the governor.

Rafael gazed into the beautiful blue-gray eyes of the woman before him, spellbound. He had never fully understood his dramatic, poetic father, but now he understood. *When the woman of your dreams appears, Rafael, you will move heaven and earth to have her. Nothing will stand in your way.*

"Darling! There you are! I was able to make it after all!" A bright, cheerful voice broke the romantic delirium enveloping Rafael, and he turned to see Westley Reid coming toward them. He was smiling and carrying a lady's storage bag. Behind him, a black porter wheeled a large trunk.

With cold shock, Rafael saw his error. It compounded with each flashing second, excruciating. He turned back to the beautiful young angel, but now he saw, to his horror, another man's wife. She looked pale and shocked, and now he understood why. He wanted to speak, to beg her forgiveness, but no words came. *Another man's wife . . .*

He felt as if the world had been ripped from beneath his feet.

Westley joined them and embraced his wife. He kissed her cheek, then hugged her again. "Evie, it's so good to see you!" The man looked around, seemingly bewildered. "What on earth were you doing in the coach section?"

She smiled but looked tense. Rafael shared the embarrassment. He wanted the earth to open and swallow him whole. "I . . ." She gulped, then cleared her throat. "I exchanged my ticket with a family—the wife was with child, and her time came while we passed through Kansas." She spoke rapidly, but her husband just listened with a smile, as if delighted and charmed by anything his wife said or did.

She drew in a quick breath and continued. "I had such a large berth, Westley, and I didn't need it, really. So I convinced the conductor to allow them my place—I had to pay him a bit extra, but he was very agreeable after that. It is important that a new mother eat well, and the coach passengers aren't served meals onboard the train, you know. We had to get off at each stop for our meals. It was interesting, really, and I ate well enough."

She was decidedly nervous, but Westley didn't seem to notice her discomfort. He beamed with pride and kissed his wife's cheek again. "You are your father's daughter. Robert Talmadge made friends of the rebels in Andersonville prison, and his daughter gives up her magnificent cabin to ride West in squalor. How I do love you, Evie!"

Westley turned to Rafael, holding his wife's small hand in his. "Rafael, I see you've already met my wife. I'm surprised you found her in this crowd." He looked around at the many passengers who still stood around the station.

Rafael wanted to run. Instead, he nodded and forced himself to smile. "Mrs. Reid and I had . . . barely met."

She glanced at him. "I had just gotten off the train."

Westley kissed her hand. "Well then, allow me to introduce Evelyn Talmadge Reid, my wife."

Rafael bowed. "It is my honor to meet you, Mrs. Reid." He had no idea what to say. He had just propositioned a married woman, not knowing her name or anything about her other than that she had captured his heart at one glance.

"Rafael has become a good friend since I came out here, Evie. I hope you will get a chance to know him. He is the pueblo schoolmaster, so I felt sure you would enjoy his company. The children adore him, despite his rather . . . warlike appearance." Westley chuckled pleasantly at this, but Rafael cringed. Certainly, he had behaved beastly enough today.

Evelyn uttered a small noise, perhaps "How very nice," then looked around at nothing.

Westley apparently sensed nothing of the currents running between his wife and friend. He turned to Evelyn and patted her cheek. "My darling, you must be exhausted. Riding in coach!" He shook his head and tsked, but he was smiling. "I will take you back to my quarters—I've established myself in a small adobe home between Santa Fe and the pueblo, which I think you'll love—and you will sleep for days if need be to recover from your journey."

"Thank you. I would like that." Evelyn carefully avoided meeting Rafael's eyes, instead keeping her gaze pinned on her feet.

Rafael felt ashamed. He had put this woman in an uncomfortable position and made a fool of himself over an unavailable woman. What had gotten into him?

Westley motioned to the porter, thanked him, and gave him an extra coin—more than the man would have made in a whole week from most passengers. Westley Reid was a good man, generous and kind. Yet suddenly Rafael found himself looking at his friend with a bitter envy he'd never dreamed possible. He pushed it down.

Westley grinned at him. "I had intended to invite you to dinner tonight, my friend. But it appears my wife has spent her last energy by sacrificing her comfort for a good cause. But you will dine with us a few days hence, and you two can get better acquainted."

Rafael's horror at this pronouncement was matched by Evelyn's expression. But neither of them challenged Westley's good-natured invitation.

Rafael stood as if in a dream—a dream that had dissipated like a soft mist before blazing sunlight—and watched Westley Reid lead his beautiful young wife away. Westley was already speaking, enthusiastically telling Evelyn of their new home and of the life they would share. Rafael stood alone, amazed that something as bright and sweet as this woman could have touched him this way, and yet vanished so swiftly.

When the woman of your dreams appears, Rafael, you will move heaven and earth to have her. Nothing will stand in your way.

He would have moved heaven and earth, yes. But the thing that stood in his way was far more powerful, daunting. It was friendship.

"Rafael has put off dining with us for two weeks. I hope he's not ill!" Westley stood in the center square of the Tewa pueblo looking around for his friend, but Evelyn cringed inwardly.

"I'm sure he's very busy with the children in his school." She hadn't seen the tall, dark man who had greeted her since their first encounter, but the fire in those brown eyes haunted her. Every time she thought of him, her nerves tingled just as they had when he first clasped her hands in his. A dinner would be excruciating. Apparently, Rafael was trying just as hard to avoid her as she was to avoid him.

"Nonsense, my dear. The man works too hard. He needs to get out more, and I want you to get to know him. He would make a good friend for you."

Evelyn fought a miserable groan. Westley shaded his eyes against the setting sun, oblivious of her mood. "I checked at the school. His little brother says he's not there."

As Westley spoke, several guards rode into the square, led by John Talbot. The officer and Westley had met at Harvard during their schooling. Upon spotting him now, Westley sighed. "What now, do you think?"

Evelyn glanced at her husband, recognizing his expression. "Why did you approve his commission out here if you don't like him?"

Westley's fair face darkened, and he shifted his bright gaze from her. "I had no choice." A smile covered his displeasure, and he shrugged. "He seemed to want the post very much. And he's qualified. What was to stop me?"

Evelyn sensed there was more to it than that, but the guards dragged an elderly Zuni man forward. Evelyn gripped Westley's arm. "What are they doing to that man?"

Westley shook his head. "I don't know." He stepped forward and called to Talbot. "What is the meaning of this, Lieutenant? What has this gentleman done?"

John Talbot sat straight in his saddle, his blue uniform in perfect order, every button polished. He motioned to the soldiers, and they stopped. He smiled at Westley, but somehow, Evelyn felt the expression didn't reveal true affection. "This 'gentleman' has been giving us trouble, I'm afraid, Colonel." Westley's new title still surprised Evelyn. He had been given his rank thanks primarily to her father's influence in Boston, and because it seemed honorary rather than earned, Westley most often ignored it.

"In what way, *Lieutenant?*" Westley's voice sounded harsher than normal, and Evelyn repressed a smile. He might downplay it to everyone else, but apparently he enjoyed reminding John Talbot of their respective ranks. "He seems a harmless fellow to me."

Talbot's mustache twitched, but the smile remained. "He has been stealing valuables from my office, and probably from yours." At this, Talbot gestured to one of his guards, who began roughly searching the old man. The guard held up a crystal paperweight, and the old man gasped in surprise. He shook his head violently and spoke rapidly in his language. The guard gave the paperweight to Talbot, who passed it to Westley. "Isn't this yours, Colonel?"

Westley nodded. "It is, but . . ."

Before Westley could finish, the guards shoved the old man against a wall, and one drew out a large whip. Westley's face hardened, and Evelyn realized that despite his gentle, soft-spoken manner, he was a strong man. "Lieutenant, this man, like any other, deserves a fair trial before any punishment as extreme or distasteful as flogging is carried out."

The smile never left Talbot's lips. "Colonel, surely you understand that time-consuming trials will never produce the effects we require here? This man isn't the first to steal from our officers. No, we must teach the inhabitants of Tewa respect." His smile faded. "This order is within the rights of my command, as my commission clearly states. I am allowed to keep order in those ways I must."

Evelyn looked desperately to her husband, but for a reason she didn't understand, Talbot's words seemed to resonate bitterly with him. Evelyn stepped forward herself. "You will not beat that man, Lieutenant. You'll have to go through me first."

Talbot eyed her with compassion. "Colonel,

perhaps you should remove your wife from this scene. She is clearly a delicate woman, easily disturbed."

Evelyn made a fist, but Westley caught her arm, and she saw the look in his eyes. "Lieutenant, there must be a better way of teaching respect."

The old man looked terrified, and Evelyn's eyes filled with tears. "Westley, you can't let them." But her husband seemed unwilling to offer more defense.

As she watched, horrified, the guard drew back his whip and cracked it across the Indian's thin back. The man stumbled forward with a cry, and Westley cursed. Through the anguish of the moment, Evelyn realized it wasn't Talbot or the guard he cursed, but himself. He stepped forward, his expression drawn with pain. It was as if in order to move, he had to fight through a great wall set against him.

Thundering hoofbeats startled everyone, and Evelyn spun around to see a great gray horse charge into the square. Her mouth opened in astonishment. The rider was masked, and a dark cape hung over his broad shoulders. Talbot shouted in surprise, summoning his startled guards. "Shoot him, damn you! Shoot that damned Renegade!"

The gray horse reared at its rider's command, then leapt to one side, evading the soldiers who swarmed toward him. The man laughed. The carved, painted mask he wore appeared to be Zuni, evoking ancient legends of a culture in place long before white men invaded the land. It seemed to Evelyn as if one of the Zuni prisoner's own ancestors had taken shape in anger and now rode to protect him.

Evelyn stepped toward the man on the horse, spellbound. For an instant only, he seemed to notice her and hesitated. Long black hair fell loose down his back, shining in the red-gold sunset. The guards aimed their weapons, but he spun his horse again. As Evelyn watched in amazement, he snapped a strange, three-pronged whip, and it cracked in the dry air, disarming two guards with one flick of his wrist.

Another guard fired, and Evelyn bit back a shriek, but the Renegade was too fast for his opponents. He cracked his whip again and yanked three guards off their feet, leaving them in a tangled pile to scramble for lost weapons. Talbot aimed his revolver, but the horseman urged his gray horse forward, charging the lieutenant like a medieval knight in a joust. As the gray horse bounded forward, Talbot tried to fire, but that strange whip flew again, wrapped tight around Talbot's neck, and the Renegade jerked him off his horse.

Talbot lay mute on the ground, the wind knocked out of him, and his assailant rode to a stop before him. Evelyn held her breath, not in fear for Talbot but in fear of what this daring, heroic man would do. If he killed the guards, if he killed Talbot, he would prove himself no better than a criminal. For the people he defended, and for her, she prayed he would not.

The Renegade coiled his whip at his side, yet no one dared move against him. He motioned to the old Zuni prisoner, who scrambled away. Before he did, though, a look passed between the prisoner and his savior, and it briefly occurred to Evelyn that though her hero was masked and mysterious, the native residents of the Tewa pueblo knew his identity. Her mind spun—surely he would be handsome, young, vigorous. In his eyes, the mystic light of his ancient people would shine bright. His body would be hard and conditioned, able to withstand the rigors of his dramatic rides to protect his people.

Evelyn gazed at him and sighed. This was the kind of man she had dreamed about as a child, presenting her with a scene not likely to occur in Boston or the East's tame cities. Suddenly her heart was fueled by dreams, though long before she had realized her life would follow a simpler, safer course. This masked rider's daring appearance and heroic rescue moved her indescribably.

"This man has done no wrong." If his actions had elicited Evelyn's admiration, his low, heavily accented voice moved her heart. It was a beautiful sound, thick with the language of his people. "Set him free."

The guards looked nervously to Talbot, who clutched at his throat as he fought for words. "Never. He is a criminal."

"Is that so?" The Renegade gestured to the guard who had first confiscated the paperweight. "If you will check your guard's pocket, you will find more of Colonel Reid's possessions, taken, I assume, to place blame on this old man. For what?"

Talbot seemed astonished, but didn't speak. Instead, it was Westley who stepped forward and checked the guard's pocket as the Renegade had ordered. He drew out a golden quill pen. "Mine, I believe." Westley grimaced, and the soldier guiltily winced. "It seems this stranger is correct. And to place blame on an old man? For what would this man require a paperweight or a golden pen? You, sir, may be instead the thief Lieutenant Talbot seeks."

The guard backed away, looking to Talbot as if he expected support. But Talbot rose angrily to his feet and aimed his pistol at the man. "Take him." The other guards hesitated, then surrounded their friend.

The Renegade bowed to Talbot. "This matter isn't over, Lieutenant. Should another of Tewa's people be unjustly accused, I will return. See that there is no need."

Talbot again aimed his gun, but Westley caught his arm. The horseman spun his great horse and galloped away. Talbot cursed and fired a shot, too late, at the departing legend. "That man is a *criminal*. He will wreak havoc upon us if we don't stop him!"

Westley watched the Renegade ride away. "He may have been in the past, but today, at least, he prevented you from a wrong, Lieutenant."

Talbot's eyes blazed with anger. "This isn't the first time he has terrorized the pueblo, Westley. By the account of many local landowners, he has troubled these people since before your arrival."

"Today, he has done no wrong."

Talbot seemed furious. "Colonel, we must go after him, hunt him down. We must learn his identity and rid ourselves—this pueblo—of his influence."

Westley shook his head. "Until I witness a true crime, I will not act against him." He paused. "What would you have me do, John, send all these people from their homes and turn it over to the local landowners? That seems to be what those men want, and what you want, too. Why?"

Talbot's face became a mask, as daunting and inanimate as that worn by the Renegade. "Of course not. I wish only to bring order to this place. But the landowners, surely, have the better claim to dictate the fate of this area."

"In this, we do not agree. I say the people who live here must decide."

Talbot's expression didn't change, and he shrugged. "Perhaps. But either way, it is my duty to ensure the safety of the people living here. The Renegade is a threat to that. And I'm sure he will prove that on his own."

The old Zuni man was released from his bonds, and Talbot rode away with his guards. Westley stood in the square with Evelyn. "Well, that was inspiring, wasn't it, my dear? This Renegade has made life more interesting, to be sure. I wonder who he is? A brave man, at the least."

Evelyn nodded, but she couldn't speak. Westley took her arm and sighed. "We might as well return to our home, Evie. It appears Rafael isn't at the schoolhouse. I'm sorry. I had hoped to persuade him to dinner tonight."

"We should go home, yes." Evelyn breathed a sigh of relief as Westley helped her into their carriage and they started away. As they rode from the pueblo, she glanced back, and the vision of the dashing Renegade flitted through her mind.

She had been so lonely: Westley had been so distracted by the pueblo's troubles, lately, and she was so far from her family in Boston. Surely that was all this attraction was. She had felt the same powerful compulsion when she'd met the schoolmaster, though for different reasons. It was best to repress these feelings. She loved her husband.

Looking over, she saw that Westley seemed lost in his own thoughts, his brow furrowed. Was something besides the Renegade's appearance troubling him? Evelyn forced herself from her own reckless imaginings. "Is something wrong, Westley? You seem preoccupied."

For a moment she looked into his heart and saw a depth of pain that she hadn't imagined. Her blood ran cold. Had he seen into her secret attraction for Rafael, or perhaps her girlish admiration of the Renegade? "Have I done something wrong?"

Westley smiled, obliterating the sadness she had seen, and he clasped her hand in his. "Never, Evie. You are an angel."

She cringed inwardly, knowing she was very far from that, but she forced herself to smile, too. "Then what's wrong?"

He sighed, and his gaze shifted to the Sangre de Cristo mountains as they became shadowed with nightfall. "I have made so many mistakes, Evie. If only I had been stronger."

"What do you mean?"

"I try to be a good man, you know, for you, for all those who have placed faith in me. I wish . . . You deserve so much more." His voice trailed off, and he sighed heavily.

"I don't understand. You have always been a good man. I am fortunate to be your wife."

He smiled at her, but he still looked sad. "I am the lucky one, my dear." His smile faded to an expression of remorse. "I'm sorry I haven't . . . shown that lately. I have left you too often alone."

"I understand. You have been busy. I'm fine." As she spoke, she knew that though she had been lonely, her loneliness couldn't solely be attributed to Westley's frequent absences. She often felt lonely even when they were together. Seeing the Renegade had brought it all back to the surface. Even as a child, she had been overrun with imaginings of what love should be like, but life could not compete with that inner drama. She knew that. She had come to accept it. Yet, apparently, the longing hadn't disappeared as much as she'd hoped.

"You're worried about something. Is it Lieutenant Talbot? He doesn't seem to be obeying orders very well."

Westley frowned. "That much is certain. But the time will come when I will stand up to him." His sweet face hardened with determination, but Evelyn wasn't sure what he foresaw, or why it would be such a task to stand up to his underling. But it seemed like a very daunting task, for his next words were weary. "In the end, my honor must be more important than anything set against me."

Her husband stopped and flicked the reins on the horses' backs. Evelyn wanted to ask what he meant, but Westley had fallen silent, and she recognized a mood best not penetrated. As he urged the carriage horses forward into the darkness, and night closed in all around them, it seemed to Evelyn that fear was closing in, too.

The Renegade haunted her dreams. Evelyn woke with a start, her body flushed and too warm. She hopped up from her bed and pulled her lightest dress over her chemise. Where was Westley? She peeked out the window into a dark, starless night. It was later than she thought. If only she hadn't seen the Renegade ride into the plaza that way! If only she didn't imagine him so handsome and so virile, when she herself was so lonely. Since the Renegade's attack, Westley had been even more distracted, and she had been often alone.

Alone meant time to dream and to fantasize, and that was proving more dangerous than she'd ever imagined. If she'd seen his face, maybe he wouldn't have such a mystic appeal. Maybe he was homely. Maybe knowing who he was would dampen the vivid pictures in her mind. The worst of it was that, because she hadn't seen his face, she was free to imagine the handsomest man she knew in his stead—Rafael de Aguirre.

Westley had finally cajoled Rafael into dining at their home. It had been even worse than Evelyn feared. He'd been quiet and clearly ill at ease, surely because of their first encounter. Evelyn hadn't even been able to speak to him without a quaver in her voice. Had he not been the subject of her fantasies, it might have been easier, but as it was, the whole evening had been excruciating. The memory of that encounter was made worse because she liked him. He spoke of the children in his school with enthusiasm, with love. He told of native legends and about the antics of his young brother, Diego. Rafael was an intelligent, caring man with a decidedly romantic outlook on life. If she hadn't been moved by some unknown power at their first meeting, this dinner with the man could not have failed to steal her heart.

Evelyn felt overcome by shame; it covered her like mud. She loved Westley dearly—they had been friends since childhood, and never in all the time she had known him had he ever been unkind. But passion never flared between them. There was only warmth and tenderness. He deserved better from her than a woman whose mind kept flitting to another man.

Evelyn went to the door and looked out. The night was strangely quiet. Westley had told her—it must have been hours ago—that he was going for a walk. She had dined alone because he wasn't hungry, and he seemed more nervous than usual, though he wouldn't explain why. She had watched for weeks as he struggled with something, never sharing what troubled him. She wasn't the kind of woman who pried or demanded—she respected his privacy—but his distance left her so lonely. What was happening to her life?

The night air felt cool, though it was July and hot of late. Tormented by her shame, she went outside hoping to clear her senses, and perhaps meet Westley when he returned. A horse stomped, and Evelyn started. The sound came from behind their small adobe home. "Westley?" She spoke softly, and he didn't answer. It had to be him, but fear accompanied her anyway as she crept around the edge of the house. For a moment, she saw nothing.

Then her eyes adjusted to the darkness. She saw a large horse silhouetted against the western horizon, riderless. It was a horse she knew. She had seen it many times in her dreams. The Renegade's gray. Her blood moved like ice as her gaze shifted to the ground. He was crouched there, kneeling beside something—a lifeless shape. Her heart stopped, and she felt dizzy. *Westley?*

His hands were at Westley's throat. Evelyn opened her mouth to scream, but he saw her and rose. He just stood there for an instant, shocked to be caught. Evelyn backed away, shaking her head. She thought she heard him say "No," but the wild rush in her mind obliterated all else.

Hoofbeats thundered in the distance. The Renegade listened, then leapt astride his gray. Evelyn ran to where Westley lay and crumpled beside him. She screamed in bitter pain—there was no life beneath her touch, no life in him anywhere. She turned her face to his murderer, hate filling her. How had she found this murderer attractive? Even briefly?

The dark shape hesitated, as if anguished to

leave, but a moment later Lieutenant Talbot and his guards galloped toward them, and the Renegade vanished into the night.

Evelyn bowed her head to Westley's silent chest and sobbed.

Chapter Two

"Lieutenant Talbot, you cannot believe my brother, my sixteen-year-old brother, is responsible for Westley Reid's murder."

Rafael de Aguirre removed his small, round spectacles and polished them with his handkerchief, but he kept his gaze fixed on John Talbot. The officer sat back in a dark wooden chair, relaxed behind his desk. Beside him, Westley's widow stood, as beautiful now as the first time Rafael saw her. From the moment Rafael entered the office, she had avoided meeting his eyes, but he felt her there as if she touched him.

"I must agree with Se-nor de Aguirre, Lieutenant. It wasn't Diego de Aguirre I saw fleeing Westley's murder." She pronounced "Señor" haltingly, as if she hadn't quite mastered Spanish inflections yet. Without his spectacles in place, his image of her was blurred, but Rafael felt her there, even more than he saw her.

Talbot glanced at Evelyn Reid, but his brief smile indicated an affection that didn't include much heed. "It was dark that night, my dear. You were terrified. And this man, you said, wore a cape and a mask."

"I am sure of what I saw, Lieutenant. The man I saw was older and larger of build than Diego."

Talbot's jaw tensed, but his tight smile remained. "Moments witnessed in such fleeting time can be misleading, Evelyn. But we have testimonial to declare that young Diego has boasted of your husband's murder."

Rafael didn't move. He fought the rising fury inside himself, combating it with clear thought and reason. "Testimonial from whom?"

Talbot's smile turned mocking. "A source who wishes to remain anonymous." He adjusted papers on his desk, aligning them into an ordered stack. "As you well know, de Aguirre, your family is held in high esteem by the local people in this pueblo. To speak against any of you might be deemed dangerous."

"It would be in this case, for the claim is a lie." Rafael's words came with more passion than he usually allowed. He had won the confidence of the local government by appearing as a soft-spoken teacher of children, quietly asserting the rights of his people, and at least seeming to back down when countered.

"You are nothing more than the pueblo's schoolmaster, de Aguirre. I suggest you leave this matter in the hands of those best equipped to deal with it."

Talbot's words were baiting, but Rafael refused to accept the challenge. "Had those in authority chosen a more likely suspect, I would do just that, Lieutenant."

John Talbot had come west soon after Evelyn's husband, appointed by the governor to gauge the trouble posed by the conflicted pueblo. It seemed to Rafael that the lieutenant's real interest was elsewhere, though what he hoped to gain from taking over the pueblo, Rafael couldn't guess.

Since Westley Reid arrived in New Mexico, a group of greedy landowners had seemed more and more bent on taking over the pueblo, and it had been during that time that the so-called Renegade began riding in defense of his people. Sometimes, he freed unfairly charged prisoners, and other times, disrupted attempts by the landowners to drive people from their homes. Though he had won every battle he'd fought, he had never killed anyone—but now he was accused of Westley's death.

Now the man who had been considered a hero by the pueblo had become an enemy to the American authorities, and Rafael's own brother was to pay the dearest price for their suspicion.

Talbot tapped the desk thoughtfully, glancing at Rafael through lowered lids. "It seems you and I differ on what actions protect the people of this pueblo. Stricter control, I think, might serve them better than cheering on the lawless antics of a renegade Indian."

Rafael straightened and stepped back from the desk. He replaced his spectacles, then adjusted them on his nose. "Each man must follow his own heart, and choose the leaders he deems worthy."

There was so little time to turn this tide that threatened to destroy his brother. Reason wouldn't help. Only the appearance of the true Renegade would break the noose. Yet who would then defend these people against the greed and avarice of their suppressors?

Evelyn shifted her weight, her hands clasped at her waist. "The Renegade may have seemed noble, Se-nor de Aguirre, but he proved himself dark of heart when he murdered my husband."

With his spectacles in place, he could see her clearly now. He almost wished he had left the sight a blur. She was a beautiful woman, the most beautiful woman he had ever seen. Her eyes were the color of the ocean in a storm—a misty gray-blue, revealing a depth of emotion to mirror the sea. She was taller than the women he knew, but slight of build, as if in her height she strained to make up for her perceived delicacy.

Since they first met, he'd seen her occasionally at a distance. He had dined once at Westley Reid's home, but after that, she and Rafael had avoided each other. After Westley died, Rafael had wanted to go to her, to comfort her, but remembering the awkwardness of their first meeting, he had written a polite, formal letter instead. She was in mourning, and the devastation of her husband's death must have been intense, particularly since he had been murdered so brutally.

"I am sorry for your loss, Mrs. Reid. Your husband was a good man."

She nodded, still avoiding his eyes. "Thank you. I do not understand why he was killed. He believed strongly in leaving the pueblo in its native hands."

Rafael replaced his handkerchief and sighed. "You would be wise to heed Mrs. Reid's words, Lieutenant. Not only is my brother too young to be the man you seek, but Westley Reid's murder happened almost a year ago—when Diego was fifteen, and well known to be small for his age." He paused, feeling his young brother's wrath from afar. Nothing infuriated him more than implications of youth and small stature. Though he was growing, the delight in teasing him never ceased.

Talbot didn't waver. His smile indicated he knew beyond question the truth of Diego's innocence. "Such a minimal argument will do little to sway your brother's sentence, I'm afraid."

Rafael sensed a dark gamble behind Talbot's threats, even more reason not to show a reaction. "If you truly believe my brother guilty, you must surely do everything in your power to assure his conviction. That will take time, of course, and I am confident I can change your opinion on this matter."

Sometimes, it was hard to speak calmly when he wanted to fight. But now was not the time for passion.

A slow smile spread across Talbot's narrow face, and this time there was no mistaking his expression of challenge. He rose from his seat and came around the desk to face Rafael. "I'm afraid it won't be as simple as that, schoolmaster. There is a dangerous criminal on the loose in this pueblo—a man who has caused major disruption since my arrival at this command." He paused to shake his head as if disgusted. "This Renegade must be brought to justice, so that peace and control might be restored. Despite his youth, we have reason to believe your brother Diego de Aguirre responsible for Westley Reid's death, as well as for donning this devilish disguise under which he torments my command. The Mexicans and Indians and other misfits of this pueblo may find his actions heroic, but I do not, and he *will* be stopped."

Rafael hesitated, surprised by Talbot's twisted logic. How could a people who had lived here so long be deemed misfits? But now was not the time for challenge. "As I said, I am confident I can change your mind on this issue."

Talbot's pale eyes glittered, but Rafael forced impassive calm over his own features. "My government agrees with me, de Aguirre. As soon as a scaffold can be erected, we are to carry out the sentence." Talbot paused, long enough for Rafael to know he felt he held all the cards this time. "Hanging, I am sorry to say. Tonight, at sunset."

Rafael didn't move, didn't breathe. He heard Evelyn Reid's sharp gasp of astonishment—she hadn't known this sentence until now, he felt sure of it. "You can't do this, Lieutenant! I told you, I'm certain the man I saw the night Westley died wasn't Diego!"

Talbot didn't take his combative gaze from Rafael. "You said, my dear Evelyn, that he was Indian, as is the man we've all seen on his brazen raids."

She stomped her foot, surprising both men. She looked ready to fight. "As are most of the people living here! Lieutenant, that's no reason. What's more, Diego doesn't look Indian. He looks Spanish."

Talbot wasn't listening to her. Rafael knew now that his prey was elsewhere, and had never been his brother. "Because a man wears traditional native garb doesn't mean his blood is Zuni."

Talbot sat back on his desktop, smug, sure of himself, lips curled in a smile. "I have never understood this legend. . . . Tell me of it, Rafael."

Rafael went to the door, then looked back. "I have no time for stories, Lieutenant. But know this—the man who rides takes on the form of an ancient warrior, he who appears to his people in times of darkness. He is not a man, but a ghost. . . ." He paused while Talbot waited, expectant. "He is not, perhaps, an enemy you wish to stir again."

Talbot seated himself behind his desk again. "On the contrary, de Aguirre—that is precisely what I intend to do."

Rafael smiled. "Then I hope you will get your wish, for the Renegade's appearance will clear my brother of false charges." He opened the door and felt the warm, dry air against his face. "I assume you will permit me to visit my brother?"

"Of course. You have until sundown."

So little time . . . And so many people in his care, people who depended on him, his reckless brother most of all. Rafael closed his eyes, and he knew despite all the people in his life, all the friends and family, he was alone. But even as the loneliness made itself known, another presence, delicate and poignant, touched his heart. He knew where it came from, and he tried to resist.

Rafael looked back into Talbot's dark office and saw Evelyn standing there. She hadn't moved since he'd first entered. There was something about her that drew his attention, just as it had when she first stepped off the train. Her beauty intrigued him, as it would any man, but there was something more, a poignant sensitivity, an ageless grace—these things compelled him closer, when closer was the last place he should be.

The impression he had of her was of a woman searching for something, vaguely, as if she had given up real hope it would ever be found.

He shook his head and went out the door, then down the stairs to the plaza. If ever there was a woman to avoid, it was Westley Reid's widow.

He found his brother in a dark cell on the level below Talbot's office. A room that had once been used to store corn had been converted into a jail, to which steel bars had been added. Guards surrounded the entrance as if Billy the Kid were held inside.

They knew the schoolmaster, and found him no threat, so Rafael was admitted without question. Diego lay on a narrow bench inside the first cell, looking restless, but only a little worried. When he spotted Rafael, he smiled as if rescued from a tedious day of study.

The boy yawned, but didn't bother to get up.

"What took you so long?" He grinned and shook his head. "So have you heard? Do you know who they think I am?"

Rafael nodded, but his heart ached. Diego believed, as he had from childhood, that Rafael would protect him from all injury, that he was safe in his brother's care. This time, it might not be so easy.

"Lieutenant Talbot has told me that you're suspected of being the Renegade. I do not think he believes it."

Diego folded his arms behind his head, frowning. "It's just a ruse to draw out the real man. Well, they have no proof it's me, so they'll have to let me go." He closed his eyes, content, but when Rafael didn't respond, he peeked over, suspicious. "Right? You did remind them of the law, didn't you?"

"The officials we've been dealing with in Santa Fe of late don't seem to hold much respect for the law. And Lieutenant Talbot is taking this to a level I hadn't expected."

"What 'level'?"

"Diego, he intends to hang you for the murder of Westley Reid. Tonight."

"They're going to *hang* me? What for?" Diego sat upright on his narrow wooden bench, aghast. His wavy black hair fell all around his face, and he seemed to have grown taller even since the previous day's dinner. Taller and thinner.

Rafael sat down beside his brother, fighting to remain calm and reassuring. "When you get home, I'm doubling your meals."

Diego's eyes narrowed and his full lips curled

into a quick, youthful frown. "*If* I get home, you mean."

Rafael looked into his brother's dark eyes. He saw the innocent pride of early manhood, struggling to conceal fear. Their Spanish father had died when Diego was seven, and their mother took them to live among her own people, the Zuni who lived west of Santa Fe. When she died, Rafael became parent to his brother, teaching him with such skill that soon all the children of the pueblo became his students.

He remembered when Diego was hurt, how he would fling himself into his brother's arms sobbing—he was a wild, emotional child, now struggling to seem careless when his death was just hours away. But the dark eyes glimmered with tears and Rafael's heart ached. He put his arm over the boy's shoulders.

They looked at each other, and Rafael forced a reassuring smile. "You know I won't let anything happen to you."

Diego placed his hand on Rafael's shoulder, and suddenly he seemed older than his sixteen years. "I never doubted that. My brother, it's not me I'm worried about." He paused and a single tear fell to his high cheekbone. "It's you."

Evelyn stood on the balcony of John Talbot's pueblo office, looking down at the scaffold his guards were assembling for Diego de Aguirre's hanging. She felt trapped, caught in a spiraling downward force that threatened her, everyone with its darkness. She wanted vengeance for Westley's death, but at what price? She had seen Diego often, a tall, thin boy with a bright, sweet face and large brown eyes. He always seemed to be laughing, tossing balls, teasing and laughing with the other boys. His manners were polite, because he had been well schooled by his older brother, but he was known for his playful mischief. He was as unlikely a murderer as she could imagine.

"Lieutenant, you know Diego de Aguirre didn't kill my husband."

Talbot didn't answer. He gazed out the window into the plaza and smiled. "Don't worry about that boy, Evelyn. I need him—that's all."

"You think threatening to hang him will bring out the real killer? Why?"

"It may be the boy is important."

"I cannot believe the Renegade who killed Westley would care about Diego's fate."

"We'll see."

"What will you do if he doesn't appear? I must have your word that Diego will not be harmed."

Talbot glanced at her, then took her hand, patting it. "Of course not, my dear. You must trust me in this. Have I not worked tirelessly to hunt down and bring to justice your husband's killer? Westley meant almost as much to me as to you. You know we were at Harvard together. He was like a brother." His gaze shifted again to the plaza below. "His killer will meet with the justice he deserves."

"Perhaps you should have assured the schoolmaster that his brother is in no real danger." As much as Rafael de Aguirre's presence unnerved her, she respected him. The letter he wrote to her after Westley died had been kind, and she knew he was a good man. She admired his dedication to the children of the pueblo and his loyalty to his brother. He had brought together an odd mix of children to his small school, from Mexican families as well as Zuni, and even a few of the Chinese who had been enlisted to build the new railroad. Even a few of the white settlers had begun sending their children to his classroom.

Talbot wouldn't think seriously of executing Rafael's brother, not in Santa Fe where their family was held in such high esteem.

"What are you going to do if you catch him? They won't let you hang him, they won't even let him go to trial."

Talbot fingered his mustache thoughtfully. "That is a problem, I agree. I will get permission from the governor to have him transported elsewhere, perhaps north to Denver."

"Whatever happens, Westley left control of the pueblo to Rafael de Aguirre. The people of this pueblo have nothing to fear from the Renegade's capture." She paused. "Maybe the Renegade is threatening them in some way."

"You admire the schoolmaster very much, my dear?"

She bit her lip and tried to appear casual. She hadn't forgotten the dangerous tingle in her veins in Rafael's presence, nor her shortness of breath when he held her hands. "I do admire him, of course. He has done good work here. Westley thought highly of him."

"Indeed, Rafael de Aguirre has ingratiated himself even to the governor—he will hear no ill of him."

"Why should he? He has done nothing but

educate his people, so well that the rail workers now bring their own to his classroom."

"A noble man, by all accounts. Yet he seemed . . . forceful in my office today, don't you agree?"

Evelyn frowned. "You are about to hang his brother, for a crime everyone knows he didn't commit. I am surprised that Rafael acted as calmly as he did."

"Perhaps he has something else planned."

As Rafael left Diego's cell, a dark tide seemed to rise against him. There was so little time. Too much pressed in on Santa Fe now, too many conflicting interests. But why the new arrivals wanted an abandoned Zuni pueblo, he didn't know. They did want it, though, badly—enough to try unscrupulous methods of driving out the people who had settled there.

It was an odd mixture who had settled in the small, abandoned pueblo outside Santa Fe. Once, it had been connected to the seven legendary cities of Cibola, those sought by the Conquistadors, a history from which his mother's people, the Zuni, were descended. They called themselves *A:shiwi,* and among all the native people, they had managed to hold best to the old ways and customs.

When Allejandro de Aguirre fell in love with the chief's strong-willed daughter, the *A:shiwi* forbade the match. Allejandro took her from her father, and they settled in the small, deserted pueblo, taking in people of all races who needed homes. Allejandro had great dreams, as did his wife, of a place where all cultures could live together in peace. He had been an imaginative man, and he inspired his eldest son with the same dream—but unlike his poetic father, Rafael had the sense and understanding of the world to bring those dreams to life.

The pueblo was now home to Zuni, Mexican, and Chinese, as well as white settlers who hadn't the money to live among their more favored brethren, and they had bonded together in a community that the larger Santa Fe lacked.

It had worked well, until the pueblo unexpectedly gained the interest of a secretive group of landowners brought to New Mexico by the promise of the new railroad. Using a grant given to a soldier during the Mexican-American war, the American government declared that the Tewa Pueblo was now the possession of David Reid from Boston.

The landowners enlisted a young officer, John Talbot, but at times, Rafael felt it was Talbot who influenced his benefactors, and not the other way around. Lieutenant Talbot proved brutal, enforcing unfair laws imposed by the landowners, and it was then that the Renegade made his first appearance, taking the guise of an Anasazi god who protected his people. The Zuni believed they were descended from the ancient Anasazi, and his arrival gave the people both courage and hope. The Renegade killed no one, but his daring rides kept Talbot and his brutal guards at bay.

When David Reid's son arrived, Rafael had feared the worst, but rather than supporting the landowner's claims, Westley Reid proved to be kind and thoughtful, inspired by the work Rafael had done. The landowners had attempted to convince Westley that the inhabitants of the pueblo should be removed, or forced to work for the landowners in payment for remaining, but Westley would hear none of it. Instead, Westley gave Rafael management of the pueblo, and had promised to return to Washington, where he would restore the land rights to the people who lived there.

Rafael had no idea why the landowners wanted the pueblo and the mountain land surrounding it so much. There was far more to be had in the mines higher in the mountains, or working with the railroad to secure their fortune. But when Westley died, John Talbot had brought in a force of guards, supposedly to catch Westley's killer, but more likely to use the Renegade as evidence that the pueblo should be put in their hands.

As of now, ownership of the pueblo was in the hands of the most vulnerable person imaginable, Westley's widow Evelyn Reid. She was as steadfast as her husband had been in her desire to leave the pueblo in native hands, but Talbot had kept her secured away, and more evident still, she wanted nothing to do with Rafael.

Many forces rose to conflict within Rafael as he tried to keep his father's vision alive, and create a better life for the people he loved. As he walked through the plaza, he felt those invisible walls closing in around him, and unaccustomed fear forming in his heart.

A soft touch on his shoulder startled him, and he turned. Evelyn Reid had caught up with him but she paused before speaking. She looked nervous and seized a quick breath before speaking. "I am sorry about your brother, Se-nor de Aguirre."

He hadn't been so close to her since the day they met. He remembered their awkward dinner with shame, knowing he had caused her discomfort by his rash infatuation. "I do not blame you, Mrs. Reid."

She nodded, quickly and looked off to the side. "I will do what I can to convince Lieutenant Talbot to change his order."

"I do not think it is my brother he's after."

"No, I know that. He thinks somehow this act will draw out my husband's killer."

Rafael sighed and looked toward the western mountains, still shrouded in mists. "And it may, Mrs. Reid. It may."

She nodded vigorously. "I hope so. It has been so long."

He looked back at her. She seemed wistful, and so alone. "You should have gone home long ago."

"I should, I know." Her gaze turned toward the mountains, too. "When I came here, I thought it would be different."

"What did you hope to find when you came here, Mrs. Reid?"

"I hoped to find myself in a place where I would matter, where I could make some difference in the world."

"You would make a difference wherever you are."

"Ah, but when I came, there was another in my place, and what I hoped to do was already done."

He hadn't realized her dreams had been specific. "Who?"

A faint smile formed on her lips. "You." He stared, and she looked at the mountains again as if it was easier than looking at him. "When I lived in Boston, I studied to be a teacher, too." She paused. "Didn't Westley tell you?"

Rafael hesitated. Westley Reid had mentioned his wife often before she arrived, but as a beautiful, delicate possession. He had seemed proud to have won her, and spoke lavishly of her family's wealth and position. Rafael didn't doubt that Westley loved his wife, for what man wouldn't? But if he knew nothing of her secret dreams, that love must have left her a lonely woman.

"I could always use help, Mrs. Reid." He liked the thought. They would work together, teaching children, and they would become friends. Perhaps this kind of arrangement might erase the embarrassment of their first meeting.

She tensed at the suggestion, as if it bore some unspeakable threat. Considering his behavior that day, perhaps she was right. "That is a kind offer, se-nor, but it is time I went home."

"There is much in the world that prevents us from doing what we wish to do."

"Yes." They looked at each other, and he saw in her a shadow of himself. Like him, she was lonely, caught in a storm she was doing her best to endure. "Se-nor de Aguirre, I will do what I can to help your brother. Westley thought so highly of you, and counted you as his friend." She sounded formal, and she didn't meet his eyes.

"Thank you. But I fear the only thing that can save my brother now is an appearance by our Renegade warrior god."

"God, indeed!" Her little face tightened with anger. "I hope that he dares show himself, though I can't think why so evil a man would care to save your brother. Perhaps it pleases his conceit to defy the law, and for your brother's sake, I hope so."

"It is my hope also that the man who killed your husband is brought to justice." Rafael paused, searching her face. "You are sure it is this Renegade who murdered him?"

She nodded vigorously. "It was, yes. I saw him myself. He was kneeling by Westley's body . . ." Her voice caught. "I do not remember what I was doing, but I was walking, you see . . ." Her words trailed and she looked away as if overcome, not by grief, but by shame.

A woman so sensitive that she would blame herself for her husband's death, for not being at his side. A low ache surfaced in Rafael's heart. How much had she loved her young husband? How much grief had she endured, waiting all these months for his memory to be avenged?

He wanted to touch her, to comfort her, but any comfort she took from him now would cause her greater pain by nightfall. Rafael stepped back and bowed slightly. "Mrs. Reid, I wish you peace, for you deserve all things blessed and sweet."

His words surprised her, but she nodded once. "Thank you."

She wanted to put distance between them—he felt her withdrawal though he wasn't sure what threat he posed to her. He sensed much unspoken between them, and he found himself wanting to confide in her, to tell her how afraid he was that one day he would fail, and someone—even his brother—might suffer because he had been too cautious, or too reckless . . .

He stilled the impulse and released her. Of all people, what madness would make him long to confide in Evelyn Reid?

They stepped apart at the same time. She turned and walked back to Talbot's office, but when she reached the door, she looked back over shoulder. Rafael's heart took an extra beat. Here, standing apart, he found what he had missed when she stood close.

They knew each other, somehow deep inside, and they were both afraid. But from the time he'd first met her, he had felt her fingers invisible against his skin, in his hair. He felt himself reach toward her as fear gripped his heart. *My brother . . .*

She met his eyes and he felt her as if some ethereal part of her touched him. Again, and not for the first time, as if her heart knew what her mind could not, as if she knew what danger awaited him at sunset, he heard her voice in his mind . . . *Take care. . . .*

Sunset came glorious in shades of red and gold. The adobe walls glowed as if they, too, were made of gold. Evelyn stood on Lieutenant Talbot's balcony, looking out over the crowd that had gathered for Diego de Aguirre's execution.

Talbot ascended the stairs to join Evelyn, partially, she guessed, to avoid the objects hurtled at him by the children in the crowd. He puffed a breath after bounding up the stairs, but he looked pleased with himself. He dusted debris off his jacket and stood beside Evelyn. "They're not taking it well."

She frowned. "Did you expect them to?"

"I didn't realize young Diego meant so much to them. He's just the schoolteacher's mischievous brother, after all. But we're going to have trouble if I put the Renegade's neck in a noose, that is certain."

Evelyn glared at the crowd. "He killed Westley."

Talbot placed his hand on her shoulder. "Westley meant nothing to these people, my dear, however good his intentions may have been. This Renegade means more. It pleases their conceit to have such a 'hero' among them."

"What are you going to do if he doesn't appear?"

Talbot looked out over the crowd, his attention fixed on the western foothills. "He will come."

Evelyn looked to the foothills, too. Where the desert met the pine and aspen forests, there the Renegade had so often ridden, always aware of his target, always fast, so mystical that some people truly did believe him a god. Evelyn remembered the first time she saw him with shame now. She had admired the Renegade, too. He came as if out of a girl's dream, tall and mysterious and strong, riding to right cruel wrongs.

And this man she had admired, that Westley had admired, had proven himself no god, but an animal instead, fighting not for good, but for his own conceit. She believed now that he was more interested in controlling the pueblo for himself than for its people, and that if he won, he would prove an even more callous leader than the landowners had been.

Beside her, Talbot's eyes lit with fire and he pointed toward the narrow path running down from the foothills. "There! A rider approaches."

Evelyn looked out and gripped the balcony rail tightly. *He* rode down from the hills, the man, the villain, who had tormented her nightmares since Westley's murder. She saw him now, his long black hair streaming loose behind his head, a black cape, and that mask of some ancient god.

In his hand, he bore a long, coiling rope. Westley had not been shot, but had been strangled. No one doubted what weapon was used, not after Evelyn herself had seen the Renegade standing over her husband's body. She closed her eyes, and remembered him crouched beside Westley, his hands at her husband's throat. He had seen her, but when she screamed, Talbot and his guards arrived and the Renegade had leapt upon his horse and galloped away.

Now he rode into the plaza like an avenging god, and the crowd cheered.

"The moment has come, my dear. If you will excuse me . . ." Talbot bounded down the stairs, dodging flying rocks, and went to the scaffold beside Diego. The guards didn't move against the Renegade, but surrounded Diego instead.

Evelyn stood watching in horror as Talbot himself fixed the noose around Diego's neck.

She shook her head in mute fear but the Renegade drew his dark gray horse to a halt. She expected violence, for him to charge and attack among gunfire from the guards. Instead, he rode slowly to the scaffold, and the crowd parted. No one made a sound as he dismounted and stood before the scaffold steps.

"It is me you want, Lieutenant. Set Diego de Aguirre free, and I will surrender to you."

Despite the noose, Diego shook his head, and Evelyn heard his plaintive "No." Who was this man, that even a boy would risk his life to protect him?

The crowd murmured in astonishment and denial, but Talbot laughed. "I'm not so big a fool as that. Guards, surround him."

Still, the Renegade made no move to flee or fight. His strange whip hung at his side, within easy reach. Evelyn hadn't seen his weapon clearly the first time she had seen him in action. Everything had moved too quickly then, and she had been too stunned by his skill and the presence he radiated. Her vision fixed on it now. Not exactly a whip, it was a thick, leather cord that split into three ends, to each of which was attached a hard, nut-shaped pouch.

Though his magnificent horse stamped as if ready for the challenge it was used to, the Renegade reined it in, and it stilled. "Release the boy."

When the guards surrounded the Renegade, Talbot pulled the noose from Diego's neck. Evelyn held her breath, and for an instant, it was as if she saw inside her enemy's thoughts. She did not perceive surrender, but a battle instead.

"His whip, his whip! Lieutenant!"

Before her words flew, the Renegade's whip snapped in the air. He wielded it like some ancient warrior god. The three ends worked as if his fingers controlled each split cord separately. The cords wrapped around one guard's leg, yanking him off his feet, knocking him into another.

Nothing could stop him. The guards faltered and fell into disarray. Talbot shouted orders that no soldier was quick enough to obey. The Renegade's perfectly trained horse spun left, then right, and the Renegade wielded his weapon so fast and with such skill that none of them seemed to know how to combat him. A guard aimed a rifle, and the three cords cracked around it, sending it high into the air.

Through the shouts, the cries, and the cheers from the crowd, Evelyn heard him laugh. Nothing could have enflamed her more than the laughter of this man who had killed her gentle, trusting husband. She moved in a blind fury. She stumbled down from the narrow adobe stairs and charged into the plaza. She shoved past the shocked onlookers, and his whip cracked in the dry air. . . .

Something slammed into her back—one of the hard pouches. Evelyn screamed with the sharp pain and the Renegade froze, his strong arm in midair. She looked up, hating him, and knew he hadn't seen her coming. The guards seized their chance and surrounded him, binding him with desperate speed, but he didn't move. He just stared at Evelyn as she crumpled to her knees in pain.

They bound his hands as Talbot came running from the scaffold to her side, but Evelyn rose to her feet, spellbound with fury and pain. She walked to him, stared up at him, surprised at how tall he was. Her hand shook as she reached for his mask. Dimly, without true awareness, she realized it was a beautiful artifact from ancient times past, tied around his head by a leather strap.

She gripped the strap in shaking hands and yanked.

Cold shock turned her blood to ice as she looked into the mystic brown eyes of the pueblo schoolmaster, Rafael de Aguirre.

Chapter Three

"Do you have the revolver I gave you, Evelyn?" Talbot spoke quietly, careful not to be overheard by even his own guards. The train whistle blew, alerting the passengers to its imminent departure, but Evelyn kept her gaze pinned on the station house where the guards surrounded Rafael de Aguirre.

"I have it."

Talbot patted her shoulder. His touch seemed eager rather than comforting. "The pueblo inhabitants have reacted even more violently to de Aguirre's arrest than I imagined. I don't want to take any chances with you."

Since Rafael had been revealed as the Renegade, Talbot had treated her as if she were precious, visiting her daily, sometimes several times in one day. More than anyone else, he seemed to understand her low, boiling fury against the man she had trusted, the man who killed her husband. Something had changed inside her that day, and she didn't know herself anymore. She had lost all sight of who she had been before she looked up and into the beautiful eyes of her husband's killer. She had seen all shame in his eyes—her own, most of all.

"I am concerned about your welfare, Evelyn. I hate to think who among his people he has enlisted against you. They blame you for unmasking him. . . ." Talbot's voice trailed, but Evelyn didn't care who blamed her. "They worship de Aguirre because it is he who now controls their land."

"But it was Westley who gave him that control."

"Your husband was a generous man, but naive. It is a shame he didn't see through de Aguirre's scheme to gain control of the pueblo. But it worked, didn't it? De Aguirre gained Westley's confidence and then killed him. And now they hold you responsible for his capture."

Evelyn hadn't noticed that the pueblo people had turned on her, but then, she had barely left her room since Rafael's arrest. She had received many letters written on Rafael's behalf, but though their support of Westley's killer infuriated her, no one had threatened her.

Most of the letters were emotional, pleading for Rafael's life, telling of the good he had done. Some were angry, condemning a law imposed upon them by white settlers. One that she remembered too clearly had been written from a student—it was perfectly spelled and articulated, occasionally abstract, but nothing concealed the admiration and pure emotion in the writing of one anonymous boy.

Talbot surveyed the area, appearing uneasy as if fearing Rafael might still manage to escape. Though he had brought in more guards for Rafael's move, and had barricaded the station, pueblo people still lined the entrance, shouting furiously at the men who would take their beloved hero away and to his death.

"They surrounded the jail continuously, they followed us from the pueblo to the station." Talbot clucked his tongue and looked thoughtful. "I fear that even taking him to Denver may not be enough."

Evelyn's muscles tensed. "Why not? You said the judge there wouldn't be biased by Rafael's reputation."

"If we get him there."

Evelyn fingered her small crochet bag and felt the cold, hard gun that Talbot had given her. "Do you think they will try to rescue him?"

"I think the 'schoolmaster' is adept at evading justice. I hate to think how many people he will kill if he escapes."

She hadn't imagined he could escape. The thought stabbed into her like knives. "It is almost over." She spoke to herself more than to Talbot, but he sighed heavily.

"Would that it were so! No, I'm afraid it will be weeks, months even, before de Aguirre faces the sentence he deserves."

Darkness as thick as fog seemed to close in around Evelyn. Hate and loss and shame burned inside her. Every word Talbot spoke fired that pit inside her, and she knew suddenly, with perfect clarity, that if she didn't act Rafael would escape.

The early morning sun rose over the adobe walls and through the mountains, glinting on the Sangre de Cristo mountain range. The train whistled again, and the train footman began to direct passengers onto the train. Valets loaded luggage, but Evelyn carried her own small bag herself. A large, gold-trimmed trunk required four men to hoist it into the storage compartment. Evelyn looked around, wondering who in Santa Fe required such elaborate luggage.

A large, buxom woman who appeared in her mid-fifties pushed her way through the crowd and addressed the conductor as he supervised the embarkment. She clutched a small, grumpy looking white dog to her ample chest, and gave the impression of a ship in full sail entering a tiny harbor. A small, rabbit-eyed man scurried behind her. Evelyn wasn't sure if he was the woman's husband or her servant.

"Mr. St. Claire demands that the greatest care be taken with our trunks and other baggage!" The woman's voice was as shrill yet robust as the woman herself. "You, there, conductor! See that those 'persons' you have enlisted understand." She eyed the valets critically. "They appear to be of the Mexican variety and I have seen at least one black-skinned man handling trunks and baggage. If any of my valuables, which I have packed with the greatest care, should turn up missing or in disarray, you, sir, will have to answer to Mr. St. Claire!"

Evelyn's heart lightened unexpectedly and she smiled at Talbot's confused expression. "I would say that the conductor is blessed if it is Mr. St. Claire he must answer to, and not his wife."

Talbot smiled, too, but his brow furrowed at Evelyn's change in mood. "Indeed." He motioned to the station house. "When the passengers are abroad, they will bring forth de Aguirre. See, the crowd already awaits him. Their adoration will fuel his conceit and with his audacity, I fully expect him to attempt escape."

Evelyn's amusement faded at the reminder of the Renegade's penchant for daring getaways. She couldn't let him escape this time, but Talbot's doubt encouraged her own.

The guards emerged from the station house, leading Rafael toward the car that had been prepared for its prisoner. She saw him there, surrounded, but taller than all the guards. The morning sun glinted on his black hair, shining on him as if even the forces of nature adored him. He didn't look toward her, nor did he seem to notice his guards. He looked straight ahead, self-contained and handsome as if nothing could truly contain his power.

Talbot squeezed her shoulder. "I will have to leave you to escort de Aguirre onto the train. Perhaps you should board the train now. . . ." He spoke as if he knew she wouldn't accept.

"No. I must see that he doesn't escape." Her voice sounded flat and empty, perhaps because she had slept so little, and that fitfully.

"Very well. Take care, Evelyn. I expect him to attempt escape. I have alerted my guards to this possibility, but as we have seen time and time again, the Renegade is a dangerously resourceful man. Perhaps I should have positioned sharpshooters, but the governor advised me to do nothing to stir the emotions of the people here any higher."

The onlookers shoved against the barricade, voices raised, and a commotion ensued inside the station. Evelyn's heart held its beat. The guards led Rafael de Aguirre forward, but the crowd pushed in, slowing their progress. Talbot maneuvered away from the angry onlookers, and stood near the entrance to a rear car that had already been set up as a jail car.

Evelyn stood frozen as Rafael emerged from the crowd. Someone shouted, a woman sobbed. He spoke quietly to them, and as if directed by a god, they silenced. He looked calm, regal, as if nothing could touch him. He inspired such love and such fury. . . .

He would escape, somehow. He had befriended her husband, he had looked into her eyes, and somehow woven a spell she couldn't deny. Westley lay dead, and she was torn apart, and he would escape as a hero. . . .

Rafael walked a little ahead of his guards, confident despite his proclaimed fate. He wasn't wearing his spectacles, but Evelyn wasn't surprised. No doubt they were part of his real disguise, that of a kind schoolmaster more interested in books than a renegade's daring deeds. Though his hands were bound, he looked strong, almost invincible.

He wore a loose-fitting white shirt, bound with a long cord. Evelyn's breath caught. It wasn't the weapon he had used in his attacks, but it could certainly be wielded with the same devastating results. His arms were bound at the wrists, but tied in front of his body rather than in back, no doubt because he would be seated for so long. The rope around his waist was poised perfectly, easily within his reach. . . . She was surprised he hadn't used it already.

She saw into his thoughts as if they were connected to her own. She had felt that the first time she met him, and maybe she was right. But she knew. He was waiting—waiting until he ascended the stairs. Then he would turn and, with his bound hands wield the rope, startling the guards. As if it had already happened, she imagined him leaping atop the train, then disappearing while the crowd cheered at his glory.

Wild hatred filled her heart. She knew what had to be done, and she knew only she could do it. He placed one foot on the wooden step, then stopped. He turned, tense like a cougar coiled for the hunt.

Evelyn seized her gun from her small bag. She lifted the revolver; it felt as heavy as a cannon. No one noticed her, because all attention was fixed on Rafael, but then as if warned by angels, he turned his dark gaze toward her.

He saw her holding Westley's revolver and he squinted to see. His perfect, sensual lips parted in astonishment. In that one instant, she felt as if he saw inside her, too, to the madness that had consumed her since his arrest, to the long months of anguish and secret shame that possessed her, and even to the endless torment into which she now walked blindly.

In his eyes, she saw not fear, but . . . sympathy.

Her whole body shook. Talbot noticed her as she took aim, but he seemed too shocked to summon his guards or stop her. Evelyn's fingers squeezed around the trigger, but as it clicked, she noticed a dark bruise covering half of Rafael's broad forehead. *He had been beaten.*

Her gun fired as if pulled by an unseen hand and the shot went awry. The bullet grazed past Rafael's head, and a board on the station roof splintered with its impact. The guards looked to Talbot, who motioned to them, and they shoved Rafael into the jail car. But Rafael himself stared at her in astonishment.

The shock of what she had done, had tried to do, swept through her. Evelyn sank to her knees and sobbed.

She had tried to kill him. And came damned close, too. Rafael sat bound in the jail car, but he ignored his guards as he looked through the barred windows. Without his spectacles, everything at a distance remained a blur. Maybe his dim sight explained his love of reading and the ease with which he lost himself in the worlds woven by pueblo storytellers. But seeing only a few clear feet in front of him prevented him from ever being much good with guns. Had he been a more advantaged hero, he might have been able to shoot the noose from his brother's neck.

Had he been armed with a long-distance weapon rather than an Argentinean bola, Westley Reid's fate would certainly have been different. And Evelyn Reid would never have aimed her small gun at his heart. . . .

She really wanted to kill him. Rafael closed his eyes, but he could still see her small face, pale and wide-eyed as if consumed by a quiet madness. He shouldn't be hurt that Evelyn Reid had come to hate him. She had every reason, or at least thought she did. But what kind of hell had she endured over these months that could drive such a gentle, sensitive woman to shoot a man?

He half believed Talbot had put her up to it, though he couldn't imagine the lieutenant would hire a sweet, shy woman as an assassin with so many trained guards at his beck-and-call. Certainly, they would be better shots than she.

There was nothing he could do now. His last chance at escape had come in its fleeting second, and Evelyn Reid had stopped him. Somehow, she had known his intention. Outside the window, Rafael saw his people, some pounding on the train only to be hauled away by the guards. He had tried to save himself before they tried for him. What would happen to them now that their fate had been ripped from his hands? Evelyn still controlled the pueblo, but with Talbot influencing her, it couldn't be long before she surrendered to his wishes, especially since the man accused of killing her husband had proven to be Westley's trusted friend.

A long, dark road lay ahead, and at its end, his death. Diego was still too young to take over as his people's protector. The boy would put himself in more danger by assuming the role of the Anasazi god than by running. But he knew his brother. The stories told by their father had affected both their hearts, and if Rafael died, Diego would certainly try to follow in his footsteps.

Too many people depended on him for Rafael to accept his own death so easily. There were other white men like Westley Reid, who weren't motivated by greed and corruption and prejudice. If Rafael could reach them, if he could be heard . . . It made too much sense to have an assassin remove him before that could happen. Those people who had killed Westley would find it much easier if he died before he was allowed to speak in court.

But to choose Evelyn Reid, of all people as his assassin?

The noise of the train increased, but Rafael calmed his thoughts. He had to clear his mind, to see his own path before him. His father's bright imagination ran true inside him, as well as his mother's deep understanding. Given time, he would find a way.

Wild emotion proved an unexpected obstacle. Had it not been for the fury of his supporters, he wouldn't have been moved from Santa Fe and could have had his chance to speak before people who understood him. Had it not been for Evelyn's desperate passion against him, he would have made his escape.

Something deeper tugged at his mind. If he hadn't stood there frozen while she pointed her small gun, so deeply moved to witness her anguish and fury, he would have used her distraction and made his escape even more easily than he had planned.

But instead, he stood there feeling her bitter pain, wishing he could comfort her and protect her.

The train pulled slowly from the station, and he looked out to the faces of those he knew so well, and loved. Without his spectacles, they blurred into a common lot as if surrounded by a mystic haze, reminding him that a greater power than himself ultimately looked after them.

For three days prior to his departure, his closest friends had stopped visiting. The reason for their absence disturbed him, because he knew it wasn't for lack of care. Though no one was allowed into his cell; they had gathered by his barred window—Diego and those closest to him had come several times a day. Then nothing.

There was nothing he could do now—but he felt with grim certainty he would soon be learning what they had been up to instead.

"Lieutenant, please forgive me. I don't know what came over me." Evelyn sat in the first class cabin, staring out the window as the train passed through the high mesa landscape. She hadn't spoken for hours. After they boarded the train, the conductor had guided her to her private berth, and she had slept until nightfall.

When the announcement came that dinner was to be served soon, she had wanted to stay in her berth, but Talbot had sent for her. She had forced herself to rise, to face what she had done, but he seemed surprisingly sympathetic.

Talbot took her hand, seeming not to be angered by her mad attempt to shoot Rafael de Aguirre. "Who could blame you for such a brave attempt? Think no more of it, Evelyn. That man murdered your husband, and has been made a hero by the ignorant people of this land. But it is fortunate that you are leaving Santa Fe, for now you will be vilified by their kind. It is lucky also that none of his followers were armed, lest you had been shot."

Evelyn didn't respond. Her memory of the madness that overtook her was cloudy, but rather than the outrage she expected, all she remembered was stunned silence. Obviously, Talbot had seen the outcome more accurately.

Talbot fingered a newspaper given to him by the conductor, but his attention wavered. "I assume that after de Aguirre has been executed, you will return to Boston with your family?"

Evelyn hesitated. There was no reason to stay now, but to return . . . to leave all she had dreamed of, and all Westley had hoped to do . . . "Settling the matter of the pueblo meant so much to my husband."

Talbot released her hand and adjusted his narrow tie. "Surely you can see that Westley's ambition far exceeded the capacity of these people? No, Evelyn, I think you must accept that, though honorable, leaving the pueblo in the hands of those now living there just isn't feasible. You must see that the landowners had the wiser intentions."

She wanted to argue, remembering all Westley had said. But then, his notions had come after long hours of conversation with Rafael de Aguirre. "Perhaps you are right."

Talbot smiled, relaxing into his seat. "I am glad you can see the situation realistically. Westley was an idealist, and I am sure his thinking influenced you. Reality, I'm afraid, rarely matches the pristine dreams of men like Westley Reid."

That much was certain. Evelyn closed her eyes, feeling the endless rhythm of the train racing over the new tracks. The buxom woman who had boarded the train in Santa Fe now occupied the berth nearest Evelyn's. She talked continuously, issuing orders directed at the beleaguered conductor, who passed the care of Mrs. St. Claire to his young porter.

The first class cabins had grand anemities equal to the finest eastern hotels. There was a library, private cabins that converted to berths at night, and elaborate meals. The coach cars boasted far less extravagant care, and were filled with miners and farmers and Indians, people on short hauls or who couldn't afford the splendor and comfort of first class.

The porter rang a bell, his round face alight with welcoming expectation. The passengers rose, led by the formidable Mrs. St. Claire who addressed the porter with both condescension and suspicion. "Mr. St. Claire is concerned that our meal will not be up to the standards assured us in the railway advertisement. Our journey westward, taken approximately ten and one-half months ago, proved to Mr. St. Claire that the proclaimed accoutrements do not always match the reality of our situation."

Evelyn glanced at Talbot, who didn't seem to notice the tiresome Mrs. St. Claire. Something seemed to be troubling him, but she wasn't sure what it was.

The porter's cheerful expression altered and he looked weary. "Mrs . . . ?"

Evelyn repressed a smile. The porter had to know the woman's name—she'd said it often enough. Mrs. St. Claire braced in offense.

"St. Claire. Agnes St. Claire. Mr. St. Claire requires reassurance that our meal will be of the highest caliber available."

"That, I can promise you, Mrs. St. Claire. Tonight, we will serve the finest cut of antelope steak, oyster soup, and plump quail."

"It sounds adequate, if the antelope isn't tough. Mr. St. Claire dislikes the harsh work of chewing, as it antagonizes the jaw."

Evelyn fought giggling, but Talbot still took no notice. She found herself missing Westley so painfully that she thought she might cry. She remembered his quick smile and easy laughter, how he loved moments like this. He would have delighted endlessly in Mrs. St. Claire and her silent husband.

The porter led them to the dining car, but as Evelyn sat down to eat, loneliness filled her heart. She had dreamt of raising children in open spaces, with a freedom often denied them in the strict, correct manner she had known in the eastern mansions.

There would be no children now, and she was returning to a world and a lifestyle that offered nothing of the raw adventure she once longed for. Her father would welcome her home, he would care for her as always. He might even encourage her to wed again, but Evelyn knew she never would. As a white-clad porter delivered her wine and oyster soup, she felt weary enough to sleep forever.

Rafael chewed a hard lump of dried bread and then sampled what appeared to be dried, salted meat. Probably antelope. He set it aside, and contemplated dying of starvation before hanging.

His guards had little better fare, but drank some form of strong beer and played cards. They had given up taunting him—domineering men seemed often to enjoy serving the law in this capacity—because he gave no response at all, and they had lost interest.

Train travel wasn't at all what the fancy brochures promised . . . but then, this was a trip he had never expected to take.

Days of monotonous travel followed. Rafael guessed by the landscape that they had reached southern Colorado. The train slowed for its next stop, then came to a grinding halt. Rafael stretched and leaned forward to look out the window. The coach passengers disembarked to seize what food they could find and to stretch their legs after long hours spent trying to sleep in their cramped seats.

Outside the train, new arrivals made ready to board. The largest group, unkempt and weary, assembled outside the coach cars. A smaller group headed for the first class entrance, but Rafael saw no bags designated for those elaborate holdings.

His heart took a sharp leap and he squinted until the group came into better view. Though he couldn't make out their faces, he knew them too well. One in constant motion, one standing peaceful. One in silent command. He wasn't sure who accompanied them—he couldn't make out if Diego was there or not, but he feared the worst.

They boarded the train, entering the car that Evelyn had first gone into. Not a one had a grain of sense, though imagination to spare. Together . . . His body tensed at the prospect. As the train pulled out of the station, Rafael leaned forward, straining to see as they disappeared from his view.

He sat back, closed his eyes, and prayed. Three of the most dangerous people he knew—for they were motivated by passion and not reason—had just entered a cabin with the woman who had tried to shoot him. The results couldn't be good.

"There is a Chinaman attempting passage." Mrs. St. Claire seized the weary conductor, who sighed audibly as he turned to face her.

"Mrs. . . . ?" Apparently, the conductor had taken the same form of resistance the porter had established. Evelyn smiled.

The angry woman's eyes narrowed to slits. "St. Claire. Agnes St. Claire. Mr. St. Claire was assured when we booked our reservations on this railroad that no such persons would be inhabiting the first class car. He feels that the ability of Chinamen to render their facial features immobile makes them untrustworthy."

Evelyn turned in her seat to see the newcomers. Their attire didn't indicate wealth, and they were undeniably a strange lot. A small, dark-haired woman wearing a strange, lumpy dress and a fedora stood before two young men, one of whom appeared to be simple and the other who appeared Chinese. The Chinese youth looked around the cabin with a faint suggestion of disdain, as if he'd expected better furnishings, but the simple boy smiled pleasantly and nodded respectfully at the woman seated nearest him.

The conductor dutifully checked the small woman's tickets, then shook his head. "They have made first class arrangements, madam."

Evelyn suspected that in any other circumstance, these strange newcomers would have been ushered to the coach cars, first class ticket or not, but because Mrs. St. Claire had become such a thorn in the conductor's side, he would place them as near to her as possible, and undoubtedly see that their meals were served before hers even if it cost him his job.

Mrs. St. Claire snatched the ticket out of the conductor's hands. She lifted a round eyeglass to inspect the ticket, and her frown deepened. She elevated her head and gave the ticket back to the conductor. "Mr. St. Claire is not satisfied, and this matter will be brought to the intention of the rail immediately."

"At your earliest convenience, madam."

The conductor scurried away, and Evelyn noticed that Mr. St. Claire, despite having such strong opinions on many subjects, never actually said a word. He looked out the window, like a rabbit conditioned to its hutch, and simply nodded when his wife sat down and began issuing a torrent of complaints.

Talbot paid no attention to the new arrivals, and instead conferred with his guards at the rear of the car. He was dressed splendidly, seeming to feel in his element among the wealthy passengers, and had even spent time in conversation with Mrs. St. Claire at breakfast. When Evelyn had questioned him later, hoping for an amusing tale, he had told her with obvious admiration of Mrs. St. Claire's vast heritage and importance in Boston, where her husband held a "major position" in the Boston Heritage and Trust Bank. Apparently, Mr. St. Claire had some connection to the new railroad, but Mrs. St. Claire had skimmed over that information.

Again, Evelyn found herself missing Westley. He had delighted in people, and would have provided a far more interesting slant on Mrs. St. Claire than simply her proud heritage. Because he had been born to wealth and prominence, he placed little value on those advantages, and saw humor where men like Talbot found nothing but splendor. But Talbot's origins lacked the presence of stately manors and sedate pride, and so their importance was that much more in his estimation.

The new group seated themselves across from Evelyn. The woman tugged at her ample skirt in a sudden burst of annoyance, and sat with her legs sprawled forward as if she were more familiar with trousers. The Chinese boy proved anything but immobile. He could barely sit still, seeming excited, chatting with his companions ceaselessly. He read every newspaper, magazine, or booklet that the porter possessed, then eyed the book Evelyn had been trying to read. She smiled at him, and passed it across the aisle. He beamed, but didn't speak.

To Evelyn's surprise, the other boy also investigated his friend's reading material, and appeared to read, too, albeit far more slowly. The small woman in the fedora helped him, revealing a patience Evelyn wouldn't have thought possible. Since Talbot was proving an inadequate traveling companion, she made up her mind to befriend them at the earliest opportunity.

She tried to catch the small woman's eye, but had no success. Once only, the woman looked her way, and the dark anger in the woman's eyes surprised Evelyn. Her hopes fell and she returned to gazing out the window at the high rock plateau of southern Colorado.

Night came after a tedious day of endless travel. Thanks to Talbot's unexpected admiration for the St. Claires, Evelyn had been forced to endure their company at dinner. Neither she nor Mr. St. Claire spoke during the meal, although Mrs. St. Claire inquired after Evelyn's history, and seemed impressed by Talbot's assurance that Evelyn's family was of the highest order.

The wild passion of anger had faded, and her spirits reached a low ebb. As she dined on quail amidst the lavish surroundings of the dining car, her mind wandered to Rafael. She didn't want to think of him, not ever again. Yet his fate was part of hers, despite everything.

The woman in the fedora seemed more restless than usual, and the Chinese boy fell silent, which caught Evelyn's attention more than anything else. The simple boy hadn't altered his demeanor, however, so maybe his silence was nothing more than the effect of tedium on someone not used to sitting still.

The passengers left the dining car, and assembled in the lounge area. Outside, the night sky bristled with a thousand stars and the full moon made its first appearance over the eastern horizon. Mrs. St. Claire established herself beside Talbot, chattering about the quality of the wine, which "Mr. St. Claire" apparently felt wasn't at all adequate.

Evelyn's mind wandered, but the bright imaginings that once consumed her had dwindled to the low ache of loneliness. Though Mrs. St. Claire's persistence seemed above and beyond that of anyone Evelyn had known, the woman wasn't an entirely unusual specimen. Her motivations and desires were obvious—money and self-importance, wealth and position. And though Talbot served the government with greater tasks, he seemed no different.

All they valued seemed so empty to Evelyn. Westley had understood that much. Perhaps he hadn't felt things as deeply as she had, perhaps he hadn't been as emotional as she at the core, but he had far more depth of character and interest than these people did. Once, she had hoped for a love who shared her deepest dreams, a man sensitive to things beneath the surface of people's lives.

But the only person who seemed remotely interested in those things had proven himself a murderer instead.

Evelyn closed her eyes, and loneliness enveloped her. The most interesting people on the train seemed to dislike her. At least, the woman in the fedora clearly did. And the life she was returning to was peopled with contrived conversation and manicured days that would make journeying with Agnes St. Claire seem almost interesting.

When the porter rang the bell to indicate that the berths had been prepared, Evelyn leapt at the chance to retire. She undressed wearily, then lay upon her bunk wearing only her long chemise. She listened as the other passengers made ready for sleep, as Mrs. St. Claire complained on behalf of her husband about insufficient toiletries. . . .

Evelyn drifted toward sleep, her thoughts fleeting as if seeking escape. Stilted whispers jarred her awake, and she sat up in her bunk. Someone passed by her berth, stopped a moment, then went on. She felt sure she had heard someone whisper, "Is this the one?" and that the speaker was a young man.

She waited for a while, but no further sound came but the endless rhythm of the train. She lay back and closed her eyes, but again someone moved outside her berth. She started to sit up, but a hand jerked through her curtain and clamped over her mouth.

Someone pulled her from her berth. She struggled to free herself, but the bright-eyed Chinese boy held her fast.

Chapter Four

The train screeched on its tracks and jerked to a sudden halt, knocking Rafael forward from his seat. The guard jerked upright, blinking in confusion. Rafael sat back quietly, hoping against hope this had nothing to do with the train's unexpected passengers.

A few moments passed, interrupted by shouts of confusion and fear. More than once, he heard the words "train robbery." Footsteps thundered toward the jail car, and a guard burst through the door, wide-eyed and panicked. "Get him," he gasped. "Bring him to the lounge car."

Rafael's guard fumbled for his gun. "What're you saying? Bring who?"

"The prisoner!" The man sounded frightened. "There's been a holdup."

Oh, no. Rafael bowed his head. Even worse than he imagined . . . His guard seized Rafael's bound hands and yanked. "So you had something planned all along, did you? Well, Lieutenant Talbot ain't going to let you get off this train, no matter who you got up there."

Rafael didn't answer. *A holdup.*

"So what do we do?" asked his guard, nervous.

"The damned conductor insisted we bring the prisoner. Talbot ain't for it, but he's got no choice. The robbers got a gun to a woman's head, and it's Reid's widow. Ain't much he can do about it."

Rafael rose to his feet. *Evelyn.* "I will speak to them."

The guards hesitated, then hauled him forward. They passed through the coach cars where people tried their best to sleep on the hard upholstered benches. A few people recoiled at the sight of the prisoner, but most ignored his passage.

The guards led Rafael to the lounge car, where a group of first class passengers had assembled behind the terrified conductor. By the exit, a too-familiar group stood holding Evelyn like a prisoner. Her hands were bound behind her back, but she didn't appear injured. He took one look at the instigator and closed his eyes. "Sally, let her go."

Sally frowned, then shoved the gun closer against Evelyn's head. Despite the situation, Evelyn didn't appear terrified. She glared at him with the same hatred he had seen at the station. She wore only a chemise, revealing more of her delicate body than he ever dreamed he would see. Her dark brown hair fell in tangled waves almost to her waist, and she looked more beautiful and more vulnerable than anything he had ever seen.

Sally nodded at the conductor. "You get those guards to set this man free, or I'll shoot this girl." She paused, administering a blistering stare upon the conductor. "You'll have her internals splattered all over your fine walls."

From the rear of the passenger group, Rafael heard a shrill cry, followed by, "This is unacceptable!"

The conductor turned nervously to Lieutenant Talbot, who glowered with dark fury. "What do I do, sir? The rail cannot have a murder taking place, not in the first class cabin."

Talbot's jaw quivered, his eyes blazing, but he seemed unable to summon an effective argument. Rafael sighed. "Sally, let her go." He paused. Was that the right decision? They had already involved themselves. Even if they freed Evelyn, now they too would be considered criminals. He needed to return to Santa Fe. There he would have the chance to find Westley's real killer, if he could find out what it was Talbot wanted so much from the pueblo.

Sally ignored Rafael. "If you don't cut Rafael's ties and set him free, you're going to have this girl's cold dead body sprawling at your feet."

A piercing voice interrupted them. "Mr. St. Claire finds it unacceptable that a prisoner was included on this journey! There will be inquiries!"

Rafael looked to the back of the lounge, squinted, and saw the robust shape of a large, blond woman. Even without his spectacles, he could see that her robe seemed to contain a substantial bustle. A small, weedy man cowered behind her and seemed to be looking for an exit. Despite his terror, the conductor paused to issue a profound sigh at her outburst, and Rafael guessed the woman had proven herself a presence during their trip.

One of the guards aimed his gun, looking to Talbot for approval. Talbot hesitated, and Rafael realized to his horror that the lieutenant might indeed risk Evelyn's life in order to keep Rafael from escaping. "I would think twice, if I were you, Lieutenant." Rafael nodded at Chen, who held a shiny white revolver in rock-steady hands. "I doubt you have a soldier who can outshoot this boy."

Talbot frowned, but Chen beamed with pride.

"Lieutenant, do something! The Chinaman is armed!"

From the corner of his eye, Rafael saw Evelyn glance at Mrs. St. Claire, and he felt an odd desire to laugh. Chen looked eagerly to Rafael. "Can I show them, sir?"

"Don't shoot anything important, alive, or inflammable."

Before anyone could react, Chen fired his gun and Mrs. St. Claire's handbag dropped to the ground. A small dog issued a wild bark, then scurried across the cabin like a mouse. Mrs. St. Claire let out a tremendous bellow and lurched back into her husband's arms as if in a faint.

Sally seemed annoyed by the delay. "Get on with it! Cut his ties. I'll give you ten seconds." Beside her, her son William began counting, slowly and accurately. Rafael wondered if he was dreaming, but the conductor hopped from foot to foot as the countdown neared zero.

"Stop!" The conductor turned to Talbot, desperate. "Lieutenant, we have no choice. You must release your prisoner."

Talbot trembled with rage, but he nodded to Rafael's guard. "Cut him loose."

The guard obeyed, then stepped back. Rafael took his place with his rescuers, and the porter, who seemed to like the excitement, opened the door to the night outside. Sally motioned to her son, who tossed several sacks out into the darkness. "It's time to go, Will."

The boy hesitated. "What about her?" He gestured to Evelyn, and Sally frowned.

"She's coming with us."

Rafael groaned. "She is not. Mrs. Reid will stay where she is."

Sally rolled her eyes and shook her free fist. "Don't you go letting your heart cloud your better sense, Rafael. We need her with us, and you know it. For one thing, she's the one who claimed you did in her husband. Without her, they got nothing on you."

"Nothing? You held up a train because of me!" He stopped, glaring. "We will discuss that later. She stays here."

If ever there was a stubborn woman, it was Sally. "You aren't thinking straight, because they've kept you tied up for weeks. You listen to me, and I hope you're hearing your mother's voice echoing in mine. We need this girl with us. That way, when they start following us—and you know they will—we can use her."

"No."

Sally ignored his protest. "Will already grabbed one of her dresses—she must have had five of them. What in the name of God does a woman need with that many gowns?" Sally glanced at her son. "You got her underthings, I assume?"

Will nodded, proud, then smiled at Evelyn. "Even got your toothbrush, miss."

Evelyn looked between them. Her voice sounded small, but clear. "Thank you."

Rafael stared at her in amazement. There was so much more to her than he knew. But he couldn't endanger her this way. "No."

Sally didn't listen. She gestured at the conductor. "Here's what you do. You get this train started and fast. We're going with the girl, but in case anyone tries anything . . ." She paused as if seeing a flaw in her scheme. She poked at Chen with her free hand. "Get one of them for a cover."

Chen bounded forward, assessed the passengers, then seized Mrs. St. Claire and dragged her forward. He positioned her in front of himself like a shield. Before Rafael could stop her, Sally shoved Evelyn through the open door. He heard a sharp, cut-off cry, and his heart clenched. Still smiling, Will followed and disappeared into the night. Sally aimed at Mrs. St. Claire, then glanced at Rafael in warning.

"You know I won't hesitate to kill this one." She looked as if she might choose to pull the trigger anyway. "You don't know what we put up with listening to her squawk."

Mrs. St. Claire screamed, directing orders at her feeble husband, who waited expectantly and made no move to rush to her rescue. Rafael glanced out into the night, then sighed. "I am sure Mrs. St. Claire's husband would be devastated to lose his wife. Move the train forward, conductor, and we will be gone." There was a chance, albeit a slim one. By the time Talbot could assemble his pursuit, they would have a head start, at the least.

Apparently realizing this, too, Talbot pointed his finger at Rafael. "You'll never get far, de Aguirre. Wherever you go, I will find you."

"You'll need horses, Lieutenant. I'd imagine you can purchase some in the town of Pueblo. That's another day's journey north, I'm afraid. But I will take your word on your pursuit." Rafael went to the door, and Chen held Mrs. St. Claire while backing through the door.

The conductor ordered the train forward, and the whistle blew. It eased forward. Rafael glanced out the door and saw Evelyn Reid standing beneath a night of a thousand stars. The full moon rose higher and shone upon her like a goddess. Her white chemise fluttered in the wind, and her long hair swirled behind her like a curtain. Life took unexpected turns, and though he hadn't asked for this one, he recognized each moment as a gift.

Taking him by surprise, the wild force of life surged within him. He met Talbot's dark gaze and he bowed, smiling. "Until we meet again . . ."

The Renegade had returned.

Evelyn watched as the rest of her abductors bounded from the moving train. The Chinese boy seemed to drop and roll deliberately, then bounded to his feet like an acrobat. The small woman called Sally jumped as if leaping from trains was a daily occurrence. Last, Rafael de Aguirre jumped down, his long black hair flying. Even without his cape and mask, he looked bold and devastatingly handsome.

The train whistle blew once more, and it picked up speed. Through the open door, Talbot fired wild shots into the night. Evelyn could see him against the lamplight inside the train, his guards beside him. She half expected him to leap after them, but he couldn't hope to assemble his men that fast, not fully armed. He would come after them, that she knew, but how soon?

The quiet, pleasant boy who had jumped with her went forward to greet them, leaving Evelyn standing alone in her chemise. She backed slowly away, then turned to run. Her whole body hurt from the fall, her bones ached, her head throbbed, and her wrists felt raw. But this might be her only chance for escape.

If she could run far enough, quickly enough, she might find cover, and she could hide until they decided it was wiser to leave her behind. If she could reach the crest of the small hill . . . Her bound hands hindered her balance, nor could she hold up her chemise—it tangled around her ankles and she fell forward to her knees. She struggled to get up, but a shadow darker than the night closed in around her, then in front of her.

She took a desperate breath, then looked up. Standing above her, his head crowned with a thousand stars, Rafael de Aguirre drew a knife.

She should have been terrified, but anger took hold instead. He had been on his way to justice, and now she lay in a heap at his feet. She glared up into his eyes, daring him to kill her. In a wild flash, she realized and accepted that she wanted her blood on his hands.

Rafael looked down at her silently. He drew a deep breath, then shook his head.

As she waited, every muscle drawn tight with the expectation of death, he walked behind her. She held her breath, expecting the sudden bite of pain. Instead, he knelt behind her and cut her ties. Evelyn yanked her arms free, then turned to face him.

He rose to his feet before her. Without a word, he held out his hand. As he had done the first time they met . . .

Evelyn stared at his hand, then at his face. His kindness cut deeper than any knife. She jabbed at the hard soil with her fists and thrust herself up without his assistance. She backed away, but Chen caught her by the shoulders and held her fast.

"I hope your wrists don't hurt too much, miss. Sally told me to tie them tight, but I didn't want to cut off your circulation. Circulation is important, you know. It keeps blood going to your heart." He peeked over her shoulder to Rafael. "Isn't that right, sir?"

A faint smile touched Rafael's sensual mouth. "Circulation is surely essential. . . ."

"The thing is, we were in such a rush, I didn't have time to check it right. So if I hurt you, miss, I'm sorry."

Sally came up from behind and struck the

boy hard on the back. He rolled his eyes, then grinned at Evelyn. The other boy joined them, carrying a sack. "These here're your things, miss. I packed everything you'll be needing. I didn't know which was your favorite dress, so I picked the one I liked best, the blue one with lace."

Evelyn stared in astonishment, unsure how to respond. "The blue one is my favorite, too."

Sally looked her up and down with obvious disgust. "Well, you'd better put something on and fast. I don't want my son seeing a girl in her nightdress just as if it don't mean nothing."

Evelyn opened her mouth to object, but no words came. She sputtered incoherently, but Rafael cleared his throat beside her. "If you'd given Mrs. Reid time to change before you held up the train, Sally, she might have found something more suitable for the occasion."

The entire event felt like a dream. Rafael, the Renegade who murdered her husband and terrorized Santa Fe, was now making excuses to his train-robber cohort over Evelyn's attire. No words stinging enough came, so she stared mutely, gathering what remained of her wits.

Sally looked impatient. "What are we waiting for, Rafe? We've got to get moving."

Rafael stood back, assessing his saviors. "There are a few things I need to know first." He paused. "Line up, all of you." He looked and sounded like a schoolmaster, not the villain she knew him to be. It seemed impossible. He glanced at Evelyn, and his dark eyes twinkled. "You, too, Mrs. Reid, as your own fate will be considered as well."

She refused to move, but the others lined up beside her, Sally at the end. Rafael addressed the small woman first. Sally gazed off across the dark horizon, more like a rebellious student than a devious criminal. Rafael fixed his gaze upon her until she squirmed. "Maybe you'd care to explain?"

Sally glanced behind her, casually, then shrugged. "About what?"

Rafael's composure shattered. "*About what?* Sally, you held up a train. A train!"

"It wasn't any trouble. Except for this damned skirt."

He towered over Sally, but she didn't seem afraid. "I am not concerned with the 'trouble' it took to arrange and pull off this insane holdup. What I find disconcerting is that you found it necessary at all."

"Well, how else would you get out of this fix, anyway?"

"I see. What next, dare I ask?" His voice took on a deep, ominous tone.

"What do you mean, 'next'? We busted you out. How much more do you want from us? The rest is up to you."

He groaned, long and defeated. Apparently, Rafael wasn't in on his rescuers' plans. "Is that so? Well, if it were 'up to me,' I'd still be on that train!"

"With your head in a noose." Despite what must have been blatant devotion on Sally's part, she didn't speak to Rafael with the awe and obedience Evelyn would have expected.

"I hoped to have my say before a judge in

Denver." He sounded as if he fought for control when he wanted to shout instead.

Sally issued a brief snort. "And how much do you think Judge Merrill *Talbot* would hear your pretty words, anyway?"

"Talbot?"

"That's right. Talbot arranged for his own brother to hear your case. Think you'd get far?"

Evelyn choked back a gasp. Talbot's *brother?* Why hadn't he told her? She had no doubt of Rafael's guilt, but when she got over her wish to take justice into her own hands, she knew she'd wanted it proven fairly.

Rafael pondered this in silence for a while, then nodded as if it clarified some mystery. "It seems our noble lieutenant cares more for my fate than I realized. I wonder why it's so important to him?"

"There's more." Sally's voice took on a different tone. "Diego is missing, Rafael."

"What do you mean, 'missing'?"

"A few days after you were captured, ten people were taken from the pueblo. Don't know who took them, or why, but since then, it's happened three times."

"Why didn't you tell me?"

"Because there wasn't anything you could do, not in jail. The best thing we could do for you was to break you out, and we had to wait until you were on the train to do it."

"Diego . . ."

"He was in the bunch that got nabbed the night before they took you. It might be coincidence, but I'm thinking it's because he's your brother."

"Maybe, but more than that is going on." Evelyn heard the tension in Rafael's voice, the restrained emotion. If he cared so much, then couldn't he have spared some of that tenderness for her husband? "Then you're right, I must return, and quickly."

Sally uttered a satisfied chuckle. The quiet boy stepped up to Rafael, looking hopeful. "Did we do good, sir?"

Rafael hesitated, then placed his hand on the boy's shoulder. "You did, Will. Thank you."

The boy seemed pleased, but the Chinese boy practically hopped with excitement. "It was incredible, sir!" Evelyn waited in annoyance for him to boast about their daring rescue. "First class is the way to go, and I won't be taking anything less from now on. I read every newspaper—you wouldn't believe the misspellings and grammar inaccuracies—and the meals! I've never had quail, but I'm going to hire my own chef once I get myself established, and he's going to prepare quail at least once a week. And I wouldn't mind having a porter . . ."

Sally swatted the boy, but Rafael laughed. "I'm sorry to deprive you of your luxuries, Chen. I'm afraid the service in my car was far less impressive."

The boy sighed, ignoring whatever hardships Rafael had endured. "Wish we could have stayed on a few more days."

Will found his pack and shouldered it. "I didn't like them oysters much. What are they, anyway?"

"You don't want to know, boy," said Sally, just as Chen offered, "Bugs."

Evelyn stared, stunned by the peculiarity of her abductors. She wanted to laugh, then realized what they had done to her. She was trapped at the mercy of a man who had tormented her for far longer than she dared to admit.

Chen spun his white gun around his finger, then stuffed it in his belt. "Got to get a holster for this soon. One with some beads on it. Or jewels. What did you think of my shooting, sir? Good, wasn't I?"

Rafael patted the boy's shoulder. "You're an impressive sharpshooter, Chen."

Chen nodded. "Figured I could make a career of it, hunting down criminals, that kind of thing. Probably make quite a name for myself."

Sally groaned. "Until you get shot yourself."

Chen ignored her. "I should be just about as good with a gun as Señor de Aguirre is with his bola."

A bola . . . The whip used by the Renegade. Evelyn wondered what it was, and why he had selected such a strange weapon.

Rafael sighed. "A shame I don't have it now. I should be able to devise something similar. But it was passed to me by my father—I am sorry to lose it."

He waxed sentimental about the weapon used to kill her husband. Evelyn had no words for her outrage.

Chen pointed at Will. "Wait a minute! Will's got your bola in one of his packs, too."

Will pulled the strange whip from a pack and gave it to Rafael. "I picked it up when the guards took you, sir."

Rafael tied it to his belt, then patted it like an old friend. "I dropped it hoping you would. Thank you, Will."

So . . . he was armed again. Armed with the weapon he'd used to kill Westley.

Rafael moved passed his cohorts and stood in front of Evelyn. Like Sally, she avoided his gaze. She remembered her minimal attire, then fiddled with the ribbon of her chemise.

"Mrs. Reid . . ." His voice trailed, and he sighed. "I am sorry to involve you in this."

She looked up, eyes narrow. "You 'involved me' when you murdered my husband. That you and your cohorts would abduct me is not surprising."

"It was not my intention." He touched her back, gently. "Your back . . . I never meant to hurt you."

His voice was so low and so gentle. Even the sound of him was sensual. "Perhaps you should have considered that before flailing that . . . *thing* around."

"Were you much injured?"

"Yes." She paused, fighting conscience. "No. But it stung badly."

"If nothing else, please accept my apology for striking you. I would sooner take the blow myself."

"How very noble of you!" He meant it. She felt his sincerity, and heard it in the quiet gravity of his voice.

Evelyn considered her predicament for a moment, then nodded to give herself assurance. There was nothing else to be done. She had to deal with her captors calmly and logically. She straightened her back, feeling taller, and addressed Rafael formally, in what she hoped was a manner of detached reserve. "So . . . You've kidnapped me. May I ask what do you intend to do with me now?"

Rafael glanced at Sally and arched his brow. "A good question."

Sally rolled her eyes and looked even more impatient than usual. "Take her with us, of course. As a hostage." Rafael started to shake his head, but Sally held up her small hand. "We need her, Rafe, and you know it. That bastard Talbot's going to be on our trail as soon as he can get horses. He'll think twice before shooting if we've got her as a shield. We can use her to bargain with, if it comes to that. And if she gets in our way, we can always shoot her."

Evelyn stared in horror. As pleasant as the boys were, Sally seemed to have no sympathy whatsoever.

Rafael winced, then rubbed his eyes as if they pained him. "It might be wisest to leave her here. . . ." He glanced at Evelyn, and she sensed his reluctance. "Lieutenant Talbot will be on our trail as soon as he can get horses," he said.

This sounded promising to Evelyn. "You'll never get far, especially not if you insist on hauling me along with you."

He ignored her, then surveyed the southern horizon's dark silhouette. "We'll never make it on foot."

Chen beamed. "We won't have to, sir. You don't think we'd hold up a train without a good plan set, do you?"

Rafael hesitated, indicating he thought them

capable of just that. "What plan?" He spoke as if he almost dreaded to hear the answer.

Chen looked around, then pointed. "There!"

Evelyn looked, too, but she saw nothing. Rafael stared into the night, and appeared as doubtful as she felt. He fell silent, and seemed to be listening. After a moment, he smiled. "Horses. Five of them. Well done."

Evelyn eyed him doubtfully. "How do you know that? I don't see a thing."

"I've gotten good at listening to make up for my other deficiencies."

As he spoke, a man emerged over the southern crest leading five horses. Rafael walked to him and they embraced, speaking in a language Evelyn didn't understand.

Chen stood beside her, chatting amiably. "That's Patukala, Señor de Aguirre's uncle, on his mother's side. He took off north as soon as we laid our plans, back when Señor de Aguirre was still in prison. He had the horses, and we had a pretty good idea where to meet. I worked out the distance and how far he could get, all that. Good planning, wasn't it?" He paused, evidently waiting for some flattery from Evelyn.

"I . . . Yes, I suppose it was."

"I'm the best student Señor de Aguirre has in arithmetic. In everything, actually. Had a hard time getting Patukala to understand, though. Good fellow, but he doesn't speak much English. I've tried to teach him, but he's proud, so he won't try to talk if he can avoid it. Just says one word here, one word there. But you should see him at a Zuni gathering! Señor de Aguirre brought his students to one last summer, so I know all about it. Patukala is the son of the chief—Señor de Aguirre's mother was the chief's eldest daughter . . ."

Chen barely paused for breaths during his conversation, but he spoke well, articulating clearly as if well taught. Evelyn recognized the source of the polite but long-winded anonymous letter she had received after Rafael had been jailed. Now she was face-to-face with a child who obviously adored Rafael, who saw only good in him. How could he understand the pain she felt, knowing this man had murdered her husband?

The night air chilled around her and she wrapped her arms around her waist. Will noticed immediately and fished around in his sack, then passed her a light cape. "Put this on, miss. It'll warm you."

Sally seized the pack, found the blue dress, and thrust it at Evelyn. "You put this on first, girl, before you go shocking Patukala."

Evelyn took the dress, but hesitated before putting it on. They made it seem as if she had done something wrong, and might embarrass them if given the chance. Even Chen nodded thoughtfully, assessing her. "She's got a point, miss. Patukala is a dignified person. Don't imagine you've got anyone back East with half his pride."

Evelyn thought of her father, and thought Patukala would meet his match in Robert Talmadge. "My father endured the Civil War in a Confederate prison, where he starved for months. I am assured by my mother and all who know him that the one thing he had was dignity."

She loved her father because the dignity he possessed he also granted to others. Though from one of Boston's most exclusive families, he had encouraged her to become a schoolteacher. Her mother had been ill, so he hadn't been able to come West as he'd hoped when Westley died, but she received monthly letters from him, giving her courage in a time when nothing else mattered.

This was the heritage she was born to. Less mystic than Rafael's, but no less powerful. Her history was honor, and dignity through horrific loss. Maybe her captors didn't understand this, but she would cling to it to her dying breath.

Chen eyed her for a moment. "The Civil War was a curious twist in American history." He sounded as if he recited from a book—or a much-admired schoolmaster. Evelyn frowned. *Curious twist, indeed!*

"Many brave men died so that others could live free."

Chen appeared unimpressed by the legacy her father had handed down to her. "Señor de Aguirre says the whole thing could have been avoided if those of European descent had been less greedy. He says the North was motivated by money and the South wanted to hold on to their slaves for the same reason."

"Oh, does he?" *The nerve!* "Perhaps your Renegade should spend less time analyzing the faults of others and concentrate on his own shortcomings!"

Chen's face twisted with youthful indignation. "He says that white people too often use violence to settle their differences."

Evelyn fumed. "Well, he should know."

Rafael came toward them, interrupting their budding argument, and she yanked her dress over her head, hoping to restore some of her shattered pride.

"We have horses, my friends. Patukala and I have discussed the best course south. I will lead them to believe we are fleeing to Mexico, then double back for Santa Fe. With luck, we'll have time to free the lieutenant's captives, and perhaps discover what brought him to Santa Fe in the first place."

Evelyn braced her hands on her hips, indignant. "Lieutenant Talbot wasn't responsible for your missing people—if they really are missing, which I doubt."

Patukala noticed Evelyn, then looked at Rafael. His brow arched. They spoke quietly, and the Indian sighed. Though she had no idea what they said, Evelyn felt offended. They looked so much alike, tall and strong, with high cheekbones and proud features, dark eyes and hair so black that the night itself seemed to shine upon it.

Westley had been blond, his skin so fair that even a short while in the sun turned him pink. Every emotion was visible on his face, but somehow, Evelyn had always felt she didn't understand him fully. Maybe it was only a dream to want to be that close to someone. She remembered those shocking, grim moments when she had seen into Rafael's thoughts.

Maybe it was a nightmare instead.

Will hurried forward and began patting a stout pinto, his own mount presumably. Evelyn recognized Rafael's horse, the Renegade's familiar dark gray. Another, equally large, she assumed to be Patukala's, but Sally went to it, slapped her gear on its back and mounted, then pointed irritably at Evelyn. "What are you going to do with her?"

Rafael hesitated, but Evelyn considered the number of horses a sudden advantage. "A shame he only thought to bring five. I will have to stay behind."

Rafael didn't answer, but when he walked toward her, she backed away. "I will fight you."

He held out his hand, which she refused to take. "Come with me."

Evelyn shook her head, but he took her arm and led her aside. Evelyn struggled, but he didn't release her. Gently, he took her shoulders and turned her to face him. She was ready with argument, but her heart beat so fast that she felt dizzy.

She expected him to speak, but to her horror, he didn't. He just gazed into her eyes, standing too close, so close that she felt the warmth emanating from his strong body. He looked so deeply inside her that she thought he saw every demon that tormented her, every dark space she'd hidden. . . . She wanted to look away, but instead she stood transfixed.

"Mrs. Reid, I did not kill your husband." Her chin puckered and she started to shake her head, but he moved his touch from her shoulders to her face. "Whatever happened between us in the past, know that I did not kill your husband."

He dared refer to that first meeting . . . "You did. I saw you there." Her voice came as a tiny whisper and she began to tremble. *I cannot let you see me weak. . . . I cannot let you ever see how weak I am.*

"I know you believe that, and you did see me, that is true. But Westley was dead when I reached him."

"What a coincidence!" She felt stronger now, and she would not be swayed by his mystical charm. "So you just happened by at an opportune moment?"

"He told me to meet him that night. I do not know why." He paused. "He knew, you understand."

"That you were the Renegade?" He was lying. Westley hadn't known any such thing. For an instant, she had almost believed him. Her doubt returned and she found it comforting. It was easier and safer not to trust. "And how did he know this?"

"He knew because I told him."

"You can't expect me to believe that. Why wouldn't he tell me?"

"Because he believed, rightly, that you would be endangered by any involvement."

"How convenient!"

Rafael smiled, ignoring her sarcasm. "It is my hope that during our journey together, you will come to believe me."

"What? I thought you were going to leave me here!"

"I was, but I have thought better of it."

She felt like crying suddenly, and she didn't know why. "Why?"

"Because, though it was not my will, I now have the lives of four people in my care. I can't say I approve of their methods, but what they did was for a good cause."

"For you."

"Yes, for me. I can't have you telling Lieutenant Talbot our plans. But I am thinking of you also."

Evelyn made a fist. "How very lucky for me! I beg you not to consider my welfare."

"If I could help it, I would not. But my heart tells me you are in more danger from those pursuing us than you would ever be with me."

She glared. "That is not possible."

"Be that as it may, you're coming with us."

Evelyn bowed her head, feeling defeated. "Why couldn't you have abducted someone else?"

"Such as Mrs. St. Claire, perhaps?"

Evelyn peeked up at him, surprised he would remember Agnes's name. "Perhaps."

Rafael smiled. "I cannot say the thought of her as a traveling companion pleases me. And I fear Mr. St. Claire would consider that most inappropriate."

Evelyn's mouth slid slowly open. Then, despite her best intentions, she smiled, too, and a tiny laugh burst forth before she could stop herself. Rafael touched her cheek, so gently that it hurt.

"I won't let anything happen to you, Mrs. Reid. You have my word on that. You and I are much alike."

"How is that?" She didn't want to ask, but the words came of their own accord.

His finger trailed along her cheek, but then he drew his hand away as if he hadn't meant to touch her this way. "We are, neither one of us, what we seem to be."

"That can certainly be said of you." She wanted to hate him, desperately. She reminded herself that the gentle schoolmaster had been the real disguise. Rafael de Aguirre had been the Renegade all along, a man capable of deceiving everyone, all for his own mysterious ends.

He didn't seem offended and seemed to accept her defiance as acquiescence. He looked toward the others, squinting. He rubbed his eyes as if he endured a headache. "We have a long road to follow, you and I. I hope by its end, you will at least understand and forgive me."

"Forgive you?" Her lips curled at his hypocrisy. "Yet you claim no responsibility for my husband's murder."

"I said that I didn't kill him, not that I bore no responsibility." He closed his eyes and tipped his head back. Evelyn tried not to look at him, but Rafael possessed an innate grace that compelled her beyond reason. "Mrs. Reid, you cannot blame me for Westley's death any more than I blame myself. I involved him in something he didn't fully understand. I should have handled it alone."

He spoke so well, so gently and so sensibly. Even in darkness, she couldn't deny how handsome he was, and how strong. He was going to bring her with him—for endless days, she would be in his company. *No*. . . .

Evelyn shoved her hands in her pockets and her fingers touched cold metal. The revolver Talbot had given her was still there, and it was still loaded. Very slowly, as if mesmerized, she drew it from her pocket and pointed it at Rafael. She stood with her back to the others, and in darkness, they wouldn't know what she was doing until too late.

He saw the gun, but he didn't shout. He just looked at her, gently, with that same empathy she had seen in his eyes at the train station. *I can't kill you*. "Let me go . . . and I won't shoot."

Again, he held out his hand, saying nothing.

She shook her head. "Let me go."

"Evelyn, I can't do that. But I won't hurt you."

"I'm the one with the gun." She wanted to be strong, but her voice wavered and he smiled.

"If shooting me is what you must do, then do it."

Her eyes swarmed with unexpected tears. "Please, let me go."

"I will see that no harm comes to you, but I can't do as you ask."

He stayed so calm and so gentle. She waited for him to leap toward her and seize the gun, but he did nothing. Tears fell to her cheeks and she passed him the weapon, defeated. "I am your prisoner."

He examined her small gun, then shook his head. He placed it back in her hand. "You keep it, Mrs. Reid. You may need it, one day, when you face a greater enemy than myself."

She stared in astonishment, then shoved the

revolver back in her pocket. "There is no enemy greater than you!"

Rafael smiled. "Mrs. Reid, I wish that were true." He didn't wait for further argument. Rafael took her arm again, gently but firmly, and led her back to the others. Sally looked between them suspiciously, but made no comment.

He rubbed his eyes again, and she wondered if he was tired. "Perhaps, if you're ill . . ."

He shook his head. "I'm fine." He blinked as if his eyes were dry, then directed her back to the others. All but Chen had mounted. Chen held Rafael's gray, but Rafael went to the other horse instead. Chen shook his head in dismay. "This one is yours, sir."

Rafael offered a rueful smile. "Same shape." He stroked the horse's strong neck. "Hello, Frank."

Evelyn choked back a laugh. "*Frank?* You named your horse *Frank?* That's not terribly impressive, se-nor, for the steed bearing the Renegade."

Rafael seemed confused by her reaction. "I liked it."

Sometimes, he could be unwittingly charming. Evelyn bit her lip to keep from commenting further.

Will let out a sharp "whoop," and bounced down off his pinto. "I'm sorry, sir! I forgot all about these." He pulled Rafael's small gold-rimmed spectacles from one of the many packs dangling off his saddle. "No wonder you picked the wrong horse. You couldn't see!"

"Again, thank you, Will." Rafael breathed a deep sigh of relief, took the glasses, and put them on as if handed a gift from God. He adjusted them, then turned to Evelyn, smiling. He assessed her thoughtfully, and his smile widened. "Mrs. Reid, I hate to broach such a delicate subject . . ."

Her lip curled to one side. She wouldn't let him affect her, no matter what ploys he tried. "Why stop now?"

He touched his mouth, an impulsive gesture that indicated he felt shy or perhaps embarrassed. "You've put your dress on backwards."

Chapter Five

Her chin high, Evelyn Reid turned her back to her abductors and straightened her dress. She scrambled around, twisting, and reorganized herself adequately. She finished the task, then stood with her hands on her hips, waiting for further instruction. She looked ready to defy whatever he said. "I suppose you'll tie me like a dog and lead me behind one of you?"

She had to know he wouldn't do that. He expected her to ride behind him, or in front of him, but when his gaze drifted to her rearranged bodice, to the soft skin shadowed in the starlight, he decided against such close proximity. "Chen, will you assist Mrs. Reid onto your horse, please?"

He spoke evenly, but her eyes narrowed as if she, too, had expected he would keep her with him. He wanted to, too much, so it was a situation best avoided. Chen held out his hand politely, and to Rafael's surprise, she took it and let the boy help her into the saddle. Chen climbed up after her, already chatting pleasantly.

Patukala took the fore, riding on ahead where his sharp vision might make out any danger. Rafael rode at the rear. He was the most likely among them to pick up sounds of pursuit.

Night prevented them from riding fast, but Rafael didn't let them stop. While the moon was full, they would use it to their advantage, gaining precious ground over Lieutenant Talbot and his men.

His mind wound ceaselessly around the people taken captive. Why? Not just to remove his brother, nor to use the boy's captivity against Rafael. This act had been done when Talbot felt sure the Renegade would no longer trouble his activities. But why?

Rafael shook off the question. He had to move fast, yet take the longer road. If they were captured, not only his life would be forfeit, but the lives of his impulsive gang of rescuers.

And there was the danger he felt toward Evelyn. Westley had given control of the pueblo to Rafael—but with Rafael executed, it would fall to her. Was it possible that Lieutenant Talbot's only interest in her was personal? She was a beautiful woman, and as a young widow, likely to attract many suitors. The thought of her marrying again surely didn't please him. Evelyn was more than a lovely ornament for a man's home. She was a vibrant soul, seeking more in her life than what someone like Talbot could offer.

When he was near her, he felt her longing. She wanted to matter, to help people, and to live as a full person, not in some constricted role laid down by her conservative eastern family.

He remembered her arguing with Chen over his interpretation of the Civil War. Strange that at such a time, in such a place, she saw fit to engage her captor in an intellectual argument. Beyond personal indignation, however, he had sensed an honest desire to teach the boy of her own history. Like him, she had been born with that desire, and it wouldn't be torn from her by marriage.

Rafael urged Frank closer behind Chen's horse. Chen was still chatting, telling her how a young man with good judgment and intelligence could make a name for himself in the world, even if his background might have set him at a disadvantage.

He had heard this speech before. It was oft-repeated as Chen tried to convince himself that it didn't really matter that his parents had died, that he had spent his childhood as a virtual prisoner of the railroads, working like a slave on tracks supposedly designed to make the land free to all.

Rafael had found him when he was nine years old, starving. He had stolen food from the rail workers, and he was being beaten in public for his crime. That day, Rafael had taken the mask left to him by his mother, and the Argentinean bola his father had brought from his homeland, and created an avenging warrior from a past remembered only in legend.

Evelyn seemed to be listening intently. "If I

might make a suggestion, you could certainly aspire to more than gunfighting."

"I'd thought of setting up my own business. What with all the people flooding in from the eastern cities, I should be able to make a fortune. Maybe I'll open a saloon." Chen stopped and sighed. "Of course, now that I've turned criminal, it might not be so easy. Don't suppose a train robber has much shot at anything but a life of crime. Still, as smart as I am, I ought to be good at it."

Evelyn issued a sharp squeak just as Rafael groaned. Somehow he had to set right all that had gone wrong. Chen deserved better, as did the others. They had sacrificed everything for him, their homes, their safety, their dreams. He had to protect them, whatever the cost.

Evelyn was sputtering as if unable to form words into speech. Rafael had a fair idea what she wanted to say. He rode up beside them. "As smart as you are, Chen, you should know that turning to crime won't solve anything."

Evelyn's lips curled to one side, annoyed. The moonlight shone full on her face, and every expression made itself dear. "Fine words coming from you! If this young man has learned anything from you, it's that turning to crime is the only solution to whatever ails you."

Chen looked between them as if weighing the value of their respective arguments. "I wouldn't say Señor de Aguirre taught us that, exactly." He paused, while Rafael enjoyed a moment of satisfaction. "Of course, he did say that when the people running the government oppress you, sometimes there's no choice but to fight back with every weapon you've got."

Rafael sighed. "That is not exactly what I meant."

Evelyn delivered a dark, knowing look his way. "Madmen throughout history have used that same logic."

He frowned. "As have saints, Mrs. Reid."

Her brow arched, and he recognized a formidable opponent. "Are you terming *yourself* a saint, sir?"

"No . . . I simply meant that sometimes the side of right differs from those representing the dominant culture."

"In other words, you take the law and people's lives into your own hands—and anyone who stands in your way is deemed expendable."

He wouldn't get far debating with Evelyn Reid, that much was certain, nor would he win her approval with words. She couldn't see past the Renegade to the man inside—or maybe she didn't want to. "For a woman held in captivity by such a dangerous criminal as myself, you seem remarkably unafraid of angering me."

Her eyes shifted to one side and she bit her lip. "That is because I have nothing left to lose."

"Or because the fear you profess to feel for me is less than your good sense allows."

Chen considered this, then tapped his lip. "Or because she knows you can't kill her because we need her as a hostage."

Rafael sighed, but Evelyn nodded. "That is true."

"Thank you, Chen." Feeling defeated, Rafael slowed his horse and let them ride ahead again. It was easier to watch her from behind than to have her looking back at him, ripe with suspicion and dislike. Eventually, she would learn that he hadn't murdered her husband. He would see to that somehow. But would she ever forgive him for a desire he hadn't been able to conceal from the moment he first laid eyes upon her?

He rode for a long while in silence, and finally, even Chen stopped talking. He knew they were tired, but he had to get a good start on any pursuit. They rode southward still; they hadn't yet reached the area where he could lead them west and into the mountains. For now, speed was essential. Once he felt sure they were well ahead of Talbot, he would alter their path and lead them where no pursuit could follow.

It was a long road to travel, and would likely be dangerous even without Talbot following them. He had to have Evelyn's trust, lest she attempt escape at every turn.

Unfortunately, since their first meeting he had given her every reason to think him a madman.

The moon sank low over the western mountains, and the endless plains surrendered to darkness. Ahead, Chen's head lolled to one side and he slumped in his saddle. He had fallen asleep. Evelyn gently prodded him and he woke, quickly informing her that people of Chinese descent could sleep while awake.

Evelyn didn't argue with this logic, but Rafael knew his brave, passionate rescuers had reached the limits of their endurance. He called ahead, and the group halted. "It is time we find a place to make camp. We'll sleep for the rest of the night, then head west into the hills tomorrow."

Patukala turned back and spoke quietly in the Zuni tongue. "Up ahead, there is a rocky area, many pines. And water nearby. We can sleep concealed there."

He led the way, and the rest followed. The ground was as Patukala said, rocky but hidden in a grove of ragged conifers. Sleeping wouldn't be comfortable, but it would be safe. They dismounted. Without a word, they commenced making camp. Patukala had brought six bedrolls—apparently, they had intended to kidnap Evelyn all along. Chen stood by, supervising as Sally and Will prepared a small meal of dried meat and native roots, but Patukala forbade them to make a fire.

Chen issued a stream of orders that Patukala ignored—though Rafael's uncle rarely spoke English, he understood it perfectly. However, he had found it in his best interest to feign ignorance, for the sake of peace and perhaps because he delighted in frustrating Chen.

Sally unfurled the last bedroll, then gestured absently at Evelyn. "So where do you want her? I could tie her up to one of them pines, or maybe nail a stake next to her."

Rafael winced at her lack of tact. "That will not be necessary, Sally."

Evelyn positioned herself beside Sally, her head high. "It will."

He had never dreamed she could be so . . . fractious. "Mrs. Reid, you need to sleep. Escape is not in your best interest." He paused, thinking of some impetus for her to contain herself. "There are . . . wolves."

"I am not afraid of wolves."

He shouldn't be surprised, but he couldn't help his reaction to her charm. "Tigers?"

She frowned, but he detected a dimple in her cheek as she resisted smiling. "I will be bound." She paused. "Perhaps it would be better to tie me to a stake. A pine might be prickly."

He contemplated leaving her free despite her claim. But it would offend her pride to think he didn't find her formidable. "As you wish."

He fixed a rope loosely around her wrists, drove a stake into the soil, and laid her bedroll next to it. She examined her ties and shook her head. "I can easily free myself from this."

A difficult woman. "You can, yes. But I shall be sleeping near you, and as you may have noticed, my hearing is amazingly acute. If you begin struggling with your ties, I'll hear you, and then bind you to the prickliest pine I can find for interrupting my rest."

He was teasing her, but she considered his threat seriously and nodded in solemn acquiescence. "Very well. I am too weary to flee tonight, anyway. It would be wiser to wait until Lieutenant Talbot and his men are upon you, then make my escape."

"Good thinking."

Rafael found his bedroll and lay it near, but not too near, Evelyn's. Chen established himself closer, sitting cross-legged beside her while chewing on salted meat. He offered her some, which she took.

"It just can't compare to roast quail, can it,

miss?" Chen sighed, then gnawed off another bite of meat. He took a long drink of water from his canteen, then passed it to her. She didn't seem to mind sharing—she drank heartily, then thanked him. Her loose bind gave her no trouble—she could easily escape if she wanted to.

Rafael ate, watching Evelyn. From the moment he first met her, she had enthralled him. He had known from the first that it was more than her beauty he found captivating. He had seen a soul sympathetic to his own, gentle and sweet. But there was more to her, clearly. Innocent charm, a steadfast determination to remain independent, a desire to matter in the world . . . These things compounded into the most alluring woman he'd ever encountered.

"The roast quail was good, yes." She spoke thickly, chewing on the tough meat. She swallowed, then took another drink from the canteen. "But at least you got to dine in peace. I, on the other hand, was forced to endure several meals in the company of Agnes St. Claire."

Chen whistled. "I had you beat, at that."

Sally walked by, returning from a moment of privacy in the bush. She cast a dark glance Evelyn's way, then moved her bedroll to the far side of their camp. Patukala came to Rafael, then pointed up at a hillock. "I'll take the watch. You sleep."

Rafael shook his head. "I'm not tired yet. I'll take the first watch and wake you later."

Patukala didn't argue. He had ridden hard and fast, with single-minded determination. He settled himself near Sally and fell promptly asleep. Will already slept, having positioned himself near the horses. He smiled even in dreams. Evelyn looked around, then sighed, gesturing at Sally. "She doesn't like me much."

Why Evelyn should care what Sally thought of her, Rafael didn't know, but she was a sensitive woman, and fair enough not to blame his rescuers when her true anger was directed at him.

Chen eyed Sally, then shrugged without interest. "She doesn't like things that happen unexpectedly. We had our plan all set. When you tried to shoot Señor de Aguirre, it shook her up." He lowered his voice. "And to tell you the truth, she's just plain grumpy."

"I see." Evelyn hesitated. "Lieutenant Talbot says the pueblo people hated me for what I did. You don't seem angry, though."

Chen's brow furrowed. "Hated you? No, miss. People understand things better than that. They know, all of them, that you thought Señor de Aguirre killed your husband. Now, if you'd known him better, you'd know that wasn't possible—as I tried to explain to you in my letter." He paused. "What did you think of it, anyway?"

She seemed confused, probably taken aback by Chen's abundant self-appreciation. She fingered a golden locket hanging around her neck as if it steadied her. "It was very well written, very moving. You elucidated your points extremely well."

Chen yawned. "I thought so. Figured you'd see reason when you got that, but I wasn't sure Talbot would let you read it."

"I was impressed, all the same."

Chen lay back, pleased with himself. Within

seconds, he was asleep. Evelyn remained sitting and seemed restless. Rafael hesitated, but he knew what he had to do. The time had come, and he had best get it over with now. He shifted, then came to sit beside her. She tensed, and a stab of remorse reminded him that she had reacted this way when they first met.

"Mrs. Reid . . ." He kept his voice low so as not to wake Chen. "It is time you and I had a talk."

"I see no need." She didn't look at him. She seemed to be fiddling with the hem of her sleeve instead, as if it held endless fascination.

"There is a need. When you and I first met, I dishonored you. . . ." A quick intake of breath told him that this matter wasn't settled for Evelyn, either. "I have never apologized to you for my error. Allow me to do so now."

She shrugged, too quickly. "It is forgotten."

"If it was forgotten, you wouldn't hide your eyes from me as you do now."

Her gaze snapped to him, then away again. "You are a duplicitous, murderous rogue. That is why I distrust you, Se-nor de Aguirre."

"Is that it, truly, Evelyn?" He fell silent for a while. Nothing was resolved. His brazen attraction to her stood between them. "I have never acted that way in my life." He paused. "You have no reason to believe me, I know. Perhaps it was the heat."

"I don't recall that day being particularly warm."

He smiled. "The chill, then?"

A reluctant smile curved her lips, too. "A weak excuse, se-nor."

"It's the best I can do. It's been a long day."

She sighed. "It has, indeed."

They didn't speak for a while, sitting quietly together. Almost imperceptibly, Evelyn seemed to relax. Or maybe she was just exhausted. "Perhaps you should sleep, Mrs. Reid. You need not fear tonight. I will protect you."

She eyed him doubtfully. "But who will protect me from you?"

"You haven't forgiven me, I see, despite my apology."

"You killed my husband."

"I only ask forgiveness for crimes I have committed, not for those I'm wrongly accused of. I ask it for my behavior at our first meeting, and yes, for involving Westley in the pueblo troubles."

"I expect he involved himself. He liked to be in the middle of things, setting matters between people. I cannot blame you for that."

"He was a good and honorable man."

"Yes." She seemed uncomfortable with this subject, but it was time they understood each other.

"Whatever else you may believe, know that I considered your husband a friend. Had I known you were his wife . . ." He stopped and sighed, looking east over the dark plains. With the moon gone behind the mountains, the stars shone brighter and his memory sparkled just as clear. "You cannot imagine . . . And perhaps I cannot explain fully what I felt that day, or why. I don't understand it myself. A form of madness infected me. But to learn the most wonderful woman I'd ever seen belonged to another man, a man I admired . . ."

He had said too much, again. She tensed, but her brow furrowed tight. "You didn't know me at all. How could you think I was wonderful?"

He gazed down at her, fighting an urge to touch her cheek. "It may surprise you to learn, Mrs. Reid, that nothing I have learned subsequently has altered that opinion."

Her eyes narrowed. "I tried to shoot you."

He smiled, but his heart filled with an ache that seemed almost part of him now. "That, most of all."

She shook her head. "I do not understand you."

"Don't you? You are a woman of substance, Evelyn, of emotion so deep . . . You alone of anyone there—the guards, soldiers, Talbot—only you sensed what I had planned."

"Then I was right. You were planning an escape."

"I was. I've gotten good at it over recent years." He paused. He liked talking to her. "I'm lucky you're such a poor shot."

Her gaze shifted as if she felt guilty over something and she didn't comment. Silence filled the space between them again, but she made no move to sleep.

After a long while, she peeked up at him. "Why have you never married?"

He liked the question, and it surprised him. "Of late, my duties have kept me from pursuing that path." It seemed wisest not to add that the only woman to interest him in over a year had been in mourning.

"Your duties as schoolmaster, or as Renegade?"

"Both."

She considered this for a while, but didn't seem satisfied. "And before?"

She was delving into his romantic history. A wave of pleasure coursed through him. "I came close to marrying once."

"Oh." She sounded casual, but he felt her bright gaze intent upon him. "Why didn't you go through with it?"

"The woman I had courted decided life in Santa Fe couldn't compare to the greater splendors of Mexico City. I went with her, but I found that the life there didn't interest me. There were endless parties, festivals, but people in her society seemed to feel the clothes they wore, the styles of their hair, and the like more important than I did."

"It sounds somewhat like Boston."

"Perhaps. But many have said the society in Mexico City is stricter than anything known in the East."

She looked up at him curiously. "Didn't they accept you?"

"I suppose they frowned upon my Zuni heritage, but my father was a man of some prestige, so my mixed blood was forgiven. What troubled them more was my profession, I'm afraid."

"Teaching children?"

He shrugged. "It is considered 'inappropriate' to have such dealings with the lower classes."

Her lips twisted. "It sounds as if their society was populated by Spanish versions of Agnes St. Claire."

"She was, I will admit, not entirely unfamiliar to me."

Evelyn hesitated. "But your fiancée wished to remain there?"

"She did, and she was not my fiancée, though perhaps she expected to be. After I realized our dreams differed so much, I refrained from proposing, and returned to the pueblo alone."

"Did you love her?"

"Yes."

She said nothing, but she didn't look entirely pleased with his answer. Again, she fingered the locket around her neck.

"It may be . . ." He didn't mean to speak or to continue this conversation, but there was more between them than could be denied. "It may be that I didn't understand the depth of love then. I didn't realize how it could envelope all your soul, own you, surround you, and become so much a part of you that everything you do, every breath you take, is filled with its fire."

If ever a man had said too much . . . He caught himself and stopped, but the expression on her lovely face answered clearly. She knew exactly what he meant. She bit her lip and shifted her position.

"Did you feel that way, Mrs. Reid, when you were married?"

He never should have asked. He had no right to ask. She cleared her throat. "Marriage, I thought, was very pleasant." She sounded so nervous. He had meant to assuage her fears, to make her comfortable in his presence. Instead he had done this. "I do not think that what you describe . . . is necessarily for the best. . . .

There is a quiet ease between people, such as I had in my marriage with Westley."

"It may not be for the best, but I cannot imagine anything so compelling as when love claims you so completely." He paused. Suddenly, it was important that she consider him handsome. He removed his spectacles and set them aside. "Can you?"

She looked up at him, her eyes wide. Her voice came as a whisper. "No."

Somehow, they were closer to each other than he remembered. Her face seemed bare inches from his. He wanted to protect her, to earn her friendship and respect, to prove to her that no matter what he had done in the guise of the Renegade, the quiet, restrained schoolmaster reflected his true self. Instead, he reached to touch her soft hair, untangling it from its loose binding. It fell in long waves around her face and down her back as she stared up at him, shocked and enchanted.

His fingers grazed across her cheek—the softest skin he had ever touched—and he bent closer to brush his mouth over hers.

She froze, astonished by his act. He tasted her and desire so strong that it stabbed through him. She trembled like a captured bird. "No," she murmured as if it were torn from inside her. That faintest whisper stopped him. Unable to move away, he rested his forehead against hers, and though he couldn't see her face, he knew she wept. Very gently, fighting the madness that he had never been able to contain, he placed his hands on either side of her face, then kissed her forehead.

"I am sorry." He didn't expect her to accept his apology now, he wasn't asking for forgiveness. He was admitting to her what she had known all along.

He was a renegade after all.

Evelyn lay curled in a ball, her back to where Rafael sat silent on watch. She pretended to sleep, but her heart hammered relentlessly. He had kissed her, so gently and so sweetly that she still tasted his lips upon hers, felt the aftershocks speeding along her nerves.

Never had a man been so demonic as Rafael de Aguirre. So demonic, and so sweet. She was terrified. If he had taken her, thrown her to the ground and had his way with her, then she would have felt nothing but hatred. What he did instead seemed worse—he infected her soul, enveloped her heart, and tortured her with a desire she was devastated to feel.

No man had ever kissed her that way. Westley had been almost apologetic about his marital rights, and their relationship had taken more the form of a friendship or of close family kinship. Those moments had been somewhat embarrassing, but not a real disturbance to her composure.

Rafael shattered everything. Why hadn't she stopped him? Like the first time they met, she had just stared up at him, stunned like a woman spellbound. She almost believed he truly did possess some power handed down to him from his godlike ancestors.

His touch sent fire all through her, his nearness sent her heart racing. His kiss had turned her to liquid inside, but his lips had barely touched hers.

Evelyn stole a quick peek at him. He sat a short distance away, his eyes closed, but she knew he was awake, listening with his sharp hearing to the sounds of the night.

If she rolled over, he would hear her. She tried to lie still, but her body ached from the ride, and she longed to stretch out. Despite the rocks, the bedroll offered enough padding for comfort. She drew a breath and rolled over, allowing her cramped legs to extend.

Rafael noticed her movement at once. He must have known she wasn't sleeping. "Are you uncomfortable, Evelyn?"

When had he stopped addressing her formally, anyway? She decided not to comment on his infraction, lest he think she noticed too much of what he said or did. "I'm fine, or would be, if you weren't hovering like a hawk over prey."

He smiled. "You are something of a captive, you know."

"And you are my guard."

"Until Patukala takes over at the watch, I'm afraid so."

"It doesn't matter who guards me." She paused. "Aren't you tired?"

"I am. But I have too much on my mind to sleep just yet."

Evelyn resisted, then propped herself up on one elbow. Her ties had loosened so much that she barely noticed them. "Such as what?"

"My brother, the people taken from the pueblo . . ."

"I know nothing of that. I'm not sure I believe it, anyway. Why would Talbot or anyone else want to take your people captive?"

"I'm not sure. But there is something—something concerning the pueblo that interests them."

"What?"

"I have no idea."

Patukala rose from his bedding and motioned to Rafael. Evelyn looked between them, sensing Rafael's hesitation. "I suggest you take your chance now, se-nor," she said. "If we are attacked by tigers, I would have you ready with your weapon rather than dozing off in your saddle."

He looked at her in surprise and Evelyn bit her lip hard. This could almost be construed as flirting. It wasn't intentional, but she seemed to lose all sense of purpose or decorum in his company.

A slow smile grew on his dark face. "I will agree on one condition."

She hesitated, suspicious. "What?"

"That you will stop calling me 'se-nor.' "

Wonderful. He attempted to reduce the boundaries of formality between them even more. "That would be . . ."

He cut her off. "Inappropriate? But it is not so much for the sake of familiarity I ask."

He paused, and she sensed he was baiting her into something. "Then why?"

"As it happens, your pronunciation of the term 'señor' is somewhat . . . lacking."

She frowned. "Is that so? I studied only the basics of rudimentary Spanish before coming

West." She felt stung. So this explained why he smiled whenever she addressed him. The nerve! She had to pretend that nothing he did affected her, but it wasn't easy. "Very well, if you prefer, I shall call you Rafael. Do I pronounce that well enough for your liking?"

"Perfectly." He lay back on his bedroll, his arms folded behind his head, and he stared up at the night sky. "Sleep well, Evelyn. Tomorrow will be long and tiring, and may have many unexpected turns."

Evelyn didn't respond. *Unexpected turns, indeed.*

She lay back and tugged the wool blanket up to her neck. She tried to close her eyes, to sleep, but instead, found herself looking at Rafael as he slept beside her.

She thought of him charging into the plaza, wielding his strange whip—the bola—with every muscle of his body acting in perfect accord. He was a man designed to attract a woman's more earthy attention.

What did he want from her? She tried to tell herself he wanted sway over her, because he needed her to escape. But he had done the same thing when they met.

When he looked at her that way, she forgot everything. She had forgotten who she was, that she was married. Everything. Tonight, she had almost forgotten that she was a widow because of him.

She had to remember that, despite his earnest denials. It was her only hope.

Somehow, she had to repel him. Evelyn tried to collect her thoughts to focus on what she knew of men. His infatuation might be intense, but it was likely superficial. Perhaps, yes, he had tired of the women available to him and was bent on seducing those of a different type. He considered her pretty—maybe that was the problem. Evelyn chewed the inside of her lip. If he saw her in a different light, when she wasn't groomed, perhaps . . .

The idea had promise. Men seemed universally attracted by what they could see of a woman. As much as Westley had loved her, it was her appearance he complimented most often. He found her charming, but she had sometimes suspected that were her personality quirks found in another woman whose appearance he liked less, he might have found them annoying instead.

This was most certainly true of Rafael de Aguirre. He had called her "a woman of substance," true, but after all, he hadn't known any of that when he first saw her. All he had seen was a slender figure, wavy hair, and an even-featured face. It was often apparent that those smitten attributed any number of charms to the object of their affection, charms that wouldn't be noticed had that person been visually inadequate.

Evelyn relaxed. Rafael was no different from any other man. From tomorrow onward, she would do her best to present herself in the most unpleasant light possible. As soon as he saw her in a less flattering light, his interest would fade.

Chapter Six

Evelyn Reid had fallen into a puddle of mud. Where she'd found mud of any kind on the dry plains, Rafael had no idea, but wet dirt covered her from head to toe.

Never had he seen a sight so charming.

She stood before him, looking deliberately casual, her cheeks dotted with even splotches of mud, her long hair tangled and suspiciously darker than normal, as if that, too, had received the benefit of her mud bath. Her blue dress had lost its natural shade and seemed more tattered than it had the night before.

"What happened to you?"

Her eyes narrowed. "What do you mean?"

He adjusted his spectacles and assessed her thoughtfully. "You look as if a tiger grabbed you in the night, mauled you, and shoved you into quicksand. Or mud."

She puffed a quick breath, unconcerned. "I'm afraid a lady's daily rituals of bathing, grooming, dressing . . . Those things must fall to the wayside on a journey such as this."

"Fall to the wayside, yes, but was there a reason to immerse yourself in the foulest piece of wet earth you could find?"

She met his eyes without wavering, a veiled challenge. But what she was challenging, he didn't know. "It keeps the bugs away."

He sniffed. Yes, she had found a particularly noxious pool. He wondered if she used this tactic to repel bugs—or him. "You stink."

She seemed pleased. "It is an earthy fragrance. You get used to it."

Sally walked by and rolled her eyes heavenward. "Should have shot her when we had the chance."

Patukala eyed Rafael doubtfully, then assembled their packs on his saddle. Patukala spoke in the Zuni language. "*What you want with that one . . .*" He shook his head. "*You are more like your father than I knew*."

Rafael wasn't sure what this comment meant. His mother had been normal, after all. Unlike Evelyn Reid. Suddenly he realized what his uncle had said. *What you want with that one . . .* So Patukala had guessed his secret desire. Maybe it was obvious to all. For Evelyn's sake, he would have to restrain his affection for her.

Rafael mounted his horse, then waited for the others. "As soon as we find fresh water, you're going in it. Headfirst."

"I'm not." She mounted before Chen, and looked more pert and satisfied than he'd ever seen her. How could a woman so filthy be so . . . adorable?

Rafael shook his head and rode off ahead of her. He was more smitten than he realized.

Her plan was proceeding nicely. A week had passed as they journeyed, first south, then west into the mountains. Patukala had left the group with Sally for a few days, apparently to set an alternate trail to confuse Talbot's pursuit. Each morning, Evelyn woke first, found dirt, and applied it to her cheeks and clothing. Unfortunately, she hated feeling grimy. Before she had slathered herself in self-made mud, she had used the clear water to cleanse thoroughly. Her morning ritual had become more arduous than anything she'd done before.

After the first day, she was more careful about the smell, but Rafael was obviously horrified by her appearance. He kept looking back at her, shaking his head when a round glob of dirt fell from her hair. When Chen's horse passed Rafael's, he complained of being downwind of her, and quickly took the rear.

Chen didn't seem to mind her foul stench, but perhaps he was too self-involved to notice. Or maybe he'd gotten used to it. After a few hours, Evelyn couldn't smell herself, either.

Rafael, however, managed to comment at every opportunity. Sometimes, his comments seemed more like teasing. And teasing felt a little too much like flirting, so she tried to ignore him.

"If you do not like my smell, Señor Rafael"— she pronounced "señor" correctly this time—

"then perhaps you should engage a greater distance between us."

Despite her obvious logic, he didn't accept her advice and rode close behind Chen's horse.

Patukala led them through the western foothills, and slowly higher into the mountains. Evelyn wanted to question Rafael on their surroundings, because he seemed to know where they were going. Often, his uncle stopped and appeared to be asking Rafael the best path to take.

By midafternoon, her curiosity got the best of her. He was riding beside Chen's horse again, quiet, looking thoughtful. "So where are you taking us, anyway?"

He glanced over at her. "West into the mountains."

"That much I gathered on my own. For what purpose?"

"There are many places hidden in the mountains known only to my people. We will find safety and trails laid centuries ago."

She considered this, and found it promising. "Very well. If you would alert me to points of interest as we proceed, I would be grateful for the diversion."

His brow rose and a smile flickered on his lips. "Points of interest? Do you take me for a travel guide, Mrs. Reid?"

"I take you for a captor and a renegade." She paused, still interested in what might be seen of ancient civilizations in these mountains. "I had purchased a guidebook for western travelers on my way out, but found it inadequate. The section on the Indian people was particularly misleading."

"How so?"

"It didn't mention a propensity to ride in the guise of ancient warriors, for one thing. Neither did it give any form of accuracy as to lifestyle and personal habits."

"Do those things interest you?"

She gazed off into the mountains, vaguely. "Yes, of course. I would like to know how people live. You, I know, are not representative."

"No . . . I can lay claim to neither a Spanish heritage, nor Zuni."

Chen looked thoughtful. "Of course, neither one is as impressive or as ancient as Chinese history."

As Chen spoke, his horse stumbled. Seated sidesaddle already, Evelyn dropped to the ground in surprise. Rafael jumped down to assist her, but she caught herself and backed away from him, then pointed at the horse's leg. "I think he's stepped on a rock."

Chen sighed as if the horse had committed an offense directed at him. "I have got to get a better mount. Perhaps a black Andulasian." He dismounted and lifted the horse's right front leg onto his knee, then examined the hoof. "I don't see a rock."

Rafael knelt beside Chen and felt around on the hoof's underside. "I'd say it's bruised, but not badly." He straightened, then eyed Evelyn. "But I'm afraid our prisoner will be forced to ride with me." He patted the horse's neck. "One rider is enough for this one."

Evelyn's breath caught. She couldn't ride

with him. Chen was one thing—but sitting that close to Rafael would be excruciating. "I could walk."

Rafael pointed to the nearest mountain. "We're aiming to reach the summit by nightfall. Are you sure you want to walk?"

She gulped. "Yes. It would be refreshing to stretch my legs for a change."

To her surprise, Rafael didn't argue. He just mounted, spoke to Frank, and headed off. Chen looked between them, then shrugged. He cantered ahead to join the others, leaving Evelyn tagging along behind. If her captors remained this lax, it would be possible to escape before an hour passed.

Apparently, Rafael shared this insight, because he kept his horse at an even walk, riding ahead and to the side of her path. For that, she was silently thankful. Already, evading the droppings of the horses ahead had become a noxious irritant. She exhaled a breath of annoyance, then held her nose as she stepped carefully around the most recent deposit.

Rafael looked down at her, shaking his head. "Any time you change your mind, you can ride with me."

"This is fine. I enjoy walking."

She hated it. Her laced boots were thoroughly inadequate for the task, and already her feet were sore and blistered. It would have been bad enough over even ground, but rocks and hills proved a torment she hadn't expected.

The labor took on the nature of an almost spiritual quest. *I will not surrender. If I do, if I give in here to him, I will give in more. . . .*

She managed to walk for three hours, until each step tore at her feet and brought tears to her eyes. She kept her head down so Rafael couldn't see, but she couldn't hide her pain forever. The tears came more heavily, until she couldn't stop them. It was more than pain that assailed her. She felt defeat closing in. She felt *him* closing in. Exhaustion crashed over her all at once and she crumpled to her knees.

Rafael leapt down from his horse before she hit the ground. He knelt beside her, saying nothing, and she cried. The others stopped, too, but Rafael motioned them onward, and they rode off on the narrowing path ahead. Still, she cried.

He reached to touch her, then stopped himself. "Evelyn, I'm sorry. I know you don't want to ride with me. But Sally's horse is flighty and bucks if you tie an extra pack to its back. Will's is too small. Patukala—I suppose you could ride with him, but he's got all the packs and it would take an hour to shift them. Please . . . you can ride behind me, whatever it takes. But don't do this to yourself."

She sniffed and nodded, then looked up at him, tears staining her cheeks. "If I had better boots . . ."

He smiled, but pity filled his brown eyes. "There's no need." He took her leg in his gentle hands and unlaced her boots. She winced as he pulled them off. Her stockings were tattered and bloody and the air stung as it touched the raw skin. She expected his anger, but instead, pain filled his eyes.

When he looked at her, she saw more anguish

than she had ever beheld, a depth of feeling that she had never shared with another person. She swallowed hard, and found herself unexpectedly touching his face. "It's not your fault. I am too stubborn."

"You are, at that." He rose to his feet, then picked her up. She shouldn't have succumbed to his tenderness. Rafael's strong arms held her, and she felt his hard chest, the throb of his heart beneath firm flesh . . . Wild thoughts circled in her brain—of kissing his neck, running her fingers over his smooth skin, nipping . . .

A small squeak burst from her and she closed her eyes tight. Rafael mounted, still holding her. "I thought . . . I thought I was going to ride behind."

He tied her boots to his saddle, then urged Frank forward. "That would mean riding astride, Evelyn, with your skirt bunched . . ."

"Say no more!" She held up her hand to stop him from more descriptive terms of intimacy. "This will be fine."

They caught up with the others and Evelyn tried to settle into his saddle as comfortably as she had with Chen. But sitting with Rafael was nothing like with the amiable Chinese boy. For one thing, Chen was much smaller and lighter of build, so they didn't have the physical intimacy.

For another, she hadn't been aware of his every breath, his heartbeat, or the way his strong thighs moved in rhythm with the horse's stride. When he spoke, she heard the deep rumble in his chest, and felt the warmth of his body against hers.

Sally noticed them together and she frowned. "So she's finally gotten you just where she wants you, eh?"

Evelyn gaped, too shocked for a retort. She felt Rafael's muscles tense as if he fought for calm. "She injured her feet walking, Sally. It was I who insisted Evelyn ride with me."

Sally sneered, then huffed. "That's what she wants you to think. Nice ploy, that. Getting your bleeding heart sympathy worked up watching her trudge along."

Evelyn exhaled a furious breath, then made a fist. "It might please you, madame, to address me directly from now on. I remind you that it was your choice to kidnap me and that I am here against my will!"

Sally wasn't impressed. "I know your kind, girl. You don't have a rat's sense of your own heart. You'd put a bullet in a man to kill off your own guilt."

"My guilt!" Evelyn stopped. There was a grain of truth in Sally's statement. More than a grain. "I wasn't thinking clearly. I should have let justice run its proper course."

"You should have stood up the day Lieutenant Talbot slapped Rafe in jail, and told him this man didn't kill your husband."

"I saw him." Evelyn felt stung, though she was sure she was in the right. "And even if I had done what you say, he wouldn't have listened. He didn't believe me about Diego, after all."

"That's because he was using the boy to get Rafe, and you know it. He didn't have to believe you—the governor would have listened. But no . . . you stood back and let them drag this man, a good man, north where no one would have a say except that bastard Talbot's brother! Why'd he want that, do you think?"

"He felt a fair trial wouldn't be possible. Talbot had discovered that Rafael was the Renegade. Who else would have killed my husband?"

"People don't look close enough to their own homes, I'd say." Sally snorted and rode on ahead.

Evelyn fell silent, pondering Sally's accusations. It came too close to the truth. Rafael touched her shoulder. "Don't mind Sally, Evelyn. She was close to my mother, and feels herself in that role now."

"It's more than that."

"Well, maybe she's a little jealous of you."

"Why?"

"Not that you look it today, but normally you are a woman of elegance. You're 'well tended.' "

She wanted to argue, but couldn't. "I have tried to be a good person, and to use the advantages I was born with to help others."

He squeezed her shoulder in gentle support. "I know that. I saw that the day I met you. To be honest, I don't know what's gotten into Sally. She's usually a kind woman, patient and good-hearted."

"I have seen that with her son. I wish some of her 'good heart' might be extended to me."

"Give her time."

Evelyn sighed. "I suppose it shouldn't matter."

"You are a sensitive woman. Such things will always matter, whether you want them to or not."

She glanced up at him, taking comfort despite herself. He looked so handsome, his dark skin warmed beneath the high sun. He looked ancient and wise, beautiful and kind. He was all she had ever admired, and all she'd thought she couldn't find.

He was a lie. She had to remember that. Beneath his compelling exterior, beyond his gentle manners, there was a man who donned a mask and took justice into his own hands. She thought of his weapon. A bola, some kind of Argentinean whip, he had said. With it, he disarmed his enemies easily—but caused them little harm otherwise. Only once, on Westley, had the bola been used to kill.

Evelyn felt herself weakening. The thought disturbed her. If she came to trust him, to believe in his innocence—then what? What would keep her from dissolving into his arms as she had longed to do? Evelyn caught herself, forbidding a memory too painful to touch.

She adjusted herself in the saddle for greater comfort, but her movement brought her closer against him. She heard a muted groan, and peeked up him. "Did I hurt you?"

His breath seemed a little too swift, and his brown eyes had darkened almost to black. In a flash, she recognized desire. He shifted in the saddle, away from her. "Not exactly pain, but if you'd sit still, this ride would be easier for both of us."

"I'm sorry."

"It's not your fault." He sounded formal, polite. She tried not to look at him, and he seemed to be avoiding her eyes, too.

"Aren't you offended by my smell?"

He looked down at her and smiled. "Deeply." He paused. "Unfortunately, your other charms outweigh your stench."

She frowned. "It has faded substantially since this morning."

"To you, perhaps."

She bit her lip. "I must be a rather unpleasant sight to look upon."

"You are filthy and small rodents could make homes in the tangled nest of your hair."

She braced in offense, then remembered this reaction was just what she'd intended. Still . . .

Without warning, he bent forward and kissed her temple. She was too surprised to react. "It was a good attempt though. I admire your effort."

"What do you mean?" He knew . . . Her heart doubled its beat. How did he always seem to know what she was thinking?

"Did you really think what I saw in you was so superficial as to be negated by a dirty face?"

"I thought it might be."

"You are more than beauty, Evelyn Reid. But if I might make a suggestion, your attempts serve only to highlight the unusual nature of your imagination. And imagination is something I have always found hard to resist."

She wasn't sure how to respond to this. For most of her life, a vivid imagination was something she felt she must curb, rein in like a horse that, given freedom, would prove dangerous. Westley had often teased that she came up with the most creative explanations for simple events. If someone was late arriving at a party, she assumed the person had been waylaid by ruffians, or eloped with the local grocer. When she arrived in Santa Fe, he had laughed because she was looking for evidence of ancient civilizations everywhere—and when a man clothed as an Anasazi warrior charged into the plaza, she had fully believed him otherworldly.

Imagination led to infatuation, to foolishness. It led to nothing but heartache. It left poets weeping in solitude, artists starving on streets beside paintings whose beauty no one else saw. If in a hundred years those paintings had more value than a castle, the artist himself was long dead.

Imagination made a woman dream of a love so strong that it would defy all obstacles—when she was better off marrying sensibly, to a man who cared for her and left those secret places inside her heart untapped.

"I have always feared that a fanciful imagination was a curse rather than a thing of charm."

"Why?"

"It hasn't served me particularly well." She sighed. "As a matter of fact, I was expelled from my first school because I spent too much time dreaming."

Rafael stared at her in astonishment. "That is no reason to remove a child from school! It's obvious that your teacher wasn't skilled enough to deal with a talented child."

He spoke with such feeling . . . Evelyn tried not to look at him, but he was incredibly compelling. "That's what my father said. He put me in another school and lectured my new teacher on what he considered my 'talents.'" She paused. "What was your father like?"

Rafael smiled. "Allejandro de Aguirre was nothing if not imaginative. He wrote poetry, staged theatrical presentations at the pueblo. He won my mother not by reason, but by singing to her."

"It sounds romantic."

"It was. She was heartbroken when he died, and her own will to live soon faltered."

"Were you very young when he died?"

"I was twenty years old, my brother seven."

"You are much older than Diego. Are there no others between you?"

"My mother bore five children after me, but all died, either before birth or shortly after. Diego was a surprise to her."

"He seems pleasant."

"He is rebellious and wild and difficult."

Evelyn cocked her brow at a dramatic angle. "He is sixteen."

Rafael smiled. "That is what I meant."

She couldn't help liking him. There was so much in his heart, so much thoughtfulness and compassion for others. "I suppose that to him, you are his parent."

"I have looked after him, yes. Until now."

She didn't want to care, not this much, but she saw pain in his dark eyes, the strain of knowing he was needed, perhaps desperately, and couldn't reach his brother. "Sally said large groups have been taken, isn't that right?"

"Yes."

She pondered this for a while, struggling to think logically. Generally her mind wandered and skipped around before seeing the whole picture. But the parts had to be viewed as forming a whole. "Then it seems to me they weren't taken to be killed, nor because of who they were. They must have been taken for a purpose, to do something. It seems most likely for some kind of work."

His brow arched. "You have a good mind, and you're right. But if for work, why not simply hire people? There are many workers available in Santa Fe now, who aren't yet employed by the railroad."

"That, I don't know. But it would seem this work is secret, and so must be done by captives. People who won't be able to tell anyone what they have been doing." Her heart chilled as she comprehended what this might mean.

"Captives . . ." His expression darkened with fear. "People who once they have completed their task . . . are expendable."

He echoed her thoughts exactly. She nodded slowly. "Yes."

"If that is so, then my brother is in great danger."

Evelyn looked up into his beautiful eyes. She wanted to disagree, but she couldn't. "Yes, I believe he is."

Rafael didn't want the day to end. Evelyn had at last settled comfortably in his lap, she was speaking to him almost like a friend. And she had helped him to understand what might have happened to his brother. She had a bright mind, taking unusual paths toward understanding truth. Her intuition impressed him almost as much as her charm. She would have made a fine teacher.

Since the first night, he had slept near to her, but never near enough. He had risen to watch her sleeping, then lain quiet when she woke. He had watched as she sneaked from the campsite. At first, he feared she would attempt escape, so he followed her. And there he had seen her busily applying mud to her cheeks. He had left her alone, understanding her purpose, and she had done likewise each morning.

He hadn't told her he knew what she was doing. It seemed to please her so well, and gave her a measure of perceived safety in his presence. More than that, Rafael didn't know what to do with his feelings for Evelyn Reid. From the moment he first saw her, his reaction had taken on a life of its own, inspiring him to actions he'd never considered before.

He wanted to know her, to be inside her, not just her body but her soul. To have her, of all people, look at him with distrust cut deep. Yet she had softened toward him—he felt it. Maybe, as they journeyed onward, he could earn her confidence. If he could restrain his desire, if he could keep from frightening her with words he hadn't meant to say . . .

Patukala had ridden back along the path, scouting for signs of pursuit, so Rafael led their party now. Frank liked the lead, and his stride extended with pleasure. Evelyn watched the path ahead, looking eager despite the grueling day they'd spent in the saddle.

"Where are we going, exactly? I've been keeping a lookout for interesting landmarks, but so far, all I've seen are rocks, juniper bushes, and peculiar-looking pine trees."

"May I ask what you were expecting?"

"I'm not sure. But something more interesting than this."

He directed Frank off the path, and up a short hill. Across a wide gorge, the western horizon opened wide before them. Rafael stopped his horse and pointed at a distant mountain. "What do you think of that, Mrs. Reid?"

She looked in the direction he indicated and then back at him. "What is that mountain?"

"It is called Sleeping Ute, and if you look more carefully, you will see the silhouette of a sleeping warrior."

"I do not see any such thing."

"There—his headdress flows to the north. His arms are folded across the chest—that is the highest point. His knees form the southern peak."

"And the smaller peaks are his toes?"

"Exactly. The Utes themselves dwell nearby. Their legend speaks of a great warrior god who fought against 'evil ones.' In his greatest battle, he braced himself for the fight and pushed up the earth, creating the valleys and mountains. He was injured in the battle, and his blood turned into living water for all creatures to drink."

"Imaginative."

"As the seasons change, and the leaves turn color, those are his blankets. When the clouds gather and the rain falls, the Utes say it is a sign that the warrior god is pleased with his people."

"How do you know these things? Did you learn this from your mother?"

"My mother, as it happens, was uninterested in legend. It was my father who found native myths a fascination."

"Is this mountain where we're going?"

He smiled. "Not so far. Our destination is close now. You might find it a 'point of interest.' "

She seemed ready to question him, but Patukala galloped up from behind, startling the other horses. Rafael brought Frank back to the path and greeted his uncle in Zuni. *"What is it, Uncle?"*

"Talbot is behind us, Rafael. He is closer than I had thought, but I covered our trail, and lay the beginnings of another. It will stall him, but not for long."

"How many are with him?"

"Ten. Perhaps fifteen. More than we."

"And they will be well armed." Rafael drew a long breath. Talbot moved fast, and was motivated by more than pursuit of justice. *"At some point, we will have to fight him. If we're successful, it will set him back, but I doubt we can stop him completely."*

"We can hide in the holds of the Ancient Ones. Stop him, then separate ourselves. Make for Taos and the Acoma pueblo. The A:shiwi will help us."

Rafael hesitated. *"My grandfather?"*

"My father. He will assist us."

"He has refused me all my life. Why now?"

"He is a stubborn man, but a wise one. He does not want his grandson shot down like a dog."

"He did nothing when I was taken prisoner."

Patukala's brow arched. *"Where do you think I got these horses? We will spend the night concealed in the houses that our ancestors created, then divide in the morning."*

Evelyn looked between them, suspicious. "What is he saying?"

"It seems your noble Lieutenant Talbot is more eager in pursuit than I hoped."

"Talbot is behind us?"

"Yes. We knew he would be sooner or later. I am sorry to say it is sooner."

"What are you going to do?"

"Hide tonight. Tomorrow, we will throw him off the trail."

She pondered this as he explained the situation to the others, then fell silent as they rode onward. After a while, she looked up at him, her small face intent as if she waged some inward war with herself.

"Yes, Mrs. Reid? What troubles you?"

Her lips twisted to one side, as if she hesitated to speak her heart to him. Then she feigned a casual expression. "There is likely to be some manner of fighting, I assume?"

"It may come to that. I hope not." He paused. "I won't let anything happen to you, Evelyn."

Something in her shadowy blue eyes told him her safety hadn't concerned her. Again, she delayed before speaking. "Lieutenant Talbot will be well armed, with long-range rifles. How will you fight him, given your propensity for fighting with a whip?"

"It is called a *bola*, an Argentinean whip, used more for herding cattle, hunting, and knocking apples off trees than fighting."

"You used it rather effectively against your guards."

"It is used to enforce and extend its user's will—that is certain." He paused, studying her lovely face. "But my 'will' has never included murder."

"So you say." Something about the way she shifted her gaze from his gave him hope. She didn't want to believe him, but she was wavering. "You're wearing your spectacles. Can't you shoot?"

"I am capable, I suppose, but I will not."

She eyed him doubtfully. "Why not? It is safer to shoot from afar . . ."

"And more deadly. Having been your target, I am well aware of that."

"I don't understand you at all."

"I will kill, if I must. Don't mistake that, Mrs. Reid. But I will not use a device that has caused such massive grief."

"Why not? It's much more effective."

"That is why." Rafael sighed. "Man gave himself a weapon that allowed him to stand at a distance and kill. And so, he no longer killed only for hunting or defense. He began to kill for greed, for power, and to satisfy all those demons that had once been restrained. A man will risk his life to save another, to hunt food. Would he risk his life for greed or for power, if he were not armed with a weapon that made it easy to kill from the safety of distance?"

She stared up at him, opened her mouth to speak, then closed it again.

"And war, Evelyn. What of war? Our ancestors fought with weapons they made themselves, with their hands. Now, look at your own society. How many thousands were slaughtered in your Great War that would not have died had those men had to face each other and decide for themselves if what they marched into battle for was truly worth the price?"

"The Civil War was motivated by the greatest honor—the freedom of all men."

"The control of a country's wealth seems the more likely ambition."

Her face knit into a tight frown. "My father was an officer in the war, and I assure you, he did not fight for money! He was an Abolitionist of the highest order, and he has lived his principles ever since."

"I suppose he has men friends of different races?" He couldn't quite restrain his sarcasm, but Evelyn braced.

"As a matter of fact, Señor Rafael, he does. You don't understand, because you weren't there. You don't know what they went through. . . ."

"And I don't want to. It is insanity, nothing more, to launch battles of such magnitude."

"They were the bravest men to ever live!"

It was plain Evelyn Reid adored and admired her father, and had been filled with all kinds of fairy tales about his bloody war. But the thought of it, thousands upon thousands of men marching into certain death, had haunted Rafael's dreams since childhood when his father had told him of the American war. His father had been a vivid storyteller, but the mass violence, the mindless orders, men cut down like wheat before a scythe—these things needed little embellishment to cause nightmares.

Evelyn, however, looked irritated and combative over the issue. "At least, my ancestors weren't in the habit of scalping their victims."

"On the contrary, it was your ancestors who taught mine the practice."

"What rubbish!" She twisted around away from him, glaring. "Its impossible to reason with you, so I shall not try."

"I was just thinking the same thing about you. If all men dealt with their problems on their own ground, without inflicting their will on others beyond, the world would suffer less anguish."

"And what do you do, oh wise Renegade that you are, when one culture of people has enslaved another? Do you leave that to be resolved 'on their own ground'?"

He had no immediate answer, so her brow angled as if certain victory was at hand. "There is always a better solution than war."

She tossed her head. "A shame you hadn't been there to advise Mr. Lincoln on your 'better solution.' He would have been much relieved."

She could be an extremely annoying woman at times. He puffed an exasperated breath. "That is not my point."

She huffed. "What is?"

"Had your culture been less domineering and aggressive in the first place, these situations wouldn't have arisen at all."

"I suppose Indians waged no wars?" She knew they had, the little fiend.

"Not on such a vast scale. I am not saying my

people are free of violence, just that we haven't made such an art of it as you."

"I guess we shouldn't even mention your Spanish side."

He paused, teeth ground together. She had him there. "No, we shouldn't."

They rounded a corner, reaching a point high on the mesa. Evelyn gestured down, and far below, Rafael saw Talbot's group filing up the same winding path. "It appears you'll have your chance to prove your theory now, Señor Rafael. The battle is coming to you."

Chapter Seven

Rafael took the fore and led them on such a confusing series of paths that Evelyn had no idea how Talbot would ever find them. They climbed sharp hillsides, then down over gorges so steep she closed her eyes lest Frank trip and send them careening over the edge. But Rafael seemed to have utmost faith in his surefooted mount, so Evelyn eventually relaxed, too.

As they progressed, she felt more and more certain that Talbot would never find them. As he had done all along, Patukala took Sally and Will, riding on alternate paths, hoping to delay the pursuit even more. Evelyn wasn't sure if she felt relieved or annoyed at their success. She wanted to be annoyed. Maybe it was because the mood of the group affected her, but she found herself looking back with fear rather than hope.

Her mind drifted from the pursuit and back to her captor. She hadn't realized he was quite so opinionated. Wrong, and sure of himself all the same. No wonder he felt he could take the law into his own hands. She hadn't been able to reason with him at all.

A tiny voice in her head informed her that she, too, might be considered opinionated, but she shoved it aside. *We are alike, you and I.*

"Not in the least." She had spoken aloud. Evelyn cringed, but Rafael glanced down at her, fighting a smile.

"Did I miss something, or are you having an argument with yourself?"

She struggled for an explanation. "I was thinking . . . I am not in the least concerned. . . ." She popped her lips, unable to think of anything.

"About . . . ?"

"None of your concern." She glared, but he was still smiling.

"Then I beg your pardon. I will not interrupt such conversations again."

"Thank you."

She yawned, though she wasn't really tired. "When are we stopping?"

"Soon."

He didn't seem chatty, for once. Rather than relief, she felt disappointment. She had hoped, without thinking of it much, to engage him in another argument. But maybe he was concentrating on the maze of trails before him. Despite herself, Evelyn preferred Rafael's attention on her.

The paths seemed clearer now, though overgrown. Many of the rocks seemed to have been laid along the way on purpose, but long ago. "Who lives here?"

"No one."

He would have to be inspired to give more than one-word answers. "Then who lived here before?"

"The Ancient Ones."

She rolled her eyes, exasperated. "Ancient sparrows?"

"The Anasazi, Mrs. Reid. My ancestors. *Those who came before*."

"Ah." She looked around. "And did they make these roads?"

"They did. Many centuries ago, my people traded as far as Mexico, perhaps beyond. They dwelt in cliffside cities, then disappeared."

"Probably driven off by my ancestors?"

"Why they left isn't certain, but the Zuni believe they moved out of the mountains and instead built pueblos, living much as they did before, growing corn and beans, making pottery, raising their families. At that time in history, your own ancestors were . . . what? Invading England?"

"My ancestors were Scottish, thank you very much. Strange that your noble, peaceful ancestors should have a renegade for a descendant. I don't think British history has any such persons."

He scoffed. "Highwaymen abound in England. But they are motivated by robbery, not defending people unjustly suppressed."

"I'm sure some acted for good causes."

"The beloved Scarecrow of Romney Marsh

was a smuggler. What good cause was there in that, other than profit and greed?"

Why had she encouraged him to talk, anyway? "How do you know these things?"

His brow angled. "I am a schoolmaster."

"I hate to think what you have taught the children about European history."

"The truth, of course. That it was a bloody civilization, infected with the sickness of greed."

She wanted to hit him. "And what of the art, the music, the stories, the poetry?"

He hesitated. "I will acknowledge a contribution in that area—although the poetry and art of my people still goes unnoticed by your culture."

"And what of the cities? When I was ten, my parents took our family to Europe, to London and to Rome, to Greece and to Austria. We traveled all over, and I have never seen such wonders as I beheld there. As interesting as I'm sure your rather dull and unchanging history is, you certainly don't have cities that compare to those in Europe."

"Is that so?"

Without warning, he urged his horse into a sudden gallop, dislodging Evelyn. She squealed in surprise and jammed her eyes shut, but he held her in place with one strong arm wrapped around her waist. Frank charged up the hill, around a tight corner, then up another slope. Rafael reined in the horse as suddenly as they'd taken off, and Evelyn opened her eyes.

A dry wind blew in her face, ruffling her loose hair. She looked out over a blue sky, then caught her breath. Before her lay a vast city. She saw thousands of stone houses, multistoried earthen homes, ancient and worn yet still glorious, built into the walls of the mountain.

"Behold, my lady, Mesa Verde. Did you see anything in Europe like this?"

She gazed out in wonder, then whispered, "No."

They hid the horses in what appeared to be an ancient storage, and Will set about tending them, bringing them water from a nearby stream, and plucking grass to pile in their makeshift stalls. Patukala and Sally arranged their camp, both disinterested in the enchanting ancient city. Many of the ancient dwellings were still intact, and Evelyn wandered around exploring their wonders. Chen accompanied her, though she suspected he was motivated by a desire to avoid work more than actual interest.

The sunset filled the canyon, and she could imagine what it must have felt like to live there, protected in this beautiful, mystical city. Evelyn crawled up a ragged step and entered one of the higher rooms. She peeked in, half expecting ghosts to emerge.

Chen followed her into the room and looked idly around. "These aren't exactly spacious, are they?" he asked, just as Evelyn inwardly reflected how much room each dwelling possessed.

"They must have felt so . . . safe, and so peaceful."

Chen kicked over a pile of rubble. "Boring. Of

course, the Chinese were about ten thousand years more advanced than these people."

Evelyn eyed the rubble. "Perhaps not quite ten thousand years, Chen." She spotted a broken urn, then bent to pick it up. She dusted it off with her skirt, revealing black-on-white pottery.

Chen seized it from her hands and examined it closely. "What a shame it's busted! Something like this might be worth a lot." He eagerly searched the room, but found nothing more than shards. Undaunted, he hurried away to search the other rooms.

Evelyn shook her head, then went to the door. A strange feeling infected her senses, as if she experienced some lingering form of déjà vu, as if she had stood in this same spot before. She looked out the door, down into the canyon. An eerie chill wrapped itself around her. Across the silent city, she could imagine ghosts. She could hear them laughing, singing, sense the busy activity all around her . . .

It was more than imagination. She felt it like a memory, as if she saw through another woman's eyes. She looked around, back into the room behind, and saw it filled with sun, herself kneeling at some task. But the girl in her mind kept looking toward the door as if waiting for something, or someone.

She went outside to free herself of the feeling and to purge her overly active imagination. Rafael came walking toward her up the narrow steps built into the pueblo wall. Her breath caught when she saw him. The golden sunset shone on his dark skin, the dry wind tossed his black hair. And suddenly she understood what the girl had been waiting for: a much loved mate.

"What are you doing up here? Patukala has arranged our bedding in the dwellings below, where escape will be easier should it be necessary to flee."

"I am exploring." She felt nervous, and glanced back into the dark room. "Chen found pottery."

"Thousands dwelt in these cliffs. I should think remnants of pottery a common find." He came to stand beside her and drew a long breath. "It isn't hard to imagine living here." He had spoken Evelyn's own thoughts, so she kept silent. He gestured to a high peak. "From there, my people sent signals. Their methods of communication were elaborate, as were their roads and trails."

"Why did they leave?"

"Drought, perhaps, though as dry farmers, it seems unlikely to me that this was the sole cause. Perhaps . . . war. Too often, it is bloodshed that ends a city's glory."

"Like Rome."

She wasn't sure he would like the comparison to European history, but he nodded. "Perhaps. And in war and in hatred, love is destroyed."

She looked up at him. It had been an odd comment, and he seemed surprised to have spoken of his history from an emotional core rather than intellectually. He shook his head as if to relieve himself of a discordant thought, and Evelyn knew with a cool shock that he was experiencing the same strange memory as she.

She felt a bond tightening around her, and

maybe around him, too. She went back into the room to distance herself, but he followed her, curious. Alone in the darkness, together, her nervousness soared, though she wasn't sure why. She backed casually to the far side of the room and almost fell into a pit.

"What is that?"

Rafael caught her arm, drawing her away from the edge. "Be careful of those, Evelyn. They are kivas, where my people performed rituals." He looked into the darkness, then knelt beside the hole. He reached in and tugged up a rope ladder. "Amazing that this is still intact."

Evelyn's curiosity overcame her shyness. "Let's go down!"

"Into total darkness?"

She puffed an impatient breath. "Can't you fashion some kind of torch?"

He didn't answer, but rose to his feet and left the dwelling. Evelyn waited, confused, but he returned bearing a torch. He was as curious as she.

He examined the rope, then decided it was safe. "You hold the torch, and I'll see what's down there."

He *would* have to go first. Evelyn frowned as he passed her the light, which she refused to accept. "I don't think so. *You* hold it, and I'll go down."

Since Rafael was already holding the torch, she had the advantage. Before he could argue, Evelyn swung herself around, adjusted her cumbersome skirt to one side, and climbed down. She looked up to see him leaning over the edge, torch in hand. He looked tense. "Be careful, Evelyn. Slow down."

In rebellion of his bossiness, Evelyn hopped off the rope ladder and landed on a hard, dry floor. She loved the excitement of exploration, of discovery. But something more elusive filled her heart with anticipation. The feeling she had been here before intensified in this dark pit. "There is something . . ." She closed her eyes, and again imagined the young woman, this time kneeling intent upon some artwork on the floor.

She felt cold, as if the spirits of the dead surrounded her. Mesmerized, Evelyn went to the far wall of the kiva and knelt as she imagined the girl doing. Her hands shook as she brushed aside dirt and debris. There on the floor, a pattern had been carved into the earth.

"I've found something. . . ." Her voice came small and quavery.

"What?"

"I don't know. You will have to bring the torch down."

Rafael descended the rope ladder and held the torch aloft. Evelyn dusted the faint lines and the image became clearer, though faded and lost in places. What she saw shocked her beyond words.

The image depicted a rider, his face covered in a mask, his dark horse rearing as he drove away enemies from the pueblo.

Rafael came around to see her discovery. He looked at it and nodded, but he didn't seem surprised. "Curious . . . It is the legend of the warrior god."

"The one you mimic during your mad sprees of crime?"

He didn't seemed offended. "Yes."

A tremor of nervousness coursed through her as he looked down over her shoulder. "She drew it about her husband."

He eyed her doubtfully. "What?"

"She was thinking of him when she drew this. When she looked in his eyes, this is what she saw." Evelyn shoved herself up and stared down at the ancient picture. Her heart beat as if a lion had come upon her, and there was only one thing to do. She didn't wait for Rafael. She hurried up the rope ladder and went out into the sun.

He came out beside her, saying nothing for a long while. "What troubled you, Evie?"

He called her by her pet name. He probably wasn't even aware that he had done so. She was too shaken to correct him. "You will think I'm crazy. Everyone does, when I see things like this."

She felt his hand on her shoulder. "I do not. What did you see?"

"The girl who drew that picture . . ."

"I hate to disappoint you, but in my culture, it was often the men who were artists."

She shook her head. "Not this time. I think . . . I think he believed in her and supported her, so she did something not common. But those drawings on the floor were hers, and she did them for him." Her voice trailed, and Rafael didn't argue. He just waited for her to continue. "She thought he could save her from anything, that he would always be there. But she was wrong."

"The legend of the warrior god is common to my people, and many other native religions. I doubt one woman was responsible for the tale."

"Maybe not, but this one was special to her. It was *him*. Her husband."

Evelyn peeked up at Rafael to see his reaction. He didn't look uncomfortable as she expected, nor did he seem amused as Westley used to be over her "fanciful visions."

"You say she was wrong . . ." He sounded almost troubled, as if he believed her.

"He went away, she thought to save her, to protect them all, but he never returned. Whatever came . . ." She stopped, as sure as if the sun shone on an ancient past and illuminated it clear as day. "It was war that came, and many were killed. Not her . . . She went with the ones who survived, out into the desert . . ."

"And the pueblo people were born."

Evelyn nodded. She felt the woman's loneliness, as she lived into old age without the man she loved, a heartache that never abated following her into death, and perhaps beyond. "She missed him so . . ."

"This is not the way history is usually divulged, Evelyn."

"Perhaps not, but I suspect it is more accurate. They couldn't come back, because they believed the warrior god had died . . . and if he no longer protected them, they would no longer be safe in these cliffs."

Rafael sighed. "That is not unlikely, I suppose. As Mesa Verde grew in trade and in glory, more and more people learned of its existence, and more and more wanted its riches. Eventually, the invaders from other lands would be too much for these people to withstand."

She missed him so . . .

The sun disappeared behind the mountains and Evelyn felt suddenly so weary she could barely stand. "You said that Patukala set up our bedding?"

Rafael studied her face, then nodded slowly. "Are you all right?"

"Tired. I think I will sleep now."

"Now? You haven't eaten yet."

She yawned. "I'm not hungry." Her eyelids felt heavy and she felt strangely weak. She started down the crumbling steps, but Rafael took her arm. She wanted to object, but it didn't seem worth the fight.

He said nothing as he led her back to the others. They had gathered in what might once have been a small plaza, eating, though Patukala wasn't with them. Sally looked up and eyed her suspiciously. "Where has she led you this time, Rafe? Into a snake pit?"

Rafael smiled. "Close."

Evelyn glanced at him. "Are there snakes in those pits?"

His dark eyes glinted. "Why do you think I told you to be careful?"

She shuddered. "I have a slight aversion to snakes."

"Then next time be more careful before you drop yourself into a dark hole, Mrs. Reid."

So he was back to formalities? She was too tired to mention this discrepancy now.

Will chewed thoughtfully on dried, salted meat, then nodded toward the lower dwellings down the hill. "I took the horses to a spring for water, and they're hidden down there now, sir."

Rafael patted Will's shoulder. "Well done. Thank you, Will."

Sally pointed down the hill. "Patukala found out where Talbot made camp. He's gone down as lookout now."

"Where?"

"Down that path to the left, but Patukala doesn't think they have any idea we're up here. Even if they did, they'd never find us at night."

Rafael nodded, then seated himself beside Will. "We'll leave before dawn, but make sure to leave signs we might still be in hiding here. Considering the size of this place, that should keep Talbot busy for days."

Chen held up a small, brown urn, his expression triumphant. "And I found this! What do you think, sir? How much is it worth?"

Rafael took the urn from his hands and examined it. "I'd say about fifty-five cents."

Chen's face fell. "What? I thought ancient stuff was valuable! You can sell it to museums or maybe an art gallery in San Francisco."

"That's true, Chen, but I'm afraid this isn't an ancient artifact."

"It's not?"

"For one thing, it's not Anasazi, or even Zuni. Anasazi art is most often black-on-white, or turquoise. I'd say this is most likely Navajo. Their hunters camp here often. I assume they left this behind"—he sniffed the urn and grinned—

"about two weeks ago. There's still traces of tea at the bottom."

Chen took his urn from Rafael, sighed miserably, and then tossed it aside. Sally rolled her eyes, but Will retrieved it, then began stuffing grass into it for the horses.

Rafael glanced up at Evelyn, smiling. She smiled, too, then realized what she had done. She was no longer a captive, she was becoming his friend. She felt as if they were guides on a school excursion into the hills, enjoying the diverse personalities of their students—together. She snapped her vision to her feet, afraid of the closeness she felt with him.

"If you don't mind, I am going to sleep now." No one seemed to mind at all. Evelyn hesitated. "Since I am your prisoner, I thought you might be interested." He'd abandoned tying her after the first night, but he had known there was nowhere she would run to then. Now, Lieutenant Talbot was camped less than a mile away . . .

Rafael gestured toward the small dwelling they had investigated. "I'll have Will put our bedding in that one. It's a good distance away, and I think it wise for us to position ourselves apart, in case Talbot makes an unexpected visit."

They would be alone, more apart from the others than they had been so far. The thought made her nervous, but his rationale made sense. If she argued, it would indicate fear of being alone with him—and since he hadn't overstepped his bounds since kissing her on the first night, that would seem as if she had given it too much thought. He had promised to maintain his distance, and so far, he had kept to his word.

"Sleep well, Evelyn."

"Good night—to you all." She felt awkward, but Chen and Will waved at her pleasantly—like schoolboys. Sally ignored her as always.

Evelyn climbed up the broken steps, gripping her skirt to keep from tripping. When she looked up into the ancient home of a people she knew almost nothing about, an overwhelming sense of familiarity enveloped her, as if after a long day she were going to a place of comfort and love.

She was going home.

Rafael waited until dark before joining Evelyn. It wasn't easy. He had wanted to follow her as soon as she'd said good night. He knew she would be sleeping, but he would watch her with the moonlight on her face, rippling on her hair . . . It was a guilty pleasure, when her sleep gave him the freedom to study her little face, her soft lips, but it was a pleasure he had stolen nightly.

As he expected, he found her asleep, curled on her side near the rear wall of the small dwelling. He liked the room. It felt familiar, as if those who had lived there, ages ago, had known a deep peace that Rafael hadn't yet experienced in his own life. These people had been his ancestors; he felt closer to them now than he had when living among the Zuni after his father died.

Even their city seemed familiar. He had found a spring near their dwelling, where he washed, and it felt as if he'd bathed there a thousand times. Walking at dusk seemed like a nightly ritual, and even the songs of the birds making ready for sleep seemed familiar. When he bowed his head to enter through the low stone door, he had felt as if even that were a much-repeated task.

Rafael laid his bedding close to Evelyn, but not touching. The moon rose in the east, casting its silvery light through the small entrance. As he had hoped, it shone on Evelyn's dark hair, over the curve of her shoulder. It was more than desire he felt for her. When she had climbed into the ancient kiva, her eyes bright with excitement, his heart had felt swollen with tenderness. He wanted to take her all over the West, to his mother's people, maybe even to other countries where she could satisfy her endless curiosity.

If ever a man was possessed of an unlikely dream, it was this. Rafael forced his attention from Evelyn and rolled over on his back, staring at the dark stone ceiling. He had been smitten before. Beautiful, charming women had captured his attention more than once. But no one had created inside him this endless ache, this pit of both sorrow and delight.

Maybe it was the circumstances—the woman he desired considered him a criminal, and blamed him for killing her husband. He was forced to keep her as a captive when he wanted to treat her with infinite tenderness. But she had to see that he wasn't a cruel man, that he wouldn't hurt her, that he cared.

Sometimes, when they looked into each

other's eyes, he felt sure she cared for him, too, that she understood him and liked him. The same things amused them both, and they were both interested in the deeper meanings of the world around them. He wondered what kind of relationship she had shared with her husband. Had they been able to speak without words? Had Westley understood her insatiable curiosity, and her intuition that that was so well attuned that she heard the voices of civilizations long dead?

He knew he should sleep. In all likelihood, he would have to face Talbot's men tomorrow, and be quick enough to outwit them. But desire kept him awake. He was a young man, and his need had grown unrelenting with Evelyn so close to him, day after day. They hadn't really been alone—Chen or Will usually slept near, and Sally kept a close eye on all Rafael's motions.

Tonight, they slept in a room that once housed an Anasazi family, where men and women had loved quietly, ages ago.

He removed his spectacles so he wouldn't see her sleeping body quite so well and tried to think of something else, but his heartbeat refused to slow. Thoughts of touching Evelyn's soft skin, feeling her breath against his neck, bringing her own desire alive, filled his mind. Night after night, he had fought his desire. Now, alone with her, it proved a futile struggle. He grew aroused and hot, and he ached.

As if to increase his torment, Evelyn murmured in her sleep, and the sound was decidedly sensual. A small gasp escaped her lips, as if delighting in some secret pleasure. She squirmed on her bedroll, then rolled onto her back, one arm curled over her head.

Rafael tried not to look at her, but the next soft whimper claimed his full attention. Her head shifted to one side, and the moonlight illuminated the curve of her lips. She was dreaming of passion, of making love with a man she adored. He knew it. In her sleep, she was feeling his hands on her delicate body, cupping her breasts. She felt him inside her . . .

Rafael sat upright and buried his face in his hands as Evelyn issued a faraway, shuddering sigh. His whole body throbbed in reaction to her mindless pleasure. He had known she would be a sensitive, sensual lover, but to think of her dreaming this way . . . He reminded himself that it was most likely her husband she dreamt of, his love she remembered. This dampened his desire somewhat, as again he felt himself an outsider in her life—as he had been the first time he met her, watching her walk away with another man.

"Please, don't leave me." She spoke, her words slurred in sleep. Rafael contemplated leaving the room until her dreams subsided into deeper sleep, but she tossed again in her bedding as the sensuality she had evidenced turned to fear.

Her expression changed—her brow furrowed and she appeared upset. Her voice came small and plaintive. "I'm so afraid I'll never see you again. . . . I shall die, I shall die without you."

She would have romantic dreams. But her small, plaintive voice touched something deep inside him. Maybe she relived her husband's death.

She moaned again, in pain and in love. "Rafael, no . . ."

He caught his breath, staring. She dreamt of him. But was it the same dream that inspired her soft moans and pleasure, or had it shifted to something darker, with him cast as the villain?

Though it seemed most likely she was resisting him even in sleep, Rafael's body reacted as though she begged him to love her. He wondered if this was part of some elaborate scheme of vengeance, to torture him this way, but Evelyn's breaths quickened and she tossed her head in sleep.

She shot up without warning, her eyes wide, her lips apart as she gasped to catch her breath. She looked around wildly, then spotted him. "He didn't come back! He didn't come back. . . . Where were you?"

He had no idea what she meant, but she seemed terrified. Fighting his own desire, he got up and dragged his bedding beside hers, then knelt beside her. She didn't resist as he drew her into his arms. He held her close, softening her tangled hair with his fingers. Her heart raced and he felt her wild pulse beneath her soft skin.

It was agony. As he had fantasized, he felt the little puffs of her breath on his neck. "Hush, Evie. You're all right. You were only dreaming."

Her breath slowed, but she made no move away from him. "I was dreaming of her."

He glanced down. "*Her?*"

Evelyn nodded vigorously. "Yes, the woman I told you about, the woman who lived in this place." Her words indicated she was at least coherent now. Maybe his own imagination had added more to her dreaming than had actually existed.

"Was she . . . with her husband?"

Her head snapped up and her eyes narrowed to slits. "Why do you ask?"

She was. "No reason."

She bit her lip, guilty, and he felt sure her cheeks grew pink, but the silver moonlight wouldn't give away that much evidence as to the nature of her passionate dream. *She had said his name.* Evelyn cleared her throat. "She was afraid for him. He was leaving, and she was afraid he wouldn't come back."

They had been making love. Rafael felt sure of it. And the husband in Evelyn's dream had worn his face. The thought restored the fire in his veins, and his groin ached with desire. "I cannot imagine he would want to leave her."

His voice came thicker than he'd intended, and she looked intensely suspicious, as if she knew he had read her thoughts. "I do not think he wanted to leave, exactly."

They looked at each other, and her mood changed. She dampened her lips with a quick dart of her tongue and her breaths turned swift again, but not with fear. All he considered wise and safe fled from Rafael's reason. He touched her face and smoothed her hair back. She closed her eyes as if reveling in his touch.

He knew why—it mimicked the sweet passion of her dream. He cupped her face in his hands and kissed her face, softly, all over, but not her mouth. He had promised not to kiss her.

He felt her hands on his waist as she twisted around in his arms.

She kissed him. Her soft, sweet mouth found his, her lips parted and she tasted him. All restraint fled, from both of them. They kissed wildly, holding each other tight. She kissed his face, she gripped his long hair in her fingers as if to hold him steady while she deepened their kiss. He wrapped his arms around her, feeling her small body close, her heart pounding.

She murmured, more sensually even than when she was dreaming, and he felt the tips of her breasts peak against the fabric of her dress. His heart slammed in his chest. Nothing could stop him, and she didn't try. Instead, her small hands worked on his loose shirt, her fingers found his skin, and she bent to kiss his neck, then his chest. It was heaven, the sweetest delirium he had ever known.

His hands shook as he unfastened her dress, then pulled it over her head. She didn't resist or try to stop him. Her chemise hung loose around her body, and he untied its ribbon, letting the soft gown fall over one shoulder. He cupped her breast through the sheer cloth, feeling its fullness and the hard peak of her nipple. He heard himself groan, and her head tipped back as he grazed the tip with his thumb.

Every muscle in her body was tight, quivering. He bent and took the concealed bud between his lips, dampening the cloth with his tongue. She whimpered and her nipple hardened still more against his touch. Her back arched, and her every breath seemed to beg him to take her and love her.

They fell back together, spread across his bedding and hers, clothing tangled as he kissed her. He wanted to ask her if it was all right, he needed to hear her voice telling him yes, but Evelyn tugged at his shirt, then ran her hands up and down his back. She arched beneath him, and her leg coiled over his, an invitation that drove him past thought of words.

Trembling with desire, Rafael yanked off his shirt and tossed it aside. He freed his erection from his trousers, but before he could remove them entirely, Evelyn reached for him. She gripped his shoulders and pulled him down to her, fumbling between their bodies until she found his thick shaft. She hesitated, almost as if unsure whether touching him was permissible.

He buried his face in her hair, his lips below her earlobe, and whispered, "Yes."

She shuddered in response and her fingers closed tight around his length. He couldn't stop himself nor temper his lust now. His hips moved, and she gasped as if he thrust inside her. Rafael pushed her chemise up to her waist. She opened her thighs for him, and in the light of the moon, he saw her pale face, tense with desire.

He slid his finger along her inner thigh, then over dark curls already dewy with feminine moisture. A low, primitive groan tore from his throat at the feel of her. When he found the tiny peak of her womanhood, her hips bucked as if she hadn't known it was there. He circled it gently, then firmer, until she cried out, wordlessly begging him for release.

She reached for him again, this time with more certainty. She gripped him tightly, urging him beyond the limits of any desire he'd ever dreamed possible. She lay back, and he gave in to what he'd wanted most since the first moment he saw her.

He entered her soft moistness with such force that he thought he would be spent all at once, but she squeezed tight around him, and his desire seemed too vast to ever be sated. Her long legs wrapped around him, her thighs squeezed, and she moved against him, her body shaking with rapture.

Rafael thrust inside her, so deep that it seemed they were joined at the core of their souls. She met him, sobbing with pleasure as her own release shuddered through her. She kissed his neck, his chest, sucking with mindless pleasure as their bodies writhed together. He felt every wave of ecstasy ripple through her, compounding until his own shattered and burst, filling her. Hot waves seared through him, on and on, lasting longer than any pleasure he'd ever experienced before, until together they subsided to lie still in each other's arms.

Silence filled the ancient room, broken only by their mingling breath and the sound of two pounding hearts. Her legs hung over his as if she was too weak to move them, but she still clung tightly to his shoulders, holding on to him as if she were afraid to let go. And then another sound grew softly, slowly drowning out all else that he heard.

Evelyn was crying, and Rafael knew then

what he had tried so hard to ignore when he gave in to their mindless passion.

He had just made the biggest mistake of his life.

Chapter Eight

"Evelyn . . ." Rafael's voice came as if torn from deep inside him, as if it hurt. "I'm sorry. Please don't cry."

She couldn't let go. Her fingers clinging into the hard flesh of his shoulders, she hid her face against his neck and felt his racing pulse. He filled her completely, still swollen inside her. Tiny aftershocks of pleasure sped through her, echoes of that wild burst of passionate energy she hadn't known her body contained.

Tears ran down her cheeks and into her hair, but still, she couldn't move or let go. It seemed like part of a dream, unreal, yet separating her from all else. She had become another woman, wild with the urgency of desire. She had betrayed her husband's memory and cursed her own soul.

Rafael pressed his cheek against her forehead, and he held her. Despite the power and sweet demand of his lovemaking, he knew what their passion had done to her. He held her gently, he kissed her forehead and whispered in his beautiful, low voice that it was all right, that he was sorry.

She barely heard him as shock set in. She had made love with him, the Renegade, the passionate young man who had looked into her eyes a year ago and made her forget who she was.

He moved to withdraw, but the friction between them sent fierce tremors through her body, and the heightened sensitivity of her secret flesh burned with the touch. She squeezed tight around his male shaft, and he groaned with pleasure. If he left, she would have to face what she had done. . . .

She murmured "no," over and over, but in rhythm with the whisper, her hips arched to draw him in. He tried to resist—she felt his effort, but it only fired her own. She kissed his neck and tasted his skin, all the while taking him deeper, feeling him grow hard and hot inside her again.

They moved together, undulating in primal rhythm, faster and harder until again searing currents of ecstasy shattered inside her, and from him into her. He slowed, his breath ragged and swift, but she couldn't let him stop. Her body found release, but that release didn't end. Instead, the sensations crashed like a great wave against the shore, retreating only to surge forward again. Rafael moaned and carried her with him, meeting her and filling her until her mad ecstasy finally abated, leaving her so weak she couldn't move.

Finally he withdrew from her, then lay beside her. He gathered her into his arms, but he said nothing now, and she didn't expect him to. How could he apologize when it had been Evelyn herself who demanded him? She closed her eyes, safe in his strong arms, her face against his powerful chest, breathing his exquisite male scent, and she knew there was no choice left to her.

She wasn't sure how long she waited as she watched the moonlight creep across the floor. Finally, Rafael's breaths slowed and deepened in sleep. Even then, she didn't move. But as the night wore on, her thoughts cleared from their mindless passion, and she knew what she had to do. His sweetness, his tenderness, and his love gave her no choice.

Evelyn moved from his embrace and he stirred. She lay quiet for so long that an hour might have passed by. Then without a sound she rose from their tangled bedding, replaced her dress, and walked barefoot from the ancient dwelling. Patukala would be on watch, but he wasn't looking for her, he was watching for Talbot's men.

Barefoot lest her boots make a sound, Evelyn slipped from their camp. Hidden in the shadows of the piñon trees, she made her way down the path to her lover's enemy.

"Lieutenant, I've told you. Rafael and his group have already gone."

She was surprised Talbot questioned her at

all. She had stumbled into his campsite, barefoot, shocking the two guards he'd put on lookout. She must have looked even more tattered than she felt. But Talbot held a lantern up as if looking for deceit in her eyes.

"I have men posted on several paths, my dear. They've reported nothing."

She wasn't sure if he knew about the city, but if he caught her in a lie, he would have Rafael surrounded before they had a chance to escape. She had fled his embrace to save herself, to escape from a guilt so overwhelming that every breath came now with effort. But she couldn't betray him.

"I believe he is headed . . . south." From what she'd gathered, Rafael still intended to go west, then turn southeast at a later point.

"Back to Santa Fe?"

She shook her head. "I don't think so. I think he means to go to Mexico."

Talbot's eyes narrowed. "After all this time in his company, you don't know his destination?"

"I was a prisoner, Lieutenant. He didn't divulge his plans to me."

"But you must have learned something."

She hesitated. "Such as what?"

"What he knows . . . what motivated the Renegade."

"I think . . . he saw himself as protector to his people."

"You speak of him gently. More gently than when you aimed a gun at his heart."

Evelyn felt nervous, though she wasn't sure why. In Talbot's company, she should be safe from the one thing that threatened her most—

her desire for her handsome captor. But instead, she felt uneasy, as if every word said posed some hidden challenge.

"I have not changed my opinion of Rafael de Aguirre, I assure you, Lieutenant. He is a dangerous man, but he is bent now on his own survival and escape to Mexico. I don't think he cares about those people anymore. His sojourn as the Renegade was just done to please his own conceit. He's just trying to save his own hide now."

She didn't believe a word of what she'd said. She had changed that much since Rafael's strange group of friends abducted her.

"You escaped . . . easily."

She felt as if Talbot was interrogating her, as if she were suspected of some crime herself. "My ties were loose. . . ." She couldn't tell him her ties were nonexistent, and that her captor trusted her because she had become his lover. "I told you, he's thinking more of his own survival. I wasn't necessary to them anymore. That's all."

"Maybe."

Evelyn looked at him in surprise. "Do you doubt me?"

"No, of course not, Evelyn. I just wonder how much you understand the Renegade's motives. I doubt very much, for instance, that his real destination is Mexico."

Her breath caught, but she kept her expression as straight as she could. "Why not?"

"Let's just say that the pueblo he defended with such ardor has more at stake than its misfit residents."

"What?"

Something about John Talbot had shifted, though Evelyn wasn't sure what it was, exactly. "Nothing you need to concern yourself about." He looked around, assessing his guards as if they, too, might be worthy of suspicion. This man trusted no one. "Let us talk privately, shall we?"

He led her apart from the others, into the shadows. Evelyn held herself tense, ready to flee, though she wasn't sure what threat he posed. "One of my captors said that people have turned up missing from the pueblo. Do you know anything about that, Lieutenant?"

A shallow grin crossed his face, but Talbot shrugged. "What does it matter? They're a worthless lot. I'm sure someone has been clever enough to put them to better use."

"You know where they are, don't you?" Evelyn felt sick. Rafael had been right. Talbot and those associated with him wanted something from the pueblo—she had no idea what. "Westley told me that any worth the pueblo was found to have should be returned to the people living there."

Talbot sneered, and the sick feeling filled the pit of her stomach. "Westley . . . Tell me, my dear, how well did you really know your dear husband?"

She felt like a cornered animal, not sure what her enemy wanted. "What do you mean?"

"What did you know, say, of his fondness for other men?"

Her brow furrowed. "He had many friends. . . ."

"One in particular."

Was he implying that Westley was in league with the Renegade? But that didn't make sense. "Are you suggesting that Westley did something illegal concerning the pueblo? Because I can assure you, Lieutenant, he was only following the instructions given to him by the government and his father."

Talbot crossed his arms over his chest. For an instant, he looked like a judge in a witch trial. In her mind, she pictured him with a gray wig, wielding sentences of death to appease some mad hatred in his own heart. "You knew nothing of it, then?" He paused to laugh. "I thought it might have explained your own affection for the schoolmaster. But no, it seems you both wore your sins privately."

"Westley committed no sin."

Talbot's eyes glowed, and the image of the dark judge seemed to fill her perspective. "He committed the greatest sin of all. He favored his own gender. He took a male lover."

Evelyn stared at him, blank, but she didn't react the way Talbot seemed to expect. "And how would you know this?"

"I was at Harvard with your husband and his friend. There were rumors even then. They were too close, too . . . emotional with each other." He paused to shudder. "You would never guess who it was."

Evelyn closed her eyes. She remembered a young man that she met only once, slender with dark hair and large brown eyes, a gentle voice, a kind manner, yet somehow . . . sad. "Randall Hallowell."

Talbot's mouth opened in surprise, then pressed shut in a pinched line. "You knew him better than I thought."

"Yes." She hadn't known, not fully, but Talbot's revelation came as no deep surprise. She had seen the same sorrow in Westley's eyes when he would gaze out the window of their home, heard his soft apology that he had come to bed after reading late into the night or that he was so often sick and couldn't lie with her. She hadn't understood completely what was missing in their marriage until she had given herself to Rafael, but it felt as if some part of her had always known . . . and understood. "My husband was a good man."

"Your husband was perverted, dark and evil. He was not fit to decide what became of the pueblo."

She shook her head. "What has his private heart to do with the pueblo?"

"He was unfit."

"He did nothing wrong, Lieutenant. Mr. Hallowell left for a tour of Europe before we married, and Westley came to Santa Fe shortly after."

"Don't be such a fool, Evelyn. You make their union seem almost romantic. He must have bedded a hundred men."

"Your imagination is darker than his life ever could have been, Lieutenant." She turned away as tears filled her eyes. Westley had been so lonely, fighting something that was innate to him, fighting love. As she had done since she met Rafael de Aguirre. They had been so lonely, the two of them, but maybe he had found comfort with her, because she never asked for more than he could give, because they were friends. *I miss you so . . .* She missed his humor and his quick wit, his kindness. Now she understood what haunted him, and her empathy only grew.

"It doesn't matter now, Evelyn, he's dead and his sickness died with him." Talbot sounded eager now and Evelyn tensed. "The landowners have every reason to take control of the pueblo, but it is in your hands now."

She looked back over her shoulder. "What do you want?"

"I had hoped, when the matter of your husband's murderer was resolved, that you would sign the rights of the pueblo over to me. It has no worth to you."

"It has value to the people living there."

He scoffed. "What? To a group of ragtag Mexicans and outcast Indians, a few castoff Chinese rail workers and their ratty children?"

"To the people who live there."

He moved toward her, then gripped her shoulder with his hard, bony fingers. "Evelyn, my dear, see reason. They were no better than criminals, worthless, led by a mixed-blood renegade Indian. Perhaps de Aguirre knows more of the pueblo's worth than he let on. . . ." He stopped himself before saying exactly what that worth was perceived to be, but Evelyn listened intently. "He had convinced Westley to give it to him, after all. And you . . . If I hadn't discovered his duplicitous identity, he would have had you eating out of his hand. Even when Westley learned that the reticent schoolmaster was the Renegade, he refused to listen . . ."

"What? You knew . . . You've known since *then?*"

His eyes shifted to one side as Evelyn pinpointed the discrepancy in the story she had been told. "Of course, I knew. But I couldn't prove my theory—he was too quick. For a year . . ."

Had that been the real reason for the delay, or was there another motivation for delaying the Renegade's capture? But what? "You knew . . . even before Westley died. . . . And if you knew . . ." She backed away instinctively, but Talbot leapt forward and caught her arm. "You killed him."

He offered no denial, but his jaw hardened. "Your husband was a twisted man, an idealist who refused to see reason. I am a realist, Evelyn. Death serves a purpose . . . even yours." He caught her chin in his hand, moving closer. "I had hoped for a different outcome between us. After that pathetic husband, you must hunger for a real man. Once we reached Denver, I had every intention of marrying you."

"And again, gaining control of the pueblo. But I still don't understand why you want it." At the first opportunity, she would escape and tell Rafael what she had learned. But she had to stay calm and not surrender to fear.

Talbot's eyes narrowed to slits. "It's a damned shame it won't work out as I'd planned. You're a beautiful woman, and your family has prestige in Boston." She suspected her father's prestige was a lot more important to Talbot than her charms. "But unfortunately, I have to hunt down your Renegade before he returns to Santa

Fe. And I can't be bothered with watching over you. I'm not sure, you see, dear Evelyn, just how much I can trust you."

Now that Evelyn knew he'd killed Westley, Talbot would feel that he had to kill her, too. But if she could delay him, then maybe Rafael would realize she was gone. Her heart throbbed. Would he come for her, knowing she had left of her own accord, fleeing from the passion they shared? He didn't know how dangerous Talbot was—perhaps he thought she'd be safer here.

Even if Rafael would come for her, it might be morning before he even woke up. She had left her small revolver in Rafael's bed—when he had told her she might face an enemy greater than himself, he was right.

Talbot had led her from his men—and if he couldn't trust them, maybe she could. She opened her mouth to scream, but he leapt quicker than a cat and slammed his hand over her mouth. "Shut up, damn you!" He hissed into her ear, then yanked her back behind a dead tree. He tore off his loose tie, then swiftly gagged her.

She struggled, but he bound her hands tight behind her back, then tied her to the tree. "I don't want you confusing my guards. It's damned hard to find trustworthy men." He paused, considering. "I'm afraid I'll have to leave you here for a while, my dear. These men are hunting down a murderous renegade—when they realize he's killed his beautiful captive, I'll have every soldier within five hundred miles hunting him down."

Talbot left her tied to the tree, and try as she might, she couldn't free herself. Tears streamed down her cheeks, but Evelyn kept twisting her wrists until she felt blood running down her fingers. She felt like an animal caught in a snare, willing to rip off its own limbs to be free.

He was going to kill her, and Rafael would be blamed. Somehow, she had to escape. Talbot couldn't murder her here, in his campsite. He would have to take her away from the others and make it look as if Rafael had somehow recaptured her. She heard him speaking to his guards, his voice calm.

"I'll take the next watch, Dan. You get some rest. But stay alert. It's likely that damned Indian will try to nab her back—and I'd hate to think what would happen to the young widow in that case."

"It's a lucky thing he's kept her alive this long, Lieutenant. Poor little thing looked torn up."

"We mustn't think now of what he did to her while in captivity, Dan. All we can do is keep her safe now, and out of his hands."

He sounded so reasonable. Such an impersonal man! It was no wonder he scorned the emotions of others. "Well, take care, Lieutenant. The Renegade is a cursed sneaky devil. He's likely to sneak into our camp before we even know it. Held up that train like it was nothing, he and his gang."

"I'm glad you're aware of it. I've hidden Mrs. Reid just beyond the horses. . . ." He gestured in the opposite direction of where Evelyn was actually bound. "She's terrified, but we'll keep her safe, won't we?"

"We sure will. Men like that Indian schoolmaster are just plain heathens, don't think nothing of killing a young lady if it serves him. We ain't letting him win this time!"

As she listened, she realized that Talbot was a master of manipulation. He could find a weakness, a fear, a latent hatred, and play on it until a person took the action he wanted. He had manipulated her, too. After Rafael's arrest, he had reminded her over and over how she had trusted and admired the schoolmaster, playing on her shame, encouraging her to hate him rather than face her own inner demons. He had given her the revolver at the train station, knowing—because a manipulator knows the dark vulnerability in humanity—that she would try to shoot the Renegade.

The guards left their positions at watch and made ready for sleep. Talbot sat with them, chatting, drinking coffee, and smoking a cigar. He seemed in no hurry. All the while, Evelyn tried to free herself, but to no avail. She considered what to do when he came for her. If she ran to the campsite to inform his men of his actions, could she be sure they'd believe her story? Talbot could probably convince them she was acting on Rafael's behalf—he had proven himself that skilled at manipulation. Her only hope was to run to the man she had fled from earlier that night, and hope against hope she could reach him before Talbot caught her.

An hour or more passed as the soldiers went to their bedrolls. Talbot waited a good while longer alone, probably to be sure they slept. He rose and stretched, then walked around the campsite. He disappeared, then came up behind her. "I think it's safe now, my dear, for our Renegade to make his appearance."

He pulled her away from the tree, holding her in front of him. He shoved her forward, but Evelyn was ready. She took a few steps, then jerked back. She kicked his knee as hard as she could. He grunted with surprise and pain, and Evelyn ran. She stumbled, and kept running, but her long skirt tangled around her legs, and with her bound hands, she couldn't hold it aside. She heard him racing up behind her. She couldn't run fast enough, though she tried.

She scrambled over a boulder, heading for the piñon trees on the path toward Mesa Verde. It was her only hope—to reach Rafael. If Patukala spotted her . . .

He caught her from behind and shoved her to the ground. Evelyn kicked and fought. She bit his arm through the gag when he reached around to get the rope over her head. He struck her, she thought, but in her fury, she wasn't sure.

"Damn you, you little witch! You'll never get away from me!"

He twisted her arms back until she choked on a scream. Evelyn fought, and she fought well. He yanked her over so that she lay on her back, but she kept kicking. He tried to pin her down with his knees, but she moved too fast. Her arms hurt—maybe they were broken, but she didn't stop. Furious, Talbot wrapped a rope around her neck, cutting off her breath.

The rope tightened around her throat, and Evelyn felt dizzy for want of air. Her struggles ceased, and in a fleeting instant, she faced her own death.

The sound of hooves thundered over the dry mesa. Out of the darkness, springing from the hidden city like a warrior god, a horseman galloped. Talbot sprang back and yanked Evelyn to her feet, holding before him like a shield. He shouted for his men, as if it had been he who had been under attack.

She didn't stop fighting. She kicked and tried to pull away, but he still held her neck in the rope, tightening until she couldn't breathe. Rafael reined in his horse, and it reared, a great shadow against the indigo sky. Talbot fumbled for his gun, but the Renegade's whip cracked through the silent air. The gun flew from Talbot's hand, and Rafael struck again, knocking him back. Evelyn kicked him hard in the groin, then jumped away.

Rafael swung the whip and the hard ends wrapped around Talbot's neck. With his free hand, Rafael reached for Evelyn. She looked up at him, amazed. He had come for her. She took his hand, then realized he rode without a saddle. With his help, she scrambled onto the horse's back behind him.

Rafael yanked his whip and Talbot fell forward. She knew he meant to kill this time. A shot rang out, startling the horse, but Rafael held fast to the whip. Another shot followed, then another. Talbot's guards had come.

"Rafael, we must go. They'll never believe that he tried to kill me. They'll think you dragged us both out here."

He hesitated, furious. "And we may not get the chance to explain . . ."

The guards raced toward them, on foot because Talbot's cries had startled them from sleep. Though they shot wildly, they were getting closer. Rafael yanked the whip free, and Talbot gasped for air. He struggled to his feet, then found his gun on the ground. He aimed, but Rafael whirled his horse around, and galloped not west, but north toward Talbot's campsite.

Evelyn held tight to his waist as the night air whipped around them, blowing his black hair around her like a veil. She heard gunshots, but Frank never slowed his pace and remained surefooted even in darkness.

Rafael doubled back, then found a trail leading into the city. He woke the others, silently. Without words, they readied their horses. Only Sally glared at Evelyn, knowing she had been the cause of near disaster, but she maintained silence as they loaded their packs. Rafael helped Evelyn to the ground while he saddled Frank, and Will brought Evelyn's bedroll and gear from the little stone dwelling where she had lain with Rafael.

Saying nothing, Evelyn began helping. She rolled Chen's bedroll and gathered the gear he had left behind, including a small bowl she had found that might truly have been an Anasazi artifact. He tied it to his horse and smiled pleasantly as if nothing had happened. Tears filled her eyes, and she knew where she belonged now.

With a renegade.

* * *

His lust had almost killed her. Rafael's heart throbbed with remorse as they rode westward in darkness. How could he have been such a fool? Night after night, he had lain beside her and not touched her. Yet when she was most vulnerable, confused from sleep, weary . . . he ravished her.

Patukala galloped up from behind, leading another horse beside his own. Rafael stopped and waited for his uncle to catch up. *"What is that, Uncle?"*

Patukala grinned. *"Theft? I thought since the young woman has decided to return, we might move faster if she had her own horse."* He reached to pat the newcomer, a light-limbed bay with a star on its forehead. *"This one seemed best for her, yes? I drove off Talbot's horses. He will catch them again, but it will take him time. And one soldier, I think, will have to go forward on foot."*

Rafael smiled. *"Because Evelyn will have his horse. Thank you, Uncle. It was well done of you to think of disabling him in some way."*

Patukala nodded at Evelyn. *"You have more important things to think of. I do what I can."* He paused. *"Does she say what she knows yet?"*

"I haven't asked."

Evelyn seemed weak, but she hadn't spoken since he rescued her. He had noticed her helping make ready to leave, but he hadn't dared question her. When he had woken and found her missing, he had known immediately where she'd gone. Only a moment's hesitation passed before he knew he had to find her, so he had leapt on his horse's bare back and ridden after her. If she had been safe, if that was where she wanted to be, he would have left her with Talbot and gone on alone despite the ache in his own heart.

But when he crept into Talbot's campsite, he had found the guards sleeping, and Talbot missing, Evelyn nowhere in sight . . .

He had no idea why the lieutenant would have wanted to kill her, but when he saw her fighting with every ounce of her courage and strength, the fury of a lion rose inside him.

Now Evelyn sat quietly in front of him, gazing out over black hills beneath a starless sky. She didn't sleep, she just stared. He wanted to talk to her, to resolve what had happened to them, but the time seemed wrong. She noticed the new horse and her eyes brightened. "Is he mine?"

She spoke eagerly, like a child anticipating a new gift. Rafael's heart warmed with affection. "He is."

She smiled, delighted. "He's very pretty."

He hesitated, not willing to let her go after having her so close for so many days. "Can you ride?"

"Of course!" She scrambled around, adjusted her dress, then hopped down. She seized her horse from Patukala, then patted its nose. Rafael watched as she leaned down and breathed into its nostrils. The horse touched her face and she closed her eyes. Patukala and Rafael exchanged a dubious look, which Evelyn noticed. "I am introducing myself to him. My uncle operates a horse farm in Maryland—he taught me to do this. Actually, I believe he learned this method from Indians."

Patukala's brow angled. *"We are blamed for so much."*

Rafael shook his head, but Evelyn paid no attention as she hiked up her skirt, placed her foot in the stirrup, and swung herself up. "You tell him that he could learn from me rather than scoffing all the time." She urged the horse forward, ahead of them. "And tell him I'm not crazy."

Rafael followed her. "He didn't say you were."

She glanced back at Patukala, who was pretending not to listen. "He thought it."

Rafael eyed his uncle. *"Did you?"*

Patukala shrugged, then turned his horse off the path again, heading off to scout for signs of Talbot's pursuit. *"Many times, my friend. Many times."*

They rode through the night taking winding paths, crossing through mountains and along canyons until their horses stumbled with weariness, and still no one spoke.

When dawn broke, Patukala rode ahead, then came back having found a sheltered spot for them to rest. *"Up ahead, we should hide for this day, then ride at night once more. I do not think he will follow us this way—the trail won't be easy to follow, and from here, it is rock. He will not expect us to take this trail, and he will follow the wider path leading south."*

They rode beneath the shadow of Sleeping Ute Mountain, its features lost as they drew close. Patukala led them to a sheltered grove, hidden behind huge boulders. Nearby, a rushing stream flowed, and they dismounted to make camp. Will took the horses, but Sally stood in front of Evelyn, hands on her hips, her face contorted with anger.

"What in hell have you done this time?"

Rafael stepped forward to defend Evelyn, but she held up her hand and faced Sally quietly. "Lieutenant Talbot murdered my husband. He has done something with your people. I do not know what. I think there is something hidden in the pueblo that is very valuable, and Talbot is after it—he and whoever he has enlisted along with him." She sounded weary, her voice monotone and low. She peered up at Rafael, her eyes devoid of sparkle. "Can I sleep now?"

"Of course."

He watched her walk a distance away, then unfurl her bedroll. She sat down upon it, gazing wistfully up at the mountain, and his heart ached with grief. Sally eyed her doubtfully, looking ready for a fight. "That girl has nerve."

Rafael took Sally's arm, holding her back. "Leave her alone, Sally. She's been through enough."

"Like hell! Rafe, it's you who's been through enough, and she's the one putting you through it. That girl doesn't think. She runs off just like she pulls a gun—all emotion."

"That's not true." Evelyn was an emotional, sensitive woman—that was part of her charm.

Sally huffed. "Is that so? Well, tell me. What were you doing last night?"

He gaped. "*What?*"

"Oh, don't give me that 'who, me?' shocked look! I know damned well the minute she got you alone, she'd have you bedded and now you've got that stupid, dewy-eyed boy in love look. She's got your heart wrapped around her little finger. She'll get you killed, Rafe, because the only thing you're thinking of is her." He opened his mouth to speak, but she jabbed him in the chest. "You listen to me, boy. Your mother told me, right before she died, that I was to look after you. She said you might seem sensible on the outside, but you were just as crazy as your father and if you got yourself into trouble, there'd be hell to pay."

He felt insulted. "This has nothing to do with Evelyn."

"Like hell. She's even crazier than you are, and you've got a hell of a lot riding on your shoulders now. You'll do something stupid, probably to save her, and you'll get yourself killed. Hell, what am I saying? You did something stupid tonight to save her!"

Anger boiled inside him. "Are you saying you'd rather I'd left her there to be murdered by her husband's killer?"

"No . . . but if you'd waited for the rest of us . . ."

"It would have been too late." Rafael turned away, but Sally called to him.

"You're a good man, Rafe. You're brave, and yes, you were right to get her away from him, knowing what a devil he is. But I'm warning you now, keep your distance from that girl. She's trouble, for both you and herself."

"I know that, and I will. But you're wrong to blame Evelyn, Sally. I am the one at fault. If not for me and what I did to her last night, she would never have run at all."

Sally sighed heavily, but Rafael picked up his bedroll and walked away. He started toward Evelyn, then realized there was no reason now to even pretend to guard her. She was with him now of her own free will. His heart felt like stone in his chest as he lay down beneath the shade of the quiet pines.

He took off his spectacles and closed his eyes, feeling the soft morning breeze on his face. It would be a beautiful day, warm and clear and dry, the kind of summer day he had always loved best. He lay beneath the shadow of the warrior god, and felt he had been through a battle more dangerous than anything he'd faced before.

What madness came over him that had made him think he could make love to her that way, and have her forgive him? Yet he relived every second, every breath she'd taken as she lay in his arms—but the rapture and perfection of their union rose up against him, preventing him from winning her trust and her love, rising up between them like a hundred-foot wall.

He had seen her fighting for her life—because of him. She was so strong, and so fragile, the most vulnerable woman he had ever known. Sally was right. They were a danger to each other. If he did nothing else in his life, he would protect her. That meant protecting her from the most dangerous man he knew.

Himself.

Chapter Nine

"Can we talk?"

Evelyn's quiet voice startled Rafael from his light sleep, and he sat upright, surprised to find her kneeling close beside him. He shoved his long hair from his face, feeling curiously shy. His hands shook as he replaced his spectacles. "Evelyn . . . What is it?"

She looked shy, too. She bit her lip, but he saw no anger. "There is something that I have to say to you."

His chest felt tight. He wanted to stop her before hearing in her own words how much he had hurt her. "I'm sorry, Evelyn. It never should have happened. I would do anything if I could change what I've done to you."

Her brow angled in confusion. "What you've done? Rafael, you saved my life. I have never been so terrified as when Lieutenant Talbot tried to kill me. I fought as hard as I could, but he was winning."

He smiled despite his anguish. "Evelyn . . ."

She puffed a quick breath. "Let me go on, please." He nodded and she seized another breath. "First, I want to thank you for saving me."

"There's no need. You wouldn't have run off if not for me."

She looked into his eyes, and she no longer looked young, but ageless and weary and filled with some emotion he didn't quite understand. "There's more that I must tell you. I knew you didn't kill Westley, Rafael. I knew it, and yet I almost shot you."

His mouth opened, then closed. "You knew?"

"I told myself you had—I wanted to believe it, you see."

"Why?"

Her chin quivered, but she didn't cry. "Because . . . because of what I felt for you." She paused. "Don't you know?"

"I'm the one whose behavior caused such grief, from the first time we met till last night."

A sorrowful smile formed on her beautiful lips—lips he had kissed, that had kissed him with a sweetness that he would never forget. "Rafael . . . What happened between us, that was not your fault. Don't you see?" As she spoke, her small voice caught and her eyes filled with tears.

"You were dreaming, half asleep. I . . ."

She was blaming herself. Women had this tendency, but he couldn't let her think it was her fault. "I took you without asking, when I knew it wasn't what you wanted. The fault is mine."

Her brow arched. "Three times?"

He pressed his lips together. She had been insistent. The memory left him tingling, and the desire he fought to ignore made itself known once more.

"You don't have to protect me. I know what I've done." Stunning him with her tenderness, Evelyn reached and pressed her palm gently against his face. "You did nothing wrong, not last night, and not the day we met. You didn't know who I was when I got off that train. There was no shame in what you said to me that day, nor in anything you've done since. It is I who bear the shame."

Rafael scratched his head. Perhaps eastern morals were even stranger than he'd realized. "That can't be. You've done nothing."

"Haven't I?" She looked at him and fell silent for a moment, then sighed. "I wanted you, Rafael. I wanted you last night, so much that I would have turned the world upside down to have you." She leaned toward him, almost imperceptibly, her eyes shining like some fallen angel confessing its most sacred crime. "And I wanted you then, too. I saw you coming toward me when I got off the train, and I forgot who I was, that I was married, everything. I knew what you were asking of me, you see. I knew what you wanted, and I tell you now, if you had asked, I would have gone. It was madness. I never knew I was capable of such things, but I learned more about myself that day than I had in all my life."

He had no idea what to say, though she didn't seem to expect anything.

"From that day onward, the thought of you obsessed me. When you came to our house for dinner . . . Every time I looked at you, I felt it like some beast inside me. Your hands touched mine, when I was serving you soup, and I felt as if struck by lightning . . ." She stopped and closed her eyes, then looked at him again. "Did you know?"

He wasn't sure how to answer. He looked down, but he nodded. "Only that there was something between us, and that you felt it, too."

She winced as if she hadn't truly been sure, but even suspecting, found his confirmation agonizing. "You have no idea how it tormented me. My dreams were filled with you." She paused to utter a short, discordant laugh. "More than that, I even imagined you as the Renegade, and the scenes I envisioned weren't so much heroic as . . ."

Rafael shifted his position. "Romantic?"

She refused to meet his eyes, but she nodded once. "You could call it that, I suppose. Perhaps it was more . . ."

His heart doubled its pace. "Erotic?" She exhaled as if relieved at last to confess her darkest crimes.

"Horribly so. I had no idea at that time that I was capable of such thoughts." She peeked up at him, embarrassed. "You inspired such a beast within me."

"A *beast?*" He couldn't quite contain his pleasure and a small smile crept to his lips. "You fantasized about me."

Her cheeks turned pink and her eyes squeezed shut. "I did. I blamed it on my imagination, which has always taken strange turns and gone to unexpected places. And perhaps I was lonely."

"I know that you were. Westley was so preoccupied trying to resolve the pueblo's problems."

She glanced up at him. "Did you know about him?"

"What do you mean?"

She bit her lip. "About his . . . secret life?"

"What 'secret life'?" If the man had betrayed her in any way . . . Rafael's eyes narrowed. He had considered Westley Reid a friend, but he would never have left Evelyn with a man who mistreated her. "What did he do to you?"

"He didn't do anything to me. You misunderstand." She looked uncomfortable, as if she'd said too much.

"What did he do? Did he have a mistress?"

"Well . . ." She hesitated. "Not exactly." She puffed a quick breath. "He preferred the company of other men, you see."

Rafael scratched his neck. "What?"

She eyed him as if wondering at his innocence. "He was in love with a man."

A short laugh escaped him before he knew what he was doing. "No, he wasn't." He paused. "Why would you think that?"

"Talbot told me."

Rafael rolled his eyes. "A reliable source, if ever there was one."

She smiled gently. "It wasn't a surprise to me. I think in some way I had known all along."

He couldn't quite believe what he was hearing. "What man?"

"A friend he knew at Harvard. Apparently, Talbot found out about it somehow when they were at school together."

He considered this revelation for a long while, then shook his head. "No wonder you were lonely."

"I don't blame him. How could I, when my own demons proved so hard to resist?"

He didn't like being termed a "demon," but he decided not to argue the point.

"I don't believe he was unfaithful to me, whatever Talbot thinks. He was just trying to be something he wasn't."

"Before you came to Santa Fe, I was taking your husband around the pueblo and he told me about you. I remember him saying that he wished he could have been the kind of man you deserved. I didn't know what he meant, and he said no more."

"Poor Westley. But we don't choose what qualities we are born with. Maybe it's what we do with those gifts that defines us, after all."

He wanted to learn more of what she felt for him. So much remained unsettled between them. "Last night . . . Why did you run off that way?"

She drew a long breath, then gazed up at the mountaintops. "I was so ashamed. It was as if the beast rose up and finally won. I had to get away from you, you see, but I was running from my own demons."

He frowned. "I'm not sure I like being compared to a demon."

She peered at him for a while. "Have you never been so confused?"

"Yes. Right now."

She smiled. "I'm sorry. I don't mean to say that you're a demon. Only that in your company, I feel as if I don't know myself."

Rafael considered this, then gently took her hand. "I understand. Even if you doubted, you thought I might have killed your husband. And given your . . . well, your fantasies relating to my disguise, I can see that it must have been painful to be taken captive by me."

"Yes."

He fell silent again and she waited quietly beside him. He scratched his chin. "There's something that I have to ask you, too."

"What?"

He felt awkward and shy and he felt sure he shouldn't be asking this now. He touched his mouth, an impulsive gesture of embarrassment. "How was it?"

"How was what?"

"Compared to what you imagined, I mean." He paused, and felt sure his own face reddened. "How was I?"

Her brow rose, but a slow smile grew on her face. Very gently, so slowly that he ached, she leaned toward him and kissed his cheek. "Rafael, you surpassed my wildest and most dangerous dreams."

He smiled, so pleased with himself that he could barely sit still. "I had to ask."

She fingered his hair as if she had longed to do so for ages. "I know."

Nothing else mattered. He wanted to draw

her into his arms and kiss her, but she looked so tired, and she had been through so much. Something else tugged at his conscience. Because he hadn't been able to control himself, Evelyn was now in as much danger from Talbot as he was. The pursuit would double its intensity now, because Talbot had to know how grave a threat Evelyn posed.

Rafael took her hand again and kissed it. "This feeling between us, Evelyn, I can't deny it, and I can't drive it away. But I give you my word, it won't happen again, not while your life is in danger. I will protect you, because if I hadn't seduced you last night, Talbot would have no reason to want you dead now."

She looked a little confused, but she didn't argue. "He may not have wanted me dead, but he intended something worse. He told me he meant to marry me once we reached Denver."

"You would have refused."

"I would, but Lieutenant Talbot isn't in the habit of accepting no as an answer. I can well imagine myself forced to wed at gunpoint, all so he could gain control over your pueblo."

"Why does he want it? Did he tell you anything?"

"No, he was careful about that, even once he decided to kill me, though he didn't mind boasting about Westley's murder. Whatever it is must be very important to him. Even his guards know nothing of his real plans. He wants something, desperately. And he didn't deny the abductions of your people, either, though he wouldn't say for what purpose they were taken."

"You didn't get the impression they had been killed, then?"

Her fingers closed around his in sweet comfort. "No, I think he needs them for something, and he made no mention of your brother. I doubt he even knows Diego was among the captives."

He held her hand close to his heart, not wanting to let her go, and knowing it was the only way. "Thank you, Evelyn. If you will forgive me for my ardor and lack of restraint, then perhaps you and I can find some measure of peace between us."

She nodded and smiled, but she looked a little sad. "I am no longer the Renegade's captive, but his friend."

The paths south to Taos proved arduous and long. Days passed, and Evelyn felt they'd made no progress at all. Sometimes, it seemed they'd circled back and faced north again, but neither Rafael nor Patukala seemed concerned. On one of his scouting rides, Patukala had learned from a group of Indian hunters that Talbot had indeed been misled, and had taken a more southern route. Rafael said Talbot meant to cut them off before they reached Santa Fe, but the pressure of pursuit had abated.

Evelyn loved the high mountain landscape, the small streams and waterfalls, the ragged pines. Sometimes, she rode beside Chen because he always had something to say, and his conversation was cheerful, filled with the bright hopes of a young man whose life was untarnished with his own mistakes.

When she wearied of Chen's high energy, she rode with Will, who spoke little, yet seemed to emanate peacefulness. From him, she learned the disposition and personality of their horses, which Patukala had brought from his father's pueblo. She learned that Rafael had found Frank as a yearling running free and had recognized Andulasian blood. He had presented the horse to his grandfather, but the old man refused to accept a gift from his mixed-blood grandson.

Evelyn felt indignant on Rafael's behalf. "Do you mean his grandfather disapproves of him?"

Will checked back over his shoulder to be sure Rafael wasn't close enough to overhear. Rafael was riding with Chen, who was filling the air with questions that the schoolmaster dutifully answered. Will seemed satisfied by this, then turned back to Evelyn. "The chief doesn't approve of most anyone, from what I've seen. Funny thing is, he gets on well with Diego, and Diego looks a whole lot more Spanish than Señor de Aguirre."

Evelyn glanced at Rafael. "He probably sees more of himself in Rafael. At times, this creates a clash of wills. Or maybe the chief disapproves of his renegade actions."

Will scrunched his face. "Ain't that, miss. What he don't like is Señor de Aguirre teaching us."

"How can he object to that?"

"If he taught Zuni children, the chief wouldn't have minded so much. But Señor de Aguirre took in Chen, boys and girls of Mexican families, and me, too, though everybody said I'd never read a word." Will paused, proud. "I read that book you gave Chen on the train."

"Did you? That's wonderful, Will." It had been a dime novel she'd bought at the train station, romantic and somewhat sentimental in nature. "Did you enjoy it?"

"I liked it fine. Thought it was real sad, Angelina losing everything and then dying all noble and pretty like that. But Chen said it was stupid and that the girl just whined about everything, and the hero should have ditched her for someone rich after her brother gambled away all their money."

Evelyn repressed a smile. "Chen's values need . . . work."

Will shrugged. "Aw, miss, Chen don't really care about the money, even though it looks like he does. He's just seen that folks with power use money to get done what they want done. That's all. He wants to get things done, too."

Evelyn just stared at the boy, amazed at his insight. He was right. There was more to Chen than boyish greed. "I suppose that's true of everyone."

Will shook his head. "It ain't true of Lieutenant Talbot and them landowners who want our pueblo."

"What do you mean? Surely it's power they want, too."

"They want power, but not to get things done like Chen. He wants to matter in the world. They just want to get control of the world so they can feel like they own it. Chen wants to be someone, to be important. But underneath, it's because he thinks other folks are important, too, and he wants to help out. You should see him at the school, miss. He runs around helping all the children—'course, he knows more than the rest of us combined, and he keeps telling us so, too. He learned from Señor de Aguirre, and though he ain't so patient, he won't give up until he's helped me figure something out."

Evelyn's heart expanded as she imagined the scene at Rafael's small pueblo school. Her eyes filled with unexpected tears and she pressed her lips together to keep from crying. Children of all races, with no thought of how wealthy their families were or where they came from, brought together by Rafael to learn of their world, and to learn they too had a place in it.

"I would love to see your school."

"It's a real fine place, miss. Señor de Aguirre and Diego built it themselves, so it sits on its own next to the old pueblo. Got windows and new desks that Diego made last year when he got bored. Chen kept telling him they ought to be fancier, but Diego got mad and they ended up in another fistfight."

"Don't they get along?"

Will made a face. "Two mad dogs get along better than them two. Señor de Aguirre is always prying them apart and sending them off in different directions. But he don't get mad. You noticed that? He just likes them all too much."

Evelyn glanced wistfully back at Rafael. He was listening patiently to Chen telling him something about setting up a shop to profit from the new railroad. "He is a good man."

Will nodded. "Figured you'd see that sooner

or later. Once you got past feeling bad for loving him and all."

The path narrowed so that Will had to take the lead. Evelyn held her horse back, staring. *Loving him.* Her heart beat in strange little leaps. After all this time, she'd never truly considered the depth of her feelings for Rafael. She had named it lust, admiration, even affection.

But Will knew. He had known all along, because he just saw things as they were. Rafael rode up behind her. "Is there some reason you're blocking the path, Mrs. Reid?"

She looked back at him, her eyes wide, her lips parted. *I love you.* He gazed at her, bemused. Evelyn gulped, then urged her horse forward down the path. She followed Will, but her mind raced, flitting from thought to thought as she faced the full realization of what she felt.

It had begun as a wild infatuation, buried in remorse when Westley had been killed. She had learned, here with him, that Rafael was as good a man or better than she had imagined, and that as a lover, he surpassed her wildest fantasies. Even more, she admired what he had done with his life and for others.

She loved his face, especially when he wore his small round spectacles. They highlighted how unusual a man he was, and when he might have been simply devastatingly handsome, the addition of spectacles gave him a quirky appearance. She loved his tall, strong body, and the way he looked so innately proud, as if nothing fate could throw at him would ever tarnish him.

She loved his gentleness, and the way he understood unspoken words, and read the hearts beneath words that were sometimes lies.

I can't lose you.

Since her escape from Talbot, Rafael had kept to his word. He hadn't touched her. He didn't even sleep close to her anymore. He was kind and polite and friendly, but not romantic.

Her guilt at betraying Westley's memory had faded once she accepted that Westley, too, had been torn. She felt sure now that he would understand how she felt, and forgive her, just as she forgave him.

Without guilt to cloud her heart's voice, she couldn't deny what she felt for Rafael. The realization that she was in love with him, and had been all along, brought with it a new intensity of doubt and fear. What if he didn't love her back?

He had said he was infatuated, that he thought she was special. She knew he was attracted to her physically, and that the sexual energy between them was strong. But he had told her that he almost married once before. What kind of relationship had he shared with that woman? Evelyn suspected his former love hadn't been as unusual as Evelyn herself, probably not given to odd flights of fancy.

Maybe the kind of woman he wanted to marry was very different from the one he wanted to bed. Evelyn stared down at her horse's neck and fiddled with its black mane, adjusting each strand to fall to the left. Maybe he wanted a woman who hadn't made so many mistakes in her life, a younger woman who was untarnished by life.

"Mrs. Reid, you look pensive. What troubles you?"

She startled at Rafael's voice and her horse pricked its ears intently as if wondering what predator she sensed in the woods. He was calling her Mrs. Reid again. She hadn't thought about it much, but maybe he was trying to place distance between them, drawing more formal lines so that neither would dare cross again.

She looked at him with no idea what to say. "I was just wondering . . . Was your former fiancée . . . sensible?"

His brow rose, alerting her to the utterly obvious intent behind her question. A smile played his lips. "Why do you ask?"

"No reason." That knowing smile grew and her cheeks warmed. She cleared her throat. "It's just that Will and I were discussing . . . literature, and he had commented that the heroine in the book I lent him was 'whiny.' Well, actually, it was Chen who interpreted her as whiny, which I can't argue with as I found her overly pious and somewhat judgmental."

She was babbling, so she stopped short, keeping her eyes wide as if nothing beyond intellectual speculation had motivated her interest. He nodded thoughtfully. "I see."

"Good."

"So you wanting to know my former fianée's nature—I thought I told you she wasn't my fiancée—this relates only to Will's reaction to a dime novel?"

She kept her expression straight. "Yes."

"I *see*."

She wanted to hit him. A small growl

emerged unexpectedly in her throat. "What was she like?"

"Nothing like you."

She turned from him and rode on, her back straight. The path widened, unfortunately, and he seized the opportunity to ride beside her. She kept her vision ahead and refused to look at him. Her lips felt tight with annoyance, so she stretched them into a semblance of a smile.

From the corner of her eye, she saw him watching her. He was smiling. She loved him. "I hate you."

She winced and cringed the moment she spoke. Rafael laughed. "I thought I had been forgiven."

She patted her chest and breathed as deeply as she could. "This is a new emotion."

"Based on my answer?"

She squeezed her eyes shut. "You are being deliberately . . . awful."

"If you would tell me the real reason for your question, I might be able to answer you more fully."

She glared at them. "No."

He waited a moment, then shrugged. "Then I'll tell you anyway. My former fiancée, who I had never actually proposed to, was indeed 'sensible.' Perhaps the term 'practical' is more accurate. She knew what she wanted in life, where she wanted to go, and what she wanted from me. Unlike yourself."

"How very nice." She couldn't help it. Her lips curled in disgust and her brow tightened into what she assumed was an extremely unattractive expression. "A shame you were forced to separate."

"We weren't 'forced.' I left because I didn't want the same things she did."

"She sounds superficial in the extreme." Now she hated herself for speaking. Evelyn clamped her hand over her forehead and groaned. "I'm sorry. I don't know what's come over me. It must be the heat."

"I was just going to ask if you'd like a blanket to wrap around your little body, since there's a decided chill in the air today."

"Can you let nothing pass?"

"Not when your mood interests me this much."

"I have no idea why you should care."

"You're thinking about me again."

It would be wrong to say "I hate you" twice to the man she had so recently accepted loving. She effected a casual expression. "We've been riding for days and days. It's only natural that I should wonder about you every so often, considering how meeting you has turned my life upside down in more ways than I can count. It was idle curiosity on my part. I am sorry I asked."

"Is there anything else you want to know?"

A million things. "No."

"Ah."

They rode on in silence. Evelyn slumped in her saddle, feeling discouraged. He hadn't quite given her the answer she'd hoped for. She wanted him to tell her that his former love's charms were forgotten now that he had found

Evelyn, that he dreamed of her as she dreamed of him.

Strange how the balance between them had shifted so dramatically in his favor since she admitted to herself that she loved him. At first, his intense interest in her had scared her practically senseless. She hadn't questioned its depth because she was too busy evading it.

He had taken her in his arms and proved to her how much she wanted him, and how much bliss they could know together. She ran, and he stepped back, accepting . . . *No*. He thought she'd said no, when all she'd really meant was "I'm terrified."

He was right. She didn't know what she wanted from him. She looked around at the people who had risked everything to save him, because they loved him. Here in the high mountains, with sparkling streams, the pines and the blue sky, she was in his beautiful world.

She knew exactly what she wanted. She wanted him to love her, and she wanted to marry him. She wanted to be with him at his little school teaching children. She wanted to bear children herself, black-haired babies just like him. Pain so intense its hurt clutched at her, an ache deeper than anything she'd felt before. It was the horrible anguish of knowing the heart's dearest desire, and also knowing, because nothing in life is certain, that it might not ever come true.

For a dark moment, her fear and doubt obliterated her hope. Emotion ruled her—clear thinking came harder. Evelyn's face puckered as she tried to gain control over her thoughts.

The first thing she had to do was find out what he wanted from her. No, the first thing to do was to show him that she was worth wanting, too.

But what if she wasn't? She hadn't exactly simplified his journey. It might even be argued that he wouldn't have been taken captive in the first place if not for her. If she hadn't run out into the crowd, he wouldn't have struck her, and he would have escaped. If she hadn't tried to shoot him at the train station, he would have escaped there, too.

"I have made life somewhat difficult for you, I suppose." She spoke out loud, not meaning to, but Rafael issued a brief huff, implying she had indeed been a scourge upon his life.

"Somewhat? You've tormented me."

Strange how he could irritate her so much now that she knew it was love she felt for him. "I have apologized for unmasking you, and shooting at you, and running to Lieutenant Talbot, and for accusing you of killing Westley."

"I'd forgotten all that."

"Then in what way have I 'tormented' you?"

His gaze shifted to her, and one dark brow arched. "There was covering yourself in filth."

"Oh, yes. That."

He leaned toward her, lowering his voice. "And for keeping me awake at night thinking of you, and for haunting my dreams, and for looking so sweet and so beautiful that I can't take my eyes off you."

Her whole body and soul and heart erupted in a smile of pure happiness. His eyes widened in surprise at her reaction. But instead of joy, he seemed uneasy. "I'm sorry, Evelyn. That was a little . . . strong."

She felt as if he'd stabbed her. The ache inside her turned suddenly cold, but she couldn't bring herself to ask what he meant.

Rafael looked troubled. "I promised to protect you, and I will."

"I sense no danger."

He eyed her, then shook his head. "You know better. You are vulnerable. You need time . . ." There was more, and he wasn't saying it.

But as they rode on in silence, Evelyn didn't have the heart to ask.

Evelyn Reid was falling in love with him. As they rode into the village of Taos, Rafael felt sure of it. The way she looked at him had changed, and if he had harbored any doubt, her reaction to his declaration of her beauty and sweetness erased it.

He had avoided her since, riding ahead with Sally, and even taking Patukala's place at scouting for the past day. Evelyn looked hurt, but she said nothing. And the ache in his own heart seemed almost impossible to endure. Since he met her, he had flown on the wings of passion, never thinking what his ardor might do to her. And it had done plenty.

He had to return to Santa Fe. His brother and his people needed him. But Talbot would arrive first, and the battle awaiting him would far surpass those nighttime raids he'd taken as the Renegade. And now he had Evelyn loving him. She had already lost one husband. Worse still, he knew she wouldn't leave him to protect herself, and that could place her in even more danger.

So he had to avoid her, for her own sake. Their one night of passion might yield a child, but not so likely as if he lay with her every night as he longed to do. The way she was looking at him now, another such magical tryst seemed all too likely. He couldn't leave her with a child, not when his own fate was so uncertain.

Maybe, when it was over . . . when their situation was resolved . . . Then he would court her and earn the love shining in her eyes. If he could just resist the warm, sensual currents running between them now . . . If he could ignore the confusion and wistfulness in her beautiful face.

In Taos, they gathered supplies at the trading post, and Chen found a buyer for a little bowl Evelyn had discovered in Mesa Verde. It proved to be worth more than Rafael would have thought, and much less than Chen wanted. Disappointed, the boy set about gambling at a small saloon, and though Rafael warned him he was likely to lose all he'd gained from the bowl, Chen's luck held and he doubled the price by nightfall.

Despite Chen's enhanced income, it was Rafael who paid for their lodging. He secured three rooms in an adobe inn, making sure Evelyn's was farthest from his own. He wasn't sure he could trust her not to come to him in the night, so he placed her with Sally. Will and Chen took the next room, but Patukala had gone to the Taos Pueblo instead, telling Rafael that the extra ride was worth it for a night without Chen's chatter.

He went to the door of his own room, but a soft touch on his shoulder stopped him. He knew who it was without looking. He repressed a groan, then turned around.

"Since you abducted me without my handbag, I would like some money, please." Evelyn held out her hand, lips twisted to one side. "I asked Chen, but he seems to have forgotten who found that bowl."

He breathed an audible sigh of relief. "Then I'm fortunate Patukala thought to bring my own." He took out a bag of coins and American bills, then deposited it in her small hand. She fingered it as if judging its worth by weight.

"This should do. Thank you."

She started away, but something in her attitude incited his suspicions. "Why do you need money? I've already paid for your room."

She rolled her eyes. "I am a woman."

As if that explained everything, she tossed her head and marched off. She aimed for the trading post, but though she didn't look back, Rafael went to his room with an ominous feeling that some feminine gauntlet was about to be thrown.

Chapter Ten

"What the hell are you fixing to do, girl?" Sally barricaded their door, scowling at Evelyn's new attire.

Evelyn fingered one of the turquoise beads on her new necklace. "I'm going out."

"Damned sure, you're not!"

"Sally, remove yourself from the door."

"You ain't going anywhere near Rafe looking like that."

"I am."

"Not in that dress, you're not. Where'd you get a thing like that?"

Evelyn glanced at her reflection in a dusty looking glass, pleased. She had discarded her tattered blue gown in favor of a pretty dress that looked Spanish. The hem of the black and red skirt was higher than usual with a pleasant flounce, and the bodice was small and snug, fitted when a loose white blouse. The effect of the bodice beneath the blouse made her breasts look fuller than they actually were. She felt exotic, and if she could pretend to be a more dramatic, enticing woman, Rafael de Aguirre might just believe it, too.

She adjusted her new bonnet and redid the tie to a fatter bow. "I purchased it from a Mexican lady at the saloon. It was helpful, because Chen had just won a great portion of her husband's money. So I bought this, and she hid the cash from him."

"Good thinking . . ." Sally stopped herself and shook her head. "So now you're marching out to seduce him?"

Evelyn met Sally's accusatory glare evenly. "Yes."

The small woman seemed surprised at her honesty. "Changed your mind, have you, just like that?"

Evelyn puffed an impatient breath. "No, not 'just like that.' But I don't think this is any of your concern."

Sally placed one hand on the doorknob. "It is if you expect me to let you through this door."

Evelyn eyed the window. It was small, but if she squeezed . . . She pictured Sally clinging to her feet, then hanging on her all the way to Rafael's door. "Oh, very well. As it happens, learning Rafael wasn't responsible for my husband's death did much to alleviate my doubt."

Sally frowned. "You knew that anyway."

"I suppose I did. And I suppose . . . I realized that Westley would understand."

"So you've got your dead husband's permission?"

Evelyn braced. "I do not appreciate your sarcasm." Sally still wasn't moving. Evelyn shifted her weight from foot to foot impatiently. "Oh, damn you! I love him! And I'm going through this door if I have to pick you up and toss you aside!"

"Love him, do you? And what are you going to do if leaving him alone is the best thing for him?"

Evelyn's spirits deflated. "You mean because he doesn't want me?"

"No, I mean because he does."

Suddenly, with no warning, Evelyn felt like crying. Tears filled her eyes, her throat tightened. She turned from the door and sank down onto the bed. She covered her face in her hands and wept, though she would rather have died than cry in front of Sally, of all people.

She heard a long, drawn-out sigh, and Sally came to sit beside her. "God in Heaven, you're an emotional little thing. Stop that."

Evelyn sniffed. "I don't want to leave him alone. You don't understand. I'm so lonely. My heart hurts so much. One minute, he's looking at me—that certain way—and then he's avoiding me. I don't understand men at all."

"Well, I do."

Evelyn peeked up at Sally and dried her eyes. "Do you?"

"Damned sure." Sally paused and Evelyn waited expectantly. "They're all crazy."

"Crazy?"

"Look at them! I don't know much about your

husband, but I do remember that he spent a lot of time away from you, giving you plenty of time to fill your head with someone better. Age don't matter, either. Look at Chen. That boy thinks money can buy him a place in the world. Hell, maybe it can, and if it does, he'll know what to do with it. My Will, he's got more sense than most, but he does most of his talking to horses. And Rafe? He can't let an injustice pass without turning it on its head. What other man do you know who would dress himself up like a warrior god and ride thundering down on his enemies?"

Evelyn smiled. "Not many." She paused. "What about Patukala?"

Sally huffed. "Craziest of them all."

"Why?"

"For one thing, he knows just as much English as I do, and maybe more."

"Does he?"

"Speaks it, too, just so long as Chen ain't around. But that ain't why I say he's crazy."

"Then why? He seems normal enough to me."

"His father wants him to marry, naturally, him being the fittest son, but the damned fool won't."

"Why not?"

"Fancies himself in love with a woman his father don't like."

"Really? Who?"

Sally shook her head. "Me."

Evelyn beamed. "How wonderful!"

"He's an idiot."

"You love him, too."

"I've got ten years on him, maybe more. I've

got a boy who talks to horses, from a husband who drank himself to death. He can do better."

"Apparently he thinks differently. Will and Patukala seem to get along very well." She paused. "Does Rafael know?"

"I suppose he might."

"But you do love him, don't you?"

Sally's beautiful dark eyes filled with unshed tears. "I do, and that's why I've told him no, time and time again. He deserves better."

Evelyn considered this awhile. "You think Rafael deserves better than me, too." Her eyes filled with tears again, but she refused to let them fall. She nodded, and took off her new bonnet. "You're right."

Sally placed her hand over Evelyn's. "I'm not saying he deserves better. But he's got a big fight coming, like it or not, if he wants to get his brother back, and if he's ever going to clear his name. To do that, he's got to put John Talbot in his place, and that ain't going to be easy. I'll admit, I thought you were more likely to get him killed than do him any good, but you've come to your senses enough to think twice, anyway."

"I have. I won't go."

Sally got up and went to the door, then held it open. "You'll go. But you remember that while he's busy protecting you, he's going to need someone looking after him, too."

Evelyn looked up, confused. "But you said I shouldn't go."

"Know what you're doing before you walk in. That's all."

Evelyn hesitated, then got up. She left her bonnet behind—it had felt a little foolish. She had done her hair up nicely, but that began to feel foolish, too. She pulled out the pins that held it in place, and let it fall loose around her shoulders. "At least, I've bathed."

Sally grinned. "Noticed that Rafe took his time at that same task, too. Even though he thinks he don't want you coming by tonight."

"Did he?"

"Shaved, washed his hair, and soaked himself in water hot enough to scald chicken."

"Perhaps he was just feeling grimy." He wasn't. He was hoping, secretly, that she would take the initiative and come to him. Evelyn felt sure of it. Hope flared in her heart as she said good night to Sally, but as soon as she walked out the door, her doubts rushed back.

Maybe he had just been taking advantage of their first opportunity for a long, hot bath, just as she had done. Maybe he had no idea she was brazen enough to visit his room.

She went to his door and stood there. She held up her hand to knock, but couldn't do it. What if he said no? What if he told her that though she had enchanted him from afar, the responsibility of really loving her, tarnished as she was, had outweighed the appeal? Maybe once he realized he could have her, he began to see all the reasons he would prefer someone else.

She had been taught that a woman must wait for the man to declare himself. He knew this as well as she did. A woman who took action first could easily be termed "desperate." If he wasn't taking action, it was because he didn't want her.

Doubt and hope warred inside her. She

wanted to be with him. Sally said he would face a greater danger than he'd ever known once they reached Santa Fe. Could she let him go, never telling him how much he meant to her?

She knocked twice, then held her breath. She heard him walk across the floor, slowly. He stood a moment on the other side and she began to tremble. He opened the door and she looked up at him. He didn't seem surprised to see her there. He wasn't wearing his spectacles, so maybe she had woken him. His black hair fell forward over his shoulders, a little messy as if he had been lying down.

He was the most beautiful man she had ever seen.

"I've come to tell you that I love you. That's all. Good night."

She spun on her heels and hurried away, horrified. *Well done, Evelyn. Exactly how you wanted to tell him!*

She wasn't sure where she was going, so she just kept walking until she came to a low adobe wall. She stopped like a horse at the edge of its paddock. He came up behind her and placed his hands on her shoulders. He didn't speak, but he wrapped his arms around her and rested his cheek against her head.

Embarrassment filled her, and fear, because now she would have to hear his answer to a question she'd been a fool to ask. And she realized painfully how often "I love you" is a question. "I'm sorry. I lost my mind. It's been a long day."

He said nothing. Evelyn wanted to run, but he was still holding her.

"Maybe you'd believe it if I said the heat?"

Curses! He still didn't respond.

Her voice grew very small. "The cold?"

Please don't hurt me. Gently, he turned her to face him. She averted her gaze, refusing to meet his eyes. He touched her chin and lifted it so tenderly that she hurt.

He waited until she looked at him. A single tear fell from his beautiful dark eyes to his cheek, and then another. He bent to kiss her, softly, asking nothing as his mouth moved over hers. Then he rested his forehead on hers, cupping her head in his hands.

He kissed her again, and she placed her hands on his waist. "Please don't cry, Rafael. I didn't mean to cause you pain. I just wanted you to know how I feel. But it doesn't mean you have to love me back."

He looked at her, surprised, and he smiled through his tears. "My dear, beautiful angel . . . How could you imagine that I don't love you, too?"

"Do you?"

He touched her cheek. "I have loved you since I first saw you. I loved you when you were another man's wife. I loved you when you aimed a gun at my heart, and when you covered yourself in mud to keep me away. As if anything in the world could change what I feel for you! Evelyn, I would love you in hell."

Her own tears resumed and her breath came in small gasps. "Then why have you been avoiding me?"

"Do you really have to ask?"

"Well . . . Yes!"

He kissed her face and softened her hair. "I've gotten you in too much trouble already."

"It could be argued that I got you in trouble first."

"Everything is so uncertain now. I don't know what Talbot is after, and I don't know what I'll have to do to free those people." He kissed her again, as if he could never be close enough to her. "I don't know what I can offer you, those things that a man should offer the woman he loves—a home, a family, a lifetime together."

She moved closer, gazing up at him filled with more love than she knew she possessed. "Then offer me now, and fill me with all that you feel, and let me love you. Please, fear can't be stronger than love. It can't."

"I know I should turn you away somehow, for your own sake as well as for mine. For mine, because I can't bear losing you or seeing you hurt if the resolution at the pueblo isn't what I hope. But I need you too much, and I want you too much to let another night go by without you."

Happiness filled her, driving away all fear and all doubt. "All my life, I have wanted to love this way. Whatever happens, I will be with you."

"That's what I'm afraid of." He paused. "If I left you here . . ."

Her brain worked quickly this time, fueled by the power of love. "Talbot would come for me eventually." She paused. "And you know I wouldn't stay."

"You are a difficult woman."

"I will try to be what you want. If you want me to be practical, I will make the attempt." She meant it, too. She wouldn't ride with him as a weak, helpless, lovesick girl. She wanted to offer some kind of assistance, though she wasn't sure what it would be. She wanted to matter.

"Evie, I love you as you are. Your imagination, your intuition, and the depth of your feeling far outweigh the benefits of practicality."

"Are you sure?"

"I'm sure."

He kissed the tip of her nose, but her intentions didn't alter. He was right. She had to learn to use her innate talents, not try to emulate another's. Depth of feeling inspired her, intuition would be her guide. Imagination—well, she would leave that for the time being, but she felt sure it would come in handy at some point. "You will not be sorry to keep me with you. And I promise you, I will be useful when you need me most."

"If you would promise to stay safe, I would feel better."

"I will be careful, naturally."

"Why am I not comforted by this?"

She felt better, truly alive. He loved her. That was all that mattered. "Because you are tired, and perhaps you are lonely, and if that's true, you should be in your bed."

He smiled and took her hand, then kissed it. "Rest will cure weariness, but loneliness?"

"I will cure that, if you let me stay with you."

"If that's what you want."

"It is."

He stood back to look at her. "Where did you get that dress?"

She felt shy and young and she fingered the

hem of her sleeve. "I bought it from a woman while Chen was beating her husband at cards. She was about my size. Maybe a little smaller."

"It's beautiful. You are beautiful."

"Like you, Rafael."

He held her hand in his, then nodded back toward his room. They gazed into each other's eyes, and in words unspoken, he promised her a night of the sweetest love she had ever known. They walked hand in hand, and he held open the door for her. As she passed over the threshold into the little adobe bedroom, she felt as if she'd stepped into heaven.

It was easier when she didn't know what he intended. Evelyn stood by Rafael's bed, her nervousness increasing by leaps and bounds. After nights on a bedroll, the bed looked fit for a king, but she couldn't bring herself to sit. When he had made love to her in Mesa Verde, it had been dark except for faint moonlight. But now the room was lit with the soft glow of lanterns and he was watching her intently.

"You're nervous."

Her chest fluttered with a shaky breath. "Not at all."

Rafael took her hand. "I am, too."

She gazed up at him in wonder. "Truly? Why?"

"For the same reason you are, I would think. What if I disappoint you?"

Her lips curled to one side. "That hardly seems likely, given how perfect you are." That was the problem. "If you were less perfect, this would be easier."

"In what way would you have me change?"

She eyed him critically. "I would make you a bit fat around the waist. Maybe a little less tall, and your shoulders less broad. I would take just the slightest element of shine from your hair, and you could at least close your eyes so that I can't see how much of your great soul shines there."

He shifted his weight from foot to foot, looking confused. "I can't do much about my height. I guess I could eat more. . . ." He paused, uncertain. "Why would these things please you?"

"Because then I wouldn't feel so . . . insufficient myself."

He kissed her hand and held it against his heart. "You are perfect. You couldn't be sweeter or more beautiful."

She eyed him doubtfully. "I could. My figure isn't entirely . . . womanly." She'd done her best to enhance her modest breasts, but she couldn't help noticing that even the slender Mexican woman filled the blouse more impressively than she. "I'm too tall, my belly isn't flat, and I'm not sure about my backside because I don't see it, but I feel certain it isn't all it could be. My hair tangles seconds after I brush it, and always waves in the wrong direction. You may have noticed? I bite my fingernails. . . ."

"But your feet are perfection."

"Are they?" She looked down at her boots, then realized he was teasing her. She clamped her hand to her forehead. "I don't know what's gotten into me. I never worried about these things when I was married. I never noticed how inadequate I am until I met you."

"Have I made you feel that?"

"No, not on purpose. It's just that when I look at you, I imagine the sort of woman you should love, and she is so much better than I am. It's not just physically, either. I've been married, so I cannot be considered untarnished. And I think it is possible that I'm older than you are." She paused. "How old are you?"

"Twenty-eight."

She sighed. "I knew it."

"Almost twenty-nine?" He was still teasing her, but she shook her head.

"I am not good enough for you."

He didn't respond at once. He looked at her, shaking his head as if considering all she'd pointed out. Evelyn held her breath. She wanted him to love her despite her faults, but she couldn't come up with a good reason that he should.

Rafael folded his arms over his chest and looked thoughtful. "When we grow old, it may be that both of us will lose some of the splendors of youth. Will you love me less when my face is lined with age?"

"You will be handsome, and I will love you just the same as I do now, but perhaps fuller because I will know you so well."

"Do you think I love you any less, or that my love is based on what you look like? My heart is not so shallow as that, Evelyn."

"I know. I don't know why I'm thinking this way."

He drew her into his arms and she buried her face against his chest. She listened to his strong heart beating and heard how fast it throbbed within him. "You're not afraid of me, Evelyn. You're not afraid you're not good enough. I think you're afraid of how strong a woman you really are."

She peeked at him. "Am I?"

"You called it a beast, but you were wrong. The thing you try to contain is a goddess, so strong that she can bring me to my knees. She can give life or destroy, and you know it, inside."

Her eyes shifted to the side, then back to him. "Oh."

He smiled. "You don't believe me, but you will."

"Good." She puffed a breath. "How?"

His smile deepened. "By facing—and exploring—the beast. How else?"

He stood back from her. She expected further reassurance, but he didn't give it. Instead, he fixed his dark gaze on her and began, slowly, unbuttoning his shirt. Evelyn bit her lip. She watched each button pop loose. His fingers were long and dark, deft and gentle. Those same fingers had touched her in such sweet, unexpected ways. . . .

Evelyn caught a quick breath and he smiled. He peeled his shirt from one muscular shoulder, then paused, almost as if allowing her time to inspect him bit by bit. Her gaze followed the skin he bared. Both shoulders, then his wide chest, the way his arms flexed as he undressed, the taut, hard muscles of his stomach.

Evelyn felt curiously warm inside. Hot. He tossed his shirt aside, and she gaped at his exposed torso. She hadn't seen him unclothed, not this way. She wanted to, and secret fantasies that had swept across her mind since she met him began coming to life.

He was a beautiful man, and if ever a mortal was fit to ride in a god's image, it was Rafael. She wanted to touch him, but she wasn't sure what she could do without offending him, or exposing too much of her own secret dreams. He said he wanted her "beast" unleashed, but he had no idea how untamed she really was.

There was something about the way that he watched her, as if he knew every thought, every wish, that stirred her senses. He unbuttoned his belt and she heard every heartbeat as she waited for him to remove his trousers. She had never actually seen her husband naked. Westley had faithfully worn a long nightshirt, so she wasn't entirely sure what that portion of a man looked like. He had never encouraged her to touch him—doing so with Rafael had been a surprise, and more still, that he wanted her to.

He was moving very slowly, deliberately. She pretended not to look at that portion of him, then stole a quick peek. He still hadn't removed his trousers, but she spotted a well-defined bulge. A sudden impulse to tear apart his trousers seized her, and she sucked her teeth fiercely, then popped her lips.

"I don't want to shock you, Mrs. Reid."

"You . . . you are a demon."

He lowered his pants, and his erection sprang free, hard and powerful. Evelyn wanted to look away, but she couldn't. Her mouth slid open. When he had made love to her for the first time, she had felt as if he filled all her self, but she had assumed it was because of her wildly heightened sensitivity.

She ached inside with a sudden, furious intensity. There was something about him that reminded her of the dark, forbidden fantasies she had once entertained when loneliness consumed her, and when her own feminine needs stirred beneath the surface of her quiet life. Now those dreams had a focus, brought to life by Rafael's sensuous male body as he stood before her, fully aroused, his dark eyes shining.

Wild thoughts awoke in her. She wanted to touch him, to run her hands all over him, to feel his skin beneath her fingertips. She wanted to kiss him and taste him. But he didn't move or do anything to make it easier for her. He just stood there, looking beautiful and strong, and virile, as if all pleasure could be hers if she would just take it.

If he said "touch me," it would be enough.

He said nothing. Evelyn checked his expression. A look that suggested she was welcome to explore him would even be sufficient. Instead, his dark eyes just burned with that ancient light, but she couldn't be sure it meant what she wanted it to mean.

He reached, rather slowly, to move his long hair off one shoulder. Her gaze fixed itself on the way the sinewy muscles in his arms moved, and on the way the warm light played on his dark skin. His chest, when viewed in motion, was a thing of such aching perfection that she almost forgot to breathe.

She stood there in the middle of his room, trembling with desire, her fingers twitching as she imagined touching him. She had dreamed of him so many times since they'd first made love, she had fantasized about him and wanted him, and here he was, the embodiment of everything she longed for.

She crossed the room and felt as if her feet never touched the ground. She placed both hands on his hard chest and looked up into his eyes. His eyelids lowered, his sensual lips curled. She ran her hands over his skin, down his muscular arms, to his wrists, and to his fingertips. She slid her arms around his waist and felt his back, and she pressed her lips to his skin beneath his collarbone.

She wanted to kiss all of him, to taste the sweet maleness of him. She kissed and tasted and nipped, her heart racing.

He didn't react, but she felt his pulse against her lips. His arousal pressed against her, hot and fully engorged. She wanted that, too. She slid her hands down between them and ran just her fingertips along the underside of his shaft, then over the tip, feeling the slick, taut skin, the texture and fullness of him.

Rafael was made of stone. She kissed him and caressed his most sensitive flesh, but he didn't move. She kissed his neck and squeezed her fingers around his shaft. His body quivered and his breath came harsh and shallow as if he endured the greatest provocation. But still, he resisted.

Evelyn went wild, like a temptress given some immovable lover, who as she seduced him, enchanted her. She moved back to examine his expression and saw his eyes were closed, his jaw tense with restraint. She reached up, took his hair in her hands, and pulled him down to kiss her mouth. She ran her tongue along the cleft of his lips, dipping in at the corner. He surrendered enough to kiss her back, and she engaged his tongue in a sensual dance. She pressed her body closer against his arousal, feeling its pulse against her skin, and he responded. She wanted more. She sucked his tongue and he surrendered.

He wrapped his arms around her, returning her kiss with the pent up intensity she'd longed for. But just as she reveled in his arms, he broke the kiss and backed away.

Evelyn stared at him, her breath coming in shuddering gasps. His dark skin shone with lust. Her gaze drifted to the core of his desire. A small bead of moisture formed on the blunt tip of his erection, heralding the wild ecstasy raging beneath his restraint.

His dark eyes flamed, but he ended their kiss. Why? She stood shivering, feeling chilled despite the fire inside her. He took a step toward her and she held her breath in anticipation.

He stopped, then reached to untie the string that held her bodice together. It parted, and the Spanish blouse came loose, too. He moved closer, and cupped her breasts through the sheer fabric, then kissed her again.

Not enough, never enough. He slipped the bodice from her shoulders, then dropped it to the floor. He unfastened her skirt and her red petticoat, and those fell to the floor, too. Her arms hung at her sides as he lifted the blouse over her head. She had left her chemise in

Sally's room, thinking it too cumbersome for the night she had planned, but as he freed her breasts from her light corset, she closed her eyes tight in embarrassment.

He said nothing, still. He must have bent down because she felt him pull off her drawers and stockings. She stepped dutifully out of them, but she didn't open her eyes.

Without warning, Rafael lifted her into his arms and carried her to the bed. She was ready. She wanted him too much to stand longer, anyway. But he didn't lie beside her as she expected. Instead, he knelt near her curved knee and ran his finger down her stomach.

"I love you, you know." His voice came low and throaty, exquisitely masculine. "You look at me and tell me you're not good enough, not beautiful enough, that you will try to be some other woman to please me. Evelyn, I will show you now, you could not please me more."

She looked up at him, unsure what to say. If he made love to her, perhaps she would forget her doubt. It had certainly not troubled her in the ancient city.

He didn't move his body over her. He moved to the end of the bed, so she propped herself up on her elbows to see what he intended. "This is an odd posture, Rafael. What are you . . . ?"

He didn't let her answer. He bowed before her, like a man worshipping a goddess, and before her words completed, she felt the warmth of his breath on her most secret woman's core. Evelyn snapped her knees together in surprise, but he placed his strong hands gently on her inner thighs, and bowed still more.

She stared, astonished, because it actually looked as if he meant to . . .

He kissed her, there.

She froze, too shocked to stop him or to register the acuteness of embarrassment. Rafael had lost his mind.

His tongue swept out to taste her, across the tiny bud that seemed especially to throb for his attention. She couldn't believe he had done it, but he did it again. He made small circles around her small peak, then over.

All thoughts fled, and she flopped back on her pillow. He kissed her and teased, and then sucked, over and over until her breaths came as wickedly demanding moans, shuddering gasps that begged him never, never to stop. All restraint fled, and she gave herself over to him.

She cried out his name, then whirled beyond speech to a world of soft gasps and ethereal moans, to rampant demand as her hips arched and twisted, and still he didn't stop. Rapture crept closer, and when its first spasm reached to seize her, he slowed almost to stopping, then resumed his torturous ministrations. He kept her like that forever, with her legs clenched, her toes curled, her hands knotted into fists. Somehow, her legs wrapped over his shoulders, and her fingers netted themselves into his hair.

He teased her and adored her, then sucked in his strange, primal rhythm. Every current in her body took fire at once and burst into sparkling fragments, undulating with waves and waves of bliss. Her voice took on an earthen quality, deep and ragged as she moaned her pleasure. He moved above her, and entered her, and every fragment caught fire once more.

Evelyn braced her hands on his wide chest as he thrust inside her, holding himself back enough to look into her eyes as he took her. He clasped her hands, and their fingers entwined as their bodies melded. She watched him, enchanted, as his own rapture swept through him and took control of him, as his black hair swung to one side when his head tipped back, his neck straining, every muscle in his perfect body taut in climax.

She had never seen a thing more beautiful than Rafael in love, his soul flying on fire because he had her so well, this way.

He stilled his movement, then looked down at her and smiled. He kissed her hands, then withdrew from her body. She was sated, sweetly.

She held out her arms and he lay beside her, and she knew they would make love again, and perhaps again.

No desperation compelled her now, as it had the first night. She would savor each moment, each beat of his heart. She would watch him sleep, and she would wake him when her hunger for him surged. But there was no need to hurry now.

They had all night.

Chapter Eleven

Evelyn didn't want to leave Taos. Rafael noted that she packed up her new dress carefully, and wore her tattered blue gown instead. As he watched, she circled their bedroom, running her fingers lovingly over the rough wooden bureau, along the bedpost, to the base of the lantern that had illuminated a night of love he would never, ever forget.

She gazed down at the bed, misty-eyed, already nostalgic. She lifted a pillow to her face and breathed deeply. As she set it back to their bed, her eyes filled with tears and she sniffed.

"If you like it so much, you could take it with you, Evie." Rafael adjusted his belt and wound his bola into a knot at his side.

She looked askance, in that way he presumed women often did when men couldn't comprehend the depth of their sentimental natures. "I want to remember everything from this room, not steal it!"

"Why are you smelling it?"

Her lips curved in a romantic smile. "It bears your fragrance. Do you know, I love the scent of you? Everything about you has become so dear."

He resisted the impulse to sniff the pillow himself to see what pleased her. He had washed in plain water, with plain soap. He always kept his hair clean, but he didn't add anything to it. But if she liked it, he had to be sure he could duplicate the scent at a moment's notice.

She liked so many things he did. As he watched her move wistfully around their room, he remembered her lying in his arms, giving herself over completely to the passion they shared. She had inspired his most sensual imagination since he first saw her, but he'd had no idea, truly, how fully she would love him. He'd had no idea what it would mean to lie beside her, feeling her fingers playing in his hair, or trailing soft lines across his chest.

He hadn't known the bliss of talking quietly to her, when she would pop up suddenly excited by something he'd said, and how he would fight to concentrate on her words while her long hair trailed over his skin. Before Evelyn, love and sex were things he considered part of life, to be enjoyed in their time. But now she was everything, the core of him, a part of him.

Lovemaking took on a whole new dimension with her, and he knew now what it meant for two souls to join as one. She trailed her fingers over the bedspread, then turned to him, smiling. He took her hand, and her fingers entwined with his.

"I will carry this night with me always, Rafael."

He held open the door and looked down at her. "Always." But as he spoke, a new fear rose inside him. One night wasn't enough. What pain would they endure if they were parted? Rather than heading out into a lifetime together, where they could build their dreams together, he was heading back to a town where he was considered a criminal. The threat that stood against him now was death.

As they followed secret paths south toward Santa Fe, Rafael found his attention less on the task ahead, and more on the woman riding beside him. Sally shot him frequent sharp looks as if to remind him of reality looming around the next corner, and even Patukala seemed concerned, though he said little. Chen and Will remained oblivious to the change in Rafael, though Will seemed to have guessed that Evelyn had accepted loving her captor.

Chen had purchased a large leather wallet, which he kept checking, fingering the money he'd won and making elaborate plans for its future. After a dutiful consideration of purchasing expensive horses, or perhaps a share in the new railroad, he had settled on opening an extravagant hotel in Santa Fe. Not a bad plan, Rafael thought—if the boy's reputation as a criminal and train robber could be erased.

He couldn't let his friends spend their lives on the run. They loved him and had acted for him, but they had their own dreams and their own paths to follow. And Evelyn, her dreams were as dear as his own. She deserved better than to be the mistress of a renegade. She wanted to be a wife and a mother, she wanted to teach at his school, and to explore the world, fulfilling her vivid imagination.

She looked thoughtful as they rode along, her brow puckered. She gazed up at the blue sky and drew long breaths. He wondered what she was thinking—maybe she, too, had realized how much they could lose if he failed when they returned to the pueblo.

Her lips made an odd popping sound, and she glanced at his belt. "Is that hard?"

Rafael's eyes widened and he looked quickly around to see if the others had overheard her comment. Maybe she'd forgotten they weren't alone. "Well . . . not just now, but we'll be stopping soon, and I'm sure . . ."

Evelyn groaned. "Not *that!*" She shook her head in dismay, but a small smile played on her lips. "I meant your weapon, your whip."

"It's called a bola."

"Yes, that. Is it hard to learn?"

"There is skill involved." He paused, uncertain why she asked, and not sure he wanted to know. "My father taught me when I was very young, four years old or even younger."

"Did he teach Diego, too?"

"I taught him, and he is proficient, though he prefers a rapier. He has more dramatic tendencies than I do. Why are you asking about this?"

"Because I want to learn."

"No."

Her mouth opened with righteous indignation, but then her jaw firmed into a stubborn posture. "Would you say no if Chen or Will asked you?" She didn't let him respond, because she knew the answer. "You would not. I trust this isn't because I'm a woman?"

Sally overheard their conversation and eyed him expectantly. Rafael felt defeated before the battle began. "It's not because you're a woman. It's because . . ." He faltered, unsure of his objections beyond a keen sense that teaching Evelyn any kind of weaponry would be a bad idea.

Her brows arched knowingly. "Yes . . . ?"

"Because I have grave doubts about why you want to learn."

"Because I want to fight, of course!"

Rafael groaned and bowed his head. "That's what I was afraid of."

Her eyes narrowed to slits. "I was only joking." She paused to utter a contrived laugh. "I want to learn because I'm bored. We stop to eat and to rest, and I just sit while the others make camp or feed the horses. Chen gives orders, Patukala scouts, you plan. My body is very stiff from riding, and I would welcome the activity."

He didn't believe her for a second, but he suspected he wouldn't get far in an argument. Beyond that, Evelyn seemed preoccupied—with worry, he imagined, so activity might distract her. "Very well. At our next stop, I will begin your lessons."

She brightened like a star, and he feared he'd added another mistake to a growing list of errors.

* * *

"Over your head, Evelyn, not . . ." Rafael ducked and cursed as Evelyn swung the bola backward like a fishing pole.

It wasn't as easy as he'd made it look. It was also heavier. The splayed ends entangled and Evelyn fought back irritation. "If you'd give me better instructions . . ."

"If you'd wait until I'm finished explaining . . ."

"We'd be here all day!" She wasn't being a good student. Evelyn grumbled as she untangled the three stone pouches, annoyed with herself for taking out her aggressions and frustrations on the man she loved. "I'm sorry." She still felt tense and irritable, but she steeled her determination and turned back to the task.

Rafael positioned himself a good distance away. "Over your head. It's not in the speed, but in the action of the wrist and shoulder."

She had practiced at every stop they made, taking small bites of her meals, then returning to her lessons. Her progress wasn't as impressive as she'd hoped. She had wanted Rafael to be proud, to remark on her quick learning and immediate skill.

Instead, she seemed to be floundering despite her most sincere efforts. She had no control over the stone pouches affixed to the split ends of the rope, yet Rafael seemed to be able to make them work together, wrapping around enemies' legs, snatching guns out of people's hands . . .

Rafael took the bola and demonstrated its uses by tossing a rock into the air, then catching it between the pouches. "The bola can be used for hunting birds or herding. . . ."

Evelyn grimaced. "I am not interested in hunting birds or herding anything." She looked around. "Maybe if I had something to aim at . . ." She eyed a pinecone on a reasonably situated branch, then flung the bola in its direction.

Rafael groaned before the weapon hit its target. The pouches wrapped around the branch and stuck on the nut. Evelyn tugged, shot a quick glance his way and offered a brief smile. "Got it."

He nodded. "Got the whole tree, by the look of it."

She tugged again, but the whip had locked itself tight around the branch. She yanked hard, and the others gathered around. Patukala saw what she'd done, sighed and shook his head, then headed off alone. Will looked confused and a little embarrassed. Sally turned to Rafael, hands on her hips.

"If you don't stop her, we will. Take it away from her, now!"

Evelyn braced. "Everyone makes a few mistakes when learning a new skill!"

Sally cocked her head to one side. "A few?"

Evelyn looked to Rafael for her defense, but he didn't appear particularly yielding. "How do you suggest we get my weapon, an item that must be deemed a family heirloom, out of this tree?"

"I will swing my body while hanging from the rope, and my weight will break the branch."

"You're not that fat."

He was definitely testy. Evelyn looked around for another supporter. One glance told her Sally wasn't likely to come to her aid. Patukala had left and Will eased away as if the whole episode had dampened his former high opinion of her. Chen was staring up at the branch as if pondering all life's mysteries.

All she needed was someone to climb that tree and fetch the bola. Rafael could do it, and probably would eventually, but she wanted to handle it herself. Inconvenienced by her long skirt, it wouldn't be easy, but she had to try. She gripped the skirt and petticoat, then climbed into the tree. Rafael moved to stop her, but she scrambled up two branches out of his reach.

"Evelyn! Get down from there, now!"

She squirmed out on a smaller branch, ignoring his protests. "It should be possible . . . Chen! If you would please grip the whip from below to steady it."

Chen grabbed the whip and began issuing instructions, which Evelyn ignored, all the while thanking him for his suggestions. She broke off a dead branch and prodded at the knot. "No good. I need to untangle it myself."

Rafael groaned and complained and then stood below her, presumably to catch her when she fell. Evelyn eyed him doubtfully. "I don't know what you think you're going to do down there. You can't catch me!"

"If nothing else, I can break your fall."

Sally uttered a long series of curses, then marched away in disgust. "I knew it—she'll be the death of you one way or another."

Evelyn ignored Sally and wormed her way

farther out on the limb. Chen positioned the whip, elevating it to take off pressure. Evelyn reached the knot, heard the branch bend with an ominous creak, and began untying the severed ends. The hard little pouches were indeed locked tight around the branch, but Evelyn refused to give up. The branch issued another menacing crack, and Rafael spewed forth commands and orders that Evelyn ignored.

Her fingers worked quickly—it occurred to her that a man with larger hands would have found the task impossible. The branch creaked again, and she knew time was short. If she crashed out of the tree, injuring herself or, worse, Rafael, she'd never hear the end of it, and her quest to be helpful would end in ignominious defeat. But if she succeeded . . .

She restrained fear and impatience, and gently unwound the tightest loop, then freed the bola. She dropped it down to Chen, who whooped in surprise at her victory. If she tried to climb back, the branch would break. Rafael was still ordering her to do something: "Be careful." She fought an impulse to groan and roll her eyes. *As if I hadn't thought of that!*

Evelyn looked back at the bole of the tree, then down at the ground. There was only one thing to do. She took a deep breath, then swung herself around. The branch splintered just as she jumped. Rafael shouted, but she sprang clear. The branch fell and struck Rafael lightly on the head.

"See? No trouble at all." Evelyn felt proud, but Rafael rubbed his head and scowled.

"You might have warned me."

"I thought you would have the good sense to move." She dusted herself off and seized the bola from Chen. It was a slight setback, nothing more. No one becomes proficient in an instant. And that last attempt, however badly it ended, had given her a new feel for the weapon. Evelyn tried again, twitching her wrist and jerking her shoulder at the same time.

The bola snapped in an unexpected direction, and caught both Chen and Will by their legs, uniting them. Chen yelped indignantly, but Will just stood quietly while she unwrapped them. She bit her lip hard and apologized, but when freed, Chen just stomped away, too offended to speak.

Will patted her shoulder, and offered a consoling smile. "You caught us up real good, miss. You're getting the hang of it, for sure."

Evelyn warmed to his praise, then glanced at Rafael, who frowned. "If you had been aiming for them, I would be impressed. But I got the distinct impression you were 'aiming' in the opposite direction."

Evelyn shrugged. "I just have to tune my style a bit. It worked, anyway." She waited, hopeful, but Rafael didn't appear convinced.

Annoyed, she tried again, but the bola reacted unexpectedly and snapped very close to Rafael's head. Evelyn winced and closed her eyes, not daring to see his reaction. She tugged, casually, but the rope resisted just as Rafael swore. She opened her eyes, slowly, and saw that she had somehow entangled one stone pouch in his long hair.

She exhaled a long, tight breath, then hurried

to free him. He stood still as stone, his jaw set, not meeting her eyes as she carefully moved his hair. "That was a close one. Sorry." She tried to keep her tone light, but his jaw shifted to one side. A last strand of hair was wrapped tight around one of the pouches, and try as she might, she couldn't free it. She closed her eyes and yanked.

Rafael jumped and cursed as the strand pulled free. Evelyn shook her head. "I hope you are more careful of the words you choose in your school."

He glared. "I've never had occasion to use such words until this day."

It might be better to end this conversation now. Her feelings were hurt, though she knew it was her doing. She couldn't give up, because she felt sure he would need her in Santa Fe, one way or another. More than that, she wanted to be more than his lover. She wanted to be like him, to know something of his strength inside her own heart. It wasn't going well—yet—but she had time.

Evelyn gathered her courage and went to her horse. "Shall we ride on? I would like to practice from my horse's back."

A collective moan arose, but Evelyn mounted despite their complaints. One try with the bola alerted her to the error of a mounted attempt. The split cords wrapped instantly around her horse's front legs, hobbling it. Evelyn hopped off and untangled the rope, her cheeks burning with embarrassment.

She straightened to see Rafael glaring down at her. "Give it back."

She held it close to her chest. "I will not."

"For the ride, Evelyn . . ."

She wasn't ready for a mounted battle, that was plain. "Will you let me try again when we stop tonight?"

He looked pained, but nodded. "I will."

They rode on in silence, and Evelyn's spirits sank. Her attempt to learn his skills was failing badly. She had irritated him, and perhaps disappointed him. She hadn't proven a very agreeable student, because she was impatient and wanted to do more than he asked, faster.

Something else was troubling her, though she wasn't sure what it was. A vague disquiet arose in her heart, and had been growing all day since they left Taos. They had given in to their feelings for each other—not to passion as they had in Mesa Verde, but to love.

Why wasn't it enough?

He rode in front of her when the path narrowed and Evelyn gazed at his strong, broad back until she ached. He had made love to her and told her that he loved her. What more did she want?

Of course, he had also told her he'd loved another woman once. She guessed he had probably made love to that woman, too. That was the problem. She wasn't sure of the depth of his feelings, or what being in love meant to him. To her, it meant everything. It meant their lives were entwined forever, and that she would be with him, always.

He had told her he loved her, but he hadn't proposed marriage. Though he seemed to understand her better than Westley had, Rafael was a more sensible person than she was. He could love passionately, romantically, but he would consider more practical concerns such as whether she could fit into his life or not. Westley's lack of understanding her true nature had its benefits—he hadn't fully realized on what unusual paths her thoughts traveled, and so he often had attributed more practicality to her actions than had actually occurred.

Rafael wouldn't make that mistake. He might find her charming, amusing, even endearing. But would he want her for a wife, for a lifetime? As they rode, she began to consider all the reasons he shouldn't. Maybe he would do better with a young woman who had made no mistakes in her life's choices, who didn't react with heightened emotion to life's obstacles and trials. A woman who wouldn't aim a gun at him because she didn't understand her own heart's voice.

She had to prove herself worthy. She had to surprise him with her skill. It wasn't enough to be his lover if he couldn't rely on her, or know she would be there to protect him when those obstacles in his path became too much for one man to bear.

She had to prove to herself that she deserved his love, most of all.

"We have to be more careful, Evelyn." Rafael whispered in her ear as Evelyn kissed his neck, and she stopped. They lay together beside a swift stream that tumbled over large rocks, concealed by night. He had been quiet and restrained, and Evelyn wasn't sure why.

Her body ached with desire—now that she knew what lovemaking could be, she wanted to discover its every nuance. Rafael's pulse raced—she felt it against her fingertips—but he seemed to be resisting. "What's the matter? I put our bedding away from the others, and with the stream rushing by, no one will hear." She kissed him again and gently sucked the skin over his throat.

He placed his hand on her shoulder and eased her back. "That's not what I'm afraid of."

"Then what is?"

"Evie, we took a chance, twice now. If we aren't careful, you will become pregnant."

She liked the thought, but didn't feel comfortable saying so. "My cycle is past the point where I am likely to conceive."

"You can't be sure of that." His voice sounded strained and hoarse. Despite his reservations, he wanted her, too.

"Not sure, no." She felt hot and congested inside, but more than that, she needed him this night. "Have you never taken this risk before?"

He held her close and kissed her forehead. "When I was young, I learned methods of preventing conception."

"What methods?"

"Nothing that I have access to now." He sounded frustrated. "There are less reliable ways—I can pull out of you at the last minute. Or we can find other ways to satisfy each other."

He was certainly proficient at *that*. Evelyn sat up and looked around. "We are a good distance away, but still . . ." She lay back and frowned.

"I will be pleased when this journey is over and we can be truly alone again."

He didn't answer. She glanced up at him. He looked troubled, but she wasn't sure why. Her words sounded as if she was planning a future. Maybe he wasn't ready for a real commitment.

His hands on her body felt warm, and he seemed to be tempted by her skin as he touched her. "Roll over."

She had no idea what he meant, but Rafael guided her onto her side, facing away from him. Evelyn repressed a sigh of disappointment, but he wrapped his arm over her and softly cupped her breast. Her pulse doubled and he kissed her neck below her earlobe. "Lie still, Evie, and hush."

He slipped his hands under her chemise, and over her skin in a leisurely fashion so that she anticipated each move he made. He teased her breasts, first one, then the other, bringing her sensitive nipples to hard buds. All the while, he kissed her neck and murmured in her ear. Sometimes, he seemed to be speaking another language, low and sensual, promising secret pleasures in an unknown tongue. As he whispered against her skin, his hand wound down over her side and to the soft curls between her legs. She was already damp and ready for him, soft pulses racing through her at his touch.

When his fingers met her slippery flesh, he groaned, exciting her further. She felt him against her bottom, hard and hot, and she wanted him inside her. His fingers played devilishly, teasing her small peak until it throbbed, but she fought her release. She moved so that he pressed against her, and his arms went taut with his own restraint. She turned her head so that she could kiss him—he responded with even more vigor than she'd hoped.

They kissed, tongues engaged in a sweet, sensual dance, and she felt his engorged length sliding between her thighs. She curled her leg back and over his, giving him access to her, but he didn't enter her. Instead, he slid himself along her sensitized flesh until she thought she would go mad with wanting. He moved faster, the tip of him rubbing over her small peak again and again, until she could no longer hold off the sweet waves of ecstasy sweeping through her. She reached back and clutched his hair in one hand and he kissed her with primal male hunger. She bit back a cry of pleasure as he slipped just his tip inside her, filling her entrance as her body reached its climax. He groaned, then pulled away. She felt the sudden heat of him spilling against her thigh, a warm pulse of his own rapture.

Sated, they lay together, his arm over her waist, her leg over his. She felt his breath in her hair and the wild demand of his heartbeat against her back. She rolled over and snuggled in his arms, her face resting on his chest. He played with her hair, but he still seemed distracted despite the pleasure of their lovemaking.

Evelyn propped herself up to study his face. "Rafael? Have I done something wrong? Besides mishandling your bola, I mean."

He smiled, but he didn't answer at once. Her heart beat in small jerks—she was almost afraid to hear what he would say. He looked into her eyes and touched her cheek. "You've done nothing wrong, Evie." He paused, and his smile grew. "Except mishandling my weapon."

Clearly, he wasn't eager to divulge his innermost doubts, but Evelyn didn't want a distance put up between them, not now. "Are you angry with me?"

His hand cupped her cheek. "Never, Evie. Never." He seemed to sense her misgivings, because he drew her back into his arms and held her close. But she couldn't help wondering if he had broken eye contact to keep close his own secret doubts.

"Please, tell me what's bothering you. I know there's something."

He sighed, torn from deep in his chest. "I don't know what will happen when we return to Santa Fe. I don't know what I'm up against."

"What *we're* up against. Rafael, you are not alone. I'll be with you. We all will. We'll scout out the situation before riding in. Lieutenant Talbot doesn't know which way you're coming from—there must be countless secret paths to the pueblo."

"Yes . . ." He answered slowly, and Evelyn felt better. He was listening to her at least. "Patukala says we should go to my grandfather in Tesuque first."

"That sounds good." And it would put off the final encounter with Talbot for a few more days. "What good can he be to us?"

"If he can overcome his dislike of me, much. He knows a great deal of the pueblo area, and more legends than anyone. He might have some idea why my brother and the others were taken—and what Talbot wants with the pueblo."

"That sounds promising." Evelyn fell silent for a while, then adjusted her position in his arms. "Is there something about me that is troubling you? I can't help thinking there is."

He huffed and nodded, and her heart crashed. "My lack of restraint where you are concerned, yes. I should be protecting you. Instead, I can't keep away."

"I don't want you to keep away!"

"I know, love. But the matter of a pregnancy concerns me. I was careful—somewhat—tonight. But how many nights can I resist you?"

Evelyn frowned. "I see no reason that you should. I know you are worried that I will have a baby. That would not displease me."

"And if my return to Santa Fe ends in death?"

"It will not." She paused. "Did you worry this much when bedding other women?"

He hesitated. "Perhaps not."

"What of your fiancée?" Before the words were out, she longed to retract them. She hoped he wouldn't answer.

"I suppose it was her desire to bed me that kept her in Santa Fe so long."

Evelyn cringed. She promised herself she would never ask such a question again, but it was too late to retract it. "Well, then . . . never mind."

He glanced down at her as if surprised by her taut reaction. "You did ask."

"And I'm sorry I did."

Of course, he had no qualms about bedding

his former lover—he had intended to marry her. He seemed more hesitant about Evelyn. Her eyes filled with tears. Often, before her monthly cycle renewed itself, she had found herself weepy and unexpectedly sorrowful. She reminded herself this was no different. Rafael eyed her suspiciously as if contemplating the strangeness of women.

"You don't understand, Evie, because you're innocent."

"I was married for several years."

"To a man who had no interest in women. Evie, I have not misused a woman in my life, nor taken a woman without accepting what might come of our union. Don't you understand?"

No. Evelyn bit her lip hard. He had loved other women and accepted that a child might come of that love. But with her, the thought terrified him. Infatuation was strong, but fleeting, and it left no trace when it was gone. What if it had been only infatuation he felt for her? And she had given him all her heart. Evelyn's breath came tight. To her, every moment with him was precious, but for him she might be just an amusement. A temporary amusement.

He touched her chin but she refused to look at him. He kissed her cheek, then her nose, softening her mood. "Evie, look at me."

"I'm thinking. Not just now."

He kissed her mouth. "Please?"

She sniffed, then forced herself to meet his eyes. "Yes?" She tried to sound casual, to conceal her hurt, but he saw through every veil she put up.

"You are dear to me, Evelyn. More dear than anything. Do you think I want to leave you with a child when there's a chance I must ride into a situation where the only victory is death?"

Her eyes filled with tears. "That won't happen." She should have known he was thinking this way. Her own fear and doubt again clouded her intuition. She put her arms around his neck and hugged him. "I'm sorry, Rafael. I was jealous to think you have loved others so well, and not thinking of you at all. But I won't let anything happen to you, I promise."

"All that matters to me is that you stay safe." He spoke as if to prevent her from risking herself on his behalf, so Evelyn didn't correct him. But she had every intention of protecting him, any way she could. He accepted her silence as acquiescence, then kissed her nose again. "As for loving another so well . . . I have never felt anything, in my body or in my heart, that comes close to what I feel with you."

With his words, Evelyn's fear of their future and his intention faded. She yawned and closed her eyes, content. "That is what I feel for you, too. I know we have dangers to face, my love. I know we can't run or avoid them. But if you love me half as much as I love you, nothing will stand in our way."

Chapter Twelve

Love was making him crazy. As they rode through the hills from Taos, Rafael wondered whatever possessed him to give Evelyn control of his bola. She practiced relentlessly, with increasingly devastating results. Her aim had improved, but her control of the stone pouches remained faulty, and dangerous. She had managed to entangle his hair twice, painfully, tripped Patukala, and snatched Sally's canteen from her hands. That would have been impressive, except Evelyn had been aiming at something entirely different.

She had blisters on her hands from working the whip, but she kept at it, revealing a determination that surprised him. He knew now what it meant to be madly in love, when his thoughts were filled with her, when he couldn't keep his attention anywhere else, when his heart warmed with affection even as she politely disentangled his hair from the whip.

She had a wild, fierce look in her eyes as she swung the bola, and she had finally become successful enough to try it from her horse's back. Rafael rode behind her, watching as she rose in the saddle to swing at a juniper bush. She chuckled to herself when she broke off a small limb.

I love you so.

He imagined presenting her to Diego, and telling his brother how he'd found love with the woman who'd tried to shoot him. Diego had admired Evelyn for her beauty and kindness, though he had once commented that Westley was "weedy," and wondered why she hadn't picked a more capable husband. Diego had always felt Rafael was too serious to fall in love, so he would be surprised by this turn of events. He hadn't liked Rafael's former lover because he considered her vain and shallow, but he would approve of Evelyn.

If only he was bringing her home to his brother and their home, and not to a battle! Worse still, he had to bring her to his grandfather's pueblo first—to a man who bore nothing but resentment for Rafael, and harbored even worse suspicions about anyone not Zuni. The old man was rude and cantankerous, but if he injured Evelyn's feelings, even in the slightest, he would soon learn that his grandson had a darker side, too.

They stopped to rest and let the horses drink, but Evelyn sat fingering the bola as if studying it. She glanced up at Rafael, her brow knit. "How is this made?"

"The pouches are stone encased in leather, and the rope is made from the skin of a large cat . . ."

She flung the bola aside, horrified. "A *cat?*"

She was picturing a soft, fluffy kitten. Rafael smiled. "A wild cat."

She grimaced. "Well, that won't do at all." She looked around. "I'll have to use something else. Can I get leather, normal cow leather, at your grandfather's pueblo?"

"I suppose so. Why do you want it?"

She looked proud and his heart ached with love. "I want to craft my own weapon."

"Then I suggest you make it lighter than mine. And shorter." That should prevent any number of disasters.

"Not shorter, Rafael. I like this length. Perhaps you noticed that I knocked some kind of green nut from that tree we passed a while ago?"

"I noticed that you came dangerously close to a wasps' nest."

She shuddered. "That would have been a mistake."

"Yes."

"Will we reach your grandfather's pueblo soon?" She was changing the subject. Rafael smiled, loving her.

"In a few days. But from now on, we'll be riding at night. The moon is almost full again, so we'll have enough light. I don't want Talbot alerted to our arrival."

Evelyn yawned. "Does that mean we'll be stopping soon?"

"Patukala has gone on ahead to find us a secure hiding spot, and then, yes, we will stop, then ride on at nightfall."

She looked a little disappointed, but resigned. "If we're sleeping during the day, then you and I can't . . ." She glanced at him, embarrassed. "I suppose it's for the best."

"Why?" Now that she agreed with him about the need to be careful, he found himself unexpectedly hurt. "We could always go for . . . walks."

She eyed him wistfully, then sighed. "No, I don't think so."

This wasn't the reaction he hoped for. "Have I done something wrong?" Maybe he'd overdone teasing her about her efforts with the bola. He'd never felt insecure before—even when his grandfather rejected him, he'd understood that it had more to do with the old man's nature than anything about Rafael himself. He'd never doubted his physical attractiveness, either, nor cared much if women noticed him or considered him handsome.

But with Evelyn, he found himself pulling off his spectacles, combing his hair with special care, and shaving whenever he got a chance. After their journey, a razor shared between two men had worn itself dull. And despite an almost total lack of beard, Chen felt the need to borrow it from Patukala daily.

Rafael ran his hand over his jaw and detected a decided stubble. Evelyn just stared at him, amazed. "Rafael . . . You feel the same way I do, don't you?"

"In what way?"

A slow, feminine smile grew on her little face. "You asked if you'd done something wrong. I keep wondering if I've done something wrong, too." She leaned closer to him and put her hand on his thigh. "It's because you are so perfect to me that I can't imagine myself good enough to deserve your love."

He nodded. She'd spoken his own heart aloud. "That is how I feel about you."

They looked at each other and the sweet warmth of tenderness filled the space between them. She squeezed his leg, then kissed his cheek. "You've done nothing wrong. It's just that I . . ." She paused and looked uncomfortable. "This morning, I discovered that I've entered the throes of my womanly way."

He remained blank for a few moments, then understood. "Ah. Well, I guess that settles the matter of your pregnancy."

She sighed. "I suppose it does. I can't help feeling a little disappointed somehow. I know, of course, this would be a very bad time, but I have always wanted a baby so much."

He took her hand and kissed it. "We have time, Evie." As he spoke, his mood altered. Did they? If he died, she would be left alone again, with no husband, no child. He knew what he wanted, but he couldn't think of a way to do it.

Evelyn's brow puckered and she placed her hand on her stomach. "I feel somewhat empty—yet utterly miserable, fat and swollen and achy at the same time. It is a shame women are cursed thus, especially since I cannot . . . be with you for a few days."

Rafael smiled. "To my people, this is a time to honor womanhood."

She eyed him doubtfully. "Perhaps they don't get so swollen and miserable."

He remembered his mother stomping around their home, grumbling and flinging pots, her good nature brought to a quick halt on a monthly basis. "I think they do. But there is no reason to deny yourself the passion between us, Evie."

She made a face. "I don't think . . ." She paused as if envisioning the exact details of his suggestion and shuddered. "I don't think you'd like that very much."

"Even at your most 'grumpy and miserable,' I find you beguiling and beautiful, and I find myself wanting you so much that I can't make a fist." Her brow angled and he laughed. "After a few days, you'll feel better, and then . . ."

She pondered this, then nodded. "It is only a few days, at its worst."

Good. Evelyn wasn't stubborn, and she was willing to consider alternatives. It boded well for their future. If they had a future at all. He had no choice—they had to make the most of the time they had, and leave the future to the greater forces that guided it. "It will be four or five days before we reach my grandfather's pueblo. We'll spend at least a day there to assess the best course to take next."

She beamed with happiness. "I am looking forward to it very much. I want to meet your grandfather especially. Will says he looks like you."

"He does, I suppose. Far more aged."

"He must be very handsome."

Rafael hesitated. "He's not a particularly agreeable man, Evie. He doesn't favor contact with . . . outsiders."

"You mean, he's not likely to approve of me, being a white woman."

"It has nothing to do with you. The people of Tesuque have resisted the influence of the Spanish, the Anglos—even other tribes who would change their ways. During Pueblo Revolt two hundred years ago, it was the Tesuque who carried messages of the uprising to the other tribes, and it was they who suffered the first losses in battle. The revolt was put down, but they have never forgotten."

"It sounds very exciting, and when your grandfather sees that I love you and respect his culture, he will accept me."

This was as unlikely as his grandfather growing wings and flying to the stars, but Rafael didn't argue. "His acceptance isn't important."

She tilted her head to the side, looking thoughtful. "I think he means more to you than you admit."

Her intuition never failed to surprise him. "I've wanted him to like me all my life. But I've learned that earning his favor is a waste of time—it is a gift he isn't likely to grant."

"Then how can you be sure he'll help you at all?"

"As it happens, he's fond of Diego. He'll want to find out what happened to my people almost as much as I do. We can work together, however reluctantly, but I doubt much friendship will be formed in the process."

"I wish that people would look beyond their differences and see the places where they're the same."

He leaned over and kissed her head. "That was my father's wish, and later, my own, and why I started my school. When the differences are shoved aside, much is lost, but when they're held up as obstacles, even more fails that might have been glorious. I want my students to be proud of their ancestry, whatever it is, but I also want them to understand the history of others, and to understand both the good and the bad of all."

"You've been less generous with the Civil War, I think."

"I can think of nothing good in that."

"My father would disagree."

Rafael didn't respond, but felt thankful that her father remained far away in Boston. Something about a Civil War officer frightened him. How cold they must have been, to send thousands of men into death, to march into death themselves! No, he would be happy if Robert Talmadge stayed far from Santa Fe, and left his beautiful daughter in the safer world of the desert.

They rode for four more nights, then made camp in the hills not far from the Tesuque Pueblo. Rafael had decided to wait until dawn to enter his grandfather's pueblo, giving Patukala a chance to alert them to his arrival. He had no fear of betrayal—but he wanted to be sure no outsiders had ensconced themselves, men who might be there as lookouts for Talbot.

Rather than nervousness, Evelyn felt bored. Her monthly cycle had waned, but there had been no private time for her to explore Rafael's suggestion. She had been surprised at her disappointment upon learning she bore no child. She had wanted children during her marriage. Though she and Westley had been married for several years, their encounters had been few and far between, and never resulted in pregnancy. Since her passion with Rafael, she had realized that Westley rarely attained the climactic moment, which explained their barren marriage.

She wanted to write to her parents, and reassure her father of her safety. By now, they must have heard about her supposed abduction and be sick with fear. She hadn't given it much thought until now, because her attention had been fixed on Rafael, but she was beginning to think of their life beyond. It might not sit well with Robert that his daughter was swept away by a renegade.

Robert was a tolerant, honorable man, but Evelyn remembered when she left home to join Westley in Santa Fe that he had warned her repeatedly to "watch out for Indian attacks." Since meeting native people, Evelyn had decided her father had a blind spot, harboring unnecessary fear of a culture so different from his own—but she would introduce the idea of Rafael slowly, preferably when the deed was already done.

Evelyn lay dozing on her back, studying the bright stars forming shapes in the sky. Rafael had gone out to meet Patukala, and the others were sleeping. She drifted in and out of sleep, then woke briefly when Rafael returned to lie beside her.

She moved closer to him, sleepy. "Did Patukala speak with your grandfather?"

Rafael gathered her into his arms and kissed her temple. "He did, and we will be admitted tomorrow morning." He fell silent, but Evelyn guessed more had occurred.

"There's something you're not telling me."

"Nothing serious."

"About me?"

"Apparently, my grandfather had heard that I abducted you."

"Oh, dear. Was he angry?"

"Not at all. According to Patukala, he was quite proud."

Evelyn frowned. "Do you mean he was pleased you captured me? I hope Patukala set him straight." Rafael hesitated, and she squirmed around to look at him. "Well?"

"My uncle considered it wisest for me to explain the nature of your abduction, and the nuances of our relationship."

"Meaning, he didn't know how to explain it himself."

"Exactly."

"He is afraid your grandfather won't accept me, isn't he?"

"He has experience with my grandfather's stubborn prejudices. Patukala has waited for acceptance for his own lover for several years now."

"Sally?"

"Yes . . . She told you?"

"She did, by way of warning me to stay away from you, for your own good." Evelyn chewed her lip. "I didn't take her advice, though I did appreciate it."

"I'm glad you listened to your own heart instead. I would rather die having loved you than as a lonely man who lived on only dreams."

Evelyn kissed his face and wrapped her arm over his chest, but his words troubled her. He truly believed he was facing death—and it was because he wouldn't back down until he'd freed his people and restored justice to his pueblo.

She remembered the shock and pain of losing Westley, but it had been so sudden and so unexpected. If anything happened to Rafael, there would be no reason to live. She drifted to sleep beside him, and the force of her will took shape. She hadn't known Westley was in danger, so she couldn't protect him. She knew what Rafael faced, and she would be there beside him. His courage placed him in peril, and had many times before.

As sleep claimed her, she knew: It wasn't his courage, but her own, that would be the deciding factor in the battle to come.

They rode into the Tesuque Pueblo at dawn. The cool sun warmed the adobe walls, and Evelyn sighed in appreciation. "It's so beautiful."

Though the sun had barely risen, women were already at work making pottery and preparing meals. Men had already begun farming, tending beans and corn in the morning air. Patukala rode in ahead, and the people greeted him warmly.

Evelyn felt nervous—this was as close to meeting Rafael's parents as she would ever come. Despite his disavowals, she knew he admired his grandfather, and she wanted desperately to win the old man's approval.

The people took note of Rafael and greeted him with even more enthusiasm than they had with Patukala. She had forgotten how beloved he was—these people knew him as both schoolmaster and Renegade, and they admired him for all the things she had once denied.

Sally and Will stayed back and went unnoticed, but Chen dismounted and stood imperiously beside Rafael. Evelyn hesitated, then dismounted, but she wasn't sure what to do so she stood beside her horse. The people noticed her, but said nothing, and she got the impression their looks weren't friendly.

Young women emerged from different areas of the pueblo, clearly to see Rafael. Evelyn glared, but no one paid any attention to her reaction. He looked so tall standing there, taller than anyone else, and stronger. No wonder they wanted to see him—he was beautiful.

As the people greeted him, two old women came out of the pueblo walking on either side of an older man. Evelyn watched as he approached. He wasn't nearly as tall as Rafael, but there was a decided similarity in the facial features. The old man's hair was flecked with gray, but it was just as shiny as Rafael's. More than that, there was something akin in their posture, straight and proud, as if no grandeur in life could compare to the nobility of their souls.

Evelyn eased forward to stand behind Rafael. "Is that him?"

Rafael nodded, but said nothing.

The chief came to Rafael and looked him up and down. He didn't look pleased. He spoke to Rafael in the Tewa language, and it sounded disparaging.

Evelyn tugged at Rafael's shirt. "What did he say?"

Rafael sighed. "He says that I went away and left my brother and my people in danger."

"Well, it wasn't your fault! You were taken prisoner yourself."

The old man spoke again, and again, Evelyn didn't like his tone at all.

"He says I have endangered everyone by my foolishness, and that I should have returned faster."

"How much faster could we have gone?" Evelyn huffed. "What a grumpy old demon!"

The old man's bright gaze snapped to her, and he spoke again.

She waited, but Rafael didn't translate. She looked between them. "What did he say?"

Rafael shrugged, hesitating. "He mentions that if I had . . . taken other measures with my captive, our journey might have been swifter."

"What 'other measures'?"

The old man leaned around Rafael. "If my grandson had staked you out, young woman, and left you for the crows, his brother might be freed already."

Evelyn gaped. The chief spoke perfect English, and had understood every word she'd said. Rafael glanced heavenward and sighed. *Perfect.* She wanted to endear herself, and instead referred to the chief as a "demon" at the first meeting. She forced a weak smile. "Sorry, sir. But I don't think you understand. We were already in Colorado before Rafael escaped. It was a long journey."

The chief looked her up and down, and his expression darkened. "What is this?"

Evelyn turned to Rafael, aghast. "Does he mean *me?*"

Rafael took her hand, but he looked pained. "Grandfather, this is Evelyn Reid, the widow of Westley Reid."

The chief glared at their clasped hands. "This woman will do no good for you. The last, at least her family had power with the Mexicans."

"Is he referring to your former fiancée?"

"Yes, and for the last time, she wasn't my fiancée."

"He liked her?" Evelyn felt hurt, though she didn't feel favorable to Rafael's grandfather at all.

"Not at the time."

The old man frowned, deeply. "My grandson has no sense with women. He picks them for frivolous reasons, for their manner, which tends to be extreme . . ." He paused and assessed Evelyn without affection. She wondered if he referred to her or to Rafael's former love. "For reasons so foolish as how pleasing they are to the eye."

Evelyn braced, but the old chief turned to Rafael, ignoring her. "A woman should be chosen for the strength of her bone, for a steady, staunch manner. You pick women who are . . ."

Rafael finished for him. "Interesting." He paused. "Like my father."

The old man glowered. Clearly, Rafael would have done better to watch his words. "Your father took my daughter, thoroughly against her will, and turned her from the steadiest, most reliable of my daughters into . . ."

"A beloved wife."

"He wormed his way into her heart and confused her."

"She adored him."

The old chief thumped his fist into his other hand. "That is the problem!"

Evelyn's brow knit. "They raised very good sons."

The chief sneered. "One good son, one renegade schoolmaster who thinks nothing of his people."

Evelyn gestured at the surrounding Zuni. There was no chance of endearing herself now, so she felt free to argue on Rafael's behalf. "It looks like they disagree with you."

"Riding against injustice is one thing—and it is meaningless when your brother is taken and fed to the wolves."

Rafael's expression hardened. "Diego is alive, and I will free him. We have reason to believe he was taken more or less by chance, with others of my pueblo, perhaps to perform some task for our enemies."

The old man looked askance. "What task?"

"That, I hoped you might know."

The chief considered this, then nodded. "We will discuss this matter at the evening meal." He said no more, and returned to his dwelling without looking back.

Evelyn placed her hand on Rafael's shoulder. "You were certainly right about him. I had no idea."

Rafael sighed. "He is a great man. He has kept outsiders from this pueblo and preserved its inherent culture. For that, I admire him, because without such dedication, my people will be lost and dissolved into those that storm across this land."

She shook her head. "There's no storm big enough to dislodge *him*. But why didn't he answer you? He was certainly quick to place blame, but not to give answers."

Patukala came up beside them, speaking in English for the first time in Evelyn's hearing. "My father has no answer, but now the question has been asked, and he will not let it go by. By evening, he will give us something that we need to move forward."

Like the chief, Patukala's English was flawless. Fortunately, she hadn't insulted him, thinking he couldn't understand, but still, Evelyn felt foolish. Rafael still held her hand, comforting her. "I'm sorry he was so abrupt with you, Evie. He doesn't see past the color of your skin to the woman beneath."

Evelyn kissed his shoulder softly, but she said nothing. Who was the "woman beneath"? In different words, in a different way, the chief had pointed out succinctly how inadequate she was as the Renegade's mate. So far, she had been more of a burden than a help, and even though she was taken captive against her will, she had chosen to ride with them after escaping Talbot.

"I suppose you and Patukala have plans to make."

Rafael glanced down at her, probably wondering at her wistful tone. "It would be wise, but I don't want to leave you alone here."

She gestured at Chen. "I won't be alone. Maybe I can make myself useful in some way."

Evelyn spotted a group of women working with baskets and pottery. An idea formed, but she decided to keep it to herself lest it not yield the results she hoped. "Maybe I can even impress that grandfather of yours."

As she headed toward the women, she heard Rafael sigh and whisper, "Oh, no."

"This is what I know of Tewa. It is now and always has been a small and insignificant offshoot of Pojoaque Pueblo—formed a thousand years ago as a result of a quarrel between two chiefs, who were also brothers. During the Pueblo Revolt of 1680, Pojoaque was ravaged and its people scattered."

Rafael sat quietly as his grandfather recited a history he already knew.

"Pojoaque was restored later, but Tewa remained uninhabited until my father decided to rebuild its ruins.

"He rebuilt them fancifully, befitting his peculiar nature, but at least he built them on the foundations of the old. What you may not know, however, despite your vast learning, is that after the Revolt failed, Tewa was taken by Spaniards."

Rafael's brow rose. "I am aware that Tewa was inhabited by the Spaniards for a brief while."

His grandfather scowled. "It was no 'brief while.' They remained there for several years, and it was the Spaniards themselves who destroyed the walls and buried the kivas when the Anglos took over. They battled with surprising energy to hold off the Anglos, but were outnumbered and succumbed."

"So they were slaughtered? None escaped?"

"No, though rumors of their pueblo continued to draw Mexicans for some time. I have never known why they cared. It was an insignificant pueblo in the first place."

"Apparently, not to the Spaniards." Rafael considered his pueblo's history for a moment, then turned to Patukala. "I would guess the Spaniards buried something in or near the pueblo—hence, their desperate defense when leaving would have spared them their lives."

Patukala nodded. "It would have been wiser to flee. The only thing they risk themselves for is gold."

The chief snorted and waved his hand in a wide gesture. "Ever have the Europeans been driven by greed, above the cost of their own lives and above all that is good."

"That can be said of all races of men, Grandfather." Rafael remembered arguing the opposite viewpoint with Evelyn, but fortunately she wasn't there to hear him speak her opinion as his own. "Nonetheless, it seems Lieutenant Talbot knows what is hidden, and where. But why take our people? To prevent them from finding this supposed treasure themselves?"

"White men have viewed us as slaves, not threats."

"That may be true, but how could Talbot have learned what we didn't know ourselves?"

The chief frowned, but then his brow arched. "The Anglos would have taken any papers or maps the Spaniards had left behind."

"Whatever papers the government has led them to believe Westley Reid was the rightful owner of the pueblo. It was his ancestor who drove out the Spaniards. Before he came West, Westley studied the history of our land—at Harvard University, attended at the same time by Lieutenant Talbot."

Patukala nodded. "Then it makes sense these men knew something of what the Spaniards had left behind."

"Westley knew nothing of it. He may have overlooked evidence, or considered it myth—but Talbot took it seriously."

"Whatever it is, the Anglos want it, badly." Patukala went to the open door of the pueblo and looked out. He started to speak again, but something caught his eye and his brow furrowed.

Rafael rose and joined him. "What is it?"

Patukala pointed down into the pueblo plaza. "Your woman."

He was almost afraid to look. Rafael drew a breath and saw Evelyn poised in the plaza center, with Chen, Will, and Sally lined up opposite her. The Zuni were lined up watching as if a ritual dance had begun unexpectedly.

Chen, Will, and Sally were each armed with what appeared to be . . . bolas. Evelyn faced them, wielding her own weapon with dramatic flair, and she appeared to be instructing them.

Patukala glanced at him, and his brow angled. "When this one is the teacher . . ."

Rafael bounded down the narrow steps and went to her. She turned to him, beaming with unrestrained pride. "Here! I won't be needing this anymore." She passed him his bola, then held up a smaller version of her own. "This is mine! I made it myself."

Rafael took her small bola and examined it. It was made surprisingly well, though the cord was made of some kind of plant stalk and not leather. At the end, she had affixed leather pouches filled with stone.

"Good, isn't it?"

He gave it back to her and nodded, too moved to say all that he wanted to say. "It is impressive." He paused. "Why did you do it?"

"To be useful, of course. I made one for each of us. It's not hard, once you get the knack of it."

Sally snapped hers with surprising skill, and Chen fingered his as if hunting might be deemed beneath him. "If you made enough of these, we should be able to sell them in shops down in Santa Fe. We'll make them souvenirs of the Renegade, and they'll go like crazy. After Señor de Aguirre whips the place back into shape, of course."

Will flung his bola unexpectedly, and they all ducked. Evelyn offered a reassuring smile, but Sally seized the weapon and gave it back to Evelyn. "My boy doesn't need a whip. He's got enough to handle with the horses."

Will appeared decidedly relieved, but Evelyn sighed, then fixed the second bola to her dress. "I suppose I could use a backup, in case mine breaks." She paused. "Of course, I still have my revolver, but it only has a few shots left."

"I'd forgotten about that." Rafael couldn't help smiling. She looked so sure of herself. Never, not for a moment in his life to come, would he ever be bored with Evelyn at his side. She was now, and always would be, a source of endless fascination.

As his grandfather stood glowering beside them, he knew the time had come to seal their fate as one.

Chapter Thirteen

"In what way did your grandfather consider your . . . the woman who wasn't quite your fiancée . . . extreme?" Evelyn seated herself on a floor mattress, cross-legged, as Rafael changed his shirt for the evening meal. Her breath caught as he tore off his old shirt, baring his broad chest. No matter how testy she might be, the sight of him never failed to stir her senses.

He glanced over his shoulder at her and grinned. "This matter doesn't sit well with you, does it?"

She felt embarrassed and small. "I am simply curious."

He tried one of the shirts his grandfather had sent to him, and found it too small, so he discarded it in favor of an open leather vest. Apparently, he noticed her wide eyes, because he tugged at the opening. "It's a hot night. But maybe you think I show too much skin?"

She fought a foolish smile. "Not enough."

His dark eyes twinkled. "You are feeling . . . better, I presume?"

A warm glow began inside her. "Completely."

"We will retire early tonight."

For a reason she didn't understand, butterflies seemed to be spinning inside her stomach. She shouldn't be nervous, not now, but she saw a new promise in his eyes. "You haven't answered my question."

"Ah. Yes. Well, I suppose my grandfather referred to her nature, which was strong-willed in pursuit of the life she wanted."

"I see. She was ambitious."

"That is a good description, yes. Her choice of clothing was also unusual in Santa Fe. She had gowns designed in Spain and shipped to her here."

"She was fashionable."

"Yes."

"I suppose she was beautiful." Evelyn's lips twisted to one side.

"She was extremely fat and her skin affected with a grotesque pox. And her breasts sagged to her waist."

Evelyn fought a smile. "She was beautiful."

Rafael knelt before her and touched her chin. "My eyes can never find more beauty than I see in you." He ran his finger over her cheek. "There are many beautiful women, you know, and each has her own appeal. In some, it is obvious, catching a man's eye from afar. My . . . not-fiancée was one such. Her clothes, her dress, her coloring—those things commanded attention. But I find that, when I look at you, there is always something more than just the sweet perfection of your little face. Your expressions are dear to me, the way your mouth moves when you speak, or how your eyes shine when you're planning something. How you look away from me when you're shy. I look at you, and I can imagine you on some Scottish moor, your hair flying in the wind, those mystical eyes filled with some dream . . ."

"Did she dance very well?"

"She did. But she wasn't so . . . sensitive and sweet as you, in those private dances that matter more."

He meant in bed, but had the good sense to pose it delicately. Evelyn ran over his words and liked them. She nodded. "I'm not a very good dancer. Westley tried to teach me, but I stepped on his toes and tripped rather too often."

He smiled. "I'm not a very good dancer, either."

"But you love so beautifully—in those private dances that matter more." She touched his face and ran the tips of her fingers along his high-cut cheekbone. "You are so beautiful, you know."

He took her hand and pressed his lips against her palm. Her senses stirred with increasing fire. "I am a mixed-blood Indian, Evie. Your husband was as close to British aristocracy as an American can get."

It was true. Westley's grandfather had held a title in northern England, a source of great pride still to his family. "Is that important to you?"

"No, but I would think it matters to your family."

"You misjudge my parents, then. They liked Westley because he was such a gentle, fair person, not because of his lineage."

"Would they have liked him so well if he were Indian?" Evelyn hesitated, remembering Robert's fear of Rafael's race, enough delay for Rafael to understand and nod. "I thought not."

"My father will like you once he gets to know you."

"With him in the East and us here, that doesn't seem likely. I can't say I'm sorry."

"I had to meet your grandfather. How much worse can it be?"

"My grandfather can be troublesome, but he has little power beyond this pueblo. Something tells me your father has a far greater influence."

"He is respected, that's true, because he made such a good account of himself during the war."

Rafael groaned and stood up, bringing her with him. "As I said, I'm lucky he's on the other side of the country and not here."

Evelyn wore her new Spanish gown, but she couldn't help feeling that Rafael's former love had more intriguing dresses. Still, his eyes brightened when she adjusted the neckline lower to enhance her breasts. He held out his hand and she took it.

"Shall we dine, love? I'll be sure to seat us as far from my grandfather as possible."

"Good. I don't relish having him watch me eat, with that critical, grumpy look on his face. He's handsome, but rarely have I met someone who can make me feel so small. Is he always this mean?"

He led her through the door, and they walked out into the plaza. "With Diego, he is gentle and kind. In my brother's company, he laughs more than he talks."

"I can't imagine that man laughing." She paused. "Why is he so fond of your brother?"

"Because Diego is so much like my father."

Evelyn stopped and looked up at him. "I thought he hated your father?"

"His logic eludes me, and of course, he wouldn't admit it. But it's true. My father was an endearing, charming man, as is my brother. As much as my grandfather complained, I believe he was devastated when my father died. He enjoyed their fights, and my father's mad scheme. I suppose he enjoyed the way my father glorified the Zuni in poetry. My grandfather was often the inspiration for his more dramatic verse."

"And he's mad at you for teaching non-Indian children? I don't understand at all."

"If it wasn't that, it would be something else. He sees himself in me, and all his vulnerabilities and pride are reflected when he looks at me."

"Then he should be proud!"

Rafael sighed. "I hope, one day, to make him so."

She squeezed his hand tight. "You will."

The old chief wasn't the only one who resented Evelyn's place at Rafael's side. Women passed bowls of beans and rice over her and around her, never offering her anything. If she spoke to someone, they ignored her. She asked Sally what she had done to offend them, but Sally just shook her head.

"They think you've seduced and misled their beloved son. No matter what the chief says, they look up to Rafael. See where the chief has seated him. At his left hand, Patukala on the right. He grumbles, but his pride is stored in those two men."

"Rafael promised we would sit far from him."

"The old man wouldn't stand for that. You behave yourself, and try not to argue, and maybe he'll forget you're here."

"I suppose that's the best I can hope for."

"Girl!" The chief spoke harshly, directed at Evelyn, and Sally slipped unobtrusively away. "What are you doing sitting at my grandson's side? You aren't his wife—you're his mistress, and a poor one at that. Get yourself up and serve his meal as you're supposed to do."

Evelyn bit her lip and hopped up, embarrassed. Rafael started to rise, but she shook her head, fighting tears. "It's all right." Before he could stop her, she darted away, seized a bowl from an older woman, and brought it to Rafael as she had seen other women do.

He looked up at her and she saw pain in his eyes. "You don't have to do this."

She glanced at his grandfather. "I do. He is right. I am your mistress, and I will do as I'm told—while I'm here."

She spooned out portions of stew and sloshed it into his bowl. Tears stung her eyes. His grandfather had found the painful spot she'd been trying to hide, even from herself. She was Rafael's mistress, something temporary in his life. Fate had thrown them together, but all her fears and all her doubts came to bitter life as she stood behind him, her gaze fixed on the man who had made it all too clear.

The chief looked at her, victorious. She felt the satisfied expressions of women who resented her, of men who felt she had somehow humbled their favorite son. Even the children playing outside the eating circle seemed to ignore her. Chen looked embarrassed, and Patukala kept his dark gaze on his own bowl. Only Sally met her eyes, and for the first time, she saw true sympathy. She understood why—she had dared to take Rafael's side, even if she hadn't known what kind of error it was, and she faced the perceived shame, while Sally denied her own heart.

Those beautiful dark eyes glimmered with unshed tears, and Sally rose slowly, setting her own bowl aside. Evelyn watched in astonishment as the small, proud woman went to stand behind Patukala. Will shrugged, then seized his mother's bowl and sloshed her stew into his. Will's innocent act broke the strain and Evelyn smiled. She tapped Rafael's shoulder. "If you don't eat now, I will take your leftovers, and you'll get nothing."

He didn't look at her. He just passed her his bowl and kept his vision fixed on the ground.

Evelyn shifted her weight from foot to foot. "I was joking."

He shook his head, and still said nothing.

The chief ignored the tension between his guests. "My scouts have learned that Talbot has reached Santa Fe, and that guards surround my grandson's pueblo. Since your departure, more people have disappeared, and none have been seen again."

"Talbot will soon learn I have returned." Rafael's voice sounded thick with emotion, and Evelyn laid her hand gently on his shoulder.

"My scouts report that a new Anglo has arrived, and appears to be their leader now."

Rafael's brow furrowed. "Over Talbot? That's odd. I felt sure this was all his idea, and that he enlisted the greediest landowners under his influence. Who is the new leader?"

"No one my scouts recognized, and they know all the officers in New Mexico."

"So he's some kind of army official?"

"He is dressed as an officer." The chief frowned until his forehead seemed etched with displeasure. "Older than Talbot, and more dangerous. Old enough to have fought in their Great War."

Rafael shook his head in disgust. "Perhaps he misses the blood."

Evelyn pinched his shoulders. "You don't know that. He may be a good man. He may not know what Lieutenant Talbot is up to. He probably thinks you're just a renegade. Maybe we can reason with this man."

"I can't risk that. No, I must find our people and free them. I will go tomorrow."

Evelyn gripped his shoulders. "I'm going with you."

The chief cast her a dark look. "You do not speak against my grandson."

"I do when he's an idiot!" She shook her fist

at the old man, fully intending to do him harm. Rafael caught her hand in his and kissed it gently.

He rose and stood before her, still holding her hand. "Before I go, alone, there is a matter I must attend to—or all else I do is for nothing."

Her eyes shifted to the side. What fiendish means would he use to keep her from following him? "You're not going to tie me up or anything, are you?"

"An interesting suggestion . . . but not just now."

"Then what . . . ?" Before she could finish her question, he led her to the center of the plaza, so that they stood inside a circle of his grandfather's people. "Rafael, this is a bit awkward."

He sank down on one knee before her, and kissed her hand, then pressed his cheek against it. When he looked up at her, she saw tears shining in his brown eyes. "Evie, I love you. I have loved you since I first saw you, and every moment since. There has never been another so deep in my heart, nor so much a part of me. You are my soul, my life, my breath. I will do what I have to do, for my people and my brother, but I cannot go forward if I do not have your promise to be with me, forever."

She eyed him doubtfully, then glanced around. "You want me to go with you tomorrow?" How odd, that he should ask her this way, after forbidding her to do just that only seconds ago!

"I want you with me always. In spirit and in your heart."

This clarified little, but Evelyn suspected he

still might refuse to take her with him when he went after Talbot. "I will go with you anywhere. What are you doing on your knees?"

For an instant, he looked shy. He touched his mouth, that strange, shy gesture he used when embarrassed. He adjusted his spectacles as if he was nervous. "Evelyn, I am asking you to be my wife."

Her mouth slid open, closed, then opened again. "You are?"

"Yes."

"You want to marry me?"

"I do. Here, in a Zuni ceremony, if you'll have me."

"Here?" Her eyes misted with tears and she clasped her free hand over her heart. "Here."

"We'll marry in a church later, if you desire it, once I've cleared my name and can enter Santa Fe as a free man. But I would have you now, and know that I am your husband, and that you are truly mine."

Evelyn touched his cheek and then sank down before him, forgetting everyone but him. "Rafael, I have been yours since I met you, in my dreams and in my heart. There is nothing I want more than to be yours in life. I was afraid, because I didn't imagine I could so truly belong to anyone as I did to you. Yes, I will marry you. I would marry you in hell if you asked it."

Rafael glanced at his grandfather. "Not quite so bad as that, love. But we may have a reluctant shaman performing the ceremony."

"Will he do it, do you think?"

Rafael smiled. "Rather than risk me marrying you in my father's church? He will."

* * *

The entire pueblo gathered for Rafael's marriage, despite what Evelyn felt sure was intense disapproval. Rafael's grandfather took the center of the great circle, and Rafael and Evelyn stood facing each other. Women came forward bearing decorative baskets. Evelyn hesitated, then inspected their offerings. Rafael smiled.

"It's corn, a fertility symbol."

Evelyn's brow angled. "Do they think I'm infertile?"

"Maybe they think you're hungry."

He was teasing her, now, at their wedding, and she was so nervous she could barely stand. The chief looked annoyed. "These are willow wedding baskets, young woman. The opening of a ceremonial basket is directed toward the east."

He spoke as if she should know, but Evelyn didn't want to recite a vow she didn't understand. "Why?"

He blew out an impatient breath. "Because the east is sacred, from which no harm is supposed to pass."

Evelyn felt pleased. "The east, from which I came."

The chief offered a dark frown. "The white man came from the east—there is no greater harm."

"Not me."

Rafael cleared his throat and accepted a double-spouted pottery urn from an old woman who smiled warmly at him, then glared at Evelyn. "One spout represents you, one me."

"How romantic!"

"The handle symbolizes our unity, the unity of marriage. We will drink from the spouts together, heralding the consummation of our wedding."

Evelyn beamed. "I like this much more than eastern weddings—I understand it."

"I knew you would."

The chief seemed annoyed by their conversation and began chanting in his language. Evelyn glanced at Rafael. "He doesn't speak with much feeling."

"But the words are sweet."

As the chief spoke, young men banged on drums in an earthy, primal rhythm. The chief's prayer wound on and on, but Evelyn's heart seemed to rise and join with Rafael of its own accord. *You are mine. I am yours. We are one thing, forever*. Marriage was more than a formal union—it was a celebration of what was, and what had always been, and what forever would be.

The chief stopped, sighed, and Evelyn looked up into Rafael's warm, brown eyes. Tears shimmered there as he bent to kiss her. He lifted the double-spouted vessel and held it to her lips, and to his own. They drank together, a sweet nectar she didn't recognize, and their wedding was complete.

"Where did you get a ring?" Evelyn lay beside Rafael, studying the silver band on her finger. She twisted her wrist to examine it in different lighting and he watched her with love filling his heart. *My wife.*

"I bought it in Taos—fortunately, before you

sped off with my money in pursuit of that gown."

Her bright eyes widened. "Before? You meant to marry me even then?"

"I did. Of course. What did you think?"

She looked embarrassed. "That I was an amusement to you, but a temporary amusement."

"You are a source of endless fascination. I would not call it 'amusement.' Although you have given me reason to laugh, it's true."

She struck him playfully, then resumed the admiration of her ring. "It's beautiful. Thank you."

"It was made by the Zuni at Taos Pueblo. They do good work."

Evelyn sat up and took off her necklace. "There is something I want to give you, too, as a wedding present."

"Your locket?"

"My father gave it to me when I was beginning to grow up. I had so many dreams, of love and adventure and a wonderful life. But I was tall and awkward, and because I was so different, so dreamy, I didn't have many friends. Boys ignored me, and I thought nothing I wanted would ever come true."

"Those qualities make you a rare prize, Evie, not odd."

"That is what my father said when he gave me this locket."

Rafael opened it. "There are no pictures inside. A locket is for pictures."

"Not this one. My father told me to store my dearest dreams inside this locket, and hold on to them with all my heart. One day, when my dream came true, I wouldn't need it anymore. I am giving it to you, because all my dreams came to life in you, because you love me."

Rafael kissed the locket and strung it around his neck. "One day, I will give this to our daughter, so that she can treasure her dreams, too."

Evelyn's eyes filled with tears. "I love you so."

She lay back in his arms and he kissed her. "You are my treasure, my sweet love, and the gift to my life."

They lay quietly together for a while, and then Evelyn stirred again. "Do you think your grandfather will forgive you for marrying me?"

"It doesn't matter, Evie. He performed the ceremony, and it's legal. You're mine, and I'm yours, and all that we do will be blessed by the Great Spirit, by God."

"We will have children."

"As many as you want."

"And we will live together and grow old together, and every dream I ever had will come true. Our children will grow up in a house of love, learning from all cultures. We'll travel together, and show them the world."

"We will." Rafael kissed her forehead, but her words triggered sadness inside him. He couldn't promise her forever, not with Talbot's threat looming over them. But if he died, at least she was now his wife. No matter what happened, his grandfather would keep her safe, at least until word could be sent to her family in Boston. Privately, he had sworn his grandfather to this promise, and the old man agreed.

"I think your grandfather has softened on the

matter of Sally and Patukala. I noticed them together, and he was speaking to them. Sally looked pleased. I suppose nothing could be as bad as me."

"My grandfather resents the world you come from, Evie. Not you. In you, he sees men of power that sweep across our land, making laws that break the heart of my people."

"I know that's true, but not of my family. My uncle in Maryland sent his best horses to the Sioux after their rebellion. His wife befriended an escaped slave during the war, and my father was among the staunchest Abolitionists in Boston, even though he was a very young man then. You may not believe it, but they are good people."

Rafael wasn't convinced, but he let the matter slide. His wife lay in his arms, sweetly playing with his hair and running her fingers across his chest. "At least they raised you without strict inhibitions."

"They did. Although the thoughts I once harbored of you surprised even me."

"What thoughts?"

She shifted in his arms and he recognized a potentially shy mood. "Oh, well, those dreams and imaginings I had of you, before I knew who you were."

This subject intrigued him as it had the first time she'd confessed her secret imaginings. "Maybe you'd care to tell me some of these fantasies of yours?"

She buried her head against his shoulder. "I couldn't do that!"

"Why not?"

"Well, they were . . ."

"Erotic? Yes, I remember you said they were somewhat more than romantic in nature."

She nodded, still refusing to look at him. "They weren't the sort of idle dreams a lady is supposed to entertain."

Rafael cleared his throat. "That's why I want to hear them."

She peeked up at him. "Why would you want that?"

So I can make every one of them come true. "So that we can truly know each other better, now that we're married."

She looked suspicious, but she didn't argue. "I don't think I could do that."

He shrugged. "Of course, I have my own fantasies about you. But no doubt, they would offend you."

She perked up immediately and her eyes brightened. "What fantasies?"

He made a face. "You can't expect me to divulge something so private when you keep your own from me."

He watched her from the corner of his eye. Her small face puckered as she debated this. "I suppose I could sum up."

"Good." Rafael rolled over onto his side, propped himself up on one elbow, and waited. "Go ahead."

"Well . . ." She was hesitant, shy. He restrained himself from prodding overmuch. If he encouraged her, gently . . .

"Did I appear as the Renegade in these dreams of yours?"

She nodded, her cheeks pink. "Most of the time."

"And what did I do?"

She smiled, guilty. "Many things."

"Like what?" His voice had deepened and grown husky with anticipation.

"Oh, you would capture me and have your way with me . . . that sort of thing. But there were others."

"Such as?"

"Some of them were more romantic in nature than others." She was hedging, the little demon, telling him the "safe" images that filled her dreams. "Especially those when you were yourself, a schoolmaster."

"It sounds boring. I suppose I was wearing spectacles?"

"At first, yes."

Something about the way she said "at first" piqued his interest. "Tell me that one."

"Usually, it began with you realizing that I am also an adept teacher."

"I have already realized that. What has this to do with lovemaking?"

She frowned reproachfully. "With *romance*." She paused and cleared her throat as if for a speech. "You invited me to teach with you and we became close. Sometimes, we would be alone together, making plans or readying papers, and you would kiss me . . ."

He repressed a yawn. "Is that all?"

"No. . . . Once, we took children on an expedition, and something awful happened."

"Tigers?"

"I don't remember what—something awful.

We saved the children. Actually, I did. You were most impressed by my courage and skill."

Did she have to be so dear, always, that his heart ached at her innocence and charm? "I am always impressed by your courage and skill, Evie. You are a wonderful woman, and I am proud that you are my wife."

She looked pleased, but a little doubtful. "I haven't proven myself yet. But I will."

He didn't like the sound of this, so he edged her back to the subject at hand. "Go on. You were saying that you'd performed some heroic deed . . ."

"Yes. You and I were separated from the others, and when left alone to struggle our way back through the jungle . . ."

"What jungle?"

"The jungle in my fantasy. We became lovers. In my fantasies, you see, I wasn't married, so I didn't have to consider the illicit nature of my actions."

"So . . . became lovers. In what way?" He wanted details, and Evelyn was hedging.

"Oftentimes, I had saved you and was healing you, and we just ended up . . . as lovers."

Rafael considered a way to inspire her to divulge more. "That's innocent enough, Evie."

"They weren't exactly innocent. You would sleep close to me, to warm me, and I would kiss you, and touch you, and then we made love."

"What did I do in your Renegade fantasies?"

She was trying to look innocent, which meant these were the ones he should uncover. "Once, I imagined that I came upon you bathing—in a lovely little waterfall."

It sounded cold, but Rafael let her continue. "Go on. I was bathing."

"Yes. And you didn't know I was there—I was hidden in bushes. It didn't really look much like New Mexico . . . more like New England."

He didn't care about the setting of her fantasies. "Then what?"

"You were splashing water on yourself." She paused, meaningfully. "All of yourself."

"Ah."

"It was very clear, in my dream, how little droplets of water would run over your chest. And then you noticed me." She sounded a little breathless. Rafael's breath quickened, too. "When you did, that part of you that I find so especially interesting, changed."

"Yes. Go on."

"Are you all right? You sound hoarse."

"I'm fine. Don't stop."

She nodded, then looked thoughtfully at the ceiling. "For some reason, you couldn't come to me, and I couldn't go to you. Fantasies are like that, you know. So you just looked at me, and when you did, you . . . touched yourself, and I did likewise. And we kept doing that, as if we were together . . ." She stopped, embarrassed.

This was a mental image he would indulge in often. Rafael exhaled a harsh breath. "That's a good one."

"I thought so."

"Were there others?"

"Many."

"Tell me another."

Apparently, she found "summing up" acceptable, so she continued. "Then there was one where you were robbing me."

"I never robbed anyone."

"It was a fantasy, Rafael. And at the time of my fantasy, I wouldn't have put it past you. Anyway, I caught you when you were stealing my jewelry. If it matters to you, in my dream you were giving all the things you stole to the poor."

"Honorable. Get to the good part."

She smiled and kissed his shoulder. "I caught you."

"You caught me?"

"Yes, and I tied you to my bedpost."

"That sounds promising."

Her eyelids lowered, sensual and teasing. "I took it upon myself to force you to reveal where you had hidden all the treasure you'd stolen."

"How?" His heart was pounding now, and he was becoming aroused. Evelyn had a talent for "summing up."

"I did things to you, and because you were tied up, you couldn't stop me."

"Why would I want to stop you?"

"I don't remember, but it's important that you resist."

"Ah. What things did you do?"

"I kissed you . . . all over. *There,* especially."

He groaned. "I like this one, Evie."

"You did in my dream, too."

"Did I ever tell you where I'd hidden the treasure?"

"Of course. Just before I let you . . . have me."

He groaned again. "I had you?"

"Over and over. Actually, it would be more accurate to say I had you."

"Were you on top of me?"

Her blush deepened. "I was."

He closed his eyes and lay back. "I need to start stealing more treasure."

"You're confessing too early, husband. I am supposed to be testing your resistance before you succumb."

He felt weak with anticipation. "Test as you wish."

His heart throbbed as Evelyn sat up. "Then lie back. In my dream, you were bound to my bed."

"I thought I was tied to the bedpost?"

"Only at first." She paused, considering. "You were standing, and I was on my knees, kissing you. But I can kiss you here just as well."

Before he had a chance to agree, she maneuvered herself around, then peeled back the sheet. He heard a soft gasp of pleasure when she saw how much her erotic imaginings had affected him.

She wrapped her fingers around the base of his erection, then brushed her lips over his sensitive tip. She stopped and peeked up at him. "Does this please you?"

He nodded and his voice caught in his eagerness. "Pleases me. Yes. Very much."

With his approval given, her tongue swept over his hot flesh, then along the underside of his shaft. She seemed to love exploring him, and she learned quickly what pleased him most. She circled the rim of his blunt tip, then cupped him in her hands, maneuvering him in the most perfect, sweet rhythm of love that he'd ever imagined. She made love with her innate sensitivity and intuition, inspired by the deep passion inside her. Everything she did was magic, because she did it for him, hearing only him, sensing every pulse his body took.

When her teasing reached its peak, when he could take no more, she took his length in her mouth and made love to him vigorously, with delight, until his whole body shook, until his every breath was a cry for release.

She sat back suddenly, her face alive with pleasure and happiness. "It works even better than I imagined!"

He caught his breath, fighting to restrain himself, to prolong their encounter when all he wanted was to roll her over and drive himself deep inside her. "What next?"

"Now, I deny you fulfillment until you tell me where you've hidden the treasure." As she spoke, she sensually massaged his length, keeping his need at a fever pitch. "Well?"

He gulped. "Well, what?"

She puffed an impatient breath. "Where did you hide it?"

"I don't know! In the hills, in a rabbit burrow. Wherever you want!"

"A rabbit burrow? That's not very good, Rafael." She massaged him more firmly, and he clenched his fists with restraint.

"Where, then?"

Wild desire sparkled in her eyes. She wanted him just as much as he wanted her. He slipped his hand along her thigh, then found her woman's core wet with her own desire. She whimpered and tipped her head back when his fingers grazed her small peak, teasing her. "Where, my lady?"

They teased each other, playing, wild with desire. It became a battle between them. She squirmed to his touch, her breath coming in swift gasps as she approached release. At its first spasm, he withdrew his hand and she squealed in dismay. "You are a devil, just as I imagined."

He smiled. "Tell me where I hid the treasure, my love, and I will satisfy you to your heart's content."

"This is not quite the way it's supposed to go." She sounded breathless. Her face was flushed with passion. He trailed his finger over her sensitive flesh and she caught her breath.

"You hid it in the pueblo kivas. . . ."

He circled the little peak again and she shuddered with delight. "Unfortunately, the kivas of my father's pueblo had been filled in long ago. Only a few remain intact."

She struck him with her small fist. "I don't care if there wasn't a single one left! In my dream, that's where you hid them." She braced herself on his shoulders, then climbed on top of him.

He loved the fierce look blazing in her eyes, the wildness of her breath and her hair falling around her face and shoulders, over her round breasts, parted over her taut nipples. "You are a beautiful temptress, you know."

"And you are a devilish renegade." She seized his aching staff and positioned it against her soft, woman's core. He waited, fighting his desire to take her. She maneuvered herself over him, then sank down, taking his length deep inside her. They cried out in unison, and she began to move, her lovely head tipped back as hot pleasure spilled through her.

They writhed together, joined in their passion, reveling in the sweetest ecstasy. Everything outside was forgotten while they loved. His rapture came in delicious, rending waves as he poured himself inside her, filling her with all the desire she had created.

Spent, she collapsed on his chest, her skin moist and warm. "You are even more wonderful than I dreamed."

Rafael untangled her hair and eased it back over her shoulder. "For ever after, you are to tell me the exact contents of your most erotic imaginings."

"I will do that." She kissed his shoulder. "But you didn't tell me yours. What was your dearest fantasy?"

Rafael smiled. "That you would tell me yours, and then we would do this. . . ." He rolled her over onto her back and looked down into her eyes. "And that everything we did was because you love me."

She slipped her arms around his neck and drew him close to kiss him. "Then both our fantasies have come true."

Chapter Fourteen

"Evie, I could stay like this forever, with you." Rafael lay on his side, gazing into her eyes, and Evelyn smiled up at him. She reached to touch his long hair, then held out her arms for him.

"It has been the best night of my life."

"You said that in Taos, love."

"I did. But this night was the most special, because now you are truly mine."

He bent to kiss her, softly, as the early morning light broke through the clouds above the pueblo. "I am."

He took her mouth in a lingering, delicious kiss and the fires kindled inside her. They had loved over and over, all night, and still she wanted him. There would never be enough nights in one lifetime to join with her husband—they would be like this forever, and still be filled with this desire to become one.

He grew hard and hot against her and their kiss intensified. A shout startled them from their embrace; then the sound of a horn blown wildly in the distance. Rafael shot up in bed and dressed in a flash. Evelyn's heart pounded. "What is it?"

He turned to her, eyes blazing. "The pueblo is under attack. The scouts are reporting invaders."

Although her pulse raced to dizzying heights, Evelyn pulled on her old blue dress and laced her boots with shaking hands. Her hair fell loose over her shoulders, but she had no time to tie it back out of her way. Rafael grabbed his bola and ran out into the plaza. Will already had Frank saddled and ready. The great gray horse stomped in the cool morning air, snorting as if to greet the upcoming battle.

Patukala joined him with a group of warriors, and old women hurried the children into kivas for safety. Despite her dislike of him, Evelyn couldn't help admiring the chief as he readied himself with a rifle, positioned in the first line of defense. They arranged their defense by the entrance to the pueblo, lining walls and buildings. They hid themselves, apparently intending to lure the enemy into the central plaza before attacking.

Though she would have thought Chen more likely to hold himself above battle, like a king commanding from the rear, he placed himself near the chief and loaded his shiny white revolver with steady hands. She smiled despite her fear. Chen was more than king—he was a Pharaoh who would ride his chariot at the fore of his army, never behind. Even at sixteen, he lived up to the size of his pride.

Sally and Will took their places, too. Patukala exchanged a quiet look with the woman he loved, but he didn't try to stop her or send her away with the other women. He admired her that much.

As Evelyn watched them make ready to defend the pueblo, she realized how much she loved them all, even Rafael's belligerent grandfather. Rafael rode to her and her heart moved at the fire in his dark eyes. "You go with the women into the kiva, Evie."

"Sally is staying out here, and so am I."

He growled and pointed at the kiva. "Now, Evelyn. I won't risk your life here."

She cocked her head to one side. "And I won't risk yours." She drew out her revolver and checked it. "Three shots."

He groaned and prepared to dismount. He would carry her into the kiva and tie her down if he had to—Evelyn guessed his intention and backed away. "They're coming—I hear their hoofbeats. I suggest you take your own place, Renegade, and let me take mine."

"Evelyn . . . You can do no good here."

She fingered her gun. "I can. And you didn't object to Sally staying to fight."

"Sally can shoot straight!"

She patted the bola hanging from her dress. "I always have this."

He rose in the saddle, about to jump down, but a shot rang out. Evelyn seized the opportunity to scramble up the pueblo wall next to Sally, leaving Rafael with no choice. He turned

Frank and headed off to position himself for their defense.

Evelyn concealed herself behind the wall, but she heard horses thundering nearer. Sally clasped her arm tight, her fingers strong and comforting. "You wait, girl, until you got something to shoot at. Pick your target, and don't panic." She hesitated, eyeing Evelyn's small gun with misgivings. "Ain't no one expecting you to do much good, but you're a brave thing to try. Maybe if you close your eyes and don't think on it, you'll hit something. Just aim at the enemy."

Evelyn frowned, but she didn't argue. Three bullets, and that was all. She had to use them wisely.

Talbot's guards charged through the entrance and into the square, but Evelyn couldn't see the lieutenant himself among them. Maybe the scouts were right, and another man now led them. But whoever gave the command, he certainly intended to fight.

The soldiers stopped, uncertain because no Zuni were visible. Evelyn held her breath as the first warrior rose from the wall. Guns fired all around, deafening in the suddenness of the explosion. Talbot's soldiers seemed better prepared than Evelyn had imagined when they rode boldly into the pueblo—they knew what they were doing.

The adobe walls burst with gunfire, shattering into small pieces, clouding the air with dirt and debris. The warriors charged all at once, led by Patukala. In a frenzy of battle Evelyn had never seen, men fought in the plaza, wild cries rang out, horses screamed. Rafael charged in among them, wielding his Argentinean weapon against carbine rifles that could kill ten men in an instant.

Evelyn's hands shook so much that she barely felt the gun in her hands. Rafael jumped from Frank's back, and fought on foot, seizing the advantage by leaping up the pueblo steps to fight from a higher ground. He snapped the bola in the dry air, sending an enemy's weapon flying over the pueblo wall. Rafael knocked the soldier down, but another man leapt onto a large barrel behind him and aimed his rifle at Rafael's back.

Evelyn aimed and fired. The barrel splintered with a burst of water, and the guard crashed into its midst. Sally looked to her in surprise. "Lucky shot, that."

Evelyn didn't respond. Two shots left. Rafael swung around and caught another two soldiers with his whip, yanked them from their feet, then wrapped their legs swiftly with another cord. He freed his bola, then ran toward the others, leaving his tangled victims tied together. He was too far away for her to cover him. Evelyn rose and crept along the pueblo wall to better defend him.

A shot rang out over her head. It appeared to come from outside the pueblo's entrance. She ducked after the shot passed, then looked to see who shot at her. A man slunk away, back into the shadows outside the gate, but she knew without seeing his face that it was Talbot.

For the first time, Evelyn understood the primal nature of battle—the blinding fear, the desperation to survive. Fear overwhelmed her and she couldn't move. She wanted to run, like the terrified prey of a relentless predator, but then saw Rafael fighting two men, and a deeper force than fear rose inside her. *Love.*

She positioned herself again, and struggled to see Rafael through the dust and the battling men. The fear didn't leave or even subside, but love was stronger. With its power, her thoughts cleared and she focused on the man she loved. Her eyes took in everything, every danger, every struggle waged in the plaza below her.

Will fought hand to hand with a soldier, and to Evelyn's surprise, he knocked his opponent to the ground. Another soldier charged up toward Will, and Evelyn shot at the wall behind him. It crumbled on top of the soldier, burying him beneath rubble and stone. Will jumped aside and whooped with delight, then scrambled to cover inside the pueblo.

One shot left. Sally came up beside her and laid her hand on Evelyn's shoulder. Their eyes met, and Evelyn saw all for which the mother had no words.

"Glad you came, girl."

"I'm glad you abducted me."

They smiled in unison, then turned their attention back to the fight below. Rafael led the pueblo defense, fighting on foot before the others. Patukala fought beside him, wielding some kind of native club. Chen knelt under the cover of a water barrel and shot with precision, and the soldiers began retreating again toward the entrance.

They seemed to be taking orders from someone outside the pueblo—Talbot, Evelyn guessed. She considered the contrast in disgust: Rafael fought among his warriors, protecting them. Talbot sent his men in alone and waited.

A soldier shouted and waved a white flag, and Rafael held his own warriors back to let their enemies retreat. Something seemed wrong. It all felt too planned. Chen lowered his gun, and Sally relaxed beside Evelyn. Evelyn gripped her revolver, and rather than relax, her fingers tightened on the trigger.

The soldiers backed from the pueblo, weapons lowered. But as they cleared the entrance, another man appeared above the entrance wall and aimed his rifle at Rafael. Not a soldier, he was dressed as a civilian. Talbot had hired a sharpshooter, and the guise of a retreat was a well-planned strategy to get Rafael in clear view.

Evelyn pulled the trigger, and the assassin's rifle flew as he clutched his arm in pain. He dropped forward into the plaza, but the other soldiers fled as the Zuni resumed their fierce defense.

Patukala seized the wounded assassin, but Rafael turned slowly, amazed, as Evelyn rose from the pueblo wall.

They looked into each other's eyes, and she saw when he realized what she had known all along: There was no sharpshooter in New Mexico any better with a gun than Evelyn Reid.

"Why didn't you tell me you could shoot?"

Rafael followed Evelyn around the plaza as she helped to bandage wounded warriors. Though many had been injured, no one had been killed despite the ferocity of the battle. Patukala had the assassin under guard, but the man was too weak to answer questions yet.

Evelyn glanced over her shoulder. Despite her even expression, he caught the pride in her eyes. "You didn't speak very highly of gun proficiency, Rafael. And I didn't want to brag."

"The first time, I attributed it to luck. Hitting the wall behind Will, I wasn't sure if you were aiming or not. But that last shot, Evie, that was amazing. That assassin is lucky to be alive."

She huffed. "Lucky, indeed! I meant to hit his hand—not to spare his life, but I was afraid if I killed him, his finger might still squeeze the trigger and you'd be dead, anyway."

"Good thinking. . . ." He paused, assessing her like a new species recently emerged from some deep forest. "How did you learn to shoot that way? From your father?"

"From my aunt, his sister. She is a better shot than he." She finished the bandage and stood up, dusted her hands on her dirty dress, then folded her arms comfortably over her chest. "This may surprise you, Señor Renegade, but a number of women fought in the Civil War, on both sides. My aunt was one, although she performed her deeds disguised as a boy soldier."

Rafael gaped. "Why . . . Why would she do such a thing?"

Evelyn's brow angled in a superior posture. "To be near my uncle, of course. I have always admired her and wanted to be like her. It has been my fondest dream—well, not quite the fondest, but still high among my fantasies—to be able to save the man I love, just as she did."

Clearly, the aristocratic families of the East

weren't what Rafael imagined. "So she taught you to shoot. But at the train station . . . You were much closer to me then than you were to the assassin today."

A slow, wistful smile crossed her face. "I know."

Rafael's throat constricted with emotion. "You could have shot me, but you didn't."

"Could I? Even then, I knew that I could not." She came close to him and laid her palm against his face. "You are part of me. It would be like tearing my own soul asunder."

He drew her into his arms and held her. "I'm luckier than I realized."

"It's not luck, Rafael. It is love, and it will never fail you."

He rested his cheek against her head. "I'm sorry I told you to hide in the kivas today, Evie. You're a brave woman, and you are right to stand up against what threatens you. But what I do next, I must do alone."

She pulled back and eyed him suspiciously. "What are you going to do?"

"I have to go to Tewa and find out where Talbot has hidden my people. I can only do that in secret, and alone."

"Rafael . . . no. Lieutenant Talbot will expect you to come for him. You can't go alone."

"He knows I have returned, and that may endanger his captives even further. This attack was hasty—there is a reason he wants me dead, and desperately. I have to go, and now."

"Now?"

"You know I can't wait. I have to go when they're still in disarray."

"What are you going to do?"

"I'm going after the source of our problem: Talbot. He stole my brother. I will capture him, and force him to reveal their whereabouts."

"He will know this is your plan, Rafael. He'll be well guarded."

"I know. But I have to try."

He knew she wouldn't like it, but they had no choice. She drew a deep breath, then nodded. "I will let you go without me, but if you're not back as planned, I'm coming after you."

"I can't be certain how long it will take. Please remember, Talbot is after you, too—maybe even more than he wants me. I felt sure some of those soldiers were aiming at you."

"They were, but I stayed low. I have no intention of letting the lieutenant catch me."

"If I don't return . . . Patukala will come after me. You stay here."

She studied his face for a moment, then nodded. "I will let you think I agree to that, but we both know better."

"That's not terribly comforting."

"Would you stay away if I was in danger?"

He cupped her small face in his hands. "I would not. So I will do what I can to return, lest I place you in even more danger than I have already."

"Do you think they'll return to attack this pueblo again?"

"Maybe, but I doubt it. Their real purpose was to draw me out, but I don't think they'll take the risk again."

"Talbot was outside the entrance. He's the one who shot at me."

"All the more reason for you to stay behind." He paused and shook his head. "What kind of leader sends his men in alone to fight, and stays in safety behind?"

"A worm. People are nothing to him—just things to be used and discarded. He thinks, but he does not feel. He acts with no thought of what happens as a result of his action. He wants, but his motivation is to exalt himself in some way—with money, I suppose. Lieutenant Talbot is a very dark man."

"He has been raised in a culture where power and gold are the strongest motivations."

Evelyn sighed. "So, my dearest love, was I—and my father before me. But thousands upon thousands of men, and a few women, too, gave their lives so others could be free, so the world they lived in would be better."

Clearly, they would never agree on this subject. "People like Talbot used your war and the Reconstruction period after it for their own gain. You must see that."

"I know that's true, but my father says the world will work itself out eventually, and move on to new struggles. The struggles and what we do within them define us. So you and I define ourselves here, as men did in the war, and always have done when confronted with a reality that doesn't live up to their dreams. Talbot, he is doing the same thing, all for a cause that will give him nothing in the end. Maybe he will learn that, one day."

Evelyn's noble father had obviously filled her head with ideals—the ideals of a man who had grown up privileged, his head in books. The kind of man who, armed with these abstract visions, would march into the bloodiest war in the country's history, taking thousands with him.

Evelyn studied him thoughtfully, then smiled. "Isn't this what you are doing, Rafael? Defining yourself in a struggle against injustice? Isn't that why you donned your Anasazi mask and began riding out to save others?"

"Yes, but that's different."

"In what way?"

"I left no field of blood behind me!"

"Then you have been very, very lucky. My father was less fortunate."

He understood the truth behind her words—if saving his brother and the other captives meant a battle ending in blood, so be it. If it meant his own death, he would face that end. "I will do all I can to come back to you, Evie. You know that I will. I've done it before. Please trust me."

"I do, but, Rafael, I'm afraid for you today, more than I ever have been before. I'm afraid you may face an enemy you can't defeat, not alone. It's not Lieutenant Talbot I fear—it's something else. Someone with a stronger power and a stronger motivation. I don't believe this raid was Talbot's idea. I think there's someone who wants you dead more than he does."

"I have no choice, Evie. I have to go."

She held tight to his hand as if fearing to let go. "I know that you do. But . . ." She closed her eyes, then opened them quickly as a new thought triggered in her mind. "She felt this way, too."

"Who?"

She shook her head impatiently as if he should know the answer. "The girl in Mesa Verde. Don't you remember? I felt her there. I dreamt of her, that first night you came to me. She watched her husband leave, and she believed in him so much, she thought nothing could defeat him. She waited, but he never returned. I'm so afraid that if I let you go, I will never see you again."

Rafael hugged her and she wrapped her arms around his waist. "Evie, I won't truly leave you. No matter what happens, my spirit is with you, and it always will be. We are one thing. But I can't gauge my actions by fear, but by what I know must be done."

She nodded and slowly released him. "I know. It's not your actions I question. It's my own."

His eyes narrowed to slits. "Evie, you stay here. There's nothing you can do."

"I know that." She sighed, her face wistful as he turned to mount his horse. "It's just that I know she felt this same way, too. And she was wrong."

"I don't like this at all. He's been gone too long." Evelyn sat miserably in the plaza with Chen and Sally while Will tended the horses. Patukala was speaking with the chief, but no one else seemed concerned.

Sally sighed. "Girl, he's been gone no more than a few hours. It's ten miles to Santa Fe from here. He'll go in at night and learn what he can. Calm yourself. He's been doing this long enough not to make a mistake. He's got to get some idea of where they've put his brother, and this is the only way."

"I could go after him." Evelyn started to rise, but Sally grabbed her arm and pulled her down.

"All you'd do is get him in more trouble. You know that man can't see straight, let alone think straight, when you're around."

Evelyn's eyes puddled with tears. "I feel that he needs me, Sally, as if he's up against something he doesn't expect."

"He knows what he's doing. He knows Talbot."

"He knows the lieutenant, yes, but the scouts said there was another officer involved now."

"Ain't nothing Rafael can't handle. You just sit tight and wait."

Evelyn didn't argue, but she fixed her gaze on the entrance. She would wait, but for how long?

As the sun set over the pueblo, she felt as if her heart had been torn out of her chest, and all the force of her soul focused on Rafael, riding somewhere out there in darkness.

The pueblo was quiet with only a few lanterns burning when Rafael crept over the stables and slipped behind a shed. The light in Talbot's office was dimmed, and he saw no movement. Guards had been posted outside the door, but not an unusual number. Yet Talbot had to know the Renegade wouldn't let another night go by without beginning the hunt for his young brother.

Rafael had donned a black cape to shield him from light, but he had left his Anasazi mask with Evelyn. There was no need to hide his identity now, and he needed his spectacles for better vision.

The guards positioned themselves in front of the entrance to Talbot's office, but no one guarded the open window. It seemed a curious oversight, but Rafael crept quietly near. Through the window, he saw Talbot seated at a desk—he appeared to be studying a map. No one else was in the room.

It was too easy, but he had no choice. Rafael climbed the jagged wall and slipped down into the room behind Talbot. From stone pillar to stone pillar, he moved like a shadow. Without sound, he drew his whip. Talbot's shoulders remained relaxed, and he took a drink from a dark bottle. If he was drunk, Rafael's task would be all the simpler.

For one second, he paused to see the map spread out before Talbot—it was the Tewa Pueblo, but beneath it were sketched in the kivas once filled over. The kivas Evelyn had imagined in her Renegade fantasy.

He had no time to waste. With a quick flick of his wrist, he snapped the bola and wrapped it around Talbot's neck. The whiskey bottle dropped from his hands and shattered on the tile floor. The lieutenant struggled, but could make no sound. Rafael yanked him back, then shoved him against a pillar.

"Where is my brother? Tell me, or I'll kill you."

"The better question is, I think . . . Where is Evelyn Reid?" A man spoke behind him, and Rafael jerked around in shock. He kept the bola tight around Talbot's neck, but the tall man who confronted him didn't back away.

The man wore an old two-breasted uniform coat of dark blue with an insignia bearing an eagle, and he aimed a revolver squarely between Rafael's eyes. He stood alone, with no guards.

Rafael's senses stirred as if in recognition, but his instincts moved quicker. He twisted the bola with a snap, and Talbot sank to the floor from want of air. Before the new officer could react, Rafael spun to the side, jerked his whip and knocked the tall man's gun from his hand, then again around the man's legs, and the officer fell to the floor near Talbot.

Quicker than any opponent Rafael had yet faced, the officer scrambled for his gun, seized it, and took aim. Rafael leapt back and raised his weapon, then looked into bright eyes, as gray as the sea in a storm, shining with a merciless light in a face both refined and proud.

Evelyn's eyes.

The man didn't shoot—he wanted something more than the Renegade's death. "Where is my daughter? You bastard, what have you done with my daughter?"

Rafael froze, astounded. Talbot was unconscious, if briefly. He could escape, but only if he left Robert Talmadge in the same state.

Evelyn had been right. For once, he had faced an enemy he couldn't defeat. Her father.

"We can't kill him until he's told us where he left my daughter!" Robert Talmadge paced around Talbot's office, and for the moment,

Evelyn's enraged father was all that kept Rafael from death.

The man was even worse than Rafael had imagined. Despite his startling resemblance to his beautiful daughter, Robert was as proud and cold and dangerous as Rafael had imagined a Civil War officer to be—maybe worse.

Talbot sat at his desk, a devious master of manipulation and careful words. Rafael hadn't voiced his own defense—not yet. Robert Talmadge wasn't likely to listen, anyway.

Talbot rose and placed his hand on the father's shoulder. "I know you're concerned, Colonel. You have every reason to be. But we've found we can't free her from the pueblo. He has likely hidden her elsewhere since our attempt failed."

Talbot would want to lure Evelyn to the pueblo, but he certainly couldn't let Robert know the true reason. The moment she saw her father, all would be lost. Rafael closed his eyes. *Please, don't follow me. Please, stay away.*

The guards had tied Rafael to a stone pillar and now stood outside, massed against any attempt to free him. Though Robert was the only reason he was still alive, Rafael wouldn't have been caught if not for Evelyn's furious father. Because of her father's interference, Evelyn herself was now in danger.

Somehow, he had to make Robert Talmadge see reason. "Evelyn is safe, but I will not tell you her whereabouts until my brother has been located." He turned to Talbot. "And until I know she is safe from danger."

Robert's gray eyes flashed, but he seemed unable to look at Rafael for more than an instant. No doubt, he believed his daughter had faced unspeakable suffering, fueled by Talbot's well-aimed suggestions. "You are in no position to negotiate."

Talbot looked between them—Rafael could see his crafty mind working. "Safe, is she? My men reported that you used her as a shield when they tried to rescue her from Tesuque."

Robert closed his eyes as if fighting pain, but when he looked to Rafael, hate sparkled like fire inside him. "If any ill has befallen her, you will pay with such torture as even your heathen people couldn't imagine."

Evelyn had spoken of her father as a fair man, but his attitude toward native people left much to be desired. "Your daughter is safe—safer than she would be if I were fool enough to tell you where she is now."

Talbot laughed. "Would you have us believe you're her 'protector,' de Aguirre? I was there when she fled from you, desperate for help. It is my deepest, most painful grief that I was not able to save her from you when you tore her from my care."

"Is that the story you've told? Then your hope must be desperate that Evelyn isn't found, Lieutenant." Rafael turned his attention to Robert. "Your trust is misplaced, Colonel Talmadge. Your daughter fled to John Talbot only to discover it was he, not I, who murdered her husband, and he who has abducted many of my people for uncertain purposes. It was he she ran from—and she ran to me."

It was worth the attempt, but Robert's expression revealed no yielding. Talbot cast a quick glance at the father, then relaxed, seeing the truth spoken by a renegade made no headway. He seated himself behind his desk and leaned back in arrogant assurance.

"Come, de Aguirre. As schoolmaster and fond of children's fables, surely you can do better than that." Talbot paused and shook his head. "It is well known by now that you have kept Evelyn as your unwilling mistress, chaining her to your bed in Taos. Yes, we followed your trail even to the inn where you kept her like a slave."

Robert's brow winced with the anguish of a helpless father. "I would kill you now . . ."

Talbot looked smug. "Do you deny using her as a shield at Tesuque?"

What could he say to convince Robert Talmadge that he, not Talbot, was telling the truth? Rafael sighed. "Yes, I deny it, and if she had truly been my 'slave,' you can be sure she would have been locked away under guard with the children. Tell me, Lieutenant, did your soldiers also report that Evelyn joined our fight, as our ally?"

Robert looked quickly to Talbot, but Talbot hesitated. "That is madness. They reported only her screams of terror."

"Then they reported in error." Rafael looked to Robert. "She fired three times. Twice, she saved my life, and once, the life of a young man who traveled with us."

Talbot laugh, but it came tight and forced. "You would have us believe Evelyn tried to protect those who abducted her?"

Rafael ignored him, his gaze fixed on Robert. "She never missed."

Talbot's brow angled in mockery. "Never missed? I've seen Evelyn shoot. A dear girl, she is, sweet and gentle. I had given her the revolver to protect her from your raging admirers, but her aim . . . ? Really, Señor de Aguirre, your stories are fanciful in the extreme. I grieve that she missed you as a target, but to claim she fought in battle? We are not such fools."

Robert didn't answer, and Rafael saw his chance. "Evelyn could shoot the flea off a dog if she wanted to." He paused and glanced at Robert. "Her aunt taught her."

Robert said nothing, but he nodded. "You know my daughter that well, at least."

Talbot's eyes flashed as he recognized an unexpected risk. "Colonel, this man has held Evelyn captive for weeks. It is no surprise that he should have forced secrets from her."

Despite his pride and self-assurance, Robert was listening. He had raised Evelyn—there must be some good, some wisdom in his heart. Rafael tried again. "Colonel Talmadge, I love your daughter, and she loves me. My people took her from the train against my will. That much is true. But no one harmed her."

Talbot's eyes narrowed like a man in a card game where the stakes were life and death. "Is that so? Then why did she flee your 'protection'? She came to my camp, her dress tattered, her face dirty, her hair tangled. I cannot imagine what you had done to her that she, the loveliest woman I know, could have ended up in this state."

Rafael recalled how Evelyn had kept her cheeks dirty, her hair in deliberate knots—all to keep him from desiring her. How horribly that had failed! He found himself smiling at the memory, but Robert misread his expression.

"Dear God, what did you do to her?"

Talbot bowed his head and turned away, a contrived gesture of shame. "There is only one reason a young woman flees a man at night."

Rafael exhaled a long breath. "Evelyn fled me in the ancient city of Mesa Verde because I made love to her."

Robert grimaced and sat back on Talbot's desk as if hearing far more than he could bear. "My child . . ."

The pain on her father's face moved Rafael's heart, but he had no idea how to alleviate the truth. "It is no source of pride to me that I would lack restraint with the woman I love more than life, but it was her feelings for me that sent her away, not my love. She was afraid because she loved me and because we wanted each other so much. I would not hurt her for the world."

Robert bowed his head into his hands. Talbot strode forward and backhanded Rafael's face. "You deserve death for such lies!" He shouted for his guards, and four men burst into the office. Talbot unbound Rafael from the pillar, and the guard dragged him to the door.

One chance . . . Rafael turned back to Robert. "She had a hard time in school—her teacher sent her home for not paying attention . . ."

Talbot struck him on the side of the head with the butt of a revolver, and Rafael fell into darkness.

Chapter Fifteen

"Chen, wake up!" Evelyn prodded Chen's shoulder. He groaned and rolled over away from her. "Please." She kept her voice low to avoid waking Will, but it wasn't easy.

All night, she had struggled with visions of the Anasazi woman in Mesa Verde. All night she had suffered with another woman's pain. Now she knew—the girl who had watched her husband ride away had one regret: that she didn't go after him and keep him safe when he needed her. Evelyn had no intention of making the same mistake. "Chen, wake up now!"

Chen opened one eye and looked at her. "What's the matter?"

"Rafael isn't back. I know they said it would take a while, but I know there's something wrong."

"So what do you want me to do?"

"I want you to come with me."

"Where?"

"To the pueblo, of course. That's where Rafael went. If Talbot has captured him, we're going to free him."

Chen groaned. "What makes you think we can do that?"

Evelyn hesitated. "Because he needs us."

His other eye opened. Evelyn readied herself for a long list of reasons why they shouldn't go after him, but Chen just sat up, sighed, and pulled on his boots. "Let's go."

"They've got him in jail again." Chen detached his new bola from a stone pillar and climbed down from the pueblo wall. He tied the whip around his waist again and sighed miserably. "So we've come full circle."

Evelyn frowned. "Not 'full circle,' Chen. I'm on your side this time."

"Fat lot of good that does us!"

She drew a patient breath. "I believe I proved myself useful during the pueblo skirmish."

He shrugged, unimpressed. "Well, you're out of bullets now."

"And so are you." Evelyn considered her makeshift bola, but though she felt she might be able to snatch a gun out of a man's hands, maybe, she knew she couldn't fight on foot well enough to hold her own. She fingered her empty gun. "If we could steal some ammunition, we'd be better able to free him."

"You can't be thinking of breaking him out by force?" Chen shook his head, dismayed.

"They've got another officer in there, higher rank than Talbot."

"How do you know?"

Chen eyed her, askance. "His uniform has a lot more braiding and gold stitched into it. Wish I had one like it. Maybe not so faded."

"That's odd, but we can't be sure he isn't in on whatever is going on, so we'll have to avoid him, too."

Chen made a face. "Good thinking."

Evelyn stood on tiptoes to see into the window, but it was too high. "How does he look? Is he all right?"

Chen hesitated, and Evelyn's heart leapt to her throat. "He's a little bruised, miss, got some blood on his forehead. But he'll be fine."

Evelyn closed her eyes in prayer. *Please, let him be all right. Let me save him.* "We have to get in there. First, we save Rafael, and then I have to get to someone who will listen to me."

"Then you need look no further, Mrs. Reid. I'd be delighted to listen to whatever you have to say." Talbot spoke quietly behind them, and Evelyn slammed back against the wall. Chen placed himself in front of her, but Talbot nodded to two guards. "Take them."

Evelyn opened her mouth to scream, but Talbot bounded forward and clamped his hand over her mouth. Chen fought, but the guards overpowered him, hitting him hard in the stomach, and one wrapped a gag in his mouth. Evelyn struggled and kicked, but Talbot held her fast. She sank her teeth into his palm, biting hard. He swore but he didn't let go. He kicked her forward, then shoved her into a dark coach.

The guards threw Chen in beside her and he slumped forward in pain.

They were both gagged, but their eyes met, and the fear she saw in Chen mirrored her own.

"Her teacher expelled her from her classes for dreaming and said she couldn't be taught. . . ."

Rafael's eyes filled with tears at Robert Talmadge's quiet words. "And she was brighter than all of them."

"She was the light of my life and her mother's." Robert swallowed hard, then entered Rafael's cell. For a long while, he looked into Rafael's eyes, almost as if he was afraid of what he would see there. "Please tell me she is safe."

"The last I saw her, she was tending the wounded of my grandfather's pueblo. But she isn't safe, Colonel. What I told you of Talbot was true, and more. He has taken a large number of my people, my brother included. There is something he wants, hidden here or near this pueblo. Evelyn is a grave threat to him. She knows the truth."

"How can I believe you? You have terrorized Santa Fe, by all accounts. Your allies held up a train. These are not the actions of an innocent man."

"They are the actions of a desperate man. I was the schoolmaster on a peaceful pueblo, Colonel. All I wanted was to run a school where children—of any race—could come to learn, to better their lives and open their dreams. But others wanted our land, and to drive us out, and so every bit of presumed justice was forgotten. People were beaten for no reason other than to terrify them—even children were beaten, and I found I was the only one who could stop it. I couldn't ride as myself, so I donned a disguise. When your son-in-law arrived, I thought we would find justice, after all. But he was killed and I was accused of his murder. That is not true, but it serves well the purposes of those who would lay claim to my people's land."

"You speak well, I will grant you that. But my daughter . . ." Robert stopped, restraining emotion. "Did you have to involve my daughter?"

"It wasn't my choice to do so. But when she came back to me, it was to keep her safe from a man who is a far greater threat to her."

"You've admitted that you . . ." The father looked away. "Defiled her."

"I didn't say that!" Rafael fought his annoyance. "I have no wish to lie to you. Evelyn became my lover before she became my wife, but . . ."

Robert's bright gaze snapped to him and his mouth drifted open. "Your . . . *wife?*"

"We were wed in my grandfather's pueblo a few days ago."

"I don't believe you."

Rafael sighed in frustration. "When she's debating something in her head, she pops her lips." He stopped and mimicked the sound. "She talks in her sleep."

This may have been a mistake. Robert glared. "This proves only that you kept her just as Lieutenant Talbot accused."

Nothing he said convinced the angry father. Rafael looked into Robert Talmadge's cold gray eyes. "What can I say to convince you if you don't believe me now? You came here, here you stand. What do you want of me if not to learn the truth?"

"My daughter . . ." The anguish in Robert's voice pierced Rafael's heart. "I should have been here for her. When her husband died, I should have come to her and brought her home. But my wife was ill—Evelyn told me she was fine and there was no need." He bowed his head in grief. A tear fell to the proud man's cheek. "I should have been here."

"Evelyn holds you blameless, Colonel. She admires you, she speaks of you often. She considers you some kind of hero for whatever you did during the Civil War."

"She used to follow me everywhere, asking questions. She learned so quickly, not about dates but about people, about why they act as they do."

"Evelyn always sees the greater picture, the greater understanding."

"You know her well, that is plain."

"I love her."

Robert bowed his head. "I don't know what to believe. I have been so afraid for her."

"She wears a locket with no pictures. When we married . . ." Rafael took the locket from around his neck and passed it to Robert. "She gave it to me as a wedding gift."

Robert took the small locket and his fingers closed tight around it. He looked up and into Rafael's eyes. "I gave her this when she was thirteen. I told her to wear it and to store her most cherished dreams inside. If she gave it to you . . ." Robert gave the locket back to Rafael.

"It is as you say. You have her heart."

"And she has mine."

Robert exhaled a long breath. "Then it's true. John Talbot killed Westley."

"I believe so. Evelyn says he didn't deny it—apparently, they weren't close at Harvard."

"No, I was surprised when John asked to join Westley out here. Westley had never spoken favorably of him, but when John made his request, Westley granted it. I have sometimes wondered if John had some kind of unscrupulous advantage over my son-in-law."

Rafael didn't answer. Talbot must have used what he knew of Westley's secret life as a form of blackmail—but it failed when the pueblo was at stake. Westley Reid had been a man of honor, and for his honor, had died.

Robert studied Rafael's expression, and Rafael wondered if the father knew more than he said about his son-in-law's private nature. "A short while after we heard the news of Westley's murder, another man died. A friend of his, Randall Hallowell, committed suicide."

As Rafael guessed, the father had known, or at least suspected. "Then I wish them both peace."

"He was a gentle man and kind. But sometimes I feared Evie wouldn't know true happiness as his wife. He never tried to change her and I believe he loved her dearly, but I'm not sure he really understood her."

Rafael smiled. "The study of Evelyn's imagination is a pursuit best reserved for a lifetime." Unexpectedly, he found a common ground with

Evelyn's reserved, dignified father—they loved the same woman.

"If you are telling the truth, we have no time to lose. Lieutenant Talbot has left during the night, since I arrived a week ago. He seems distracted, and I believe he is planning to leave the pueblo—perhaps for Mexico."

"My grandfather believes the Spaniards left gold or some such treasure hidden somewhere near this pueblo."

"Then the lieutenant would have to take it to another country to reap its full benefits, and to protect himself from our laws. I would guess your missing people are being used in the task of digging or perhaps transporting whatever he has found in these hills."

Rafael rubbed his temple. "But where? No one has reported any of my people leaving the pueblo, nor have they been seen anywhere else."

"I will help you to find them. But I must get you out of here first."

Talbot appeared like a grim specter in front of the jail door. He slammed it shut and locked it. Robert leapt up and grabbed the bars. "You won't get away with this, Lieutenant!"

"Won't I? By now, these soldiers know they have far more to gain by sticking at my side than by betraying me. No one else will know what's become of you, Colonel."

Robert glared at Talbot. "So you intend to kill us?" Evelyn's father sounded more disgusted than afraid. Rafael couldn't deny a tremor of admiration.

Talbot glanced over his shoulder, an instinctive response of a man who must always watch his back for the many enemies his actions have earned. "Kill you? Eventually, yes. But this must be handled perfectly." He eyed Rafael. "It suits me well to have the Renegade held responsible for all the deaths that will come in this battle."

"Such as my daughter's? You are a dark soul, Lieutenant."

"Your daughter has willed her own fate by becoming the Renegade's whore." Robert's breath came as a hiss, but Talbot laughed. "I will keep you here for the time being, 'safe.' Then when the time is right, the Renegade will 'break out,' killing Evelyn's innocent father. He will, of course, be shot down at last, by my own hand—and in that moment, I will truly glory, de Aguirre. You have been a thorn in my side, and in the side of righteousness. You may not understand this, either of you, but what I do now is just. It upholds a balance, the structure of power, that both of you have defied."

Rafael shook his head. This man would never see any reason but his own. "You serve only yourself. You desire a structure that places you in command, and power in your hands that has been stolen from others. You seek power outside yourself, Talbot, in controlling others. You even attempted to control Evelyn's emotion toward me—but you failed, because her heart is pure. Until you look within, you will remain forever powerless."

His words bit deeper than he expected. Talbot's eyes burned with hate. "Powerless, am I? Yet I have the favor of the governor, and everyone else now, de Aguirre—and you are branded a criminal. I have power over everything that matters to you—both of you!" As he spoke, he leaned toward the cell. "I have power over Evelyn."

Robert clenched his fist in helpless anger. "If you dare attack the pueblo again, without permission from me, you'll bring the whole government of New Mexico territory down on your head, Talbot."

"Attack the pueblo? Why? Oh, to capture Evelyn?" Talbot ran his finger deliberately across the bars. "But, Colonel, there is no need for that. The Renegade's beautiful lover has come to me." Rafael leapt to his feet beside Robert. "What have you done with her?" He was shaking with fear; Evelyn had come for him, and been captured.

"Let us just say she is in the same place as your brother, and her fate will be as grim. I'm sorry to say it, because I can think of ample reasons to keep her with me."

Talbot placed the cell key into his coat pocket, then left. Robert paced, but Rafael sat with his head bowed, struggling against fear to think of a way to reach his wife. The two men who loved her most were now powerless to save her.

Robert banged his fist on the door, a futile gesture born of fury. "Now what?" He eyed Rafael without affection. "This is your fault, Renegade or not. If you love her as you say, why didn't you hide her?"

Rafael glared. "If you loved her so, why did you let her learn to shoot? Her confidence is extreme."

Robert couldn't argue. He seated himself beside Rafael, at the far end of the stone bench. "I begged her to come home after Westley died, but she promised to return as soon as the Renegade was captured." He paused. "You."

"I found Westley dead. I didn't kill him."

"I should have come out sooner and forced her to come home. When word came that her train had been held up and Evelyn had been kidnapped, I came as fast as I could. But too late . . ." Robert assessed Rafael's long black hair and Zuni vest. "You are not the kind of man I would have selected to replace her husband." Robert sighed and bowed his head into his hands. "It may not be fair, I know, but I have harbored such a great fear of your people. My grandfather told me stories of Indian raids when he lived on the New York frontier. They filled my nightmares when I was a boy—raging madmen with painted faces, wielding hatchets and bows . . ."

Rafael angled his brow. "As it happens, I also harbored a boyhood fear of your kind."

Robert looked surprised. "Why? My family is among the oldest and most respected in Boston. We are imminently civilized."

"Is that so? A thousand men, mowed down like wheat in a field—that is the stuff of nightmares, Colonel, not a few hunters on a raid."

Robert's eyes widened, but then a slow, ageless smile formed on his aristocratic face. "We harbor the fear of the ages, my friend—born of ignorance. But it was as you say." He stopped and sighed heavily. "No, it was worse by far. Did you say a thousand? Twice as many Union soldiers died in one day at the Battle of Antietam Creek, where I was captured. The Rebels lost almost as many. Among us both, that day left almost twenty thousand wounded. The power of our armies' weapons far outreached our general's outmoded strategy and their soldiers paid the price. Your nightmares couldn't compare to the loss I saw that day."

Rafael stared at him. Here was a man such as he had scorned all his life—an officer, a survivor of the bloodiest war on American soil—and yet he listened spellbound to the man's grim memories. "Why did you fight?"

Robert closed his eyes. "For honor's sake, and nothing more."

A cold and impersonal answer, based on idealism just as Rafael had suspected. "I see no honor in mass death."

"Do you not? We fought for the honor of all men, to live *as* men, free men. It was not without its price. I lost friends, relatives . . . One cousin died, another lost both his legs at Gettysburg."

Rafael grimaced. "And you compare this to an Indian raid? What kind of life can this man lead now?"

"A good one, surprisingly. He lives on his former commander's property, he married a Rebel girl he met during the war, and they have several children now. He has joined in partnership with a Rebel officer and they have formed an architectural business. So it could be said together they are rebuilding the soil they fought upon."

Rafael would never understand these strange

easterners, but something in Robert Talmadge's soft voice inspired admiration. He meant every word he said. No wonder Evelyn respected her father.

"Your government has neglected to extend its 'honor' to my people, Colonel. Instead, it seems bent on destroying us and all we hold dear."

Robert didn't argue. "It is fear and greed that makes it so. For this reason, many who fought in conditions nigh onto hell in Virginia refused to come west during the Indian Wars. I do not defend it, though again I say it is ignorance and fear."

"Those things, I have tried to combat in my school, so that those who will one day lead will look at each other as equals, and not for the sum of their differences."

Robert smiled. "Your profession must please Evelyn. She hoped to become a schoolteacher herself, you know."

"I know. And she will. . . . Somehow, she will."

Robert hesitated, then placed his hand on Rafael's arm. "We will find her, you and I. If we can overcome our fear of each other, then the same love will guide us where we need to be."

"Where in hell are we?" Chen's voice echoed in the dark tunnel as a guard shoved Evelyn forward. She bumped into Chen's back and he sneezed. "God's teeth, it's dusty in here!"

Evelyn squinted but she could only make out huddled shapes along the edges of a rough-hewn tunnel. Parts of it seemed old, as if crafted hundreds of years ago, but as they progressed farther inward, it seemed newly opened and the dirt was fresh.

The guard pushed Chen to his knees, laughed brutally, then retreated back up the tunnel, taking his lantern with him. After he left, someone held up a faint candle, and a long, deliberate sigh followed.

"Of all the people I didn't want to see here . . . You!"

From the ground, Chen groaned and muttered in Chinese. He lifted his head and squinted to see the man who spoke. "They might as well have dumped me in hell."

Evelyn stepped forward and her heart bounced with joy. "Diego!" Before he could react, she ran forward and hugged the surprised youth. "You're alive. Oh, thank God! Rafael will be so happy."

Diego gaped. "Mrs. Reid?"

"It's me, yes."

"Where is my brother?" Diego paused, and she knew he was fighting emotion. "Is he . . . all right?"

"Rafael is fine. He's wonderful. . . . but Lieutenant Talbot has imprisoned him again. We don't have much time."

He eyed her suspiciously. "What are you doing here?"

Evelyn hesitated, unsure where to begin. "It's a long story."

"This . . . this is unacceptable!" Another voice penetrated the darkness. Evelyn reacted much as Chen had to Diego's presence in the mine.

"Oh, no." In unison with Chen, Evelyn turned. Diego elevated the lantern, and she caught his expression as he rolled his eyes.

Evelyn seized the lantern and went to the far wall of the newest tunnel. "It can't be! Mrs. . . . *St. Claire?*"

The matron lifted her chin, as proud as if addressing the porter in the first-class cabin. "Mrs. Agnes St. Claire. And you are . . . ?"

Evelyn's angled her brow. "Perhaps you don't remember me, Mrs. St. Claire, but I was on the train to Denver with you, just a few weeks ago."

Mrs. St. Claire looked disgusted, as if Evelyn's survival offended proper decorum. Evelyn knew why—everyone would assume she had been raped, and to people like Mrs. St. Claire, that would tarnish Evelyn as much as her attacker. "It was commonly assumed, Mrs. Reid, that you were left dead on the plains." Her tone implied this would have been the more honorable fate.

"No, I'm fine." Evelyn paused, feeling foolishly pleased. "Actually, I am Evelyn de Aguirre now."

Diego hopped forward. "You *are?* You married him! Well, well. Of course, I knew it all along. He's been mooning about after you long enough."

Mrs. St. Claire held up her hand. "I do not desire to be party to this information."

Evelyn eyed Mrs. St. Claire. "How did you come to be trapped here, Mrs. St. Claire?"

Diego pressed his way forward. "Agnes here got dumped in the mines by her husband." He lowered his voice and bent close to Evelyn. "Can't say as I blame him."

Evelyn's mouth dropped. "Mr. St. Claire *left* you here? On purpose?"

Agnes braced, turning her head from Diego as if his presence pained her. As stridently conventional as Agnes had seemed on the train, met by Diego's blunt independence and his unwillingness to conform to anyone's rules but his own—the match couldn't be good. "Mr. St. Claire has been . . . confused . . . by a person whose name I will not mention, not now nor in the future, nor ever again as I live."

Diego nodded. "That would be John Talbot."

Agnes winced, but Diego rolled his eyes. "The lieutenant isn't a favorite of any of us, Ag. You don't have it any worse than we do."

Agnes's already formidable shape seemed to extend outward from her chest. "Young man, I am accustomed to a far more refined existence than any persons here might be expected to imagine."

Chen shrugged. "She's got a point." Before his words were out, Diego struck Chen, who leveled a superior glare his way. Diego affected a taunting expression, and Chen swung a quick blow, which Diego ducked.

Evelyn seized Chen and pulled him back behind her, then fixed a warning look upon Diego. Diego restrained himself, somewhat to her surprise, then went on talking as if nothing had happened. "Agnes's husband is in some kind of partnership with Talbot."

"Really? They did seem to know each other on the train." Evelyn stopped and looked around. "Where are we, anyway?"

Diego shrugged. "I'd guess we're in an old

mine—Talbot's men have had us digging since you left."

"So your people were abducted to dig these tunnels. . . ." Evelyn pursed her lips thoughtfully. "Then these must be the tunnels dug by the Spaniards after the Pueblo Revolt."

Diego nodded. "I'd say so—parts seem old."

"But what does Mr. St. Claire have to do with this excavation?"

"From what I've gathered, he's the one who hired Talbot to find some supposed treasure hidden by Spaniards—under this pueblo."

Evelyn considered this. "But how did Mr. St. Claire find out about the treasure in the first place?"

Agnes looked proud. "Mr. St. Claire is kept abreast of many such discoveries due to his position in the Boston Heritage and Trust Bank. He has served for many years as vault manager."

Evelyn glanced at Diego, who shrugged, then back at Agnes. "What does this have to do with Rafael's pueblo?"

Agnes hesitated. "Mr. St. Claire didn't find it necessary to share all details of his project . . ."

Evelyn bit back a retort, but Diego chuckled, "Apparently not."

Agnes ignored him and continued. "The Heritage Trust keeps many of its long-deceased customers' important documents—those secured and claimed by Westley Reid on behalf of his ancestor were among them."

Evelyn sighed. "I see. And when Mr. St. Claire found a tempting map, he chose not to include that among the other items given to my husband." She paused. "So much for 'Trust.' "

Diego laughed, but Agnes darkened and refused to comment. Chen shook his head. "I guess picking the right bank is going to be important once I get my fortune started."

Diego met Evelyn's eyes as if to check her reaction to Chen's single-minded fixation on success. Evelyn repressed a grin. "I'm sure you'll find the right bank, Chen. Or start your own."

Diego huffed. "I'm keeping my money in my pockets."

Chen grimaced. "And that should be more than enough space for what you're likely to earn!"

Evelyn remembered Will telling her of Diego's and Chen's squabbles. Clearly, Will had been kind and restrained in the description. "Never mind that." She hesitated. "I don't understand why Mr. St. Claire put his wife in here, however."

Diego coughed. "Don't you? Spend a few more hours here and you will."

Evelyn frowned reproachfully, but Diego's blunt charm was hard to resist. No wonder Rafael loved him so. "Mrs. St. Claire has had a very hard time, I'm sure, what with her husband betraying her and all."

Agnes appeared offended. "Mr. St. Claire has been confused and led astray by that dark tormentor of the soul . . ." She offered a pregnant pause where Talbot's name belonged. "I will set him straight as soon as this young man finds a suitable way out of here." Apparently despite her scorn of Diego's manners, the sharp-sighted Agnes St. Claire had realized Diego de Aguirre was her most likely savior. "I have offered to reward him handsomely."

Diego sighed heavily and shook his head. "And I told her I'll get us out of here for the sake of my own skin and my people. I don't want her money."

Evelyn touched his shoulder. "Rafael will be proud of you, Diego."

Diego grinned. "He told me about you, of course."

"He did? What did he say?"

"That he'd made a damned fool of himself trying to sweep a married woman off her feet."

Mrs. St. Claire issued an offended sputter, but Evelyn sighed with romantic bliss. "He was so . . . compelling."

"It's like him, you know. He ignores women for years, then falls to his knees over the one he can't have." Diego looked pleased with himself despite his surroundings. "I knew he'd get you eventually, though. One way or another. Sorry your husband died—I figured you'd just divorce him."

Evelyn winced at his youthful callousness, but there was something so direct and forthright about Diego de Aguirre that nothing he said could be held against him for long. It occurred to her that he must be popular with young women himself. "As I understand it, he almost married once before."

Diego rolled his eyes. "Marina, yes. I think he wanted to be in a relationship like our parents'. She wanted him, all right, but she wasn't willing to give up anything to keep him. She wanted him in her world—she didn't have the imagination to go into his."

"So . . . you think I am better suited for him?" Evelyn puffed with pride as she anticipated Diego's confirmation.

"I think you're crazy enough to understand him."

"I'm not crazy!" Evelyn pouted, forgetting the joy of their reunion. "And Rafael isn't crazy, either."

Diego cocked his handsome head to one side and angled a brow dramatically. "Oh, no? He dresses up as some kind of Anasazi warrior—he took after the Zuni side, you know. I got the Spanish good looks and flair. Not crazy? Half the time he's a schoolmaster with his nose in a book—then he's a legend come to life."

Chen braced. "Señor de Aguirre is pursuing justice, not his own self-interest." Chen's pointed tone implied that Diego thought of nothing else.

"At least I don't price everything I touch for how much I can get out of it!"

"You don't have the sense to realize how much good can be done when one has established oneself with power and influence!"

Evelyn placed herself between the two boys. "I cannot believe you two are bickering here, of all places. Behave yourselves!" She held up the lantern and studied their most recent excavation. Her heart pounded with purpose again as a new plan formed. "How close do you think we are to breaking through?"

Diego pointed back into the tunnel. "We've got three branches up ahead, which the landowners made us start separately. They've got some kind of map they're following, but they won't let us see it."

Evelyn pondered this, tapping her lip thoughtfully. "What if we break off and start a fourth path, unbeknownst to the guards?"

"We could. Why?"

"To escape."

Diego liked the idea—she saw it in his eyes—but he shook his head. "We'd have to wait until we're almost through and that will be another day, maybe a little less. But if we start pouring out, they'll shoot us down. Besides that, they watch us down here and keep a close check on our progress."

"They can't watch all of us all the time. And I don't mean to 'pour out.' It only has to be big enough for one person to squeeze out."

"And do what?"

"And free Rafael, of course. What else?"

"As soon as one person escapes, they'll clamp down on the rest, but we'll have to risk it. A few of us tried fighting when they first brought us down here." Diego stopped, emotion riddling his young face.

"What happened?"

"They took a man, one who had started the fight with me, and they shot him in the head."

Evelyn touched his arm gently. "We'll get out, Diego. Now that we know what Lieutenant Talbot is after, we'll know how to combat him." She paused. "I wonder why he didn't kill me?"

Chen considered the matter. "He needed his guards to catch us both. I doubt they'd look kindly on him killing you. Maybe he told them he's doing it for your own good. Or maybe he needs you for something down the road. I've got a feeling there's more to this than we realize. He didn't kill Rafael, either. He probably wants to set you up again, so that it looks like Rafael killed you. That way, he can be rid of both of you, and be free to transport his treasure out of here safe and sound."

Diego listened with a frown. "Or he just needs another hand down here. I doubt the landowners are planning to let any of us go once we've dug up whatever they're after. It won't be any trouble at all to collapse the mine on top of our heads."

Diego's blunt assessment brought a rush of fearful whispers, but he paid no attention. "But your plan is the best, Ev. Let's get to it."

Chen looked too appalled to speak. "Your brother's wife is to be addressed as . . ."

Diego cut him off. "Any way I see fit." He jammed a shovel into Chen's hands. Chen eyed it as if it might come alive and bite him.

"Your total disregard for any kind of formality or polite interaction will keep you from making a mark on this world."

"Your total disregard for physical labor is a pain in the neck." Diego elevated his own shovel as if to strike Chen. Evelyn groaned and smacked the shovel down.

"You two just need to accept that your ways are different. You will both make your mark on the world—I shudder to think what it will be, but I'm sure it's true."

Diego scoffed. "He'll have everyone lined up and start bossing them."

Chen sneered in response. "And you'll find out what everyone is doing, then turn around and do the opposite."

Both paused, reflecting on the other's bitter accusation. Evelyn watched in amazement as equal small smiles appeared on both their faces. She gazed toward heaven and sighed. "Poor Rafael, if he had to put up with this." But she smiled to herself, because she knew her husband had loved every minute. She picked up a shovel and went to the end of the tunnel to start digging.

Inspired by her efforts, Chen joined her, making surprising progress. Evelyn dug until her hands blistered, until her throat burned from want of water, but she wouldn't give up or stop. Diego gave her water from a small canteen—apparently, the guards often forgot to replenish their supplies, so the water was hoarded jealously.

As she worked, she thought of Rafael and the life they would share together. All she wanted was within her reach, and the people he loved were beside her. For him and for them, she had to find a way to free him. Love fired her courage, and she dug through the night.

Chapter Sixteen

"You know, if you dug together in unison, you'd make better progress." Chen had set aside his shovel to survey the work of the others. He stood with his hands on his hips, shaking his head. Diego stopped digging and turned slowly. Evelyn gripped her shovel, ready to intercept them if the need arose.

The need had arisen three times already during their night of work, generally when Chen issued an order, or Diego refused to cooperate. Chen had grand schemes in his head—such, Evelyn imagined, was the thinking of the first pharaoh who imagined a pyramid built in his honor. Taking part in the building had never entered his thoughts—the great vision was enough. Diego was as independent as Chen was imperious. They were bound to clash. Yet Evelyn sensed a curious symmetry between them—

two boys, so fully and perfectly *themselves,* ready to launch into life and become great men.

While Evelyn, Chen, and Diego dug the secret passage, the other captives worked more slowly on the wider tunnels to the kivas. Each time the guards came below, a lookout called, and they hurried back to the main tunnel, concealing the new passage in the darkness.

Diego stopped to rest, and Chen went in reluctantly. "The ground is softer up here." He banged his shovel against the tunnel's ceiling. "I wonder if we could break through?"

Diego shoved him aside and tested the area. "It's possible. But where will we come up?"

Evelyn bit her lip. "I hope it's not under Talbot's office."

Diego shook his head. "Not likely. My father didn't rebuild the oldest parts of the pueblo, and that's where most of the buried kivas were located. If I'm right . . ." He jammed his shovel, and rocks tumbled down. Evelyn grabbed his shirt and yanked him out of the way.

They scrambled quickly from the collapsing earth, but more fell. A chest slammed down from above them, then burst open. Evelyn stared, then looked at Diego, whose mouth slid slowly open. "That's not gold."

She shook her head.

Transfixed, Chen walked forward, then knelt, fingering round gems, amulets, and ancient jewelry. "It's worth . . . a fortune."

Diego picked up a golden collar and studied it. "This looks Aztec. Interesting. Perhaps my ancestors stored their treasure here."

Chen cast him a disparaging look. "Your fine

Spanish 'ancestors' pillaged this treasure from the Indians in Mexico and stored it here."

Evelyn shifted her weight from foot to foot. "What do we do now? The guards must have heard the crash, and there's no way we can hide this tunnel now."

Diego rubbed his head. "There's only one thing to do. Tell them what we've found—and imply there's a whole lot more where this came from."

Chen looked up eagerly. "Do you think there is?"

"No . . ." Diego rolled his eyes. "But we don't want them to know that, do we?" He spoke as if Chen were an idiot, and Chen grit his teeth.

Evelyn patted Chen's shoulder. "There may be more, but we don't have time to look. What matters now is getting out. I don't like the idea of leaving all this treasure with Lieutenant Talbot, but we have no choice just now. It rightfully belongs to the pueblo and these people. Chen, I'm sure Rafael will want you to have a share."

"I did find it."

Diego frowned. "Why don't you just stuff your pockets now, and I'll summon the guards?"

Evelyn repressed a groan. "This is the perfect opportunity for me to escape. They'll be so excited about your find that they won't notice I'm gone. Here's what we do. Help me up, and I should be able to push through those rocks. I'll climb out, and then you fill it in again. Hopefully, the guards won't realize we're that close to the surface. Then I'll free Rafael, and together, we'll come back for everyone else."

Chen sighed and let a fistful of jewels slip through his fingers. "You're not going alone. I'm coming with you."

Evelyn eyed Diego. "Rafael will want you freed, too, Diego."

He shook his head. "I can't do that, Ev. You tell him I'm fine, but I have to stay with our people. They need me. They'll be terrified if I desert them. I've been like a rock to them." He paused. "Tell my brother that, too."

Chen looked between them. "He's right, Ev . . ." He caught himself and coughed, but Diego laughed.

"What's more, the guards know me."

"Because he's been such a troublemaker."

Diego ignored Chen's interjection and continued. "They'd notice if I'm missing. I can get one of the other women to pose like you and stuff her back-to in a corner like she's sleeping maybe. You're dark-haired, fortunately, and if you leave your scarf, it should be enough." He waved at the crowd of huddled women. "Josephine! Get over here!"

Chen waved his arms wildly. "And he calls *me* bossy!"

Without asking, Diego seized Evelyn's wrap and tossed it at the other girl. Evelyn didn't wait. She used her bola as a rope ladder, and scrambled up the rocks. Chen passed her the shovel. She prodded in several places until they crumbled again. She ducked, covering her head, then looked up to see the midnight sky.

She was free.

* * *

"Two guards. Now what?" Chen shaded his eyes against a lantern hanging from the office wall. The first gray of dawn peeked over the horizon. Evelyn bit her lip. They had so little time.

"We have to disable them somehow."

Chen rolled his eyes. "And how do you suggest we do that?"

Evelyn sighed and pulled her bola from around her waist. Chen groaned and bowed his head, but Evelyn patted his shoulder in a comforting gesture. "Don't worry, Chen. I taught you well."

"Well, I'd feel a whole lot better if someone had taught *you*."

Evelyn stiffened and eyed him like a schoolmistress. "Rafael taught me. Yes, I know it took me a while to learn, but no great master is created in an instant." She paused. "All we have to do is sneak up on either side of the office entrance—it's lucky that it sticks out a bit—and then, together, we'll snap our weapons, which will wrap around their necks. At least, it works that way when Rafael does it."

"Wonderful. Maybe the guards can use these things for our hanging!"

"We can do it. Rafael needs us."

"And after that? Do we just march in and politely request that Talbot hand over the keys to the jail?"

"I've explained this, Chen." Evelyn felt sure he was delaying out of nervousness, but being so proud, he wouldn't want to admit that. "Lieutenant Talbot has gone to the mine to see the treasure—we saw him leave. There will probably be a guard inside, but he will most likely be sleeping. If we're quick and quiet, we should be able to gag him and tie him up before he knows we're there."

"That's a lot of 'ifs,' miss."

"I know, but it's the only way." It wasn't the most solid plan, but it was the best she'd been able to come up with. Better to turn Chen's thoughts ahead. "As soon as we break him out, you get a horse—yours should be in the stable with Frank—and ride to Tesuque for the others."

Chen sighed long and heavily, then nodded. "As you say, miss."

Evelyn readied her bola, and Chen did the same. They crept along the wall, then separated. Chen climbed onto the pueblo roof, then dropped soundlessly down on the other side. Evelyn pressed herself against the adobe, then made her way to the corner. She waited for Chen to get into place and give the signal.

After a few moments, she heard a faint whistle. She took a deep breath and returned the signal. She counted to three, then jumped forward and around the corner. A wild flash of fear blinded her. *I can't do this*! The guards whirled, one left, one right, and they drew their revolvers with practiced skill. For an instant, Evelyn looked into her opponent's shocked eyes and almost quailed with fear.

Rafael had done this so many times—disabling opponents for a higher good. He must have been afraid the first time, too. And he was part of her . . .

Evelyn snapped the bola back over her head, then jerked her wrist. The three pouches wrapped around a guard's neck and he dropped his gun, instinctively reaching to tear away the cord that tightened around his neck. Chen moved less quickly, and smacked his target across the face with the pouches instead.

Evelyn yanked her guard so that his eyes widened with the pressure. She jumped forward and kicked Chen's guard in the back just as he opened his mouth to shout for help. She met Chen's eyes and nodded encouragement. Here, as her heart throbbed in terror, as seconds rolled by like hours, she focused her attention on the boy . . . like a schoolmistress. *You can do it, try again*.

Chen bit his lip and cracked the bola again, a steadier try. He caught the guard around the head rather than the neck, but the cord worked effectively as a gag. Evelyn shoved open the door and they yanked their victims inside.

As she'd predicted, another guard sat sleeping in a chair by the jail door, keys hanging from his belt. The two captive guards struggled and the man woke, but Evelyn drew her gun. Her heart beat so fast that she felt dizzy, but she kept her voice even and low. "I think I remember you, sir, from the attack on the pueblo." She glanced down and saw a bandage on his head. He wouldn't know who shot whom during that wild battle. "In fact, I believe I shot you once already. I missed that time, but you are much closer now. I should have no trouble at all."

From the corner of her eye, she saw Chen stare at her, mouth agape, but she lifted her chin and affected a dangerous leer. "Don't say a word, and don't move." She passed Chen the end of her bola and he positioned himself behind the two captive guards, holding the ropes tight around their necks. Evelyn aimed her empty gun at the seated guard and moved cautiously toward him. To hide her fear, she allowed herself to smile, slightly.

"Take your revolver from your holster and toss it over here." Evelyn held her breath. What would she do if he refused, if he fought back? "Now!"

He hesitated, then obeyed. Evelyn bit back a gasp of relief.

"Put your head in your lap."

He leaned forward, tense. With a cool thrill of power, she realized he was trembling. She fought a feminine urge to reassure him. "Very good." She restrained an element of guilt and put the gun to the back of his head. "Should you move . . ." Her voice trailed dangerously, and again, his fear touched her sympathy. Evelyn bound his hands behind his back, then tied him fast to the chair. She gagged him, then looked to Chen, who stared at her as if she'd tossed off some long-worn disguise and emerged as a new being entirely.

She nodded, but he didn't respond. "Bring those two over here. We'll tie them back-to-back."

Evelyn worked quickly and gagged both men while Chen held them immobile. She aimed her gun while Chen tied them seated together on the floor. She checked the ties, then seized the keys from the guard's belt. She looked around the room, locked the front door, then turned to Chen. They stared at each other, stunned by their success, then smiled in unison. Evelyn started toward the jail door, then turned back and picked up the guard's discarded gun. She emptied it of bullets, then loaded her own.

The guard's eyes widened and she offered him a pert smile. "Thank you for these—I'm afraid I ran out at the pueblo." She paused to enjoy his anger, then bowed with dramatic flair, waving her hand as if tipping a nonexistent cap.

Chen grinned and shook his head. "Did you learn that from Señor de Aguirre, too?"

Evelyn hesitated, puzzled. "Taunting my enemies, do you mean?"

"No, the bow. He does it, too, the same way you did."

Evelyn clasped her hand to her breast. "Does he? I never noticed." She sighed with romantic bliss. "We really are one."

Chen seized the keys from her hand and unlocked the jail door. "That's scary, miss."

Evelyn found Rafael's bola and held it close to her heart. She took a lantern from the wall and they went into the back room. There were two cells, one empty. Evelyn's heart throbbed with anticipation as Chen unlocked the second cell. He pulled open the door and Evelyn rushed past him. Rafael leapt up and caught her in his arms, lifting her from her feet. "Evelyn! You're here."

She didn't wait to explain. She kissed his mouth and his face, and his mouth again. "Rafael, I've missed you so." She kissed him again and hugged him but tears of pent-up emotion burst free. She buried her face against his chest and sobbed.

He held her and kissed her. "You're all right. Evie . . ."

She sniffed and drew back to look into his eyes. "I love you so. . . ." She touched his bruised forehead. "They've hurt you."

"I'm fine. It's nothing."

She pulled him close and kissed him, savoring the feel of him against her body. "I've missed you so. I had to come after you, you see, because she didn't—the girl in my vision. That was her mistake—she believed he would protect her from anything, but when his time came, she wasn't there to save him. Do you understand?"

He smiled. "I'm afraid I do."

They kissed again, but a man hidden in shadows behind Rafael cleared his throat. Evelyn jumped back and squealed in shock. It hadn't occurred to her that another shared his cell.

"I suppose I will have to accept your claims of matrimony now, Señor de Aguirre."

Evelyn's mouth parted in astonishment as Robert Talmadge came forward. "Papa!" Her eyes welled with tears and she swung herself into his arms. Robert hugged her, and his chest caught on harsh sobs.

"Evie . . . My dear child."

She brushed away her tears. "What are you doing here, Papa?"

"In jail or in New Mexico?" He smiled but tears glittered on his cheeks. "I came West as soon as we heard that you'd been abducted from a train by a renegade Indian and his gang of outlaws."

Chen looked proud. "That would be me, sir."

Robert clasped Evelyn's shoulders and studied her face. "It appears you've joined them."

"I'm afraid I have." She beamed. "Chen and I disabled three guards to get in here." She heard Rafael groan, but she elevated her new bola and waved it at him. "We used these."

Robert eyed her whip with misgivings. "What is that?"

"An Argentinean bola, Papa. Rafael uses it in his Renegade attacks because he doesn't favor guns, and it is also useful in hunting, herding, and picking nuts off trees." She paused. "I made this one and Chen's myself."

Rafael placed his arm lovingly around her. "You are a woman of many skills."

She nodded. "I am."

Rafael hugged her as if afraid ever to let her go again. "Evelyn, what happened? Talbot said he captured you."

"He did. We've been in tunnels beneath the pueblo. And, Rafael, Diego is there."

He closed his eyes in relief and she pressed her lips together to keep from crying again. "He's fine. He seems to be some kind of leader."

Chen huffed. "At least, he thinks so. Don't know how the other captives feel about it, though."

Rafael shook his head, smiling. "What are they doing in tunnels?"

Evelyn pulled him toward the door. "Lieutenant Talbot has them digging for treasure."

Chen exhaled a wondrous sigh. "And we found it, sir! A whole chest of it—rubies and golden necklaces, bracelets. I think I saw a diamond or two. I can't even begin to think what it's worth."

Evelyn met Rafael's eyes and smiled. He

glanced heavenward and sighed. "So you've enjoyed yourselves, then?"

"It was interesting. . . . Especially finding Mrs. St. Claire."

"What?"

"It seems Mr. St. Claire tired of her company."

"I can't imagine why."

"He has formed a partnership with Lieutenant Talbot—he stole a map from the bank before giving Westley the pueblo documents. I'll explain it all later, but we have to get out of here. The sun is rising, and we don't have much time."

Rafael took the lead and they left the cell. He noticed the three bound guards. "Good work, Evie. I couldn't have done it better myself."

"Chen remarked that I had emulated your example very well."

He looked around the office, then found his own bola and affixed it to his belt. He nodded at the seated guard. "Tell the lieutenant that the tables have turned."

Rafael went to the door and Robert went out into the plaza with Chen. Evelyn followed them, but turned back to see Rafael bow and wave his hand at the bound guards. The Renegade had returned, and he was part of her.

Rafael concealed himself behind a boulder and assessed the entrance to the secret tunnels. At least twenty soldiers mulled outside, picking their way among ruins of the ancient pueblo. Lieutenant Talbot wasn't in view, but a coach waited higher on the hill, and Rafael could make out a bald, rabbit-eyed man overseeing the soldiers' progress. He held a small white dog, and his chest appeared more puffed than when he had lived in his wife's formidable wake.

Evelyn shaded her eyes. "That's Mr. St. Claire. I don't suppose he's come for his wife."

Rafael smiled. "I would think not."

Chen had found his horse and was riding for the others in Tesuque. Robert had gone the five miles to Santa Fe, where he would enlist the governor against Talbot.

They couldn't wait for help. As soon as Talbot learned of Rafael's escape, he would take action quickly to save himself. The soldiers appeared to be working at some uncertain task, piling boulders and hitching pull carts to horses.

Evelyn crept up beside Rafael. "What are they doing?"

"I'm not sure. I don't see Talbot anywhere."

"Diego is going to convince him that there's more. I hope he's willing to wait for it."

"When he learns that your father and I have escaped, he won't wait, Evie. Even if he could convince the governor that you and I were lying, he knows he can't challenge a Civil War officer."

He felt her knowing look and pretended not to notice. She issued a contrived "hmmm," then nodded. "So you've found he's not quite the villain you imagined, have you?"

"I never imagined your father as a villain." He had imagined exactly that. "However, his take on the war was . . . illuminating."

"Meaning you are beginning to understand despite yourself."

She sounded so smug. He wanted to kiss her.

"How did you get past all these guards?"

She arched her brow pointedly so that he knew she hadn't missed his deliberate change of subject. "Diego, Chen, and I dug a small hole in the roof of one of the tunnels. It's not far—in amongst some old ruins. Maybe we could call down and alert them."

"And Talbot? We can't risk that, Evie."

"I suppose you're right." She glanced toward the tunnel entrance. "What are those soldiers working on? It worries me, somehow."

"I believe . . ." Rafael closed his eyes as fear flooded his senses. "Evie, I think they're preparing to collapse the mine."

Her face whitened in the cold morning sun. "Do you mean, they didn't listen to Diego about there being more treasure?" She sounded as frightened as he felt, but she touched his arm in support beyond words.

"I don't know. They aren't working in any particular hurry—not yet. But they will, and soon, when they learn I've escaped."

"Maybe I should have left you there."

"Talbot knew his time was short anyway, once he imprisoned your father. And I'm the only one who can free them." He kissed her hand. "You did well, Evelyn."

"What are we going to do then?"

"It may be time for the Renegade to ride again."

Evelyn clutched his arm. "No! Rafael, there are too many. You can't. Please, let's wait for Chen to return with Patukala and the others. Then we can fight them together."

Rafael gestured toward the laboring guards.

"We don't have the time to wait. When they're finished with that rock pile, it will only take Talbot's order, and all those people imprisoned in the mine will be killed."

Evelyn drew a long breath, then fished around in a pack she kept tied at her side. She pulled out his mask and handed it to him. "I brought this with me. Lieutenant Talbot was in such a hurry to get rid of me and Chen that he didn't bother with our gear."

Rafael took the mask, then bent to kiss her cheek. "I love you, Evie. I won't tell you not to worry, because we both know what we're up against."

Concealed behind the ruins of a forgotten city, Rafael embraced her and held her close to his heart. Everything he wanted was within his reach. His brother was safe, his people were as yet unharmed. Beyond hope and dream, Evelyn was his wife. Now he had to risk all he held dear to stop a man whose only purpose was greed.

Evelyn looked up at him. "You're asking me to trust you, and I do. So I'm asking you to trust me, too."

He didn't like the sound of this. "In what way?"

"I need to go back into the mine." He started to shake his head, but Evelyn placed her fingers against his lips. "Someone has to warn them so we can overwhelm the guards inside and get everyone out. If they can collapse the mine at a moment's notice, we'll have to be quick. Rafael, you know I'm right."

"I can't let you risk . . ." He stopped and touched her face. "I promised you once that I would respect your courage. Now is such a test." Rafael drew a long breath. "Show me the point where you emerged and I'll help you."

"It's not going to be easy—I dug out at night, but it's not well concealed. In daylight, I think the guards would see us." Evelyn gestured to where the guards were digging. "It's close to that point."

Rafael hesitated, then smiled. "I have an idea. Wait here." He touched Evelyn's shoulder, then crept from boulder to boulder until he came up behind two soldiers who had paused to rest. Rafael drew his bola, assessed his target, then flicked his wrist, catching both men by their necks.

He yanked them back behind the boulder and saluted. They looked terrified, but Rafael smiled. "Don't fear, gentlemen. I'm not after your lives today."

Evelyn joined him, expectant. "What are you going to do with them?"

"Borrow their clothes."

He didn't have to explain further. She beamed and proceeded to unbutton their tattered brown shirts. "You are so clever, Rafael." She passed him one of the shirts, then hesitated. "How do I get their trousers?"

"My own are fine for me." He didn't like the idea of Evelyn undressing another man. He gestured to the smaller guard. "Take off your trousers, friend." The guard hesitated, so Rafael twisted his wrist. "Evelyn, look the other way."

She rolled her eyes, but obeyed. The man pulled off his pants with shaking hands and Rafael gave them to Evelyn. She scurried behind a boulder and emerged looking more charming then he'd ever seen her. The guard's shirt hung off her slender shoulders and his trousers bagged low over her hips so that she tugged them repeatedly. "He doesn't have a belt?"

Rafael repressed a grin. "I'm afraid not."

Evelyn wrapped her bola around her waist. "This will do fine. Useful things, bolas."

"I love you, you know."

Her face formed a wistful expression of love. "I know." She went to him and kissed him while the two bound guards looked on amazed. Rafael left them tied together concealed behind a boulder. He tore off his shirt and put on the guard's, then tied his hair back and placed the guard's wide-brimmed hat on his head.

Evelyn seized the other guard's hat, pulled her hair up, and placed the hat carefully on her head. She stood back to study Rafael's appearance thoughtfully. "You look like a cowboy."

Rafael grimaced. "So do you."

He looked into her eyes and for a moment, all was forgotten but his love. He remembered when he first saw her, beautiful and sweet in the train station, then anguished beside her dead husband. He remembered her fury when he abducted her and the passion in her eyes that she couldn't quite conceal.

Rafael touched her cheek, then bent to kiss her. She tipped her hat back to reach his mouth and their lips brushed softly together. He didn't need to tell her what to do. Together they emerged from behind the boulder and took their places where the captured guards had been.

Evelyn picked up a shovel and began to dig,

edging ever closer to the area where she had escaped the night before. Evelyn found the boulder she and Chen had rolled over the hole, but as Rafael bent to move it aside, a rider galloped wildly toward the waiting coach.

Evelyn caught her breath. "It's Lieutenant Talbot."

Rafael closed his eyes. "Sooner than I'd hoped." Talbot leapt from his horse and spoke to Mr. St. Claire. He shouted orders at a guard, and the man raced toward the mine entrance.

Evelyn looked wide-eyed to Rafael. "What's going on?"

"He's learned of my escape, and he's going to try to collapse the mine, as soon as they complete their setup."

Evelyn gulped. "Then we don't have much time."

Even as she spoke, Talbot shouted orders at his guards. Mr. St. Claire gestured at the mine, probably worried about the treasure and not his wife. Evelyn clasped Rafael's arm. "They won't wait, Rafael. Look, they're bringing out the chest we found."

"I know."

As Talbot conferred with Mr. St. Claire, Rafael seized their chance. He bent and shoved the boulder aside. Dirt fell inward, revealing a small hole. He jabbed the shovel in and the hole collapsed.

Evelyn drew a taut breath. "This is it. You'll have to fill it in after I go down."

"If I do that, there will be no way out except through the mine entrance."

She met his gaze evenly. "I know, but even if

you left this hole uncovered, only one person can get out a time. That would mean everyone else would be left behind. You know I can't do that, any more than you could."

He wanted to hold her and he couldn't. He wanted to stop her from going down in that hole. The desire to protect her was so strong that his muscles clenched with restraint.

Rafael hesitated, then pulled his Anasazi mask out of his pack and gave it to Evelyn. She shook her head. "You need it."

Rafael smiled. "Do I? No one will doubt who wears the Renegade mask now, Evie. And I would prefer my spectacles in place for this ride."

"What do you want me to do with it?"

He bowed his head, then looked at her again. "If I should fall . . ." She opened her mouth to stop him, but he placed his fingers over her soft lips. "If I should fall, give this to my brother. It is a treasure not meant for one man."

Evelyn pressed her lips together, but she took the mask. They waited until the guards' attention was elsewhere, and then Evelyn wedged herself into the hole while Rafael stood guard above her. She looked up from the pit and her bright eyes were filled with tears. "Take care, my love. . . ."

Evelyn dropped down and disappeared, but her words echoed in his mind. She had comforted him once before, unspoken, before either one had known how much they could love. He had heard her voice in his mind, *Take care.*

As he turned to begin his own task, he knew there was no true parting between them. They had been connected all along.

Chapter Seventeen

As Evelyn dropped down into darkness, she heard voices echoing from farther down in the tunnel. She waited as Rafael filled in the hole above her, then closed her eyes in prayer. *Please, let him be safe. Help us, please.*

She crept forward until she could see the other captives. Diego stood arguing with a guard, and he sounded desperate. "Look, we just found another one. Got to be twice the size of that last chest."

"Get back, boy."

"That's a lot of gold you're letting slip through your fingers, Sergeant."

The soldier hesitated and looked behind Diego. "I don't see nothing."

"It's still half buried. It will take another day, at least, to dig it all out."

The soldier shook his head. "All of you, back in that tunnel, down to the left."

Evelyn squeezed her eyes shut. The tunnel branching left was closest to where the guards worked above, readying the mine to collapse. Diego refused to move, and the guard drew a gun. "You're a damned arrogant bastard, boy. There ain't no reason I can't snuff you out before the others." He aimed the gun at Diego's face, but the boy didn't back down.

Evelyn's heart seized in fear. She ripped off her cap and ran forward. "Are you sure you want to do that, Sergeant?"

Diego startled, his beautiful Spanish eyes wide when he saw her. "What . . . ?"

She caught his eye and shook her head, and he silenced.

The guard eyed her attire doubtfully. "What the hell . . . ?" He didn't seem surprised to see her—apparently her absence hadn't been noted.

She puffed an impatient breath. "You may not be aware of this, Sergeant, but digging is made considerably more difficult when wearing a skirt. I found trousers more comfortable."

Fortunately, he wasn't bright enough to ask whom she'd borrowed the trousers from, but Diego angled his brow and smiled. He turned to the sergeant and his youthful assurance returned without hesitation. "We tried to get Mrs. St. Claire to wear trousers, too, but she found it unacceptable."

The guard looked suspiciously between them, then waved his gun toward the deepest tunnel. "Get in there, now."

Evelyn stepped forward. "It will take a few minutes, Sergeant. We have people working back in the other branches, too."

The guard hesitated. "Get them out here." He looked nervously up at the roof of the mine, then backed away.

Evelyn lowered her voice. "Was there another chest?"

"No."

Evelyn bit her lip, then scurried after the guard and tugged on his shirt. "If I were you, Sergeant, I would at least alert the lieutenant to the second chest. It's practically bursting with gold. He won't be pleased if he thinks you've kept it from him."

The guard didn't respond, but his eyes narrowed. He shoved Evelyn back, then left. Diego came to her side. "Did you find my brother?"

"He's outside. He's going to attack, but if we can't get out of here to help him . . ." She swallowed hard, fighting tears. "They're set to collapse the mine. We have to get everyone together, and as soon as Rafael rides in, we have to break out of here."

Diego didn't wait. He went back and gathered the others, then stood before them like a young king. "Look, all of you, I know you're scared, but we've got one chance, and one chance only. Talbot has this mine set to crash down on our heads." He paused, interrupted by gasps of shock and a subsequent shrill cry from Agnes St. Claire, who shoved herself in front of the others.

"He would not . . . He wouldn't dare!"

Diego frowned. "What do you think he put

you in here for, anyway? A holiday? Face it. Your husband wants you dead, Agnes. I assume you're worth a lot of money?"

Her chin squared, but tears filled Agnes's round eyes. Evelyn felt a stab of pity. "My family is among the oldest and most respected in Boston."

Evelyn touched her pudgy arm gently. "Don't worry, Mrs. St. Claire. Rafael is coming to save us, but you have to keep your head so we can all work together."

Agnes recoiled. "Do you expect me to rely on that Renegade?"

Diego snapped at her in anger. "Well, you didn't get far relying on your husband!"

Evelyn winced at his lack of tact. "This is what Rafael does—this is what he's always done, protected people in need when greed and avarice overwhelm them."

Diego glanced at Evelyn. "You came back alone. Where's Chen? I assume nothing happened to him?"

Evelyn smiled. Despite their mutual antagonism, Diego cared. A friendship between them was still possible. "Chen has gone for your uncle and Sally. And we need their help, Diego. There are so many guards. I'm afraid Rafael can't handle them all alone."

Diego patted her shoulder, but she saw his fear. "My brother knows what he's doing." A long pause followed. "I hope."

Rafael found his dark gray horse tethered to the tree. Frank looked up and exhaled a deep breath as if to say "not again?" Rafael stroked the powerful neck. "Once more, my friend. She is waiting. My brother is waiting. Once more, we ride."

He mounted and turned his horse toward the mine. In one hand, he readied his bola, but he looked up into the sky. Above him and all around, he felt the power of his ancestors and the ancient warrior who lived inside him. The Renegade he was and had always been came to life and filled his soul. . . .

He drove his heels against the great horse, and it leapt forward. They charged down from the hills like the wind on fire.

"All of you, get ready." Diego stood with Evelyn, ahead of the other captives. He took her hand. "There's a good chance they'll start shooting, Ev."

She nodded. "I know. But I have this." She held up her bola, which Diego assessed with misgivings. Evelyn gave him her gun. "We can hold our own until we get to the entrance."

Diego nodded and offered a gentle smile of reassurance. He seemed older than his sixteen years, and she realized that despite his youthful selfishness, Diego's strength came because he truly put others before himself. He was more like his brother than he knew.

He touched her shoulder. "Let's go."

With the other captives behind them, they made their way up along the tunnel. The guards at the entrance caught sight of them, and someone shouted, "Lieutenant!"

Evelyn heard Talbot outside. "Get them back! Shoot them!"

Diego dropped to one knee and fired. A guard

fell, and the next drew his gun. Evelyn whipped the bola and sent his gun flying. Unarmed, the guard raced from the tunnel, but another came in, shooting with no target. Diego fired again, shattering the man's arm. The guard grunted and fell back.

Evelyn saw Talbot outside the entrance. "Put up that barricade, you fools!"

The guards unleashed a rock slide, blocking the entrance. Diego shot again, but the boulders rolled into the entrance, leaving only a sliver of sunlight showing through. Talbot shouted orders at his men. "Pull the braces, now! Send it down on their damned heads!"

Evelyn looked desperately to Diego, and in his eyes, she saw the shadow of their defeat looming.

A wild cry rang out from outside. Shots rang out, and Talbot swore. Evelyn closed her eyes. "Rafael . . ."

"The Renegade should delay them!" Diego turned to the others. "Hurry up, all of you! We've got to move these rocks."

Even Agnes lent a hand as the captives fought to move the boulders. Deeper in the tunnel, they heard the mines collapsing, a chain reaction that would soon bury the entrance and everyone inside.

Evelyn worked beside Agnes, shoving boulders with as much strength as she possessed. Agnes was stronger than she looked. Her square face set in grim determination, she thrust her ample body against a rock as big as she was. Evelyn came to her aid, and the rock gave way.

"We've got a hole here, Diego!" Evelyn flung

herself at another rock, and Diego scrambled to her side, then shoved the rock back into the tunnel behind them.

He dropped back among the other captives and started herding them out like cattle. "Everyone! Through here! Get out, as fast as you can, and no shoving!" He sent the youngest boys and older women first, and to Evelyn's admiration, no one pushed to be first. They helped each other—a boy no more than twelve stopped to help an older man up the rocks. Diego stood at the rear even as the wall behind him began to crumble.

Evelyn helped Agnes out into the sunlight, then grabbed the young boy's hand. The older man faltered and stumbled, but Diego caught him and helped him over the rocks and to freedom. Two women supported another who was injured—Evelyn recognized Josephine, who had donned her scarf as a disguise. Their eyes met and Evelyn smiled.

I am part of you, these people are my family now. . . .

Dirt and rocks flew and filled the tunnel with blinding dust as the mine crumbled around them. She couldn't see Diego, but she heard him as he encouraged the last of the captives toward the dwindling exit.

Almost forty people had been abducted and forced to work in the mine. Evelyn held out her hand and helped another woman to freedom. "Diego! How many more?"

"Three. Get out, Evelyn! I'll get the rest."

Rocks crashed all around, but Evelyn refused to leave. "Hurry up!" Three boys scrambled between the rocks, and she helped each one. "Diego, they're all out! Hurry!"

He started to climb up, but the roof collapsed in a blinding crash. Evelyn screamed as Diego fell back. Rocks struck her back so hard that she fell to her knees, but she crawled down to him. He was alive, but pinned beneath a boulder.

"Evelyn, get out of here!"

She was crying, she couldn't see through the dust, but she thrust all her weight against the rock and shoved. It gave way, but Diego's leg was twisted. He grimaced with agony, but she grabbed his arm. "Come on, lean on me."

He shook his head. "I can't, it's broken."

"I know." She met his eyes and saw the tears of pain on his cheeks. His face looked white and she feared he might faint with the severity of his injury. "We need you. Rafael needs you."

By the strength of his will and nothing else, Diego shoved himself up. Evelyn caught him and dragged him through the rubble.

She winced in the sunlight as they emerged. The ground shuddered, threatening to give way beneath their feet. The old man Diego had helped came to them with the three boys and together they carried Diego from the falling rocks.

Evelyn turned to see the entrance collapse amidst a storm of dust and flying rocks.

She scrambled after the others, to a slope where the captives had gathered. Below, Rafael fought alone. He had led the guards into the old ruins, where their numbers provided less advantage. Armed with sticks and rocks, the captives charged the guards in support of Rafael.

Evelyn left Diego with the old man, then ran toward Rafael, ready to fight on his behalf.

Talbot and a guard shoved the Spanish chest into Mr. St. Claire's coach, but Evelyn's heart held its beat when Talbot yanked another prisoner from inside the coach.

"Papa! No . . ."

Rafael saw Robert, too, as Talbot shoved his gun against Robert's head. "I'm afraid the governor never got your message, de Aguirre. A damned shame a war hero like Colonel Talmadge would turn traitor for a chest of gold."

Evelyn scrambled down the hill toward her father, but Talbot jammed his gun against Robert's head. "Stay back, Mrs. Reid, unless you want your father's head blown off his shoulders right here."

Rafael rode from the ruins. "What do you want, Talbot?"

"I want you, de Aguirre. You're coming to Santa Fe with me, and I'll have you hanged in the plaza before a crowd that should have seen your death a year ago. Surrender now, or Colonel Talmadge will pay for your crimes instead."

Robert shook his head, but Evelyn fought back tears. "No, Papa . . ."

Rafael leapt from his horse. "You'll never get away with this, Talbot."

"No? But I think I will. Drop your weapon, Renegade. Now!"

Evelyn ran forward, but Rafael saw her coming and he threw aside his bola. She cried out as he surrendered to his enemy. "Rafael, no!"

Robert shoved Robert aside and his guards

surrounded Rafael. They flung ropes around him and dragged him into the coach. Evelyn ran toward the coach as Talbot leapt in the door beside Mr. St. Claire. "Do you dare to follow me, Evelyn? I think not. You've seen your Renegade lover for the last time, I promise you. I'm sorry you won't be able to witness his hanging—I need this done perfectly, you understand."

She shook her fist. "I will stop you!"

"Will you? I think not. The governor will be outraged that the Renegade killed both you and your heroic father—and used his own people to dig for a treasure that didn't exist."

"He'll never believe that! There are too many of us."

Talbot shook his head. "But unarmed, Evelyn, you don't stand a chance."

The driver lashed at the horses and they surged forward. With Rafael taken, the guards resumed their attack, this time at the unarmed captives. Evelyn's heart beat in sick fury, but there had to be a way, somehow, to save Rafael. . . .

Fear couldn't overwhelm love. She had known that since she first looked into his eyes.

Evelyn readied her bola and raced back up the hill. "Everyone! Take cover!" A guard shot at her, but she dove behind a boulder, then sprinted to where Diego lay.

Despite his agony, he readied her gun and fired. "We'll never hold them, Evie."

She was crying so hard she could barely see, but Evelyn wouldn't give up. "We have to try."

The beauty and courage of Rafael's people rose before her as the old man hurtled a heavy rock toward the guards, and the boys took up stones to do the same. Evelyn bounded toward a guard as he ducked from the stone onslaught, and swung her bola at his revolver. She caught it, then yanked it back into her own hands.

Another shot rang out, but Diego fired back over her head. They couldn't hold out for long, but the fire in Evelyn's heart refused to give up. Robert knocked a guard down with a pole, then took his gun. She saw her father fighting amidst flying dust, and she knew what he had been as a young man, heroic and strong.

The guards surrounded them, and the captives backed in against the rubble of the collapsed mine. Evelyn took her place beside Diego, and Robert came beside her. She would die here, with her beloved father, with Rafael's courageous young brother and the people he loved. But she would die fighting.

A whoop sounded from the northern rim of pines that surrounded the mine. The guards looked up, startled, and Evelyn's heart lifted. A charge of Indians galloped toward them. She saw Sally and Will riding beside Chen, led at the fore by Patukala. Galloping along on a stout pinto, the chief himself drew back a bow and shot into the thronging guards.

The pueblo attack was too much for Talbot's soldiers. They threw down their guns and surrendered.

Rafael stood on a scaffold in the central plaza of his father's pueblo. Talbot stood quietly by as Mr. St. Claire recited the grim results of the Renegade's final attack before a crowd filled with landowners from Santa Fe, and not his own people. Guards held back the remnants of his people, who wept at the loss of the captives as Talbot had described.

Rafael listened in disbelief as he was accused of murdering not only Evelyn and her father, but Mr. St. Claire's much-adored wife—all because when posing as a schoolmaster of the pueblo, he had discovered a link to treasure. He had used his own people in its discovery.

Talbot gestured and two guards came forward bearing the Spanish chest—filled not with the gems and jewelry Chen had described, but a few gold nuggets worth not a fraction of the actual treasure.

"How pointless his acts, and how futile!" Talbot spoke like an orator, then bowed his head. "Even now, the beautiful Mrs. Reid lies upon a stone field of death with her father—a man you remember from the Great War, Governor. Let us be done with this Renegade now, and let her soul and her father's rest finally in peace."

Mr. St. Claire dried his eyes with a white handkerchief. "My dear, dear wife . . ."

The governor bowed his head in acquiescence, then looked up to meet Rafael's eyes. "I was a fool to think your father's dream continued in you. Let it be done."

A guard fitted the noose around Rafael's neck, but he couldn't think of his own death. Where was she? Had the guards overwhelmed her, killed her, and did she lie on that cold stone field alone? Grief overwhelmed him—Talbot's brutal taunts had finally hit their mark. Rafael couldn't imagine that Evelyn had survived. He had seen his brother lying among the rocks, unable to fight back. All those he loved, he had failed them.

He could not think of his own fate now.

Rafael turned his eyes to the western mountains. He felt the warrior's spirit within him, lifting, as if giving its energy to a greater force. It had stayed with him for so long, but it left now as if reaching to some higher part of him, something more . . .

The wind swept down from the mountains and carried with it the sound of hoofbeats. At first, like an echo they came, and then stronger. The crowd awaiting his execution took notice, and Talbot turned, shocked as the sound of approaching riders filled the plaza.

A murmur of astonishment rose from the crowd, and then of fear. People ran from the plaza to take shelter. The governor rose and gaped as three riders charged into the square.

The three riders stormed the square around Rafael, dressed in black capes bearing coiled whips in their hands. The one in the center wore a mask—Rafael's mask—and the faces of the others were covered with black cloth.

The leader leapt from his horse—and the horse he rode was Frank. Rafael stared, stunned, as the new Renegade bounded up the pueblo steps as he had done so many times himself. The new Renegade took position, swinging a bola with precision and fury, knocking the gun from one guard's hand, then sweeping it around the feet of two more.

The other renegades worked on either side of the crowd, so quickly that Talbot had no time to arrange a defense. Another group of riders galloped into the pueblo square, led by Patukala. Rafael's heart throbbed. Where was she? His grandfather had come, but he didn't see Evelyn or Chen anywhere.

The leader snapped a gun from another guard's hand, then caught it in midair. With hands as quick as light, the Renegade aimed and shot the noose from Rafael's neck.

Will jumped from his horse and shouted. "Senor! Over here!" Rafael turned and caught his own bola.

The wind returned and carried with it his own soul. He bounded down from the scaffold and caught Talbot around the neck. Mr. St. Claire backed away, but the smallest renegade rode up behind him, reached down, and placed a light bola around the rabbit-eyed man's trembling body.

Patukala's warriors surrounded the plaza, and the remaining guards threw down their weapons. The governor looked terrified, but he didn't try to flee. Rafael dragged Talbot before him. "I'm afraid you've been misled, sir, as to the nature of my crime. It is Lieutenant Talbot who murdered Westley Reid, thanks to the clever find of this man. . . ." He nodded toward Mr. St. Claire. The smallest renegade hauled the quaking St. Claire forward, too. "The Spaniards who retook this pueblo after the Revolt stored a handsome treasure here and buried it in kivas—those that remain in the ruins behind the pueblo now. No gold bars, but antiquities taken from an Aztec fortune."

The other black-masked renegade nodded vigorously, but said nothing.

The governor hesitated. "Can you prove any of this, Rafael? I have only your word against Lieutenant Talbot's—and a field of blood to consider."

"If you will take my word, perhaps?" They turned as Robert Talmadge drove a small cart into the pueblo. The governor gasped, and John Talbot's eyes turned black with the powerless fury of defeat. Diego lay in the cart and Rafael shoved the end of his bola into the governor's hands and ran to his wounded brother.

Diego looked pale but he smiled. "Colonel Talmadge set my leg—he says he learned quite a bit of medicine when he was in Andersonville prison during the war. He has a different view on the war—I thought you should know."

Rafael touched Diego's forehead. He sounded odd, his voice toneless. Robert climbed down from the cart and stood beside Rafael. "He'll be all right, Rafael. He's weak, but it was a clean break. He'll walk with a limp, but he'll live."

Tears stung Rafael's eyes as he bent to kiss his brother's forehead. Diego smiled again, then drifted toward sleep. Rafael straightened, then forced himself to look at Robert.

"Evelyn . . ."

Robert smiled and nodded behind Rafael. He turned and the renegade leader placed hands on narrow hips. A cool thrill sped through Rafael's veins, but he couldn't speak. The slender Renegade came to him, waiting. Rafael's hands shook as he pulled away the mask and looked into the mystic blue-gray eyes of his wife, Evelyn de Aguirre.

"You make an exquisite Renegade, my love." Rafael followed Evelyn into his bedroom and closed the door. Evelyn sat on the edge of Rafael's bed, happier than she had ever been in her life. All clouds had lifted from her life, nothing dark closed in on her now. They were free to love.

"Thank you. I thought Chen and Sally performed admirably, too."

"So admirably that my grandfather has invited Sally and Will to live at Tesuque. It is only a matter of time before she and Patukala will marry."

"Love triumphs, after all." Evelyn sighed, but Rafael unbuttoned his shirt, distracting her attention from their conversation. "I still don't understand why Agnes convinced the governor to free her husband. He tried to have her killed."

Rafael pulled off his shirt, set his spectacles aside, and splashed water from a basin over his face. Evelyn licked her lips as small droplets escaped his cupped hands and ran in intriguing rivulets over his hard chest. He glanced back at her, smiling at her expression, then shrugged. "I can't say I understand her choice, either. But I suspect Mrs. St. Claire is far more capable of exacting punishment over her husband than the government could."

"She was very angry. For a while, in the mine, I thought she'd softened. I felt sorry for her. I thought her heart was broken. But I feel sure by the time they return to Boston, she will have a story concocted to explain it all away."

"No doubt." Rafael seated himself beside Evelyn, but he didn't touch her. She pretended not to notice the way his black hair hung over his shoulders, nor the way the muscles in his back flexed with even the slightest movement. "Is there something that interests you, Señora de Aguirre?"

He was teasing her. The fiend. "Everything in your pueblo interests me, Rafael. I like your school very much."

With the treasure unearthed, Rafael had set about adding on to the pueblo—after giving fair portions to his grandfather and those who had helped him. Chen had taken his portion lovingly and was still debating its best fate.

"Then you don't object to my adding on another room for your use?"

Delight flooded her, but she bit her lip to maintain dignity.

"What shall I teach?"

"My students could use a differing viewpoint on your father's war. Since he is returning to Boston soon, you might tell the story in your own way."

"That would be good. What else?"

"With your plentiful gift of imagination, I would think you would be the perfect person to encourage their own ability to tell stories."

"I could do that, yes." She liked the idea. "I would like to take our students on excursions, too."

"So we can save them from tigers and then get lost ourselves?"

She smiled. "If the occasion should arise . . . But nothing too active for now."

"Why not?"

Evelyn placed her hand on her stomach. It felt flat, firmer than it had been before her journey with Rafael began. Yet still . . . the strange, distant emptiness she once felt at odd times had disappeared, replaced by a sensation that told her life was about to take a new turn.

Rafael peered at her stomach as if it might grow round before his eyes. "Do you think . . . ?" He stopped and gulped, but a tiny smile formed on his sensual lips.

"I'm not sure." Evelyn smiled, too. "I hope so."

He looked into her eyes, but still he didn't touch her. His gaze swept to her lips, then back, and her pulse quickened. "You are beautiful, you know." His voice lowered, almost imperceptibly, and grew sensual. "I want to see you here, Evie, free, on my bed. Here, I have dreamt of you so many times."

Decidedly lower, almost husky. The sound sent shivers all through her body. "I'm here." In contrast, hers had risen slightly higher.

"You are." He reached to unravel her hair from its ribbon, then eased it forward around her face. His finger trailed over her cheek, down her throat, and to her collarbone. But as she held her breath waiting for his touch to drift lower, he moved his hand away and continued to watch her, a smile playing on his lips.

"Do you know, I have wanted you since I first saw you?" She knew but she liked hearing it as often as he would say it. "Do you know what it means to me to be here with you, knowing that you want me like this?"

Evelyn bit her lip. "I do."

He moved to kiss her, but not her lips. Instead, he kissed the side of her forehead, then her eyelid. His lips moved so softly, so sensually over her skin. He kissed her cheek, then touched her chin. He kissed either side of her mouth, tasting each corner like some treasured morsel.

He slid his fingers through her hair, but he didn't deepen their kiss. "We will be like this forever, Evie, forever." The sound of his voice was seduction, the touch of his fingers bliss. "When I'm with you, nothing else interests me. Only you."

"I love you, Renegade. But if you don't make love to me now, I will don that mask and bind you and . . ."

His eyes widened in expectant delight, and Evelyn laughed. "Later, my love. Later. We have time. All our lives, because of you." She caught his long hair in her fingers and drew him close. She kissed him, and he held her. They fell back onto his bed together, and all the world outside was forgotten while they loved.

Together, their two souls met and mingled, engaged in a sweet, delicious dance that had simmered between them since she first looked up and into the eyes of a Renegade. He filled her with himself, and she wrapped around him, and when at last he lay still beside her, Evelyn knew that every journey their souls took would lead them back to each other.

Epilogue

"I'm leaving the pueblo in good hands—when Evelyn and I are in Spain, I will be assured that no danger awaits here."

Diego sat in a high-backed chair staring glumly out the window. "I don't know what good you think I can do if something did happen."

Rafael knelt beside his brother and placed his hand on Diego's knee. "You broke your leg, little brother, not your soul or your courage."

Diego's eyes shifted to Rafael and he frowned. "What about my fencing skill? What can I do, hopping around on one leg this way?"

"You walk with a limp, Diego. It's not an insurmountable obstacle."

Diego sighed. He hadn't bounced back from his injury as Rafael had expected. After the courage Diego had shown saving the captives from the mine, Rafael and Evelyn had both believed he would emerge unstoppable. Instead, a year later, he had become quiet and withdrawn. It wasn't self-pity, but self-doubt that assailed him now. He wasn't sure who he was or where he belonged. Part of the reason Rafael was leaving the pueblo was so that Diego could find out—outside the shadow of his Renegade brother.

"Will you accompany us to the train station?"

Diego shrugged. "If you don't mind helping me into the coach."

Rafael rose and opened a small chest. Diego waited, grumpy, as Rafael returned and passed him the mask of the Anasazi warrior. "It's been a while since I wore this—I doubt I'll have the need again. But greed and avarice didn't stop with John Talbot's arrest. Other forces, even darker than his, may confront the pueblo. I believe our father would want you to have this."

Diego fingered the mask, then shook his head. "Give it to someone who can live up to it, Rafael. Maybe Chen."

Rafael angled his brow doubtfully. "Chen would sell it at the first opportunity, as soon as he realized how much it's worth. I want you to have it."

Diego took the mask and set it aside. "I'll keep it here until you return, but don't count on my wearing it."

"I'm counting on the man behind the mask, not the mask itself. I know you, my brother—you have more courage in you than you know."

Diego stared at his feet. "I'm the little brother of a great man. I'm selfish, callous, tactless—I have nothing of your depth of feeling, Rafael."

"You're seventeen."

"Almost eighteen."

"Yes."

"You have your dream, Rafael. You have Evelyn, you have your daughter. You're a good man, and I know you expect more from me. But I'm not the kind of person to become a hero. Look at how I am with women!"

Rafael smiled. "I try not to. But you haven't met the one yet who moves your heart beyond such . . . physical interest."

"If such a woman exists, which I doubt, it wouldn't matter anyway. I know myself better than that. You went through hell to win Evie. I think you'd do anything for her. I'm not like that."

Rafael remembered speaking these same words when he was seventeen, and he recalled his father's reply as if it still echoed in the wind. "When the woman of your dreams appears, Diego, you will move heaven and earth to have her. Nothing will stand in your way."

Diego didn't appear convinced. He scratched the back of his neck and exhaled a weary breath. "Hope she doesn't mind a lame husband."

Evelyn sat close beside Rafael in the first-class cabin of the Atchison Topeka and Santa Fe rail as he held their daughter in his strong arms. Surrounding them, a group of Rafael's schoolchildren chattered in excitement, eager for their trip to begin. "I'm glad Diego came to see us off. He's been so gloomy."

Rafael looked out the window. Diego stood leaning on a cane beside Chen and Will. Will waved vigorously while Chen supervised the porters loading trunks onto the train. Sally stood with Patukala, holding hands as befitted a newly married couple. Even Rafael's grandfather had come to bid them farewell on their journey, though he had objected several times to their destination.

"My brother has a long road to travel on his own journey. But a spirit like his can't be quenched by an injury."

"I don't think it's his injury, love." Evelyn reached over and patted her daughter's tuft of black hair. "When we were in that mine, Diego gave his all. He got everyone out of the mine and he survived."

"I don't understand."

"Don't you? He did everything he could, and yet you were taken, and the rest of us were almost killed. If Patukala and Chen hadn't reached us in time, the guards would have killed us. That truth haunts your brother—because his 'all' wasn't enough."

Rafael looked out the window and Evelyn saw his dark eyes fill with tears. "I don't know how to convince him otherwise."

Evelyn clasped his hand in hers. "That's not for you to do. Diego has to learn for himself. He has to learn that sometimes you need someone else to win. You had to learn it—I did, too. But for him, the lesson will come hard."

Rafael sighed. "He has good friends."

"Chen will look after him."

Rafael shot her a skeptical glance. "Or kill him."

"That, too."

The whistle blew and the train chugged slowly forward. The rest of their lives opened wide before them, and Evelyn rested her head on her husband's powerful shoulder. They would travel together, raising their baby daughter with all the love they shared.

Evelyn peered once more out the window and saw her friends waving. In Diego de Aguirre's hands, he clasped the Renegade mask. She saw him as if the future offered a glimpse of itself. "He will wear it one day, you know. And the Renegade will ride again."

Rafael kissed her forehead, then cuddled their baby close to his chest. "When his ride is done, he will give the mask to another." He kissed the baby's head and smiled. "Maybe even Catherine will wear it."

Evelyn shuddered. "I had another future in mind for our daughter."

"What? Pleasant tea rooms, mansions in Europe, a prince to save her?"

"Something like that, yes."

"Then you misunderstand. The Renegade blood runs strong in my family, Evie. It runs strong in you. Our daughter has no choice. For all the mansions and all the princes, Catherine won't rest until she serves the fire of her own heart."

Evelyn nodded, and he knew she understood. "The heart of a Renegade."

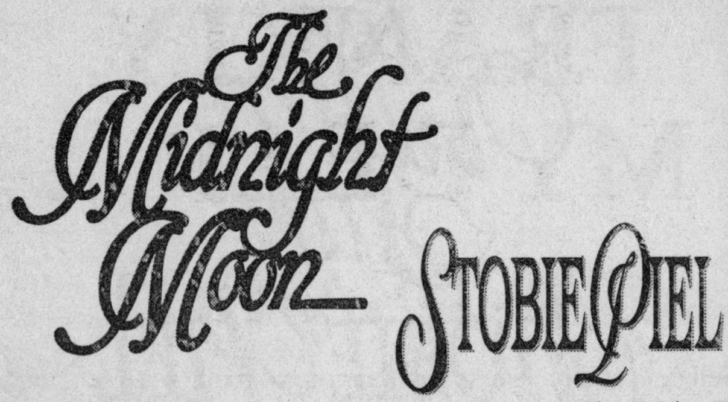
The Midnight Moon
STOBIE PIEL